# The Dedalus Book of Finnish Fantasy

Edited by Johanna Sinisalo
and translated by David Hackston

Dedalus

Dedalus would like to thank FILI, the Finnish Information Centre in Helsinki, the Finnish Embassy in London and Grants for the Arts in Cambridge for their assistance in producing this book

Published in the UK by Dedalus Ltd,
Langford Lodge, St Judith's Lane, Sawtry, Cambs, PE28 5XE
email: info@dedalusbooks.com
www.dedalusbooks.com

ISBN 1 903517 29 X

Dedalus is distributed in the United States by SCB Distributors,
15608 South New Century Drive, Gardena, California 90248
email: info@scbdistributors.com web site: www.scbdistributors.com

Dedalus is distributed in Australia & New Zealand by Peribo Pty Ltd,
58 Beaumont Road, Mount Kuring-gai N.S.W. 2080
email: peribo@bigpond.com

Dedalus is distributed in Canada by Disticor Direct-Book Division,
695 Westney Road South, Suite 14 Ajax, Ontario, LI6 6M9
web site: www.marginalbook.com

First published by Dedalus in 2005



Printed in Finland by WS Bookwell
Typeset by RefineCatch Limited, Bungay, Suffolk



A C.I.P. listing for this book is available on request.

## THE EDITOR

Johanna Sinisalo is one of the leading Finnish authors of her generation. She is the author of many highly acclaimed short stories and her first novel *Not Before Sundown* (called *Troll – The Love Story* in the USA) won the prestigious Finlandia Prize in 2000 and has been translated into English, Swedish, Japanese, French, Latvian, Czech, German and Polish. The book also won the James Tiptree Jr. Award in the USA in 2005. Her second novel *Sankarit* was published in Finland in 2003 and transfers the national epic, the *Kalevala* to the twenty-first century. One of her stories is featured in the anthology.

## THE TRANSLATOR

Since graduating from University College London in 1999 David Hackston's work as a translator has focussed largely on the stage and he has translated Finnish drama for theatres around the UK including the Gate, the Royal Court and the Royal National Theatre. He is a regular contributor to the journals Books from Finland, Swedish Book Review and Nordic Literature. He currently lives in Helsinki where he is working on a thesis dealing with theatre translation. He is also an active composer and viola player.

ACKNOWLEDGEMENTS

The editor and translator would like to take this opportunity to thank a number of people whose help has been instrumental in the completion of this book. First and foremost our thanks go to Iris Schwanck and her staff at FILI, the Finnish Literature Information Centre, and the Arts Council of Great Britain for their tireless work and financial support. Thanks go also to Eric Lane and all at Dedalus Books for the opportunity to present this selection of Finnish fantasy writing to the English-speaking world. Our gratitude goes to the featured authors for their comments and advice and to the numerous rights holders for their cooperation. Many thanks to Hannele Branch – a truly inspiring Finnish teacher – and to Emily Jeremiah, Casper Sare and Oliver Wastie for their invaluable comments at various stages of the translation and for their support, moral and otherwise. Finally we would like to express our warm thanks to each other: this project has been a fascinating journey into a world building bridges between languages and cultures, and working on it together has been a true pleasure.

Johanna Sinisalo
David Hackston

For more information on Finnish literature and a link to Books from Finland, a quarterly journal of writing from and about Finland, please visit: www.finlit.fi/fili

CONTENTS

Introduction by Johanna Sinisalo 7
Aino Kallas: *Wolf Bride* ('Sudenmorsian', 1928) 11
Aleksis Kivi: *The Legend of the Pale Maiden* ('Tarina kalveasta immestä', 1870) 35
Mika Waltari: *Island of the Setting Sun* ('Auringonlaskun saari', 1926) 41
Bo Carpelan: *The Great Yellow Storm* ('Stormen', 1979) 59
Pentti Holappa: *Boman* ('Boman', 1959) 65
Tove Jansson: *Shopping* ('Shopping', 1987) 101
Erno Paasilinna: *Congress* ('Kongressi', 1970) 109
Arto Paasilinna: *Good Heavens!* ('Herranen aika!', 1980) 116
Juhani Peltonen: *The Slave Breeder* ('Orjien kasvattaja', 1965) 128
Johanna Sinisalo: *Transit* ('Transit', 1988) 141
Satu Waltari: *The Monster* ('Hirviö', 1964) 160
Boris Hurtta: *A Diseased Man* ('Tautimies', 2001) 182
Olli Jalonen: *Chronicles of a State* ('Koon aikakirjat', 2003) 195
Pasi Jääskeläinen: *A Zoo from the Heavens* ('Taivaalta pudonnut eläintarha', 2000) 219
Leena Krohn: *Datura* and *Pereat Mundus* (1998–2001) 239
Markku Paasonen: *Three Prose Poems* (2001) 258
Sari Peltoniemi: *The Golden Apple* ('Kultainen omena', 2003) 262
Jouko Sirola: *Desk* ('Kirjoituspöytä', 2003) 283
Jyrki Vainonen: *Blueberries* ('Mustikoita', 1999) 293
*The Explorer* ('Tutkimusmatkailija', 2001) 306
Maarit Verronen: *Black Train* ('Musta juna', 1996) 320
*Basement, Man and Wife* ('Kellarimies ja vaimo', 1996) 328

# *Introduction*

Literature written in the Finnish language is surprisingly young. Despite the fact that both a thriving folk culture and a highly creative tradition of oral poetry have existed throughout our history, it seems incredible to think that written literature in Finnish has existed for little more than a few centuries. The earliest books written in Finnish, dating from the mid-16th century, were all of a religious nature, and so those who could speak only Finnish had to wait until the 19th century for the publication of secular literature. Finland's geographical position caught between two great empires created a strange climate in which the national language was subordinated at times to Swedish, at others to Russian, and this in turn resulted in that even the most respected Finnish writers wrote mostly in Swedish – a language which still has official status in Finland and from which many respected writers have appeared and still appear to this day.

The rise of the Finnish language to a 'real' and true literary medium only began in earnest at the end of the 19th century. With such a short history it is striking to see how broad and rich the scale of writing and reading in Finland has become today. In a country with little more than five million inhabitants literature is read, bought and borrowed from libraries more than almost anywhere else. Statistically Finns are among the most literate people in the world.

To generalise slightly, one could say that Finnish literature is dominated by the tradition of realism. In Finland realism is widely seen as the correct way to write, whilst other genres are deviations from this norm – some would claim that these deviations do not represent 'respectable' literature. All too often one hears the Finnish reader shun works including elements of fantasy on the basis that such things are 'not true'.

The overwhelming strength of the realist canon has made some readers forget the fact that even realistic literature is made up; that it is every bit as fictitious as the most unbridled fantasy literature.

Realistic narrative is solidly anchored in the empirical, in that which can be proven and authenticated, and this is perhaps one of the reasons for its popularity in Finland. We are a small nation with a difficult, broken past. One of the greatest functions of literature in our country has been the depiction of history and human destiny in a form both easily approachable and recognisable; literature has thus become an important part of the Finns' collective memory.

Still, Finnish literature has given rise to – and, indeed, continues to give rise to – writers who wish to look at the surrounding world through the refracted light of fantasy. It was easy to find dozens upon dozens of authors who have taken bold steps into the realms of surrealism, horror and the grotesque, satire and picaresque, the weird and wonderful, dreams and delusions, the future and a twisted past. Far more difficult, however, was the task of making a final selection from this marvellous and wide-ranging group. This anthology presents the work of twenty authors, though it would have been just as easy to present the work of twice as many authors of the highest calibre.

In making these decisions it was fascinating to note that, regardless of the great respect felt towards realism, the presence of elements of fantasy in a writer's work has not prevented them from attaining the highest possible status in literary life. Of the twenty authors in this volume, six have received Finland's most prestigious literary award, the Finlandia Prize, and many others have been shortlisted. Amongst the present authors there are some whose works have already been translated into numerous foreign languages.

In making these decisions I have tried to build up a cross-section of Finnish fantasy, both thematically and chronologically. The oldest texts date from the dawn of our literature, whilst the newest were written within the last few years. In addition to writers with a long and distinguished career behind them, I have also included works by a number of promising young writers.

Once I had whittled the writers down to twenty I assumed that the diversity of the authors would automatically produce a selection of radically different texts. On one level this is indeed the case: the spectrum of styles, subjects and originality represented in these texts is impressive. Yet at the same time I observed that certain distinctly Finnish elements and subjects recur throughout these stories, albeit in a myriad of different ways, but in such a way that we can almost assume that, exceptionally, they comprise a body of imagery central to Finnish fantasy literature.

One of these elements is nature. To this day Finns live in a very sparsely populated country, surrounded by lakes and large expanses of forest. Every Finn appears to have very close, personal ties to nature. In Finland culture and nature do not struggle against one another, they are not mutually exclusive, rather they encroach upon one another, they merge and influence one another. In the present fantasy stories the theme of nature often manifests itself through the very active role given to forests and animals.

Another recurring element is that of war. Throughout the length of its history Finland has lived between two great empires: Sweden to the west, Russia or the Soviet Union to the east. Both have taken turns to conquer our country, and the struggle to maintain our precarious independence has led to wars whose scars are far from healed. Here the theme varies just as much as the treatment of nature: in addition to the many direct references to war, its ghost can be seen in the themes of power, slavery and control, or even as a post-apocalyptic vision.

In any case, it is a joy to present here twenty different voices, each of whom draws open the curtain of reality and offers us a glimpse into their own highly distinctive worlds.

*Johanna Sinisalo*

# *Wolf Bride*

Aino Kallas

*Aino Kallas (1878–1956) is well known as a writer of poetry, short fiction and novels. She spent the majority of her life in Estonia, where she was inspired by local history and folklore from which she drew inspiration for many of her ballad novels. The theme of destructive love is central to all her works and in the novel* Wolf Bride *('Sudenmorsian', 1928), from which the present extract is taken, she combines the motif of illicit desire with ancient Estonian religious beliefs. As no literature was written in Finnish during the mid-17th century – when events in this novel take place – Kallas' work constitutes a highly original, creative vision of what such a written language may have been like.*

## *Chapter Four*

Yet just as the day has two halves, one governed by the sun and the other by the moon, so there are many who are people of the day and who busy themselves with daytime deeds, whilst others are children of the night, their minds consumed with nocturnal notions; but yet there are some in whom the two merge like the rising of the sun and the moon in a day. And all this shall be known in good time, when Fate thinks it fit.

And so it was that at first no one had a thing to say about Priidik, the woodsman of Suuremõisa, or his young wife Aalo, nor in the mill of chatterers and babblers was there a drop more water than in the island's rivers during summer-tide. For they lived a quiet life in loving harmony, in amity and accord with the villagers, and like good Christians they went often to church and received Holy Communion, and showed respect and loyalty to the law and to the estate in everything they did. No one spoke ill of Aalo, for she rose early in the morning and was good and gracious, neither rude nor rash nor indignant nor aloof, but good-mannered and in every way as calm and clement as a meadow breeze. Though in sooth many a man was vexed by the pallour of her appearance and the colour of her hair, so like the autumn-rusted juniper it was, though it was cropped short and covered in winter-tide with a woollen hood and in summer-tide with a long and narrow scarf with lace ribbons hanging on both sides upon her shoulders, as befits a wedded woman.

Thus when Priidik the woodsman and his young wife Aalo had been married almost one year Aalo bore their firstborn, a daughter, who was duly baptised in the church at Pühalepa and given the name Piret.

But the Wicked Spirit, who despises peace, had already chosen this bride for his own, just as a lamb is marked out from the flock, and cunningly lay in wait for the moment upon which he could shape her in his image.

For as from the same piece of clay a potter may fashion either a pot or a tile, so the Devil may shape a witch into a wolf or a cat or even a goat, without subtracting from her and without adding to her at all. For this occurs just as clay is first moulded into one, then shaped into another form, for the Devil is a potter and his witches are but clay.

And so it was that in the month of Lide (the villagers' name for *Martius*) a great wolf hunt was to be held in Suuremõisa once again, as soon as the ice across the strait of Soela had begun to thin and could no longer bear so much as a wolf's paw, thus cutting off his only escape.

Indeed, like other public festivities, this event had been planned for many months, and ale and spiced liquor brought for the villagers to the inn at Haavasuo, with bagpipers too, for at the hunting feast there is also much dancing.

And so lookouts were sent to the swamps and to the marshes, and in every village old wolf spears were sharpened and cleaned of their rust.

But it was not only the villagers who waited eagerly for the wolf hunt: Satan's minions rejoiced too, as this came at a most opportune moment for them.

Thus one morning a lookout, who had been keeping watch from atop a tree, brought news that the wolves had been sighted.

And thus all the men from Kerema, from Värssu and from Hagaste, from Puliste, from Vahtrapää, from Sarve and from Hillikeste were summoned to the hunt, two or three from each and every house, some eight hundred souls, womenfolk and children notwithstanding, and all of Suuremõisa's woodsmen, with Priidik amongst their number.

Thus a biting, spring day dawned, sunshine melting the snow in parts yet holding still the lowlands in the grip of frost.

When at daybreak Priidik the woodsman arrived at Haavasuo, the inn was thronging with folk as it does on market day, all turned out in their best attire as if for a grand banquet.

Aalo too had come to follow the hunt and the festivities, clad in a loose and wide-sleeved jacket, and beneath this a skirt of lamb-grey, cross-striped and pleated throughout. Though because there still lay frost on the ground she wore upon her head a brown hood, such that is called a *karbus*, draped with pretty red ribbons. And around her waist hung a belt of brass, made of rattling coins, holding on the one side a knife tethered in a tin sheath and on the other a pin box.

Yet little did she know of the trap set upon her path as she stepped out in all her finery, and that morning she was as gay and graceful as a young doe and her pretty countenance was a joy to behold.

First the spearsmen were sent out with their nets to the hunting ground, they dashed headlong saddled upon their steeds at full gallop, their spears outstretched, like a horde of Cossacks or Kalmyks.

Soon after them left the wolf hunters themselves, known as the *loomarahvas*, in a great circle around the island of Hiidensaari, hollering at the tops of their voices and firing their muskets, thus to fright the wolves from their hiding places, if indeed they had taken cover amongst the thicket or on the islands upon the swamp.

And thus a great clamour and commotion spread across the boggy lands of Hiidensaari, where ordinarily none but crane and curlew sing, and where the wild wolf howls.

But Priidik the woodsman sped towards their agreed hunting ground upon the vast meadow. At one end there stood a high stone wall, and behind the wall were hunting nets hidden from view.

And so Priidik and the other huntsmen crouched amidst the coppices on either side of the meadow, waiting and making not a sound.

Then all of a sudden there came a warning cry from a blackbird high in the treetops and at that moment, herded by the *loomarahvas*, the two wolves came into view and the shouts and cries at their heels pealed out. Nor could they hide any longer amongst the thick bushes, for the fierce barking of the hunting dogs quickly spurred them onwards. And so they both began to gallop faster, their jaws open and their dark, ominous tongues dangling low to the ground.

And with that Aalo, wedded wife of Priidik the woodsman, standing amongst the crowd of villagers, looked on as the pursued wolves dashed past her, gripped in the fear of death.

And though at times they were obscured in gunpowder smoke, as shots rained in from behind them and from the sides, Aalo could see that the first of the wolves was smaller in stature, whilst the other was a large, powerful beast, its legs tall and its body long and grey, its muzzle sharp and its forehead wide, its wild, slanted eyes full of the fury of the forest.

Then, all at once, Aalo heard quite distinctly in her ears the words:

'Aalo, Aalo my lass, will you follow me to the swamp?'

At this she shuddered, as if she had been shot in the side, for she could not see the speaker of these words. But both her body and her soul were shaken by a mighty wind, as if a great force had whisked her from her feet and lifted her into the air and like the finest fowl's feather spun her in a sacred storm, until she began to gasp for breath and all but swooned upon the spot.

And all this happened faster than a beat of a gull's wings above the sea.

Once recovered, Aalo saw the first of the wolves, every last fibre of its body strained in gallop, its head and legs and tail forming a single straight line as it leapt headlong twice the height of the stone wall, believing there to be sanctuary and salvation on the other side, though what awaited was in fact a certain death.

But then the larger, more powerful beast, running behind the first, as the men's eyes were fixed upon its companion, sped off to one side and escaped deep into the forest, thus breaching the men's barrier.

With this Aalo hurried to the foot of the wall where she saw the wolf struggling in the net, shrouding its body like a cloak, all hope of escape extinguished. And such did this ensnared beast pant as if its sides were about to split, and spittle frothed from its black, foreboding jowls and between its curved fangs as the villagers scathed and scorned it.

And Aalo saw the men with their spears raised aloft, ready to strike deep into the wolf's side, and amongst their number stood her husband Priidik.

And at that moment she heard those same words once more; fainter, perhaps further off, as if someone had cried from the wilderness, yet she alone could hear:

'Aalo, Aalo my lass, will you join the wolves at the swamp?'

Like a calling did these words reach her, like a coaxing cry from the swamp.

And thus at that very moment a dæmon entered her and she was possessed.

And this Spirit is called *Diabolus sylvarum*, the Spirit of the Forest and of the Wolf, whose home is by the swamp and in the wilds; brave and fearless, a spirit of strength and freedom, and yet also of rage and violence; mystified beyond all comprehension, winged like the storm clouds and ablaze like the heart of the earth, yet forever caught in the shackles of Darkness.

But at that same moment Priidik the woodsman thrust his spear through the net and into the side of the thrashing wolf, and many of the other men too, and with that the beast's blood spurted high into the air.

Yet not even did the dogs dare touch the wolf's flesh, for it was foul and vile to their throats, and was thrown as carrion to the birds.

And late into the night came the sounds of rejoicing, the wheeze of the bagpipes and the booming of muskets from the inn at Haavasuo, for there, fuelled with ale and spiced liquor, did the villagers celebrate their wolf hunt, and the lads and the maids danced in time.

## *Chapter Five*

O ye witches, ye who before the Incarnation of Our Lord and ever thereafter have celebrated Satan's Sabbath, who can count your number! Simon in the Holy Bible, Circe and Medea, Caracalla, Nero, Julian the Apostate – all emperors of Rome – and last of all Faust and Scotus! How then could little Aalo of Pühalepa in Hiidenmaa have resisted the Might of Darkness?

And so it was that from the time of the great wolf hunt at Suuremõisa Aalo, wedded wife of Priidik the woodsman, had begun to yearn for the swamp and for the company of wolves; how she longed to leave behind her all humanity and the Christian union into which she had been conjoined at the Holy Font and through a number of other Sacraments. For so strongly did the Spirit stir her which had entered her; like bellows it fanned the flames in her blood, making her obey the command of the Devil and transform herself into a wolf. As evening fell, and in the dusk the wolves began to move closer to the village settlements, so their howl carried in across the wolds and upon the cottage threshold Aalo stopped amid her chores and stared out into the forest, and to her ear their howl sounded as soft as the sweetest music, for she too was a sister of their spirit.

Yet all the while she pleaded with her husband Priidik the woodsman to fasten strong hatches at the barn door and for safety's sake to place thick iron bars behind them, and she acquired a new and ill-tempered guard dog. Neither did she once allow the shepherd boy to take the cattle beyond the pasture, though in sooth during summer-tide the wolves have other prey than merely cattle, such as hares, foxes, hedgehogs and woodland birds. But this Wolf hungered neither for cows nor sheep nor even for young foals: the body and soul of one young bride was its only prey, for it was an envoy of the Underworld.

And so that spring Aalo took care never to go alone to the swamp or deeper into the woods, for she knew that danger lurked there. As yet she had not wholly forgotten the union of her Christening and the effects of the Holy Water still protected her soul. But such a time did she spend caught between fear and desire, that the fire inside her ripened her, like the sun beating upon wheat in the field, waiting for the hour of its coming.

And throughout this time, as she endured this struggle, her thoughts strayed often to realms of death and darkness, as if she had sensed and forseen her premature, sorrowful demise. For unto her was everything filled with prophecies and omens, from which she divined signs and warnings and applied them to her own plight.

Thus in the mornings she would say to her husband Priidik:

'The eagle owl was hooting high in the birches last night – what does this foretell?'

Or she might say:

'Black ants came through the crack in the steps and marched across the threshold – surely this does not bode well.'

However she did not expect an answer to such questions, she merely uttered them to relieve her own anxiety.

But one day she returned from the paddock and said:

'I saw strange things in the forest today: a Mourning Cloak Butterfly rested upon the yellow sand amongst the junipers. It had black wings, black as the finest cassock of the minister at Pühalepa, but their edges were the golden colour of honey and their spots the blue of the sky. Who now is going to die?'

Yet the Devil's wicked arrow, which long ago had struck her, slowly clouded her mind with its poison, and the dæmons and their Master rejoiced in Hell, for their prey was entrapped and victory was near.

Thus it transpired that over Midsummer Priidik the woodsman was to leave for Emaste for two days to welcome a firewood merchant ship, and Aalo was to remain at home with their little daughter Piret, an old servant woman and a young shepherd boy.

But the night of the solstice has since pagan times been full of witchcraft, for then the dæmons wander freely and witches carry out their dark deeds under the shadow of night. For upon this night they convene at the crossing of paths and at the meeting of three fences and smear potions upon gates and stable doors and tie the corn in magic knots, reading spells and thus damaging both cattle and crops. And islandfolk say that on Midsummer's Eve the water sprite Näkki can be seen in the body of a young woman searching for her drowned child.

And so upon this Midsummer's Eve did the young folk of Suuremõisa and the neighbouring villages make their way to the swings and solstice fires, and the young maidens collected handfuls of nine herbs hoping to dream of their husbands-to-be. And the old too remained awake and kept watch over their houses, ensuring that no one came inside to work spells or cast an evil eye.

But Aalo, wedded wife of Priidik the woodsman, had nowhere to go that evening and sat in the cottage doorway.

And so the evening drew on and the bumble-bees rested in the trees bearing their golden goods, and all were fast asleep: the servant woman in her bed, the child in her cradle, the shepherd boy by the warmth of the stove, just as the handmill, the loom and the fishing nets hung upon their poles, and not so much as a wisp of smoke rose from the outdoor hearth.

Only the linen cloth, which Aalo during winter-tide had woven into strips, lay spread across the grass to whiten and stretched back and forth across the length of the yard like a pale yellow path.

And then, upon the cottage steps, Aalo saw the sun, the eye of the Lord, setting lower and lower in the sky, as low as the berries on the forest floor, then disappearing altogether, and with that evening soon chilled into night.

Then suddenly Aalo's ears rang again with those same words she had once heard at the wolf hunt:

'Aalo, Aalo! Aalo my lass, come join the wolves at the swamp!'

But this time they did not sound like a cry or a calling, but like an overwhelming command which had to be obeyed, lead though it may to death and damnation.

No longer could Aalo resist, and thus she dismissed her Holy Union and the fact that Christ our Saviour suffered and died upon the cross for her sins too, just as the people of Israel turned their backs upon God and their redeemer, that brave hero Gideon.

And so she gladly gave up her spirit, her body and her soul to the dæmons and let them lead her onwards.

And not even the whimpering of her innocent child could rouse her, for she was deaf to all but the call of the wolves.

Thus she took off her shoes, for it was late and dew lay heavy upon the ground, and set off barefoot along the cattle tracks towards the swamp, a distance of almost three versts.

Yet these paths were trodden by the cattle and they twisted and twined hither and thither, and all the time Aalo's heart throbbed like a bird in her breast.

After walking for a time Aalo finally arrived at the edge of the great swamp, which seemed to be enveloped in a thin white mist, so covered was it with blossoming marsh tea and cloudberries and hare's-tail. And here the sounds of the village could no longer be heard, nor the crowing of the cock nor the barking of the hounds, nor even the peal of the church bells.

And the swamp appeared to have a hundred eyes, between the tussocks, their dark surfaces staring silently at this young wife as she wandered through the night.

But Aalo skipped from tussock to tussock, as dwarf birches and cranberry tendrils tugged at the hem of her skirt as if to hold her fast.

And so she finally arrived at the small island in the centre of the swamp, where pines and blackthorns and rowans grew, where great anthills stood and where the ground was hard and covered in pine cones and needles.

Then Aalo recalled the ancient charm, snapped a branch from the blackthorn bush and waved it thrice across the quagmire.

And lo, she looked on as the bracken at the swamp's edge burst into a blue flower which shone like a blue flame.

For the villagers say that bracken only flowers once a year, on Midsummer's Eve.

And thus around this blue bracken flower, which flickered like blue fire, as if the heart of the swamp had lit up, danced the grass snakes, some with their heads held up high, some twisting in circles on the ground, and there were many hundred of their kind. And all the gnomes and will-o'-the-wisps of the forest bowed down on either side of the flower as if it were a sacrificial flame.

And upon the island in the swamp was a large group of wolves, even though it was summer-tide, as if all the wolds of Kõpu and the shadows of Kõrgessaare had released their wards, and all the wolves of Muhu and Saarenmaa and from as far afield as the mainland had joined their pack. They were sitting in a large circle, as if at a meeting of elders, their bushy tails at their heels and their thick coats tangled, but no longer did they howl.

At once Aalo perceived a large wolf sitting towards the front of the group, and realised that this was the very same wolf which at the hunt at Suuremõisa had escaped through the line of men; she knew it from its great, powerful frame and from the wild gleam in its eyes, and she understood that this was the leader of their pack.

Then she noticed, hidden within a large rock, a pristine wolf skin a deep colour of grey and yellow.

And thus at that moment the Devil snuffed out all that was left of Aalo's former life, as quickly as if the swamp had sucked her deep into its embrace for the rest of time, and no longer could she recall her husband, her child, the servants, the cattle, neither the Word of the Lord nor His Mercy.

(For such powers has the Devil bestowed upon his dæmons that they may conjure up hail, frost and wind and can poison the air and the water, and even turn people into wolves.)

And with that Aalo threw the wolf skin across her shoulders and soon she felt her bodily form becoming all but unrecognisable; for her white skin was covered in a tangled coat; her dainty little face narrowed into the long muzzle of a wolf; her small, pretty ears grew into the pointed ears of a wolf; her teeth turned to ferocious fangs and her nails to the curved claws of a beast of the wilds.

But so skilfully does the Devil in his infinite cunning fit a wolf skin around the frame of a human that the claws and the teeth and even the ears each fall at exactly the right place, as if she had been taken from her mother's womb thus and entered this world as *Lycanthropus* – a werewolf.

And in the form of the wolf, so Aalo also began to develop the cravings and desires of wolves, such as a thirst for blood and a rejoicing in slaughter, for her blood too had become the blood of wolves, and with this she became one of their number.

Thus with a wild and raucous howl she joined the pack of wolves, like a prodigal daughter she understood that finally she had found her like, and to a chorus of howls the others greeted her as their lost sister.

## *Chapter Six*

And so it was that upon this light Midsummer's night Aalo, wedded wife of Priidik the woodsman, ran for the first time as a werewolf.

For barely had she been transformed into a wolf and joined their number than the wolves left the island in the swamp and the whole pack galloped through the wilds, crossing heath and bog as they headed north-east towards Kõpu and Kõrgessaare, Aalo amongst them.

And Aalo sensed that both she and the world around her had changed through and through, everything felt new and fresh, as if her mortal eyes were glancing upon these things for the very first time, in the same way as our foremother Eve, when at the snake's bidding she plucked and ate the apple from the Tree of Knowledge in Paradise.

For now the muscles in her loins and the sinews in her sides were tensed with a new, mighty power, and now no distance was too long for her; she leapt lightly across the quagmires and over felled trees and in her gallop there was a pace as terrific as the Western Winds.

Both swamp and forest were brimming with scents which, in her human form, not once had she noticed, and these scents excited her greatly, for she was compelled to run after each and every one of them. For in some strange way, which defies all explanation, she knew precisely which scent belonged to which animal dwelling in the forest. And so her nostrils were filled with the now familiar scents of far off creatures: squirrel and fox, snipe, grouse and capercaillie, even hare and hedgehog.

But as on their nocturnal flight they neared a solitary hut in the woods or skirted far around the village, thus a wave of new and wonderful smells flooded towards them, making Aalo's blood flow all the quicker, for now, amidst the smell of cattle, she sensed the smell of ewes and kids and young foals, and this made her swoon and her blood boil, for now she too was one of the wolves.

Still one more scent came their way, wafting out forebodingly from between the forest huts, and so strange and pungent and frightening was this smell that she felt her new wolf's heart shudder in her breast. At this she saw the other wolves, her sisters and brothers, stop still for a moment, sniff the air, then redouble their speed as they galloped onwards, as if this scent brought with it certain death and destruction and was a sign of the sworn enemy.

For as between the snake, that worm of old, and humans, so the Creator also established an eternal hatred between wolves and mankind, and in this way they are destined to despise each other always.

And at that moment from a far corner of the village Aalo's

sharp lupine ears heard a short crack, followed shortly by a flare and a loud boom like thunder, and with that, blind with fear, they dashed headlong into the darkest shadow of the forest.

Yet even in her new form Aalo too was suddenly filled with true caution; everything was suspicious, as if danger lurked all around her. Thus she carefully sniffed every twig and branch upon the path, as if a wolf pit may be hidden beneath them or a trap may lie set behind the bushes.

Never in her former life had her blood bubbled with such golden glee and freedom's fancy as now, galloping across the swamp as a werewolf. For such a fury of freedom is unpredictable and forged by the Devil himself, so that he may lure his young victims into the chasm of destruction.

And when she looked more closely at her companions the wolves, as together they ran that Midsummer's Night the length and breadth of Hiidensaari, to her great surprise she saw amongst them a number of people well-known from her human life.

For running abreast her was another werewolf, the Valber woman from the village of Tempa, and beyond her was the churchwarden and a wealthy landowner from the manor at Suuremõisa; and she knew she was not mistaken, for with her wolf's eyes she could see more clearly than ever she had with her human eyes. As she ran by, Valber bared Aalo her sharp, curved fangs as if to greet her old acquaintance.

Then suddenly they heard the bellowing of the cattle and noticed a heifer that had strayed from the flock at the edge of the meadow.

And upon that very moment Aalo knew that her lupine nature thirsted and craved for that heifer's blood.

She saw the large wolf, the leader of the pack and much more powerful that the others, as it ran ahead and set upon the heifer, tearing at the veins in its neck.

Thus Aalo was engulfed by a great fever, and she could no longer understand anything clearly as she cast off the final remnants of her former human nature. And at that she joined her sisters and brothers in attacking the heifer, and together they tore it to pieces.

They slaughtered many cows that night, and ewes and young foals too.

And this baptism of blood is the Baptism of Satan as thus he strengthens his union with that which is human.

But as they galloped further and further towards the north-east and the great wolds of Kõpu appeared on the left and Kõrgessaare in front and the open sea began to loom ahead through the white night, the wolves, which had until now remained close together, dispersed and began running alone or in twos.

And at this Aalo found herself running alongside the greatest of the wolves, which she had seen evading the hunt at Suuremõisa.

With that she realised that this was the wolf which had thrice called her to the swamp that evening and which had finally come for her.

And to her surprise Aalo felt that she was the equal of this great, potent beast, and that she could follow his every step though he quickened his pace, and they seemed to be flying across the heaths and the marshlands.

For it was that same ferocious fire burning the blood flowing through their lupine veins and that same glorious glow making their lupine hearts race.

And together these two were the noblest and most splendid of all the forest and of all St. George's beasts.

Thus in the early hours, just before dawn, their journey took them to the wolds of Kõpu, to the heart of the ancient spruce forests, where man's axe had never struck and where age-old lichen-covered trees hid the mossy forest floor beneath their dark shadows.

The wind rustled through the treetops, sighed a great sigh, then died down once again.

At that moment the wolf with whom Aalo had been galloping suddenly changed his form.

Through the forest there gusted a mighty wind, living and breathing, as if an enormous lung had sighed, and all the wilds shuddered to the thud of unseen footsteps and a pair of great wings, whose span no mortal has ever measured, which more than the tops of the ancient trees shrouded the forest in a clandestine darkness.

For this wolf was *Diabolus sylvarum*, the Spirit of the Forest, though he only chose to reveal his true form now.

And upon this such a bliss came over Aalo as has no bounds and her soul was filled with an overwhelming joy, such as cannot be described in human tongues, for nothing can compare to the wonder and wealth of her elation, a fountain for those who thirst. For at that moment she was one with the Spirit of the Forest, that potent dæmon who in the shape of a wolf had chosen and claimed her for his own, and thus all boundaries fell between them and they became one, like two drops of dew which, once thus conjoined, cannot be put asunder.

And Aalo evaporated into the hum of the forest spruces, she oozed as a golden resin from the red trunks of the pines, she disappeared with the green dew upon the moss, for now she belonged to *Diabolus sylvarum* and had fallen prey to the Devil.

But when Aalo next awoke, she realised that she was resting upon the side of a large rock close to their cottage in Pühalepa, and beside her lay the wolf skin. As the sun rose from its short repost that summer's night, Aalo quickly hid the skin in a hollow in the rocks and hurried home to her bed before anyone could notice that she had ever been gone.

## *Chapter Seven*

And from this night forth Aalo was the daughter of damnation and in league with the Devil, and like the witches of Blocksberg she began to run as a werewolf, for now it was as though she had two lives: one as a wolf and one as a human.

(If any man of a doubtful disposition should question whether these events are possible, may he read for his enlightenment what the *philosophus* Pomponatius has written and published, or the works of Theophrastus Bombastus Paracelsus and Thomas Aquinas, or indeed what the Council of Ancyra *Anno* 381 proclaims in a treatise, which begins with the words: *Quisquis ergo aliquid credit posse fieri . . .*)[1]

Thus during the hours of daylight she remained in her former human body, and no one noticed anything amiss in her appearance, though she was perhaps paler than before and there was less expression in her eyes, as if she were staring into secret, forbidden depths. And when in the evenings she took off her headdress her hair seemed ablaze with an even ruddier glow than before, like fire raging upon pine logs.

But in no way did she neglect a single one of her chores, but took care of everything like the dutiful housewife she once was, from the first chores of the morning to the last of the evening. And so she milked the cows, ground the handmill, suckled her child upon her breast and hoed and ploughed the fields as did all the other women of Hiidensaari. Indeed, it appeared that she was twice as diligent in everything she did, her hands and feet twice as nimble and her words to her husband Priidik all the sweeter. And many a man who saw her skipping back and forth across the garden to the well, like a bobbin between the threads of the loom, thought in his heart what a lucky fellow was he who could call this fond and fair woman his wife.

But when night came and Priidik had drifted into the heavy, weary sleep of a woodsman, so began his wife Aalo's other life, which during the day was carefully hidden, just as bats and moths awake from their slumber at night and nocturnal flowers begin to blossom for the night alone.

And this was the life she led at night, for it was of the night, of darkness and of the Devil.

For no sooner had Aalo noticed her husband Priidik drifting into sleep than she could feel her wolf's instincts bubbling in her blood, as if her other nature, by day suppressed deep within her, at night awoke and overwhelmed her with its potency.

For she, who once had been meek and mild, was now bold and blood-thirsty; she, who once had been timid, was now

[1] 'He, who believes that something may happen . . .'

untamed; she, who once had been chaste, was now brimming with lust.

And now every night Aalo, wedded wife of Priidik, surrendered herself wholly to her new lupine nature, and as her husband slept soundly she leapt from their marital bed and ran through the forests as a werewolf.

Then, as upon Midsummer's Eve, she willingly took part in the wolves' nocturnal journeys, and there was no bloody deed as would have appalled her nature, no Devil's dance in which she would not have whirled like a flake of snow blown by a gust of dæmon's breath.

At night the Spirit of the Wolf and of the Forest was wild within her and she was ready to do whatsoever *Diabolus sylvarum* commanded her to do, be it robbery or murder, or even blasphemy against the Almighty.

For now she belonged to *Diabolus sylvarum* in a strange and secret way, with all her body, with all her soul, as strongly as if she had entered a blood union with him.

Yet although Aalo celebrated the witches' Sabbath and ran through the forests as a wild beast each and every night, at first no one so much as noticed she was gone, for before the crow of the cock each morning she had returned and was lying beside her husband Priidik. Neither did any of the villagers realise that she had any part in the disappearance of kids and lambs, for they blamed the real wolves.

But if the Lord in His forbearance now and then allows Satan and his henchmen to run wild, in time He will nonetheless clench His fist around their tether once again and pull with all His might.

And it so happened that one morning the innkeeper from Haavasuo stopped by the cottage of Priidik the woodsman and as they exchanged words of greeting he said:

'My finest ewe is lost once again, for last night it was savaged by that forest cur.'

Thus Priidik the woodsman asked:

'Tell me, dear man, how has such a dreadful deed come to pass?'

And to this the innkeeper replied:

'Last night, when I heard bleating coming from the paddock, I went outside to look and saw that beast amongst the lambs. So I quickly looked for my musket and aimed it at the fearsome foe, and perchance I struck it in the foot, but alas the beast had already caught a lamb for itself and leapt limping into the forest.'

But barely had these words left his lips than Aalo, wedded wife of Priidik the woodsman, entered the cottage carrying a pail of water limping on her left ankle, which was bloody.

At this the innkeeper from Haavasuo fixed his eyes upon Aalo's ankle and said:

'Of course, it could also have been a werewolf, for nothing can dispatch them but a silver bullet or elder heartwood. I fear the spread of werewolves has already reached Hiidenmaa, for Valber from the village at Tempa was found to have run as a werewolf and has been delivered into the hands of the gaoler and the executioner.'

And he spoke further, as he continued to stare at Aalo and her ankle:

'Only this morning did Valber float in water as light as a goose or a reed, even though both her hands and feet were tied and crossed, and only when the local executioner began using the thumbscrew did she confess to running as a werewolf and visiting Blocksberg. A black man approached her in the forest, she said, first in the form of a haystack, then clothed in fine attire, as she sat binding brooms, and he offered her some sweet roots to eat; at first this tasted as sweet as nectar upon her tongue, then as foul and as foetid as Satan's spice, and then, from a vole's den beneath a rock, the man produced a wolf-belt and gave it to her.'

But upon hearing him speak Valber's name, Aalo's eyes froze for a moment, and she turned her back on the others.

To this Priidik the woodsman replied:

'This is indeed a woeful tale for the ears of good Christian folk, yet still the Count of Suuremõisa keeps aspens growing in his forests to ward off the wizards of Blocksberg. Why, my good innkeeper, have you ever seen a wolf-belt?'

And the innkeeper from Haavasuo replied:

'I have heard talk of them, though I have never seen one. Sometimes it is made of a wolf-skin, sometimes the skin of the hanged, and it is adorned with twelve dozen star constellations. And it is said to be tied around the waist using a buckle with seven tongues, but if even one of them is opened, the spell will be broken.'

At this Priidik the woodsman cried:

'Alas, that sin should be the burden of our birth! Why, others say a person need only crawl thrice beneath a tree trunk or run thrice around a rock speaking spells and he will be a werewolf made.'

The innkeeper then replied, shaking his head:

'When Valber was threatened with death by fire and faggot she cried out: if I must burn at the stake, then verily others shall burn with me. What may these words mean? Surely that Valber is not the only werewolf upon Hiidenmaa and that her sisters still run free!'

Thus Priidik the woodsman asked:

'How can we tell those who run with the wolves, what are their signs and features, so that we should know to beware of them?'

And to this the innkeeper from Haavasuo replied:

'Many say that werewolves are more pallid than natural people and that often their eyebrows meet above their noses, upon what folk call the Bridge of Beelzebub. And I have heard also that they have witches' marks upon their bodies, scratches made by Satan himself as he claws at them, and that they do not feel pain, not even if you stick them with a needle. And if a person is found slain in their bed, a small bite upon their left side, this too is the work of a werewolf and means that they are near at hand.'

And all the while, as the men spoke amongst themselves, Aalo stood perfectly still and silent, just like the water in the well.

But before he left, the innkeeper from Haavasuo stretched forth his arms and solemnly sighed:

'Help us, Heavenly Father, for in the words of Josaphat we beseech thee: wilt Thou not judge them? There must indeed be something woefully wrong with this world, crooked as the roof of Mustapeksu's barn, and the end nigh for all, when the children of God run in the woods as the Devil's whelps.'

And with those words he went on his way.

But when Priidik the woodsman and his wedded wife Aalo were once again alone in the cottage, Priidik too looked at Aalo's ankle, doubt burning his brains, and said:

'Why are you limping, wife? You were fine yesterday.'

But Aalo replied meekly, as was her wont:

'I knocked my ankle upon a sharp stone at the well, and look how it bleeds!'

And with that she tore a piece of linen and bandaged her wounded ankle to stop the bleeding, and they spoke no more of it on that occasion.

For Aalo was still surrounded by a magic force, full of the secrecy of witches and the Devil, and it was such that no mortal could yet break asunder.

## *Chapter Eight*

But one night in the month of August, not long after these events, as the harvest was almost ready and the nights began to darken, Priidik the woodsman awoke in his bed, a draught making him shiver. And as he was fumbling for the wolfskin he realised at once that he was alone and that his wife Aalo's place beside him lay empty.

At this a strange shudder shook his soul, like a shadow cast across the room darkening it for a moment, he prayed thrice and said:

'May the Lord and His Holy Angels look over her so no harm shall come to her, neither to her body nor to her soul, for she is as fragile as the finest glass, though her body is young and strong.'

But sleep no longer touched his eyes, and all night he remained wide awake, waiting for his wedded wife Aalo to return.

Thus finally the cock crowed in the farm, then another on the neighbour's grounds, and finally a third further off as a signal that night was gone and morning arrived.

And at that very moment Aalo his wife stepped through the door into the cottage and made straight for her bed.

Upon this Priidik the woodsman, pretending to be asleep, opened his eyes and said:

'Where have you been, wife? Whence do you come?'

And Aalo replied:

'I was in the birch grove tying up bath whisks, for tomorrow is Saturday and we shall bathe.'

And in her clothes and in her hair hung the scent of the forest and of marsh tea, of moist boggy moss and of marsh mud; heavy and dizzying, like bog and bilberry.

At once Priidik sensed this strange, fragrant scent as it filled his nostrils, as though the forest and all its inhabitants had been brought inside and filled the cottage, and he said:

'Day is for daytime chores, and night is for sleep and rest. Never before have you wandered to the woods at night.'

But when Aalo threw herself upon the bed, so the scent of the forest and of the swamp in her hair grew stronger, as if a wild forest beast had lain in the bed beside him, and not a young woman at all.

And he felt a secret surrounding her, one he could not explain, and his soul sensed in this secret a formidable foe, just as wild creatures sense a brewing storm.

With that he pushed his wife Aalo from him, so repulsed was he by this scent that he could not accept, for like a foreign Element it was against his nature.

At this he said:

'How comes the scent of the swamp in your hair?'

And Aalo replied:

'I went awandering by the swamp and gathered marsh tea in my apron to boil medicinal water. I may have had a branch in my hair for a moment.'

But Priidik the woodsman felt his heart tremble with pain that his wife should so brazenly lie to his face that he sat up in bed and said:

'You are lying, woman! You smell of wolf and not of the woods! Where have you been?'

And when Aalo did not say a word in reply lightning flashed through his soul and he shouted:

'Surely you did not spend the night running as a werewolf?'

But as soon as he had uttered these words Aalo began to quiver, so determined was her husband in pursuit of the truth.

And with that Priidik realised that he had indeed uncovered the truth, as easily as had he ensnared it in a trap, and shouted:

'O, my woeful wife, have you fallen into the hands of He who ravages the spirit? Was it you who took the innkeeper's sheep? Are you in league with the werewolves and the witches of Blocksberg?'

To this Aalo replied:

'What nonsense you speak, else it is the ale inside you talking.'

And Priidik said:

'My wife, there was a time you did not know how to lie, and your speech was nothing but the yea and the nay of the righteous!'

And at this he demanded:

'Do you run with the wolves or not?'

Thus Aalo finally replied:

'And if I do run with the wolves, if it is wolf's blood which burns in my veins, then there is nothing any of you can do, for the bliss and the damnation in my soul are mine alone.'

At this Priidik shouted:

'Thus you confess, you are indeed a werewolf, cut off from the company of Holy people, and Christ nailed in vain to the cross for your soul!'

And unto this Aalo said:

'Listen to me, Priidik, for my breast burns like coals in the fire! Though I spend the hours of day with other people, and though I have a human form, so my spirit yearns for the company of wolves whenever night is near, for only in the wilds have I such freedom and joy. And thus I must go, for I am the kin of wolves, though indeed I may be burnt at the stake as a witch, for this is how I have been made!'

But Priidik replied:

'Do not blaspheme the name of your Creator, woman, for you have been shaped by Satan himself.'

Yet search though he may as he looked upon his wife Aalo, he could see in the eyes of the Devil's child neither insolence nor brazen impenitence, for the woman beside him was timid like a forest creature and a beautiful sight for her husband's eye to behold.

But at that same moment he recalled that the beauty of the face is also Beelzebub's bait, as the wise Syrach forewarned: 'Turn away, my sons, turn your eyes from beautiful women, for many a man has their beauty maddened.'

And thus he further cursed his wife Aalo and said:

'Is this the meaning of the mark beneath your breast shaped like a night butterfly? Fie, what a fool I have been, that I did not notice this before and take heed. For truly it is a witch's mark and the fingerprint of the Evil One himself!'

To this Aalo replied:

'It is not a witch's mark; my mother took fright as the barn was ablaze, and thus my breast was marked inside her belly.'

At this Priidik scoffed:

'The Devil has indeed marked you at birth with his branding iron, so that he will know his own.'

And further he asked:

'When you are in the forest, do you visit the Devil?'

And Aalo replied:

'The Spirit of the Forest comes to me.'

And Priidik asked:

'In what form does he come to you, as a man or as a wolf?'

And Aalo replied:

'Neither as a man nor as a wolf, for he has neither form nor body: he is everywhere, invisible, like a spirit.'

Thus in his bitterness Priidik said:

'Who are you, my wife? Do you truly have two natures, one meek, one wild as the forest beasts, each taking their turn to overpower you, one thirsting for blood like the wolves, whilst the other has all the virtues of a wife!'

And at this his soul was consumed with darkness as he thought of how those beautiful limbs had been abused by Satan for his shameless deeds.

And thus he asked:

'Do you drink blood with the same lips as kiss your husband and take the Holy Communion?'

And Aalo replied:

'When I am a wolf, I do the deeds of wolves.'

At this Priidik the woodsman exclaimed in a booming voice:

'That my eyes should see the wife I first beheld as a young maid amongst the lambs now attack those same lambs as a werewolf and drink their innocent blood!'

And with that he quickly stood up, reached for his musket hanging on the wall, and threatening his wedded wife Aalo he shouted:

'Out of my sight, wolf's whore! Go and join your kin!'

And thus Aalo's hands dropped from the side of the bed, to which in fright she had clung, as a drowning man clings to a log as the waters swallow him into their depths, just as her soul now left her body, leaving forever the community of Christ and the protection of the church.

Thus Aalo hurried past her husband, through the door and into the garden, and from there into the forest she ran, along the pathless paths of the wolves to join her sisters and brothers in joys which belong not to humans, but to wolves, and are eternally shrouded in secrecy.

# *The Legend of the Pale Maiden*

Aleksis Kivi

*Aleksis Kivi (born Aleksis Stenvall, 1834–1872) is widely considered the father of the Finnish novel. Kivi also wrote poetry and plays which are now considered classic works, but* Seven Brothers *('Seitsemän veljestä', 1870) is his seminal work and without a doubt* the *classic of Finnish literature; indeed it was the first full-scale novel ever published in Finnish. Although it is written in the spirit of realism, the novel demonstrates through the brothers the extent to which the world of myth and legend was very real and palpable, and fundamentally rooted in the Finnish mindset of the day. In the extract presented here the brothers recall how their village Impivaara (literally 'Maiden Hill') acquired its name.*

*Simeoni*: Listen to the hoot of the eagle owl in the wilds – his hooting never foretells of good. Old folk say it bodes of fires, bloody battles and murders.

*Tuomas*: It is his job to hoot in the forest and it bodes nothing at all.

*Eero*: But this is the village; the turf-roofed house of Impivaara.

*Simeoni*: And now the seer has moved; look, there he hoots upon the mountain ridge. That is where, as legend tells us, the Pale Maiden prayed for the forgiveness of her sins; there she prayed every night in winter and in summer.

*Juhani*: This maiden gave Impivaara its name. I once heard this story as a child, but I fear it has mostly faded from my mind. Brother Aapo, tell us this tale to while away this sorry night.

*Aapo*: Timo is already snoring like a man; but let him lie in peace. I will gladly tell you this tale.

And thus Aapo recounted to his brothers the legend of the Pale Maiden:

In the caves beneath the mountain there once lived a terrible troll, bringing horror and death to many. Only two passions and pleasures did he have: to see and behold his treasures hidden deep within the mountain caves and to drink human blood, which he craved fervently. But only nine paces from the foot of mountain did he have the strength to overpower his victims, and thus it was with stealth that he undertook his journeys into the woods. He could change his form at will; he could often be seen roaming these parts, sometimes as a handsome young man, sometimes as an enchanting maiden, depending on whether it was the blood of a man or a woman he craved. Many were ensnared by the demonic beauty of his eyes; many lost their lives in his abominable caves. In this manner did the monster lure his hapless victims into his lair.

It was a fine summer's night. Upon a green meadow there sat a youth holding in his arms a young woman, his beloved, who like a resplendent rose rested upon his breast. This was to be their final farewell, for the boy was to travel far away and leave his bosom friend for a time. 'My love,' spoke the young man, 'I must leave you now, but barely shall a hundred suns rise and set before we meet again.' And to this the maiden replied: 'Not even the sun as it sets looks with such fondness upon its world as I upon my beloved as we part, nor as it rises does the blazing sky shine as gloriously as will my eyes as I run to meet you. And all that will fill my soul each bright day until then is the image of you, and through the mists of my dreams shall I walk beside you always.' – Thus spoke the girl, but then the young man said: 'You speak beautifully indeed, yet why does my soul sense evil? Fair maiden, let us swear eternal fidelity to one another, here beneath the face of heaven'. And thus they swore a holy vow, sworn before God and the heavens, and the forest and the hillside listened, breathless, to their every word. Yet alas as day broke they embraced each other one last time and parted. The young man hastened away, but for a long time the maiden wandered through the forest twilight, thinking only of her handsome beloved.

And there as she wanders deep amongst the thick pine woods, what strange figure is this she sees approaching? She sees a young man, noble as a prince and as resplendent as the golden morning. The plume upon his hat shines and flickers like a flame. From his shoulders hangs a cloak, blue as the sky and like the sky lit with sparkling stars. His tunic is white as snow and around his waist is tied a purple belt. He looks towards the maiden and in his eyes a burning love smoulders, and most divine is the note in his voice as he says to the young lady: 'Fear not, fair maiden; why, I am your friend and can bring you unending happiness, if but once I may take you into my arms. I am a powerful man, I have treasures and precious stones beyond number – I could buy the whole world, if I so wished. Follow me as my beloved and I shall take you to my wonderful castle and place you by my side upon a glorious throne.' Thus spoke the man in a charming voice and the maiden stood in awe. She remembered the vow she had just sworn and turned away, but soon turned back towards the man once again, and a peculiar worry filled her mind. She turned towards the man, covering her face as if looking into the glaring sun; again she turned away, but glanced once more at the strange figure. His powerful charm beamed upon her, and all at once she fell into the arms of the handsome prince. Off sped the prince, his prey lying spellbound in his arms. Over steep hills, through deep dales they travelled, and the forest around them became ever darker. The maiden's heart throbbed restlessly and drops of pained sweat ran down her brow, for suddenly she saw something beastly, something terrifying amidst the captivating flames in the man's eyes. She looked around as thick spruce groves flew past as her bearer dashed on apace; she glanced at the man's face and she felt a terrible trembling throughout her body, yet still a strange attraction burned in her heart.

Onwards they travelled through the forest until finally they could see the great mountain and its dark caves. And now, as they were but a few paces from the foot of the mountain, something horrible took place. The man in his regal cloak turned suddenly into a terrible troll: horns burst forth upon his head, his neck began to bristle with thick hair, and the forlorn girl could feel the sting of his sharp claws in her breast; and thereupon the maiden began to shout, to struggle and kick in frantic agony, but all in vain. With a wicked cry of joy the troll dragged her deep into his cave and drank every last drop of her blood. But then a miracle occurred: her spirit did not leave the maiden's limbs, and she remained alive, bloodless and snow-white; a plaintive ghost from the realm of shadows. The troll saw this and, thus vexed, lashed out at his victim with his claws and teeth, with all his might, but still he could not bring death upon her. Finally he decided to keep her for himself, deep in the eternal night of his caves. But what service could she perform for him, what use could she have for the troll? He commanded the maiden to polish all his treasures and precious stones and to pile them endlessly in front of him, for never did he tire of admiring them.

And so for years this pale, bloodless maiden lives imprisoned in the mountain's womb. Yet by night she can be seen quietly praying high upon the ridge. Who could have given her such freedom? The power of the heavens? – But every night, come storm, rain or hard frost, she stands atop the mountain praying for the forgiveness of her sins. Bloodless, snow-white and like a picture, so motionless and silently she stands, her hands crossed upon her breast and her head bowed deeply. Not once does the poor maiden dare raise her head towards the heavens, for her gaze is fixed upon the church spire, far away at the edge of the forest. For always in her ear there whispers a voice of hope; though nothing more than a distant murmur across thousands of leagues, she catches a glimpse of this hope. And thus she spends her nights upon the mountain ridge, and never can a word of complaint be heard from her lips; nor does her praying breast rise or fall with sighs. And thus the dark nights pass, but come daybreak the ruthless troll drags her back into his caves.

Barely had a hundred suns shone upon the earth when the young man, the maiden's beloved, jubilantly returned home from his journey. But alas his fair maiden did not rush towards him to welcome him home. He enquired where his beauty may be, but not a soul knew of her whereabouts. He searched for her everywhere, every day and night, tirelessly, but in vain: like the morning dew the maiden had disappeared without a trace. At last he lost all hope, forgot all the joys of life and for many years he wandered these hills as a silent shadow. Finally, as another shining day broke, the endless night of death extinguished the light from his eyes.

Frightfully long were the years for the pale maiden: by day polishing incessantly the troll's treasures under the gaze of her cruel tormentor and piling them before his eyes; by night atop the mountain ridge. Bloodless, snow-white and like a picture, so motionless and silently she stands, her hands upon her breast and her head bowed deeply. Not once does she dare raise her head towards the heavens, for her gaze is fixed upon the church spire, far away at the edge of the forest. Never does she complain; never does her praying breast rise or fall with sighs.

It is a light summer's night. On the mountain ridge stands the maiden, remembering the agonising time she has spent in captivity; a hundred years have passed since the day she parted from her betrothed. Horrified, she swoons and cold pearls of sweat run from her brow down to the mossy soil at the foot of the mountain as she thinks of the terrible length of those bygone decades. At that moment she felt the courage, for the first time, to look up to the heavens, and a moment later she discerned a blinding light approaching her like a shooting star from the furthest outreaches of space. And the closer to her this light came, the more it began to change its form. This was no shooting star; it was the young man, transfigured, a flashing sword in his hand. And with that the maiden's heart began to beat feverishly, as the wonderful familiarity of that face dawned upon her; for now she recognised the face of her former groom. But why was he approaching with a sword in his hand? The maiden was vexed and said in a weak voice: 'Will this sword finally end my pain? Here is my breast, young hero, strike your shining blade here and, if you can, bring me death, which for so long I have yearned after.' Thus she spoke on the mountain ridge, but the young man did not bring her death, but the sweet breath of life, which like a fragrant, whispering morning breeze enveloped the pale maiden. The young man, his eyes filled with love, took her in his arms and kissed her, and at this the bloodless maiden felt the sweet ripple of blood running once again through her veins, her cheeks glowed like clouds at the glorious break of day and her fair brow brimmed with joy. And with that she threw her head of fine locks across her beloved's arm and looked up to the bright heavens, her breast sighing away the suffering of the bygone years; and the young man ran his fingers through her locks as they swayed gently in the breeze. How wonderful was the hour of her salvation and the morning of her deliverance! The birds chirped in the spruce trees along the sides of that steep mountain and from the north-east shone the first radiant sliver of the rising sun. This morning was indeed worthy of the morning the couple parted on the green meadow for so long a time.

But then the angry troll, his tail on end with rage, climbed up the mountain to drag the maiden back into his caverns. But no sooner had he bared his claws at the maiden than the young man's sword like lightning struck his breast, whereupon his black blood spurted across the mountain. The maiden turned her face away from this sight and pressed her brow into her beloved's breast, as shrieking wildly the troll breathed his last and plummeted down the mountainside. And so it was that the world was saved from this terrible monster. And upon the bright edge of a silver cloud the young man and the maiden rose up to the heavens. The bride rested upon the knee of her groom and with her brow against his breast she smiled with joy. Through the skies they flew, and into the infinite depths below them sank the forest, the mountains and undulating valleys and dales. And finally, as if into blue smoke, everything disappeared from their view.

And thus ends the legend of the Pale Maiden, which Aapo told his brothers that dreamless night in the turf-roofed cabin in the glades of Impivaara.

# *Island of the Setting Sun*

Mika Waltari

*Mika Waltari (1908–1979) was a prolific writer who, in addition to his many novels, published hundreds of short stories, poems, columns and scripts for stage and screen. He wrote a number of international bestsellers, the most famous of these being* The Egyptian *('Sinuhe, Egyptiläinen', 1945) and his works have been translated into over 30 languages, including English. Waltari was fascinated by mythology, mysticism and the nature of love and desire, and he made particular use of such elements in his early output. At the age of 17 he published the collection of horror stories* Kuolleen silmät *('The Eyes of the Dead', 1926) under the pseudonym Kristian Korppi (the word* korppi *means 'raven' and is presumably an allusion to Edgar Allan Poe's poem of the same name). It is from this collection that the present text is taken.*

I, the final king of the vanquished Viking tribe of the Valley of Three Suns, have commanded Father Anselmus, newly arrived from the land of the Gauls, to commit to posterity that which I am about to impart: the tale of our journey to the Island of the Setting Sun; else it shall be lost, it shall disappear along with me into the land of eternal shadows, where my ancestors have stepped before me, and in whose footsteps I, the last of my kin, a few years hence must follow.

My mother belonged to the Celts, ennobled in lore. My father brought her home as the glorious spoils of a great sea voyage and made her his wife, so in love was he with her eyes of deepest green and her body that smelt of seagrass. Throughout the long winters, when the sun was banished far from our snow-covered valley, my mother would sing in a strange, soft and wistful language peculiar songs which I did not understand, but which filled my heart with a yearning for far-off lands.

And so I grew into a young man, and the learned men amongst our slaves taught me the wisdom of eastern and southern lands. And when my father's time was done and in a burning ship he set off upon his final journey, so I became king of our valley's feared and powerful tribe.

My mind was ablaze with thoughts of battles and a soldier's honour. Many a summer we undertook great sea voyages in our dreaded longships to fertile southern climes, to the fruitful land of the Gauls, down to the blue waters of the Midd Sea, where the sky glowed and the sun was hot. There on those fertile shores we would fill our ships to the brim with treasures and mothers would fright their children in my name.

But all this had my ancestors done before me, and I was not content with the heroic honour of old. On dark evenings, as autumn storms raged out at sea and thick black clouds passed above us like great, shrieking birds, in the king's quarters people drank from goblets of pure gold the heavy, spiced wine of those southern, sun-kissed groves to the sound of dice rattling, strange tales and songs of heroism. But my mind was far from them. I thought only of the Land of the Setting Sun, guarded by monsters of the sea, where no man had ventured before. Neither heroic glory nor the spiced wine; neither the tense, fierce game nor the gentle bodies of maidens with silken skin and in whose flesh there lay an intoxicating pleasure – none of this could contain my yearning. On the contrary, in their every pulse, in every momentary glance and in every curve and fibre of their bodies I sensed this unknown land.

I told the others of my longing and of my secret intention. Some said that I had lost my wits, some that I had been possessed; but a number of them, the red thrill of adventure running in their veins, decided to join me.

And so when spring finally arrived and the sea broke free of its icy shackles and was born again, young and unbridled, as the storks sped in great arrows across the sky, their cries full of an untamed longing, we set sail. We pushed our most gallant dragon ship out to sea, and as the wooden boards wailed we felt as formidable as gods at the beginning of time taking their first valiant steps into an unknown world.

On the day of our departure the sun was hidden behind grey clouds and from atop the fells owls hooted menacing words. Those who stayed ashore were sullen and melancholic. But as a hundred slaves took up their heavy oars and the bow of our dragon ship began to cut through the murky, green water like an eagle soaring across the infinite sky, we let out a cry full of life and adventure, and that cry shook the sheer cliffs above the heavy clouds, and no longer were we burdened.

We rowed day and night, with a hundred slaves at the oars and our purple sails bulging in the wind. And we felt the thrill of racing ahead and sang proud, menacing songs.

We steered past the familiar shores of the lowlands. At the sight of our feared ship and the ruddy shadow of our sails people would flee into the forests and the dull sound of warning bells would peal out from towers across the towns. But we cared not for them, and soon the jagged edges of those towers were nothing but ghosts on the horizon.

We sped past the misty shores of the isles of the Celts on the wings of a storm from the east. After we had helped ourselves to food and water from the outermost point of the land of the Gauls, we finally arrived at the great ocean which only few ships have sailed. With the stars as our guides we set off towards the sunset.

The final shore disappeared behind us. We were a mere spot between two infinities. But we were not afraid, for the wild, red blood of sea-kings flowed through our veins.

The wind had abated and an invisible swell gently rocked our ship, sailing ever forwards. There was not a sound, save for the creaking of the oars in their locks and the ferocious singing of the half-naked slaves.

We loved the sea and every evening we made a sacrifice to it as the sun was setting and a red twilight descended upon the green water. It was as though we were crossing a bloody bridge towards the sunset and the heavy clouds which had fallen between the sea and the sky. And at once we knew that the gods were dead and that the last of the living were aboard our ship and steering ahead into the emptiness. But we were not afraid, though the fear of emptiness wrenched our hearts like an iron clamp.

After we had left our final shore, the sun had set fourteen times when the first of our slaves died. Morning was breaking, sky and sea had become one, a pink mist shrouding everything in its wake. Like shadows the slaves' bodies crouched forwards, then strained back again, their contours blurred through the mist, and not a sound could be heard, not even the splash of the oars. Then one of the slaves fell backwards, his back arched unnaturally across the bench; with a thud his head struck the thwart plank after which his body did not so much as shudder. We untied him from his shackles without stopping the others' rowing. He was healthy, young and strong, his body did not reveal the slightest wound or mark, but he was dead and so we threw him overboard into the sea. Through the mists we saw his body sink immediately, but we did not hear the slightest sound, nor did the water splash up into the air. Soon afterwards the sun dispersed the fog, but it was not a normal sun: it was an enormous sun, tinged in a dim red, like a shield rusted in blood.

The sun remained like this for several days and the motionless sea gradually turned restless. Strange sounds could be heard from the water; moaning, the roar of a giant war horse, making our ship's masts tremble.

For a long time we had not seen a single living creature in the sea. The water's surface had been still and motionless, our ship's progress slow and exhausting. But now froth and enormous bubbles began rising to the surface; as they burst they made a low, strange gurgling sound. We recalled tales of giant sea monsters and tremours ran the length of our bodies. But we were not afraid.

The following morning a second slave died in the same manner as the first.

The nights were as black as the gates of hell. The darkness seemed to thicken around us so that we could touch it. We tried to light torches, but they would not burn. We could barely hear each other's voices, for even the loudest yell sounded as powerless as the faint whisper of a child.

Only the stars shone in the sky above. Like our shields they were great and they glowed like embers in the hearth. We recognised them no longer. But we were not afraid and we refused to turn back, for we were the kin of heroes. Bravely we steered our dragon ship towards the setting sun. Yet our songs did not ring out as before, and almost every morning another slave died for no apparent reason.

After we had been at sea for forty-two sunsets, a storm broke. Both sea and sky turned black and we tethered ourselves to the masts. Waves the size of mountains crashed around us and the water blinded and deafened us. It felt as if our sails had swollen and we were gliding up and down along the slopes of the waves towards the setting sun to the creaking and howling of every join and plank. At every moment we expected the ship to split asunder, but as if protected by some strange power it remained intact and at an unimaginable speed we travelled onwards.

None of us knew how long the storm lasted. The ropes with which we had tied ourselves fast cut deep into our flesh and the salt water stung our raw wounds. We could see neither the sun nor the stars. We were nothing but a boat of shadows amidst the thick blackness, at the mercy of a maelstrom of darkness shaking us like the hands of the fell spirits. All that could be heard above the thundering storm were the agonised cries of the drowning slaves as they prayed to their own gods. But we did not pray, for we knew that here the gods were dead.

Finally we too cried for death, for our pains were too great. But suddenly the storm abated. The sun once again shone across a radiant blue sky, as if a great hand had swept the clouds behind the horizon. And our boat rocked gently upon a smooth swell, as the water heaved in the wake of the sea's rage.

The ship had survived unscathed. A few yards had been snapped, some of the railings broken, but none had lost his life. And we realised that, carried on the wings of the storm, we had covered such a distance as would have taken an entire month to row.

At that moment the slaves began to cry out: 'Land! Land!' And across the ridges of the gentle waves, far away towards the setting sun, we could see the spires of three stone towers.

The sun was brighter, the sky bluer and the sea shimmering greener than ever before. We sensed our destination was near. But we did not rejoice, and we no longer had gods to whom we could offer thanks.

The slaves rowed onwards with renewed vigour and resumed their ferocious singing which echoed out across the waves. The towers gradually became greater and from the sea there rose an island, and never before had we seen anything as beautiful.

Once again we were consumed with the heroic deeds of our Viking forefathers. We hankered for a great battle. As we sharpened our blades and the slaves polished our shields, rusted by the salt water, we sang the old war songs sung by our ancestors as they had once approached the rich ports of foreign lands.

The dull clank of our shields was ominous. It felt as if, after we were gone, not a soul would sing our songs again. But we strove to believe that our clanking boded ill for those who stood against us. And we strove to take pride in the red blood flowing through our veins.

Night fell. We rowed steadily onwards and discerned images of battle in the stars. By morning the sea was engulfed in a green mist. Once it dispersed we saw in front of us, but a stone's throw away, the Island of the Setting Sun.

We noticed what a beautiful and rich island it was, with great, unknown trees growing upon it. In its centre stood a mountain, a green trail running up one side; a road laid of strange, coloured stone. At the mountain top was a triangular temple, and its three towers stood silhouetted, dark green and sharp against the sky.

Ahead of us was a harbour built into a small cove in the bay and around this lay a town, its buildings carved from green stone. Bushes grew right up to the water's edge and their red and white flowers were reflected in the clear water. We could make out the seabed beneath us; great brown reeds swayed there gently and little fish darted in between them. Everything was perfectly still. Not even a puff of smoke rose from the chimneys in the town and we did not hear a single voice. It seemed that the entire town was dead.

Then we saw them: a group of soldiers standing in thick, motionless rows was waiting precisely where we were to disembark. They were clothed in green and bore round shields, edged in green and with an image in the centre the features of which we could not clearly make out. The points of their spears were bright and from the belt of each and every soldier hung a short, wide sword. There were at least four hundred of them; we were a mere forty in number not counting the slaves. But we were puzzled by the silence and stillness of these troops. They stood unflinchingly at the edge of the forest; we did not see banners, nor did we hear the cry of the battle horn nor a single shout of defiance.

A strange fear came over us as we watched them. But the sun was shining across the glaring blue sky and we rowed the rest of the journey, water rushing past our bow. Through the clear water we could make out the shadow of our boat racing ahead. We let out the Viking battle cry, the flank of our ship struck the harbour, hewn from green rock, with a thud and we jumped ashore protecting our heads with our shields, consumed with a battle fever upon once again feeling dry land beneath our feet.

A cloud of spears rained down towards us, but we repelled them with our shields. Still we did not hear a sound. As I looked at our adversaries I felt a strange shudder. Their faces were deathly pale, almost transparent, like marble from the sunny shores of the Midd Sea; their mouths were thin and their lips tightly pressed together; their noses narrow and arched downwards; their eyes long, oval and dark. Each of them was a head shorter than us.

But men they were all the same, those green-caped enemies. There was something sombre and deeply disturbing about their silent resistance. Not one of them moved from his position. We waded through blood, blunting our swords. None of them prayed for mercy or surrendered as a prisoner. And when finally we rested, exhausted and gasping for breath, the shore was awash in bodies and blood and broken weapons. Not a single man survived amongst our enemies. Even the wounded thrust blades into their own chests, silently straining to end their suffering.

We rested and buried our dead before pillaging the town, and we gathered weapons and jewels from the bodies of our adversaries. We collected a hoard of rings and buckles, crafted of gold and an unfamiliar, heavy, pale metal. And now we saw that the figure on our fallen enemies' shields was that of a woman in a green cape, her hands raised towards the sky and the sun.

And so the sun set once again behind this island, and it was blood-red from the blood that had been shed that day. Night fell. The slaves gathered wood and on the shore we set great pyres alight. The slaves made torches to light our path as we plundered the town. It was a magnificent and rich town, and upon the shore we gathered piles of gold and precious stones and strange, unknown metals. Never before had any Viking ship amassed such treasures.

We also found women hidden in the vaults of the buildings. Even as we dragged them out of their hiding places, they did not utter a word. They stood before us in silence, their brown hair hanging tousled around their green capes. They were indeed beautiful to our eyes. In these underground vaults we discovered small firkins carved from brown, shining wood, each filled to the brim with a strange wine giving off the pungent odour of unknown herbs. In the light of the pyres we spent the rest of the night celebrating our victory, drinking wine and sharing our spoils. And the wine entered our blood making us wild and berserk.

I saw my men and our slaves tear the clothes from the island's womenfolk in the red light of the pyres; their white bodies trembled on the damp ground and they covered their faces with their brown hair. But not a sound passed from their clenched lips, though our slaves' iron hands ravaged their fragile young bodies.

The following morning the shore was a scene of destruction, littered with the remnants of our feast. However, at the site of the battle there was no longer a single body to be seen. This surprised us greatly, but we understood that the women must have buried their dead overnight. Above us on the mountain top loomed the green temple, dark and foreboding against the bright rays of the sun, and its towers cast a black shadow across the slaves sleeping on the shore.

We set off upwards along a wide path of green slabs. The path was lined with great, strange trees. We tasted their fruits but discovered that they had a sharp, bitter taste. In a small field nearby grew an unknown crop, and its ears were the red hue of rust.

Not a single animal did we see on our journey. Once, however, something flew across our path, like a great, green bird, whose shadow brushed each and every one of us. We also heard a cry of pain, something which sounded like the drawn-out wailing of a dying man. We decided it must have been the soul of one of our fallen enemies. At this we laughed heartily and sang the victory song of heroes as we slowly climbed up the mountainside.

As we finally reached the temple the sun was shining from the very centre of the sky and our shadows were nothing but small, dark patches around our feet. The temple had been carved into the green rockface, for in all its high walls there appeared not a single seam or join. A great gate, depicting soldiers and the same green woman as on our enemies' shields, lay wide open. We stepped through this into a triangular courtyard, and at the centre of this stood a round building surrounded by green pillars.

Just as we were walking into the courtyard, one of my men fell to the ground with a yell. We examined him and saw that a wound he had sustained in the previous day's battle had reopened during our long ascent and now his blood ran into the cracks in the rock beneath us. Soon after this he perished.

The courtyard was triangular and its two sides pointing west were the longest. It was surrounded by a wall and in each corner stood a triangular tower. I climbed alone into the western tower, through dark stone staircases, and realised that it was empty. Only once I reached its flat roof did I discover a number of charred bones, which surprised me, as we had still not sighted a single living animal on this island. From the tower a view opened up across the whole island. It too was an irregular triangle shape. There was no other settlement on the island other than the green town at the base of the triangle.

As I descended from the tower my eyes became accustomed to the dark green light in the staircase and inscribed on the walls I could make out strange, intricate patterns and a repeating text in a lettering resembling Greek. Our slaves the learned men had instructed me in deciphering Greek script as a child, but the tower was too dark for me to understand anything of this text.

Upon stepping out of the doorway I caught sight of a woman dressed in a green cloak, her white arms bare, leaving the round building at the centre of the courtyard. She stood between two pillars and raised her hands towards the sun. Never in all my days had I seen such a beautiful woman.

She did not move, nor did she avert her eyes as we approached her. But as the sun shone into her eyes – and she endured the glare of the sun – we saw that her long, oval eyes were a deep shade of green.

She lowered her arms and turned to look at us. But she did not see us, for she was blind. Her body shuddered slightly as I approached her and placed a slave's shackle around her wrist. And I was surprised to see blue veins running the length of her pale, translucent arms. She then left us, knelt at the foot of one of the pillars and hid her face with her hair. And we stepped through the dark doorway into the temple with swords in our hands, our shields clanging against one another.

The holy room was a round room edged once again with green pillars. A pale green dimness hung along the walls, but there at the centre, lit through skilfully placed openings in the walls and ceiling by the bright sun, stood the image of a goddess on a low pedestal, and upon seeing this we stopped and stared in awe.

It was carved entirely of green stone; the figure of a woman, her face and arms raised towards the sky. Her body was shrouded in a green cape reaching down to her knees and attached around her neck with a golden brooch, just like all the women on the island. The cape was embroidered in gold with strange patterns, of which I could only recognise the symbol of infinity, a snake biting its own tail, inside an irregular triangle. Her perfect body arched gently backwards, as if opening up into a great embrace.

The statue was the size of a human, but the strange lighting made it look considerably larger. Her face was unfathomably beautiful, her lips half open, yet expressionless. Her eyes were two frosted green jewels, glowing with life in the beams of sunlight. The pedestal was inscribed with the same maxim that I had seen on the tower walls. I knelt down to examine it. It contained three words, but I could not make them out. A letter was missing from each word making it impossible even to guess their meaning. This same maxim was carved into each of the twenty-seven stone pillars. Each of them was also missing the same letters.

The statue seemed almost alive. In the shimmering sunlight its body seemed to tremble. We felt that at any moment it could step down from its pedestal. And yet we knew that it was nothing but dead, cold stone.

It was a god, but it was the god of a vanquished people. I took my sword and with a single slash I cut the cape from around her neck and it fell to the ground. Before us stood the green goddess, disrobed, naked, her arms and body extended as if in a passionate embrace. This effigy truly was more beautiful than all mortal women.

We had hoped to curse the god of this thwarted land, but now we stood in silence before its beauty. We felt as if this statue were alive, radiating a mysterious potency and a strange passion. We stood up straight and our muscles bulged with a longing to feel that embrace. I knew that she must be warm and alive, and, my hand burning with desire, I touched her breast pointing rebelliously, defiantly forwards. But it was hard and cold. At that moment I was like a child so much did I want to cry with disappointment.

Just then, around her delicate, left ankle, I caught sight of a thick bangle, fashioned from that same unknown, white metal. The jewels sunk into its sides flashed and gleamed in the sunlight. The others tried to remove it, but did not succeed. But then I noticed a seam in the bangle and touched it. It opened immediately. I placed it around my right wrist and it locked shut with a click. And since then I have never managed to open it again, but have worn it for the forty-eight winters that have passed since that day, and shall wear it until the sun has finally disappeared from this life and this my arm is but dust among dust. But there on the goddess' ankle, where the bangle had been, there was now a white mark, like a circle drawn on human flesh with a hot iron.

As we stepped out into the courtyard we saw that the woman at the foot of the pillar had died. We lifted our dead brother-in-arms and carried him upon our shields down the mountainside, singing a song of eternal shadows. But I could think only of the green goddess' beauty and I sensed that my companions were thinking of her too. And at that moment I realised that I despised them all.

Once again the sun began to disappear behind the island. Down in the harbour and in the houses of this devastated city we celebrated our victory, wine frothed in golden goblets and dice rattled against one another. We played for women and we played for gold and the treasures of the Island of the Setting Sun. We felt powerful and we knew our blades were sharp. And in secret we watched one another, but no one spoke a word about the green goddess. Yet every second we knew that there she stood up above, wondrous, alone, her divine body arched in a great, naked embrace. The towers atop her temple were framed in the setting sun, turning them black and green and blood-red.

The pale green dusk thickened into night. In the sky stars

lit up and on the shore great pyres burned. The new moon rose from the sea, red and immensely heavy. But we did not find peace, for our breasts were filled with a restless yearning. My companions began to fight amongst themselves for the first time since we set off. None of them, as yet, drew his sword.

Some time before midnight I made my decision and told my comrades of my plans to return to the mountain. At that same moment I forbade any of them to follow in my steps. I was the king and my word was the law. The men grumbled in response, but none defied me. I set off and took my sword with me but left my heavy shield at our camp.

Once on the path, out of sight of the others, I began to run up the mountainside, for my yearning was great. The moon shone red and a fire burned in my heart, the like of which I had never felt before, hindering my ascent and making me gasp for breath. Walking past unknown trees I picked their fruit and ate them; they burned my throat, but this to me was sweet. Strange shadows danced before my eyes, but I was not afraid, for I was consumed with a new strength, making me run and my muscles swell with renewed power.

In the moonlight the green of the temple towers and the walls acquired a deep red tinge. At the foot of the pillar lay the woman's dead body, contorted, but now her face had turned towards the moon, her head twisting unnaturally over her shoulder, her eyes wide open. But the sanctum was bright red from the light of the moon.

I stopped in the purple shadow of the pillars. The statue was as it had been. Her body was caught in the grip of passion and on her left ankle was a ghostly pale stripe where the bangle had been. I caressed her body, her breasts and the curve of her hips, and their frigidity so blinded me with rage that I wished I could die. And I, king of the greatest and most feared land, knelt before the goddess of this vanquished tribe and prayed to her and hit my head against the stone floor begging her to appear to me and to surrender to me the wonder of her green, shimmering body. For I loved her and my blood burned for her.

From the door I heard a clatter, the faint sound of metal against stone. And when I turned around I saw one of my comrades, the one I loved dearest of all; my blood brother, for once he had saved my life in the land of the Gauls. His whole body trembled as he looked upon the naked goddess, bathed in dark red moonlight. I saw his clenched fists and my bile rose. I raised my voice and threatened him with my wrath for disobeying my orders. And with that I commanded him to return from whence he had come.

Yet he did not heed me or my words, he barely heard my voice, but approached the goddess and touched her naked shoulder. I drew my sword and so the blood of my closest friend flowed into a black puddle on the floor and I saw the fire in his upturned eyes die away. Yet I felt no remorse, for I could see that the goddess had turned her head and was smiling at me and that on her face was an expression I could not fathom.

At this I tore at my clothes, I bared her my breast, brown and strong. And I knelt on the cold floor and vowed to forsake my kin and the place of my birth and everything that once I had cherished, if only she would love me.

And at this the goddess stepped down from her pedestal. Soon I sensed that her green skin was soft and warm and fragrant. Her long, oval eyes looked at me, searing through me, drowning my thoughts in their green fire. As I felt her wonder against my body I whispered hot, passionate words into her ear. And as I clasped her to my breast I heard the last drops of blood slowly trickle from the body of my closest friend and fall to the stone floor.

When finally I lay back on the cold floor, a last throb surging in my veins, she had returned to her pedestal and raised her hands towards the stars. I understood that she was cursing me and my companions and my tribe and everything I held dear. Her eyes glowed with a hatred of which I had never seen the like. But nothing could stir me; I fell into a sweet, languid sleep which was not sleep at all, but a deathly slumber.

The sun was shining high above when I awoke to the

sound of three of my companions entering the temple in search of me. They were pale and sad and my mind was filled with dark misgivings. They were shocked at the sight of my friend's body on the floor, but no one uttered a word as I commanded them to bear forth the body.

My men reported that the previous night, after I had left, a quarrel and a fight had broken out amongst the men. The discord had soon turned to bloodshed. The men all believed the others had betrayed them, and eventually the smallest move of the dice had resulted in a brawl. The slaves had then begun arguing over wine and women. As a result barely half of the slaves and only a handful of others remained alive, and these three companions implored me to leave the island without delay, for here strange and malevolent forces reigned.

I looked at the goddess and the men looked at her too. I understood that her arms were extended in a curse and that there was wicked rejoicing in the expression upon her face, but my companions could not see any change in her. In their eyes fear and desire merged into a wild glow.

At that point I let it be known that I wished to take this green effigy as a token of our victory. The men took fright, but when I said that all I wanted was the statue and that they could share between themselves all our treasures, they became happy again. But still they were not content.

I ordered them to carry the statue down to the ship and each tried in turn, but not one of them could move it. Then I took hold of it myself and I felt it rise into my arms. I carried it just as the Viking warriors had once carried home their stolen brides. My companions were amazed at my strength, though I did not feel the weight of the statue in the slightest. And on its ankle there was a pale stripe and upon my wrist the heavy jewelled bangle.

As we marched through the devastated city, the statue of the green goddess in my arms, the women tore at their clothes and rubbed earth into their hair. But when they saw the goddess' bangle upon my arm, their eyes were filled with horror and astonishment and they knelt on the ground and bowed down before me.

I carried the effigy on to the ship and stood it upon the foredeck. We buried our dead in a mass grave and ordered the slaves to assemble a cairn at the site. The bodies of the slaves we threw into the sea. All in all there were only a dozen of us left and a score of slaves.

We loaded our treasures on to the ship and it heaved beneath of the weight of gold and precious stones. In addition we took water, grain and fruit. But we did not rejoice.

Night had already fallen, but we did not wish to remain on the island a moment longer. We raised the sails and, guided by the stars, we slowly began rowing towards the sunrise. Behind us the Island of the Setting Sun disappeared into the dark night, but still the shadow of its towers was cast upon us and we felt the weight of that shadow.

The sun rose many times and set many times, the moon died and was reborn. A virulent disease erupted amongst the slaves, and they died one after the other, their bodies covered in terrible boils. The sea was menacing and there was no favourable wind. And my companions were filled with dread, afraid that we would never find our way across these unknown waters.

The nights were pitch-dark and every night the green goddess would wake from her stony sleep and I would clasp her to my chest upon the ship's rolling deck. Her love was destructive, but its wonder was great.

One day my companions came to me and said that we would never again see the land of our birth unless I threw the green goddess into the sea; the statue which brought us only misery and destruction. But I did not agree to this. And when they attempted to take her by force I fought to protect her. Thus I slew my remaining companions and commanded the slaves to cast their bodies into the sea. I had not been wounded, but now I was alone.

The disease continued to spread amongst the slaves, though I myself killed and threw into the sea every one of them at the first sight of a boil upon their skin. They perished one after the other. By the next full moon I was the only living creature aboard the ship and there was no one to attend to the sails.

I sailed through these unknown waters and allowed the ship to drift with the wind. A frozen loneliness surrounded me turning my thoughts wild and senseless. But every night I embraced the green goddess, though our embrace was filled with hatred. Her love sucked all the life and sense from me, I could feel it. And often I thought of the misery she had brought me. I no longer had friends nor a birthplace nor a belief in the benevolence of the gods. Yet despite this, as evening fell, I would throw myself into her arms regardless.

Finally I resolved to bring it to an end. So intensely did I loathe her naked, green beauty, in whose name so much noble blood had been shed, that one day I suddenly cast her overboard into the gleaming, green water. I watched her sink, her long, oval eyes staring unblinkingly back at me through the water. But once she had disappeared into the infinite depths below I regretted my deed and cried and with my sword cut wounds into my flesh and rubbed them with stinging ash.

A storm broke and the waters churned like a witch's cauldron. I raised every sail, fastened the rudder and roped myself to the mast. The ship raced forwards, the squalling waters carrying it through the darkness in an unknown direction, and I wished it had sunk so that I could have perished with it. Eventually I heard the bulwarks break, the bottom creak and the yards snap, and at that moment I knew nothing and cared for nothing.

When once again I felt the warmth of the sun I was in what remained of the ship, amidst the cleft boards and the broken, splintered masts. At the bow there no longer stood the proud carving of the dragon. I was taken aboard a passing Hispanic ship, upon which the men wore bright tunics and carried long, curved swords, and I became their slave. I did not resist, for I no longer cared what happened to me beneath this sun.

At the orders of many different masters I was forced to travel the breadth of the southern shores and I became acquainted with their knowledge and wisdom. Yet nothing could satisfy my mind. My body was crippled with longing. Only once I was an old and tired man was I rescued by my tribesmen the Vikings and was able return to the land where I was born to be king. But my tribe had been defeated and had disappeared. Our enemies had devastated the valley where I was born, now nothing but plague and famine raged there. I know that it is I who have brought this curse upon my people, but I care not, for I am an old and tired man.

Father Anselmus, who at my behest has written this account on thick parchment, has told me tales of the fair Jesus Christ who was gentle and good. On bright days he has brought peace to my mind. But all that peace I would give, if but once I could feel against my skin the wonder of the green goddess' naked body and in remembrance of those days of glory once again whisper passionate words into her ear.

Forty-eight times has spring blossomed since then, forty-eight times has the sea been born again, but never has my longing faultered nor my yearning died. Every night I kiss the diamond bangle upon my arm and long for the land of eternal shadows, so that in a burning boat I may sail forth on my final journey across the blue and dazzling sea in search of her, whose long, oval eyes longingly call to me, shining through the gleaming water from the infinite depths below.

# *The Great Yellow Storm*

Bo Carpelan

*Bo Carpelan (born 1926) is a Finland-Swedish novelist, poet and translator. In terms of form and content his work displays a continuous desire for experimentation, breaking boundaries and a linguistic richness. Themes common to Carpelan's work are the nature of memory and dream. Both his poetry and his prose have been translated into a dozen or so languages. In 1977 he was awarded the Nordic Council's Literature Prize and in 1993 his novel* Urwind *(also available in English under the same title) was awarded the Finlandia Prize for Literature. The short story here is from the collection* Jag minns att jag drömde *('I Remember That I Dreamt', 1979).*

I remember dreaming about the great storm that one October evening, over forty years ago, shook our old school house near Havsparken. My dream is full of churning skies and mournful, anguished cries, booming echoes and strange occurrences, a witch's brew still bubbling and steaming in remembrance of the day of the great yellow clouds.

Our mathematics' teacher – a small, sinewy woman who looked as if she had swallowed a question mark and had always wondered where the dot had gone, and who therefore instructed us in a low voice and with crest-fallen eyes as if we did not exist, yet whose black little eyes saw everything that went on in the classroom and who would be in front of you like a weasel if you did not obey her – was standing writing out the seven times table on the blackboard when the classroom was filled with a strange light. We looked up towards the window: it seemed as if the whole school had suddenly been transformed into a railway station. The building trembled and shook, a whistling noise seared through the thick, cold stone walls, swathes of smoky clouds raced past the high windows and shunted our classroom forwards as if we were sitting in an aeroplane. Our teacher stopped writing and raised her dark, gaunt head. Without a word she walked up to the window and stood looking out at the driving clouds.

From out in the corridor there came shrill cries and the sound of doors slamming. Our desks were faintly trembling and, as if at a given signal, we all rushed towards the windows, climbed up into the deep bay windows to follow the wind's onslaught. It had a deep, dark voice and another, higher and more shrill, and these two voices were woven together like rope lashing the trunks of the old linden trees, tearing the final leaves from their branches, leaving the park resembling a collection of black brooms, scattering dust, bent backwards like bows under the weight of the enormous boulders rolling in from the sea.

In your seats! came the sharp voice of our teacher, but still we clung to the windows. The driving skies had disappeared, outside a thundering darkness fell and the six white lamps on the ceiling lit up only to go out once again. In your seats! she shouted and we reluctantly made our way back to our desks. Write! came the voice from the corridor. The lamps suddenly lit up again, glaring at full power, and the door was flung open. We raced towards it and were sucked out into the dark corridor and began to barge our way towards the exit.

All of a sudden there came a great boom, drowning out the sound of smashing glass, the murmur of a thousand voices from the great yellow wind. Through the windows in the stairwell we watched as, with a screech, the school's gleaming corrugated roof was wrenched free of its rafters and flew out towards the sea like a billowing sheet. On its way it sliced the tops off a row of linden trees and disappeared with a roar over the observatory, high upon the wavering hill which rose out of the quaking park. And no sooner had the roof disappeared than it was followed by a cloud of report cards and essays, collected in the school attic for a hundred years. Like feathers from an enormous cushion; that is what this swirl of white paper looked like as it rose above the school and was blown out to sea and swept inland at an incredible speed. How strange nature can be! It turned out that these essays – "My Summer Cottage", "Sunrise", "What The Sea Means To Me", "My Favourite Author", "Flowers Indoors And Out" – and others like them were blown out to sea and have been read fondly by the light of an oil lamp on autumn nights by several generations of fishermen. For a long time, my mother said, they carefully dried out the soaked blue jotters suddenly spiralling down over small outcrops and islands, and tried to decipher their beautiful calligraphic script, while hunters and farmers in the north could read about "The Hero King Karl XII", "Europe's Influence on American Culture", "Mussolini: A Statesman" and "Electricity As A Power Source".

Once the cloud of report cards and essays – no one gave them a second thought afterwards, they simply disappeared and were gone, perhaps they were used for starting fires – had been seen rising above our shamelessly naked school, the headmaster – a tall, thin man who could contort himself into the most remarkable shapes – dashed up the stairs to the attic and the entire school loyally followed behind him. The school's old caretaker tried in vain to stop us: we streamed past him and charged up to the attic, which had suddenly fallen silent. The school had been caught in the eye of the storm and a terrifying silence fell over what remained of the school archives. But along the walls there still stood cabinet upon cabinet filled with the pride of the whole school: a collection of stuffed birds donated by the previous headmaster. Climbing on to a table the headmaster shouted to us to carry the birds to safety. The storm will be overhead again soon! he shouted, his white hair standing on end like in an altar picture I had once seen in church. The man in that picture had been holding a sword, but the headmaster was merely brandishing his pointer.

How right he was! No sooner had we opened the door to the cabinet containing small birds, wild ducks and titmice, swans and razorbills, storks and ibises, gulls and eagles, crows and long-eared owls, than the wind gusted once again. Across the clear sky a crimson glow shone towards us, and with a howl a booming wind whirled through the giant room and swept the birds from our hands.

And what birds! It was as if all these years of silence collecting dust they had simply been waiting for the signal to break free! With a unison cry like the sound of a gigantic thousand-stringed harp they flew along the familiar walls, rose shouting and twittering, quacking and chirping, yelling and shrieking, piping and cooing into the air and disappeared from sight. With deafening wings, flapping wings, swooshing wings, with blinking eyes and necks outstretched, with legs stretching backwards and their talons extended they whistled in circles above the headmaster, who reached out a long, pale, powerless arm towards them, before they disappeared like the leaves of a tree, up and away, out into the depths of the sky, and their cries gradually died away in waves of strange echoes, whilst we managed to crawl against the heavy, muted gales and move back down the staircase.

Then suddenly we noticed that all we could hear was our own voices, our booming steps; the wind had stopped as quickly as it had whipped up for the second time, and outside a great, milk-white silence had fallen. The doors out to the yard slid open almost by themselves. Twisted into the most remarkable shapes stood the lamp-posts around the playground, and our strict gymnastics' teacher shouted: No looking at the lamp-posts, do you hear? But his voice sounded isolated and powerless – why should we not have looked at the destruction around us, at the old school with its thick, scratched, dirty walls, at the rafters jutting up towards the pale red sky like the ribs of an old whale, at the trees standing bare and leafless, their branches broken, at a world that had perished and had risen once again? If I shut my eyes I can see them all, the boys in their golf trousers and jackets that were too tight, the girls in their gingham dresses and stockings round their ankles, their plaits and jumpers – I can see them all if I shut my eyes, the way they were standing in the playground, the way their faces lit up after the storm; the enormous yellow storm, which I later heard had only been localised and no other schools or other parts of the city had suffered but ours . . .

I awoke to find our mathematics' teacher standing by my desk holding her short flexible ruler and sat up drowsily.

'Is Carpelan sleeping during class? Don't you know what happens to those who sleep during class? Answer me!'

The class was absolutely silent, everyone was staring at me.

'They dream,' I whispered.

'Louder,' she bellowed, utterly exasperated. 'Louder!'

'They dream,' I shouted.

'They dream,' my classmates exploded, shouting and cheering. 'They dream, they dream!' The class descended into shouts and laughter and I was given a detention.

But as I was walking home through the dark playground I found a wet blue jotter, and on its cover there stood in beautiful handwriting the words: "The Great Yellow Storm". I stood beneath the lamp-post, the upright, untouched lamp-post in amongst the flaming linden trees, every leaf patiently waiting to fall at the first hard frost. My heart was racing and I began to read: "I remember dreaming about the great storm that one October evening, over forty years ago, shook our old school house . . ." After that only the blank, white pages stared back at me. There was no name on the cover. I took the jotter with me and hid it in my desk drawer. Still, I had to show Mother the note from my teacher: "Sleeps during class and answers obtusely."

Mother looked at me helplessly: 'What am I supposed to do?'

'Sign your name at the bottom.'

'But what did you say, then?'

'I said I was dreaming.'

'Doesn't everyone do that when they're asleep?'

I was unable to answer. We looked at each other helplessly. 'So what were you dreaming about?'

'The great yellow storm.'

'The great yellow storm? Well then . . .'

And with that Mother nodded and wrote: "Have seen the great yellow storm myself."

Then beneath that she signed her name.

But every time the wind begins to howl and the clouds

race across the sky I remember the day the school's roof flew off and the birds disappeared, the day Havsparken was plunged into a menacing darkness and everything wailed and shook at the force of the mighty wind, still stalking us, waiting for the chance to transform itself and shake everything that comes in its path.

# *Boman*

## Pentti Holappa

*Pentti Holappa (born 1927) is one of the central figures of Finnish modernism and has enjoyed a long and respected career as a writer. He has written both poetry and prose, often tinged with political or social critique. Characteristic of Holappa's work is the presence of an underlying ethical dialogue, which he fuses with elements of fantasy. He is particularly interested in the dynamics of human relations, both of people on the margins of society and of those searching for perfection. His works have been translated into many languages, and particularly in France he has enjoyed great success as a poet. In 1998 Holappa was awarded the Finlandia Prize for his novel* Ystävän muotokuva *('Portrait of a Friend'). The short story in this anthology is from the collection* Muodonmuutoksia *('Metamorphoses', 1959).*

I might begin my story by saying: I once owned a dog called Boman. But I might also begin by saying: I was once owned by a dog called Boman. These two sentences reveal two different truths about the same matter and this a good way to begin the story of Boman, as what happened to her has often caused me to doubt many things I once held to be true. Allow me to point out that I was by no means the only person who thought they owned Boman. As far as I am aware, many people believed they had that particular privilege. This often happens to creatures that are well-liked.

Boman was a female mongrel. She had a shining black coat, a tail with a joyful curl and two ears that stood up vigilantly. She was small. Initially I had thought taking her in was merely an animal-friendly gesture: I had thought I was saving an abandoned puppy from certain death. I had no idea of the significance this was to have. Enjoying a somewhat macabre sense of humour, a group of friends and I christened her after a poem telling the story of a civilised animal. Needless to say, this name proved far more than simply an omen.

People have always assured me that dogs need to be trained, and perhaps I did not have the strength of character to take this claim with a pinch of salt. Thus by chiding, complimenting, rewarding and disciplining her, I began to teach Boman civilised manners, I began to shape her in my own image. I had no comprehension whatsoever of the bewildered look in her brown eyes, I merely persisted with her training, even though the initial results were nothing special. Boman had to ask to be let out when she needed, Boman was not allowed to bark, Boman was not allowed to chew my slippers, Boman was not allowed to run about the neighbour's garden and so the list went on. A dog living in a civilised society has to learn a surprising number of different things. And because dogs cannot ask 'why', they cannot be given any explanations. They simply have to accept these demands as they are, as if they were humans – a race whose entire culture is based on mindless submission.

My bookshelves contained a variety of books with detailed accounts of how best to instill a dog with human values. Of an evening I would often leaf through these books whilst Boman lay at my feet. Every now and then she would give an unfriendly growl and look me right in the eyes. It seemed that she was behaving as if she had understood what I was doing. I decided to tell my friends about this to show them what an intelligent dog I had. However, I had not had the chance to do so before Boman gave me a most unpleasant surprise.

On the day in question I had shut her in my study as I had gone into town to run some errands. When I arrived back home the room was covered in mutilated shreds of paper, and there was Boman lying on the floor with part of a book cover in her mouth. Of course the first thing I did was give her a thorough telling off. Boman accepted this punishment as if it were perfectly natural: she did not try to defend herself or even hide under the bed. She clearly understood the matter and I gullibly believed this would suffice. Every one of the dog training books states that once a dog knows what is permissible and what is not, it will start to behave properly. I finished telling her off and began to tidy the room. Only then did I notice that the only books missing from the shelf were those dealing with dog training. All the other books were still stacked neatly exactly where they had been left. An odd coincidence, I thought, and decided to tell my friends all about it.

At that time Boman was about six months old. It was summer, though I decided not to travel anywhere, staying instead at home working and not going outdoors very often. To put it plainly, I was gloomy. There is however no point in talking about this any further; after all, human sorrows differ very little from one another. I tried using books to, as it were, vaccinate myself spiritually: I would seek out gloomy books, something which was hardly difficult. Almost all good books are gloomy. I read stories about people who committed murders and suicides; people who suffered from famine and illnesses; people who rotted away in prison and died with not a soul to remember them; people who refuse to accept the so-called joys of life, who flaggellate themselves, who indulge in other sacred rites and who gradually wither away in their studies. Surrounded by such novels and other entertaining reading I revitalised my spirit with philosophy, which convinced me all the more that all people are essentially evil, that life is meaningless and that our every action merely brings about more suffering. Still, sometimes it occurred to me that my own fate was after all reasonably bearable, and to tell you the truth I took some amount of delight in the plight of those fellow beings worse off than myself. Nonetheless this offered me only mild comfort and did not bring me any true enjoyment. After work each day I would often spend the evenings gripped in a melancholy stupour. When Boman became restless and started scratching pointedly at the door, I would begrudgingly leave the house, and walking through the woods or along the shore I would try to shut out the sound of the birds singing or the roar of the waves, and I would blind my eyes so as not to see the grass, the trees or the sky dotted with stars.

I cannot say how long this would have continued if Boman had not awoken me. She declared open war on my books, the very foundations of my existence. After the books dealing with dog training, she chose to tear up my books on popular psychology, then philosophy, steeped in the sweet smell of death, then the gloomiest of my novels. Naturally I was incensed at the dog's barbaric behaviour. I was no longer content with merely reprimanding her, but became furious and enraged at Boman, who always remained perfectly calm during my outbursts. I did not know how to shake her self-assured animality and had therefore to resort to the sorts of measures common only to bad educators.

I began hiding the books I thought to be in the greatest danger. At first Boman was unperturbed. Instead of those hidden away, she destroyed books within her reach. I realised that I had categorised my books wrongly. The books Boman had destroyed were of greater value to me that those I had hidden. Finally I was left with no option but to lock all my books away. It was an extremely time-consuming, frustrating job, and I was made all the crosser by the sight of Boman lounging on the floor with an openly mischievous glint in her eyes as I toiled. I took to reading in much the same way that secret drinkers practise their vice. I would attempt to creep up to the locked bookshelf without Boman's noticing, I would hide the title of the book I had chosen and would not put it down whilst lighting a cigarette, going to the kitchen or answering the telephone. This was an awful lot of bother, but it meant I was enjoying reading more than ever. Many's the time I would spend the wee hours of the morning with a book in my hand in the grip of a wicked, clandestine excitement.

Once, as dawn was approaching, I startled upon noticing Boman's muzzle peering inquisitively over my shoulder at the book in my hand. I gave a start and snapped: 'You're just pretending. You can't read.'

Everyone talks to their dogs; there is nothing out of the ordinary about it. Be that as it may, it is perhaps less common for the dog then to reply. In fact, it may very well be that such a thing has never happened – never before. In any case, Boman replied in a beautiful, cultivated voice, with perfect diction:

'Of course I can read. I learned the alphabet when I was three months old.'

'Then you did it without my knowledge,' I snapped angrily. 'It's inappropriate for a dog to learn things it isn't taught. You might have kept your skills to yourself, but of course with your vanity you had to tell me. Don't you remember that modesty is a dog's greatest virtue? Dogs should lie down at their masters' feet and dutifully obey his commands.'

What a fine sermon, I thought, and was surprised to hear quite how beautifully a little moral indignance made my voice resound. Boman listened politely, but did not seem the least bit disturbed, not to mention showing any signs of slinking under the bed in shame. After my speech she replied politely, yet with an ironic smirk:

'I'm surprised that all those books haven't instilled you with a greater love of the truth. To keep your self-esteem intact – something which, I must say, seems to be built on very shaky foundations – I am prepared to remain silent, though you will have to forgive me if I yawn from time to time. Your company can be very dull. I do have one request, however. When we go for walks, please do not throw sticks expecting me to retrieve them for you. I find it a most tedious and unimaginative game.'

I had already raised my hand and was about to teach my rude dog a lesson she would not forget, but the calm look in Boman's eyes made me relent. Instead I shrugged my shoulders, picked up my book once again and tried to read. I had in fact proved the existence of a very rare phenomenon – talking, literate dogs were not to be found in every household. Not for a moment did I think I was delusional, or that I had been swept away by hallucinations. Besides, there was no reason I would conjure up 'voices' to speak to me in such a haughty, offensive manner – the way Boman had spoken to me. A moment passed, and once I felt slightly calmer I turned to look at the dog.

'Let's agree that you may only use these linguistic skills of yours when we're alone. I do however expect a certain amount of respect, and a polite tone of voice. I am your master, after all.'

'And so do I. After all, I am your dog.'

Another argument was about to erupt, but I managed to control myself.

'In fact, your powers of speech could be very useful indeed,' I said in a more friendly tone. 'You know very well that my finances are not in the best possible shape, and this might just be the answer. People will pay a great deal of money to see anything new and out of the ordinary. I would say that a talking dog, who can also read, is fairly out of the ordinary. You could recite beautiful poems in front of an audience – that way we would also be doing the arts a noble favour. You could read texts handed in by the audience: we have to prove that you really can read, you see, and that you haven't just learned it all off by rote. Perhaps we could even hire you a singing coach. This has true potential: we need to appeal to a young audience, and nowadays all they seem interested in is popular music. Italian songs are very much in fashion. You might want to liven up your performance with a little dance routine: you would become the first dog in the world to dance the mambo.'

'Yes, a splendid idea,' said Boman. 'You should hire an enormous circus tent. It would be full to capacity every night.'

'Absolutely,' I cried excitedly. 'Soon we won't have a care in the world.'

Boman carried on talking calmly despite my enthusiasm.

'I can see it all in my mind's eye. The tent is packed full, the crowd is waiting eagerly. Then suddenly you appear in the spotlight, with me on the lead, and urge me up on to the stage. Thunderous applause. You bow to the audience. But what happens next?'

'You'll begin your performance, of course.'

'Yes,' said Boman. 'If I feel like it. I can't say for certain whether I'll always be in the right mood.'

'You mean you'd refuse?' I shouted angrily. 'You're the most ungrateful creature I think I've ever met. I saved you from a certain death, I've shared my dinner with you, sometimes I even allow you to sleep at the end of my bed. And this is how you repay me for the trouble!'

'I didn't say anything final, I merely wanted to highlight a likely scenario. A true friend will never give too rosy a picture of the future, but will always remind others of its shortcomings. And a dog is a man's best friend; I'm your best friend. In any case, you might think of becoming a ventriloquist just in case. Masters of ventriloquism are very rare indeed.'

At this I was very hurt.

'Me, a ventriloquist? I hope you don't think I'd turn myself into a clown just for money. I do have some self-respect, you know.'

'You would only have to be my stand-in,' Boman gently pointed out.

For a while I said nothing to her. I needed all the self-control I could muster, because it was not easy dealing with a dog which, in addition to all its other attributes, can think. This plainly obvious fact was the most difficult for me to accept, as my dog training books, all written by skilled animal psychologists, had imprinted upon me the tenet that dogs necessarily lack such symbolic cognition. They did not, however, appear to be right.

As I sat there Boman's slender muzzle brushed against my knee and her brown eyes looked up at me as gently as only a dog can. Those eyes had made me forgive the destruction of many of my most beloved books, and her self-deprecating gaze did not go unnoticed this time either. I lay my hand on her neck and scratched her gently under the collar. We were friends again and, as if by mutual agreement, decided to forget our previous conversation.

'You should take better care of yourself,' said Boman in a friendly tone. 'To tell the truth, I've often been worried about the state of your body and soul. You're a young man, yet here you are wasting the best years of your life surrounded by books, many of which – if you'll forgive me – are of questionable quality.'

'Perhaps you're right. I don't see other people very often and I'm on edge rather a lot.'

'I'm not surprised. People no less than dogs ought not to neglect their needs during the mating season.'

'The mating season. Who told you about things like that? As far as I can see you're still a minor.'

'Mother Nature is an excellent teacher,' she said with a smile in her eyes.

We talked for a long time and had a very pleasant conversation. An untamed animal instinct sometimes shone through Boman's opinions and this upset me a bit, but still I tried my best to tolerate it. I had noticed that Boman did not find my humanity entirely pleasant either. We avoided the subject of philosophy, as we held utterly opposing views. Boman only had to remind me of the inspired words of one of the great thinkers of our age, referring to "the stars up above and humankind down below", and I realised that, ultimately, human wisdom was not intended for wise dogs.

I'm sure I need not point out that Boman was anything but a well-behaved dog. Being too well-behaved would have become tedious after a while and Boman could certainly not be accused of that. Now that we were on a level pegging, so to speak, she began to take ever greater liberties. She would pass the time by chewing at my slippers or lounging in my favourite armchair leafing through my books. She flicked the pages over with her long tongue, often complaining that the paper and ink tasted foul. This made Boman almost as uncomfortable as the bad style of certain writers.

The duality of Boman's life gave rise to many amusing games. When in other people's company she very much enjoyed pretending to be a normal dog. Whilst walking outside I would let her off the lead and she would walk by my side, behaving impeccably. I lived in a small residential area on the outskirts of Helsinki and only a few steps away from my garden there was a path leading to a quiet pond in the woods and beyond that to an uninhabited part of the coastline. This was our everyday route and we very rarely met other people along the way. On one occasion the lady from next door walked past us; Boman did not like her. The reason for this was perfectly understandable: the woman had once kicked Boman when she was a puppy because, despite her friendly smile, she did not like dogs. I greeted her politely, but Boman started to growl. She drew back her muzzle in a snarl revealing her great set of teeth – an imposing sight indeed. Boman then began to approach the woman and leant back on her hind legs as if preparing herself for an attack. The lady gave out a shrill, frightened cry and leapt off the path and into the woods with Boman barking frantically at her heels. What a sight it was! A sophisticated woman, dressed in a tight skirt, stumbling comically amongst the thicket. I laughed so much it echoed through the forest. After a while Boman appeared once again, winked mischievously and said:

'I didn't lay a paw on her, I just got a bit carried away.'

After this incident the woman next door never said hello again and her husband would scowl at me every time we met.

There were many other people whom Boman very much enjoyed winding up. On sunny days she would lie out in the garden and frighten debt collectors, the most malicious old gossip-mongers in the town and several of our neighbours who were known to be teetotallers. Boman did not hold any personal grudges against these people, rather she acted out of a sense of duty, knowing my natural antipathy. Over time she acquired quite an array of fervent enemies, and it would hardly have surprised me if someone had tried to offer her a treat laced in deadly poison. Boman would not have been tricked by such a thing. She never accepted treats from the hands of nasty strangers. Despite this Boman never turned general opinion against herself, because she could be as adorable as only profoundly mischievous creatures know how. Children were Boman's sworn friends, so she had nothing to fear: children are the true rulers of suburbs like these.

It was during this time that Boman first met Pertti, a schoolboy who lived on the other side of the woods. I never met the boy myself, and all I know about him is what Boman has told me. Pertti's story was so appalling that it sounded almost like an old-fashioned fairytale, the kind that people nowadays find slightly trivial.

Pertti's mother had died and so his father had married a nasty woman, who became Pertti's wicked step-mother, and who had soon filled their little apartment with children, Pertti's wretched half-brothers and sisters. Even Pertti's father no longer cared for his eldest son. That in itself was a sad enough story.

Boman had first met Pertti down by the shore. It was a beautiful Sunday afternoon and Pertti's eyes had lit up as he stood looking out at the yachts, which seemed to be flying through the blue sky, as in the bright sunshine he could not tell where the sea and the sky met.

'They're flying,' he said to himself.

Boman sat down next to him and the boy continued:

'Why don't people have wings? Why can't they fly too?'

'Why don't people just grow themselves wings?'

Only then did Pertti notice Boman; he turned and looked at her reproachfully.

'But they can't.'

'Have you tried?'

'I've sometimes wished for them.'

What followed was such a truly beautiful conversation about wings that only the most gifted poets would be able to repeat it. I listened in silence. When Boman told me about this encounter, I saw a romantic gleam in her eyes for the very first time, as she would not normally allow tears to cloud her intelligent eyes. Even now she seemed annoyed at how moved she was, and who else could she turn to to talk about such a thing if not to me?

'Why do the bourgeois insist on having pets?' she asked. 'Animals have an imagination of their own, they have fantastic, wild dreams, and all the bourgeois offer them are sweet pastries and a warm home. In return they expect their pets to whimper as their master leaves the house and to jump with joy when he returns, because people like that do nothing for free.'

There was something very endearing about Boman's

outburst, and I did not have the heart to remind her that she too was especially fond of sweet pastries and more often than not demanded that I procure them.

I had to admit, however, that Boman's position as my dog was far from easy. I believe the majority of my friends to be moderately intelligent, but they too have their limits. Those of my friends who considered it a great merit to have been born a human put me in a very awkward situation. With them, it was human-this and human-that from start to finish: 'We humans . . . human rights . . . humanity . . . humane . . . super-human'. Only rarely did the word 'animal' interrupt this stream of humanity, and at this the speaker's voice would become tainted with disgust. Once in a while I would become indignant on Boman's behalf, but this was in fact unnecessary. In her intellectual independence my dog did not require the help of others. Boman proved this convincingly to me and a guest of mine, who thought himself a genius as he proclaimed that dogs do not understand the meaning of words, rather they respond to the speaker's tone of voice.

'And is that then less praiseworthy?' I asked. 'Many humans only understand the meanings of words, but they don't listen to the tone of voice. Tone is also a part of speech.'

My guest listened neither to my words nor to my tone of voice, so excited was he over his revelation.

'Let's see,' he said. 'I'll demonstrate that I'm right.'

He bowed down to Boman and very softly said:

'Go to hell. Go to hell.'

Boman had dozed off during our conversation. She looked my guest up and down, but after noticing my warning glance, she decided not to resort to violence. She got up, stretched, trotted over to my guest and lifted her hind leg at his shin as if it were a lamp-post. This of course was merely a harmless gesture, as Boman was a bitch, but my guest failed to understand the joke, despite being an intelligent and well-read man. He put on his jacket and left, and I have not seen him since.

'Training humans is very hard work,' Boman complained. 'They never seem to learn anything from their experiences.'

She gave me a friendly look and added: 'Still, with some perseverence one can achieve astounding results. Sometimes I almost forget that, for instance, you are a human. And I haven't completely ruled out the possibility that one day you might even begin to think.'

It was not often that Boman in any way complimented me and I felt flattered. I was grateful for any attention Boman showed me, because her life had begun to fill up with other matters. More and more often she would spend entire days and nights out on her own. I was worried about her, but I also knew she would not put up with any infringement of her freedom. There were many times she would come home and tell me astonishing things. She had talked to many different people, and I wondered how it was possible that the newspapers were not running stories about a mysterious talking dog. Clearly a talking dog was not considered an appropriate topic of discussion in our society: it was one of those things that everyone was aware of, but that no one dared talk about. This, of course, was very convenient for both me and Boman.

A suicidal young man was one of the many people Boman had met on her lonely treks. There was a time when it seemed that hanging oneself was something of a national pursuit. Local legend and numerous folk songs are testimony to this. Whenever I have travelled through the beautiful Finnish countryside, the locals have always pointed out some protected tree growing by the side of the road, saying: 'That's where John So-And-So hanged himself in the year such-and-such by the full moon in autumn'. Any story beginning like that is then told in full, the speaker revelling in every detail, and often ends with the fact that the lost soul in question has never found lasting peace, but to this day haunts the cowshed behind his old house. On the whole they are young men or men in the prime of their lives. I have seen young people abroad, all of them brimming with vitality, and I felt envious on behalf of the young people back home, whose duty it seems is to at least attempt to commit suicide. Over the years hanging has made way for sleeping pills, gas and other modern methods, but Boman's story revealed that the old tradition is still going strong.

Boman had just taken Pertti home, but decided to run about the woods out of sheer canine joy. All of a sudden she noticed a young man sitting in a tree placing a noose around his neck. Boman did not have time to intervene before the young man jumped from tree, but the jump did not go quite as expected. The rope was far too long, so the young man did not hang from the branch; instead he fell to the mossy ground with a thud. There he sat dejectedly and burst into tears. Boman carefully approached him and said:

'What bad luck you've had.'

'Yes, and this is my third attempt,' replied the young man, sobbing.

'Dear oh dear,' said Boman. 'Isn't that too much? Maybe you should measure the rope before jumping.'

'What do you mean?'

'Check that you can stand freely under the rope whilst it's dangling from the branch.'

Only then did the young man realise that he was talking to a dog. He hurriedly removed the noose from around his neck and backed off from Boman. He had stopped crying and with a shrewd and suspicious look in his eyes he said:

'Why, you're a talking dog, and you're very keen to help me kill myself. I know who you are.'

'Yes, I am a talking dog.'

The young man was not listening; he continued speaking, his teeth clenched together the way bad actors often do: 'You came here to wait for my demise, but it seems you've shown yourself too soon.'

'Too late, I would say. You said this was your third attempt, and I sincerely believe that both people and dogs succeed in everything they do on the first attempt. Though it has to be said, dogs very rarely hang themselves.'

'I'll make the sign of the cross and you will disappear.'

'I could disappear without it, but I could also stay. You might still need my help – in measuring the rope, perhaps.'

'No, don't go,' said the young man. 'I've never met the Devil himself before. I'd like to talk to you.'

'Thank you,' Boman replied. 'I've always liked nicknames, but I don't have very many. Devil sounds good.'

'That's it, I see you're trying to be funny. Well, humour is the Devil's work, I've always known that. But you still wish me dead.'

'No I don't, quite the contrary. Bodies hanging from trees are not a pretty sight.'

'In that case you're the first creature not to wish me ill.'

The young man looked almost moved, but Boman interrupted him.

'I don't wish you good or bad. I don't know you. Only a moment ago I didn't know you even existed. I can only tell you what I wish you after we've got to know one another. So let's get to know one another. You could start by telling me why you tried to kill yourself.'

The young man readily began to explain; all he needed was a listening ear. He had committed a grave sin, a crime. He had stolen. The previous evening he had gone to visit his elderly uncle, an old sea captain who had sailed the seven seas. His uncle was as miserly as the Devil himself (at this, the young man glanced sheepishly at Boman), but still the young man knew that one day he would inherit his uncle's wealth. This was not an insignificant amount, it would be enough for him to live happily for the rest of his days. That night they had sat up talking, as on many occasions before. Suddenly, over his uncle's shoulder on top of the bookshelf, the young man had noticed a golden Buddha staring down at him. The statue, about a span high, had probably been there for years, but the young man had never noticed it before. Now he felt that the Buddha's mysterious smile was meant for him alone, and the metal statue began to glow, its dazzling light filling the room. The young man was convinced that there was a secret power hidden within the statue, and that it would bring both wisdom and happiness to its owner. After all, did not his own uncle think of old age and his approaching death with surprising calm? This explained everything. And because the

Buddha was clearly made of gold, it was surely priceless. So once he had pondered on these thoughts for a moment, it was not surprising that he began to covet the small golden statue for himself. Acquiring that statue became vitally important to him. So when his uncle was not looking he slipped the Buddha into his pocket, bid the old man farewell and hurried off into the night with his new treasure. As soon as he got home, he took the statue out of his pocket and spent that whole summer's night sitting on the edge of his bed staring at the Buddha. Its smile had captivated him, and the night seemed to pass in a daze. It was only in the morning that the young man realised what a serious crime he had committed, and at his job in an office he spent the whole day on edge. He was convinced that there would be no way of making up for his deeds; there was only one solution. Death.

As he recounted his story the young man had taken the fateful statue out of his pocket and was now staring at it fixedly. He had clearly forgotten all about Boman, and gave a start as she said:

'Can I have a closer look?'

The young man held the statue out towards Boman; she inspected the Buddha carefully and asked to see underneath it.

'You're right,' she said finally. 'In its own way it is a very beautiful statue. I can see it has enchanted you. It's impossible to explain that smile; I don't think there's anything there, but I can imagine how it might contain a secret I can never reach.'

'It does contain a secret,' he replied instantly. 'That smile doesn't just hold the key to life, but to existence itself.'

'I believe you,' Boman agreed. 'If there is a secret, its key may just as well be hidden in that smile as anywhere else. The key to your secret is, however, hidden right here.'

The young man clutched the statue tightly against his chest and shouted half sorrowfully, half rejoicing:

'Think how unhappy my uncle must be. He has lost the meaning of his life, the key to his existence. I don't believe he will ever recover from this blow; he'll die soon.'

'Oh I don't think so. I rather suspect that this statue only holds special significance for you. Your uncle probably hasn't even noticed it's missing.'

'That's impossible. Even if he hasn't understood the statue's significance, he'll still be frantic, out of greed. He'll be thinking of the money he could have made by selling the statue, and now he'll think it's lining my pocket.'

'Yes, I noticed,' Boman replied. 'But as far as I can see you have overestimated the value of this statue. This metal isn't gold, it's brass. Bite it and see; it's an old method for identifying gold. In addition, the words "Made in England" are printed on the statue's base. You know what this means. To anyone else your treasure is just junk, but this doesn't matter to you. What's most important is that for you it is the key to existence.'

At first the young man did not understand Boman's words, then he began to shake as if he were consumed with a terrible fever. His hands trembling, he turned the statue over, squeezed it and finally let it fall to his feet.

'I've been cheated, cheated,' he shouted, hopping up and down with rage. 'I've been terribly deceived.'

'I don't understand what you mean. Surely you're not angry at yourself.'

'You damned cur, get out of my sight,' shouted the young man. 'You're the Devil himself and this is all your doing.'

In his rage the young man tried to kick Boman, though naturally he missed as Boman was able to move very nimbly indeed.

'And here I thought I was doing you a favour,' said Boman feigning innocence. 'I'm sure your uncle would gladly give you that statue, or at least he would sell it to you for next to nothing. Just think – once you owned the Buddha of Secrets you would be both wise and happy. You would be able to think more calmly about death, as it draws closer every moment, though you're still so young.'

Boman uttered those final words to herself, as the young man had bounded off deep into the woods and would not have been able to hear Boman for the gnashing of his teeth. The brass Buddha lay on the ground. Boman would gladly have taken it home with her, but carrying a metal object in her mouth would have been most unpleasant. There was also nothing she could do about the noose still hanging from the branch above.

'I do hope it doesn't prove a fateful discovery for some other desperate chap,' said Boman solemnly as she rounded off her story.

Boman spent the vast majority of her time with Pertti. He had nothing to do during the long summer months and people at home were glad the longer he stayed out of their sight. I am not sure quite what the two of them got up to, but I am certain that a little boy and a dog see far more on their walks in the woods than adults. Pertti and Boman were both so close to the ground that nothing could escape their notice amongst the trees, the bushes and the moss. And they both had a very similar imagination. I knew that Boman dreamt of running through great forests, across open fields and along high cliffs. At times like this her paws would tremble restlessly and her nostrils would sniff around for strong new scents arising from the depths of her dream.

When autumn came Pertti had to go to school. After this Boman spent days on end in my company and looked frightfully bored, even though I very often neglected my work to spend time with her. I did what I could, but because starting a conversation was suddenly so difficult I decided to read her stories and poetry. Though I went out of my way to entertain her she was not the least bit grateful, but instead made derisory comments about my choice of texts, which eventually made me feel a certain distaste towards writers and poets whom I had previously held in high regard.

'I'm bored to tears by your stories,' she grumbled. 'The suspense stories are ridiculous, because who on earth would feel suspense at a mere story? All the tragedies have the same lofty ending – something offered to the reader like a sugar cube to sweeten the pill. The only function of the baudy stories is to titillate those with one set of morals for the living room and another for the bedroom. And as for the poetry! These old-fashioned poems with their clumsy rhymes creak like a rusty set of cogs and modern poets are just as pretentious as poets throughout the ages. They whine on and on about the same old things: the setting sun and the morning dew, lost innocence, even though no living creature is ever innocent, and wise old men, even though wise old men are merely tired human beings.'

I gradually realised that it was not within my power to make Boman happy. I left her to her own devices and did not notice that she would slip out of the open window when the children were let out of school. Sometimes Boman would show her affection by telling me how sorry she was for Pertti. Strangers did not think Pertti was handsome, they found him rather sickly and they did not understand that the glint in his eyes was a sign of his wild imagination. It was not only at home that Pertti was made to suffer: the boys at school teased him and his teachers thought he was stupid and badly raised.

'They're proud of their own excellent upbringing,' Boman scoffed, 'and by this they mean that they have all learnt to speak, behave and think in exactly the same way.'

One day Boman informed me that she and Pertti had decided to run away together. In telling me she was in fact breaking her promise. It was a secret. Boman's eyes smiled at me and she looked happy for the first time in a long while. I understood that it was a secret for Pertti's sake, thus I was flattered I had been told and took as much comfort from this as I could.

At first however I did not think of myself; I was worried for the young pair of conspirators. I tried to explain that their plan was insane and highly dangerous. Boman was responsible for a boy too young to understand the consequences of his actions.

'Does anyone understand the consequences of their actions?' asked Boman nonchalantly. 'Did you understand what you were doing when you took me in?'

Eventually this conversation ended like every conversation in which Boman and I had differing opinions: Boman finally had her way.

'This is my gift to him,' she deigned to point out. 'Pertti

needs an adventure he can remember for the rest of his life. It doesn't matter if things turn out badly, but when he becomes an adult he will remember the time he grabbed hold of freedom, something that would never have been offered him otherwise. It'll give him strength.'

I tried to question Boman's noble arguments. I said that it was she who needed the adventure – she had always rebelled against the security of the bourgeois lifestyle. But these were empty words. I was already packing Pertti a knapsack I had bought in town especially. I made sure to pack warm clothes and enough food for a little boy and a dog. As night drew in I took the knapsack outside and placed it on the step, left the door ajar and bid Boman farewell.

'Think of me, won't you,' I said and did not dare look at her.

I shut myself in my study. When I appeared a few hours later Boman was gone and the knapsack was no longer on the step.

Needless to say, the days that followed were very upsetting for me. I tried to read, I made more of an effort to spend time with my friends, but nothing seemed to amuse me. After they had bombarded me with their wit for a number of hours they began to look askance at me, thinking I was hopelessly demented. I was sad. A few days later I read a small announcement in the newspaper about the disappearance of a little boy called Pertti. This told me very little and it was only much later that I heard about their adventures in more detail.

First off they had gone into town. Although it was only some ten kilometres from our suburb into the centre of town, to Pertti Helsinki was an unknown city. Its streets, restaurants and cinemas excited his imagination. Boman had accompanied me into town on a few occasions, but had never particularly enjoyed it. She had complained of people stepping on her toes, and in general she looked down upon people who flocked together in this manner.

The journey into town had been an adventure in itself. Walking along the street they had to be careful not to talk within other people's earshot, and at first they had found this secrecy a fun new game. As they arrived in town they stopped outside display windows and cinemas looking in awe at advertisements and foreign pictures. Their glances and gestures convinced one another that everything was incredible, fun and exciting. Boman acquired a taste for straining at the leash and running up to lamp-posts, which she then sniffed with exaggerated enthusiasm. No one walking by could have imagined what a fun game this was.

Once they arrived in the centre of town the adventurers were a little confused. They had reached their destination and there was nowhere to continue their journey. Before they had set out Pertti had tried to explain to Boman that adventures would come along of their own accord; they would meet weird and wonderful people and they would be carried away by the very flow of events. But now most people hurriedly darted past them, and those leaning on lamp-posts or loitering around the streets looked so hostile that the pair dared not approach them. Pertti and Boman tried to play at the railway station. They would walk along with the crowds of people arriving, then with those leaving on a train and try to look hurried and important, but before long they became tired of this and sat down on a bench in the waiting room. Now they had the time to see that these travellers were all grey and weary. Being on the move did not feel fun or exciting any more; they would much rather have been asleep in their own beds thinking of nothing. The little boy and the dog tried to escape their melancholy in the cold park, where they sat eating from their knapsack.

The park was empty and they could have talked freely without fear of anyone overhearing them, but they had nothing to say to one another. Such a thing had never happened to them before. Boman silently examined Pertti's thin face, blue with the cold, and for the first time in her life she felt guilty of a terrible deed. Boman had steeled her wits against the human sense of guilt, something she had often referred to as cheap, useless emotional rubbish. Now she felt responsible for not dashing Pertti's expectations from the outset, for not drawing the grey curtain of reality over his future.

In silence the adventurers returned to the streets, loitered aimlessly by a hot dog stand and witnessed a number of street fights. They then began to look for a place to spend the night and before long they found an open stairwell. They climbed up to the top of the stairs and lay down to sleep huddling next to one another. The darkness was impenetrable and in its protection Pertti plucked up the courage to speak to Boman.

'I shouldn't have dragged you along with me. You have a good master and a safe home.'

'A safe home can seem like a prison to someone who wants to help his friend discover a new world.'

Boman's voice was gentle but defiant. It made Pertti speechless and Boman felt a few warm tears drop on her muzzle. After he had calmed down, Pertti said:

'There is no new world. We saw that this evening.'

'If it doesn't exist, we'll have to create it,' said Boman without a shadow of hesitation in her voice.

In only a few sentences they had said all that needed to be said. There they fell asleep and awoke in the morning under a glaring light to find someone trying to wake them up, bellowing angrily. It was the caretaker.

'Up you get, boy, and be gone with you. Quick smart! And take that dog with you, unless you want me to call the police.'

The fright woke Pertti and Boman in a flash. Pertti grabbed the knapsack and the adventurers flew down the stairs. The chortling of the caretaker boomed around them and followed them out into the street as they instinctively ran away from the town centre and out towards the sea and the park land along the shore. Once in the park they stopped and took a bewildered look around. They were welcome here. The trees were decorated in a wonderful display of colours to celebrate their arrival: red, yellow and orange leaves lay scattered along the path forming a soft carpet beneath their feet. A fresh sea breeze caught Pertti's hair and caressed Boman's shining coat.

All of a sudden both the little boy and the dog were once again filled with the joy which had died out the day before; they could enjoy the luxury of their freedom. They frolicked about the park laughing, at times holding ceremonious silences. They irritated the seagulls by mimicking their cawing and tried to tame the already tame squirrels as, startled by Boman, they darted up into great tall trees. Then they would laugh at the arrogant little sparrows. In the harbour, grey, asthmatic boats wheezed their own importance, dainty yachts, stripped naked, swayed back and forth around the pavillions and lonely island fortifications sulked out at sea.

'What an angry man,' said Pertti referring to the caretaker.

'Let's forget about him,' said Boman. 'Let this be our revenge. We'll forget all about the angry caretaker and the old world.'

'Yes, let's,' Pertti agreed.

On they frolicked through parks and docks and over bridges. They gradually left the town behind them and found that walking around here was far easier. The sea played with them, momentarily disappearing behind hills and capes, then suddenly swelling back beside them, accompanying them on their journey, the waves beating in time with their steps, leading them over bridges across the bay. Further out to sea they could make out small, friendly looking islands, also decked out in resplendent autumn colours.

'That's where I'd like to go, to those islands,' said Pertti.

'I've been waiting all this time for you to start wishing to go there.'

They winked at one another and left the road to follow the shore. They soon discovered a cove containing lots of little boats, but only in one of them were the oars unlocked. They decided to take that one.

'I really ought to warn you,' said Boman. 'This is a crime and you'll be held responsible for it. I'm a dog, I can't be accused of anything.'

'I'm sure an owner who has left his oars unlocked can't be mean. He'll understand that someone else might need his boat.'

Thus began their journey through the archipelago. They decided not to go ashore on the first island, as they did not want to barge their way in; instead they waited for an invitation, a sign. Before long one of the islands revealed a friendly cove, and the wind gently blew their boat towards it. They hauled the boat safely on to the shore, sheltered under a group of spruce trees, and set off along the paths on the island. The firm, dry land supported their steps, the forest was almost silent. The most skilled summer songbirds had already flown south, and in the silence the solitary chirping of the remaining grey singers resounded with desolate calm.

There were many summer houses on the island, but not one of them contained any inhabitants. The owners were in town, but their houses were glad to welcome the small travellers. In each of the houses there was an opening just big enough for a dog, a simple latch, steps and a door opening silently. So the houses welcomed them with open arms, laid out soft carpets in front of them, offered them armchairs and sofas, bathrooms and balconies. Pertti and Boman welcomed the houses' hospitality and in return they created a history for every one of them. They conjured up noble masters living in the houses, each with a sprightly dog of his own; they imagined strong bonds between the different households, bringing them together and keeping them apart. They charted every inch of the island, its knolls, its spruce groves and bays, and gave each of these places an ambiguous name. And all this time their senses were aroused by the smell of salt and they were caressed by the icy hand of the wind coming in across the sea.

In this way the little boy and the dog created their new world, but all the time they knew that danger was not far away. Every now and then they would take a cautious look out across the open sea between the island and the mainland and as evening drew in they saw a motor boat heading towards the island. They quickly hid themselves near the boat concealed in amongst the spruces, and before long they could hear the sound of strange footsteps thumping the ground. Soon afterwards they heard angry shouts and cursing, people rushing past them. Cold and hungry, Pertti and Boman huddled against one another and waited for night to fall. Protected by the darkness they pushed the boat out to sea and headed off towards new islands.

All in all Pertti and Boman lived this precarious life for a few weeks: at times they were welcome guests, for whom houses opened their doors and offered the wonderful treats in their pantries and cellars, at others they were fugitives, spending days on end hidden in the forest or amongst the rushes. They learnt that there were two realities on the islands; one was of their own creation and the other was a strange and brutal reality, something in which they wanted no part. They spoke only of their own reality, of banquets and high dramas played out in the great rooms of these houses and on the shores, decked out in festive splendour.

Over time they became too tired to try and forget about the cold, the hunger and the fear attacking them from the old world, and one night Pertti no longer had the energy to row the boat to the safety of another island, but lay down instead at the bottom of the boat and fell asleep next to Boman. The sea rocked them first gently, then with ever greater waves, and they dreamt of sailing along far off shores on a ship with enormous sails. When they awoke the following morning all they could see was blue, the cold blue of the sea and the sky. The waves had died down to a soft swell, lazily rocking back and forth out towards the horizon. High above them were sparse clouds, which the wind had combed into thin trails across the sky. Both boy and dog were exhausted. It had been a long time since their last meal and their hunger had gradually turned to weariness.

'There is another shore on this sea, isn't there?' Pertti whispered softly into Boman's ear. 'Do you think we'll ever reach it?'

'The shore will find us soon enough. We simply have to wait,' Boman replied just as softly.

They fell asleep once again. A patrol boat spotted a small boat, which looked empty, drifting out to sea. It was only once they came closer that the patrol men noticed a little boy and a black mongrel sleeping next to each other at the bottom of the boat.

Boman had been on her travels for about three weeks. One day there came a knock at my door; outside was a policeman in uniform holding Boman on a leash. He told me that they had seen from her collar that Boman belonged to me. Some little rascal had stolen the dog and taken her with him. I thanked the policeman, he saluted me and went on his way. Only then did I dare take a closer look at Boman. The end of her muzzle was dry and she looked generally ill and feverish. I stroked her gently, but did not want to show her quite how happy I was to see her again. I placed her on my bed and she fell asleep in an instant; she slept there for a long time, semiconscious, her legs twitching. I guessed she was dreaming about continuing her flight at Pertti's side. Boman recovered from her fever a few days later with the help of the penicillin prescribed by the vet. After eating the first square meal since her return, she told me she was going out. I did not try to stop her.

This time she was not away for long. She returned with a small letter in her mouth, left for her at an agreed hiding place by Pertti. I was allowed to read the letter, which read simply in heavy, childish lettering: "They're sending me to a borstal. Pertti." The letter also contained the name of the borstal and a clumsy, hand-drawn map showing where it was situated.

Once I had read the letter, Boman and I looked at each other in silence.

'It's a long journey,' she said.

'It's too long,' I said, as I could see what she was thinking.

We did not speak about Pertti for a long time after this. Boman tried as best she could to adapt once again to her role as my dog, but as I listened to her witty banter I would often turn and look out of the window, and I would feel like crying. It was as if we were playing out a tragedy, in which the function of the lines is merely to hide the characters' pain. Boman had lost the happy, mischievous gleam in her eyes, she no longer smirked like a naughty young rogue. Sometimes she would ask me to read her poems about the sea, the wind and friendship. As she listened she would often remain silent for entire evenings at a time.

'I think your taste is falling to ruin,' I said, trying to sound jovial. 'You never used to like literature with such pathos.'

Boman did not reply.

On our walks she would plod compliantly by my side, she no longer ran around under the trees sniffing at the moss and the tussocks. On one occasion we stopped by the shore and watched the seagulls' noisy capers.

'Seagulls can fly very fast,' said Boman.

'And they are beautiful,' I added.

I had hoped that Boman was gradually beginning to see beyond herself, so I was not overjoyed when she said:

'I wonder whether it's difficult to grow oneself wings.'

'It's impossible.'

Boman sneered and glanced over at me.

That same evening I was reminded of the fact that Boman was almost a fully grown dog. As we had left the house I had caught a glimpse of some dogs running loose near our garden. I did not pay any particular attention to this, because Boman had said something and my attention had been drawn elsewhere. As we arrived back at the house I realised that she had done this on purpose. It was dark and in the garden I could see several pairs of eyes shining motionlessly. I sensed that they were staring at us and quickened my step. Boman reluctantly followed me, but followed nonetheless.

Once we had got inside I asked almost angrily:

'What were they?'

'Dogs. Males.'

'I didn't you were that way inclined.'

Boman did not respond, and despite her normal ready wit she seemed at a loss for words. I remained silent for a moment, then asked reticently:

'Would you like to go out?'

'I don't think so,' she said.

She struggled against herself, asked me to read poetry to her again and tried hard to listen, but suddenly gave a start at a sound from outside and began pacing restlessly around the house until she finally went up to the front door in the hallway and started sniffing it. Every now and then she would let out a coarse, mournful sound, then a reply would be heard from outside. She glanced over at me, then crept into a corner of the study.

This indecision lasted two days and two nights and throughout that time the dogs kept a vigil outside the door. At night the scraping of their paws could be heard on the front steps and during the day they would retreat into the woods, remaining in view the whole time.

On the third evening after we got back from our walk Boman said:

'You and your books have taught me that one always has to choose between two or more options.'

'That's true,' I replied. 'Life is about making choices.'

'Maybe your life and your truth. I want to choose both options, so I'd like to go outside.'

'By all means,' I said. 'Please, no one is stopping you.'

'Then would you open the door,' Boman growled angrily.

'Sorry, I didn't realise it was shut. Please remember to be careful, it would be terrible if those wild beasts were to bite you.'

'I will take care of myself, and I know those wild beasts. I am a wild beast too. You don't know anything about these things.'

I opened the door and Boman disappeared.

In the morning she returned looking awful, covered from head to toe in dirt and with blood stains matted in her coat. She had prepared herself for a dressing down, so she was behaving as arrogantly as when she had left, but in her eyes I could see her silent distress.

'You see?' she said. 'Nothing out of the ordinary went on.'

'Really?' I retorted and went into the kitchen.

I made her a substantial meal and she tucked in heartily, then walked over to the darkest corner of my study and went to sleep. I thought she was just resting after the events of the previous night, it was only later that evening, when she refused to leave the house for our daily walk, that I began to worry. The same happened the following day as well. Boman did not want to stay outside for more than a few minutes at a time, and when I offered her food, she would turn her head and slink off to the furthest corner of the room. There she spent day upon day, not sleeping, but staring blindly in front of her. She responded to my speech the way dogs normally do: she stared at me with questioning eyes, and it was impossible to tell whether she had understood anything at all.

In my mind I was beginning to formulate tragic theories of how moral decline can destroy the spiritual fabric of a well-developed being. Boman had given in to the beast inside her, and because of this had returned to her base animal level and had lost her ability to speak and most probably her ability to think. I returned to my books, which had lain untouched for some time, and they supported this view in every respect. For safety's sake I never spoke out loud about these thoughts, because you never could tell with Boman. Perhaps she would still understand what I was saying. After a while I became worried about the state of her health. Regardless of whether she was once again a normal dog, tied to her animal needs, things were not at all the way they should have been. As a dog, surely she should recover from her moral crisis and wait calmly for its natural consequences. In no way was she behaving like a healthy dog and I began to worry whether she might have received a serious internal injury during her adventure that night. I decided it was best to call the doctor and as I picked up the telephone I told Boman my decision, the way I had always informed her of such matters in the past. To my surprise she raised her head sharply and said simply:

'No.'

So she could still speak after all. I did not know quite what to think. Had I yet again tried to find too simple an explanation for things with all my books and life experience? Nonetheless I left the dog in peace and waited.

A week later Boman became tormented, she began whimpering quietly to herself and there was a pained look in her eyes. At first I pretended not to notice anything, but after a while I could restrain myself no longer. I approached her and she made no attempt to run away. She allowed me to rest my hand on her neck and stroke it. It was then that I noticed for the first time that two large lumps were growing on her back, right on top of her shoulder blades. As my hand lightly touched them she winced and turned to give me a stern look.

At that moment I understood. I remembered the seagulls along the shore and I remembered the first time Pertti and Boman met. "Why don't people just grow themselves wings?" Boman had asked. She had said she wanted to choose both options and had then opted for her nocturnal fall from grace. I looked at her fondly and tears welled in my eyes.

'My friend, you are the first true hero I have ever met,' I said.

At last I understood how to relate to Boman. I talked to her a lot, even though she just lay silently in the corner and did not respond. I tried to encourage her: I told her that her will was stronger than that of any other living creature and every day I remarked on how the lumps had grown. The day her wings would hatch was drawing close.

Boman appeared to perk up when I kept her company and it seemed that the worst of the pain was over. She had stopped whimpering, and although she still refused to talk she would give me signs and make it clear when she wanted to go outside. On our walks she would lead me towards the shore. We would often stand on the rocks by the shore as evening approached, the surrounding landscape was deserted and pale grey light trickled from the sky. The seagulls had not disappeared, they continued to swoop noisily above the shore, their delicate wings like sails sketching masterful patterns in the wind. Boman sat on the rocks watching the birds for hours at a time. Sometimes she looked as if she might have wanted to join them, but then she remembered and looked at her back, and her eyes would fill with helplessness.

It only took a few weeks for her wings to mature. First of all, her coat around the lumps disappeared to reveal soft, silken skin, through which two small black wings protruded. On the day the wings hatched came the first snowfall. Boman had again been very restless the previous night, she had whined to herself and paced up and down through the house. In the morning she came to show me her wings; she was both humble and proud, like a mother showing off her newborn child or an artist who is convinced of the unique qualities of a new work. The wings themselves were still very small and delicate and were a shade of bluish black, like the feathers of splendid woodland birds.

'I knew you could do it,' I said.

Boman turned her head and examined her wings, then lay down on the floor and slept solidly for two days. I bought her a jacket made of red fabric, as I did not want the neighbours to see me walking about with a winged dog.

When she awoke Boman seemed to be herself once again. She chatted happily and intelligently and we would go out for many a long walk. She had nothing against wearing the jacket, because she could not yet fly, even though her wings were growing visibly bigger. Still she was impatient.

'They're growing so slowly,' she complained. 'I'm in a hurry.'

I too was restless. I was worried that Boman's adventure that night would not be without its consequences. I suggested she practise flying – this would help strengthen her wings.

One moonlit night we went into the woods and Boman climbed up a small hill, whilst I remained down below waiting. Once at the top Boman stretched out her wings, shook them and finally dared to let them carry her weight. On her first attempt she only managed to fly a few metres before falling to the ground and rolling down the hill with her wings still outstretched. She yelped excitedly and stood up, nothing serious had happened. I very much enjoyed watching these practice flights, though I was not having as much fun as Boman. I think I was slightly envious of her, and sometimes I secretly touched my own shoulder blades, but the slightest lump did not appear to be growing.

The day soon came when Boman could fly impeccably. Although it was highly risky we even started going out during the daytime. Boman would jump from the rocks and with only a few flaps of her wings she would rise up amongst the seagulls. She had hoped to make playmates of the seagulls, but they were startled, cawed loudly in distress and swooped out of Boman's path. Then they flew away to a distant shore frantically flapping their wings. The seagulls' panic was perfectly understandable as Boman's wing span was almost two metres and in the air she was a frightening and awesome sight.

As she returned to me Boman was dissatisfied.

'It baffles me that creatures as stupid as birds should be blessed with such noble limbs.'

'Perhaps flying alone does not make us blessed,' I replied dryly.

'There is of course a difference between flying and flying. For some it is merely a way of moving, for others it represents freedom.'

I was happy for Boman's triumph, I felt that I had had some part in the birth of her wings, but at the same time I was uncomfortable. I knew she had not grown wings for the sheer sake of it. Several times I found her examining a map, and would try to back off as quietly as possible. On one of these occasions she noticed me and followed me into the study; she lay her head on my knee and said:

'Don't be sorry.'

'I'm not,' I lied. 'We're still friends.'

'Of course we are. I don't want to make excuses, but it's not easy being a dog with wings, a talking dog and a normal dog all at once. Many things have become inevitable. My adventure that night, you remember, was inevitable and soon I will inevitably have to fly away.'

I nodded and we sat there for a long time, neither speaking nor moving. I gradually moved my hand on to her neck and rested it there. Boman gave a start and said:

'In fact, I will have to go now.'

'Wait a moment, I'll open the door.'

This was the only farewell we bade each other. On that day the clouds were very low in the sky, dragging across the treetops, and Boman flew hidden safely amongst them for the majority of the journey. Only a few times did she fly low enough to take her bearings from certain landmarks: lakes, railway tracks, towns. Someone idly wandering the streets noticed her black wings outstretched against the clouds and shouted: 'Look, a black swan!' But no one heard him and so the wanderer was branded a liar as he told his friends and neighbours that evening that he had seen a black swan flying north at this time of year. Such a thing is impossible.

Only once did Boman land to rest. She chose a bare hilltop amidst the great wilderness, where all the eye could see was dirty brown pine swamps and bluish forests. Everything was still, never before had Boman heard a stillness like this.

It was late evening by the time she reached her destination. She circled above the borstal several times before landing in a nearby forest, where she spent her first night. The forest floor was covered in spruce branches and the remnants of the felling season, and from these Boman made herself a shelter and hiding place. In the morning she made an early start, crept up towards the edge of the forest and followed any movement from the borstal. The building looked just like any country house, it was not cut off from the outside world by a wall or a high fence. The boys, still drowsy with sleep, assembled in the forecourt, they were given tools and split into groups, after which they went off in different directions towards the field, each group under the close supervision of one of the masters. The boys moved slowly and from a distance it looked as if they were wearing shoes far too big for them. Sometimes whilst the masters were not looking the boys would push and shove one another, not so much to let off steam, but simply because they resented those with whom destiny had thrown them together.

Boman spent a few days watching these events from a distance before she caught sight of Pertti, who appeared with one of the groups near the edge of the forest. The fields were narrrow and the ditches in between covered in thick willow bushes. Boman had already concluded that she would have to use those ditches to her advantage. Now she put her plan into action; she easily managed to come close to the group, but had to wait for a while until Pertti was far enough away from the others that she could speak to him. Before long a suitable opportunity presented itself.

Pertti managed to conceal his excitement from the other boys and the masters, for he had long since learnt the art of pretending. He was only able to whisper a few words, but

Boman spoke to him for a long time. I do not know what they talked about, but I do know that there was no chance for the two of them to meet in private. Pertti may have wanted to try and escape, but that would have been a desperate thing to do and Boman did not wish to cause her friend any fresh difficulties. Even so, the mere knowledge that Boman was nearby gave Pertti strength. He stood up straight, the former bluish gleam returned to his eyes and he laughed happily at the taunting of the other boys and masters. 'He's been taken by the Devil,' said the nastiest of them. The others simply wondered what had come over him.

On her first excursion, Boman spent about a week with Pertti, sleeping hidden away in her shelter under the spruce branches. She also had to fend for herself. Boman had never acquired a taste for raw meat and she had never before killed a living being. Now, however, she had no choice in the matter and began with stupid, ugly animals; her diet thus consisted for the most part of crows. She could catch them easily in flight and force herself to eat, though the taste of blood disgusted her.

After a week had gone by Boman returned to me, not to stay but to rest at my house. She gave me only a scant outline of what she had been doing. Sometimes we would chat generally or talk vividly about our shared memories, but at other times Boman seemed strangely wild. On days like this she would sleep through the daylight, while at night her eyes would begin to glow. She would not let me brush her and if I came too close she would growl angrily. The next day she would once again be like any other dog: playful, mischievous but always considerate. She would also not want to talk about the previous day whatsoever. Sometimes she would ask me to read aloud to her, poetry about wings, clouds and friendship, and at times like this she seemed to cry to herself – without shedding a tear.

Boman made many subsequent visits to Pertti, though these visits were not as long as the first. I was worried about her and kept a close watch on her, and before long I realised she was expecting puppies. Soon she would be unable to fly at all.

Talking about hunches is normal between humans, but what humans had mere hunches about, Boman knew as fact. Of course, she had nothing to hide from herself; her role as both a dog with a collar and a winged animal were in constant interaction. Boman knew this and made sure I also knew this as she softly began to speak.

'I don't seem to have complimented you very often,' she said.

'But why would you have offended me?'

We both sneered quietly, sadly, both of us understanding. Then Boman continued:

'If you had no imagination, I wouldn't exist. I would have been born, of course, but imagine what would have happened if I'd had a master who couldn't believe his eyes or his ears! He would have predefined the limits of my being. In that respect I would never have existed.'

'My friend,' I said. 'You're making this conversation very difficult for me. Perhaps it's my turn to tell you what a great service you have done me, a dog who can cross the boundary between the possible and the impossible as if it weren't there.'

'Oh I believe you, I'm hardly modest. To tell you the truth, I have also fulfilled my nature as a dog, in everything I've done. It's because of you that I learnt to speak, and you also played an important part in my wings – they belong equally to you, although they are on my back.'

'In my mind I've often flown with them. This is not a gift many dogs have given their masters.'

'Most dogs would be only too happy to do so, but such a gift needs a recipient, or else it won't exist. In any case, I hope that, even as you walk alone, you will always hear the patter of my paws beside you.'

These words, which sounded so like a farewell, dispelled the smile which had rippled across our eyes throughout this solemn exchange. I wanted to ask, to implore her for an explanation, but could not bring myself to do so. Boman left that same day without my noticing, leaving me alone to spend my time longing for her. I did not read very much during this time; I found the self-importance of books, searching for something eternal, somewhat objectionable. I settled instead for newspapers and numbed my brain by reading their every last word. Soon after she had left I noticed a small announcement in the paper warning people of a wolf or a wild Alsatian moving in the vicinity of Borstal K. The local authorities were to arrange a hunt, in which the military would also take part. The paper fell from my hands.

The following day the newspaper reported the wolf as fact. There had been many reported sightings of the animal and people were afraid it would break into a barn and ravage their cattle. A wolf hunt was underway. Dozens of men, each of them armed, combed their way through the forest from dawn till dusk. The wolf was behaving strangely: it did not flee the area, as many unarmed people had seen it, and it refused to be caught in meticulously laid traps. Newspaper articles gradually became more and more fanatical, the wolf was suddenly front page news, men in both the forest and the editorial office were in a frenzy. An animal, which so skilfully evaded its pursuers, had to be dangerous. One person even used the word "criminal" to refer to this stubborn animal, which refused to give itself up and be killed.

I waited and thought of Boman. I knew she could have fled if she had wanted to. She could have spread out her black wings and risen out of reach, but I also knew that she would not flee. I remembered the glow in her eyes of late, I understood why she had kept quiet about certain matters. She was free, she had grown herself a set of wings, she could fly and be with her friend in a fantasy land, a free land. Yet at the same time she was tied. She was tied to me and she was tied to her pregnancy. Boman lived in a world in which all three of these levels cannot be realised at once: whilst one represented freedom, the others were shackles. Two represented crime, only one making amends. Boman firmly believed in the strength of her own will. She had grown herself a set of wings, she wanted to force the men on the wolf hunt to accept the fact that the animal they were hunting would not be trapped, that it was smarter, more cunning, and freer than the people stalking it. I could imagine Boman, emerging triumphant from this furore, landing one day in the market place, gathering her black wings and walking off calmly along the high street.

This is what I imagined as I waited. I thought that by her very existence she might force people to accept certain truths: there is a dog with wings, there is a dog which soars above our heads towards freedom, descending once again into our midst, or joining other dogs in their untamed games.

I did not sleep well at night, but despite this my hearing was far from acute. One morning I opened the door and found Boman lying on the step. She was already cold, there was a wound in her right side. Her black wings lay dishevelled, helpless, beside her.

# *Shopping*

Tove Jansson

*The Finland-Swedish writer and artist Tove Jansson (1914–2001) is perhaps best known throughout the world as the mother of the Moomins. Their adventures have been translated into over 30 languages and have been made into numerous film, television and stage adaptations. Jansson was also an acclaimed writer of 'adult' literature and her novels, short fiction and memoirs deal in great depth with themes of childhood, family and the problems of human relationships, most particularly in* The Summer Book *('Sommarboken', 1972; English translation 2003). The present short story is from the collection* Resa med lätt bagage *('Travelling Light', 1987).*

It was five o'clock in the morning. The cloudy weather showed no signs of abating and the awful stench seemed only to be worsening. Emily took her normal route along Robertsgatan to Blom's grocers, shards of glass crackling under her shoes, and she decided that one of these days she would have to try and clear the street somewhat. So long as she had time for her endless shopping. At present they had a good many tins of food in the kitchen, but you never know these days, she thought. Surprisingly enough the big mirror still stood outside Blom's; she stopped for a moment and adjusted her hair. Nobody could say she was actually fat anymore, more like plump – or buxom as Kristian would say. Her overcoat certainly fitted her better. It was green and matched her shopping bags. Emily clambered up a pile of bricks and cement and in through the window. Inside the stench was that of rotten food. Straight away she noticed that they had been here again, the shelves were as good as empty. They hadn't bothered taking the pickled cabbage; Emily packed all the remaining jars, picked up the last packet of candles, and on her way out a new washing-up brush and some shampoo. They were out of juice, so Kristian would just have to put up with water from the river. She could always have gone down to Lundgren's to have a look, but it was such a long way. Another time. So as to make the most out of the morning Emily popped into number six, left her shopping bags on the ground floor and went up one flight of stairs to Eriksson's. It was impossible to go any further than that. It was a good job the Erikssons had left the door unlocked as they had left. Emily knew there was nothing there to be had, she had been here shopping so many times before, but it was nice to sit down and put her feet up on the lovely sofa in the living room. Still, it was far from lovely now, stained and ripped to shreds with a knife; they had done this, the others. No matter, Emily had come here first and she had held such respect for the peaceful beauty of these rooms that she had not taken anything but food. Later, once everything had been soiled and destroyed, she had decided to save one or two items to make their kitchen look nice and surprise Kristian. This time she picked up a rococo wall clock which had stopped at five, her shopping time. No one else was out at five o'clock; it was a good, safe time.

Emily began to make her way back home; she wondered whether Kristian could eat pickled cabbage, especially now that his stomach had become so sensitive. Halfway home she put down her heavy shopping bags and looked out across the changed cityscape, the diminished suburb she lived in – there really wasn't very much of it left. Across the river there was nothing at all. Strange that the leaves in the trees hadn't come out yet.

And then she saw them, far away at the other end of Robertsgatan, nothing but two tiny specks, but they were moving, very deliberately: they were coming. Emily started to run.

Their kitchen was on the ground floor, they used always to eat at the kitchen table and they had just sat down to dinner when it happened. The rest of the flat had been blocked off altogether. Kristian's leg injury had been entirely unnecessary; as far as Emily could see there had been no reason for him to rush outside and have half a wall come crashing down on top of him like that, it had been nothing but macho curiosity. He knew perfectly well what people were expected to do, there had been warnings on the radio saying: Remain indoors in the event of . . . and so on. And so there he lay on a mattress Emily had found in the street. She had hung a rug across the blown-out window and had later propped it up with some timbers she had found in the rubbish outside. It was sheer luck that their tool box had always been kept in the kitchen. Anyone could have come in through that window. For extra security she had spent hours piling up camouflage on the outside of the window too. Kristian lay on his mattress listening as Emily barricaded them in and he couldn't stop thinking that she was enjoying herself – almost enjoying herself. He tried to avoid frightening her. He slept a lot. His leg injury didn't seem too serious but it ached and he couldn't put any weight on it. What plagued him far more was the darkness.

Now he was awake and fumbled for a candle and the matches on the floor beside the mattress. He lit the candle taking great care not to let the match go out. There lay the books from Eriksson's, unread books from a world that no longer had anything to do with him. He wound up the clock, something he did every morning. It had just gone six o'clock, she would be back at any moment. They didn't have very many matches left.

I really wish, he thought, I wish we could talk about what's happened, give it a name, talk openly and honestly. But I don't have the heart. And I dare not frighten her. Still, we could at least open that damn window.

And with that she arrived. She locked the kitchen door, placed her bags on the kitchen table, gave him a smile and showed him the gold-plated clock from Eriksson's, a truly frightful piece. 'How's your leg? Did you sleep well?'

'Very well,' Kristian replied. 'Did you get any matches?'

'No. And the juice is finished. They've torn up the sofa at Eriksson's.'

'You're out of breath,' said Kristian. 'You've been running. Did you see them?'

Emily took off her overcoat and replaced the new washing-up brush for the old one on the hook. 'I'll have to fetch some washing water from the river,' she said.

'Emily? Did you see them?'

'Yes. There were only two of them. They were far away at the corner of Edlund. Maybe folk have started going into town now that the shops are empty.'

'The corner of Edlund? But you said it wasn't there any longer. Nothing left past the petrol station, you said.'

'Yes, I know, but the corner's still there.' Emily laid a tray with some crispbread and tomato juice and placed it on the floor next to him. 'Try and eat something. You've become far too thin.' She picked up the housekeeping book and logged the new jars on the page marked 'Vegetables'.

Kristian soon started talking about the window again: they had to open it, clear it and let in some daylight, he could not carry on in this darkness any more.

'But they'll come for us!' shouted Emily. 'They'll find us in no time and take all our shopping. Kristian, please try and understand once and for all. You don't know the things I've seen out there. The sofa at Eriksson's . . . Piles of smashed porcelain, some of it antique by the way . . . And anyway it's very dark outside too.'

'What do you mean?'

'Yes, it's getting darker and darker. Only a few weeks ago I could still go out shopping every morning at four o'clock, but now you can hardly see a thing before five.'

Kristian became very uneasy. 'Are you sure? It's really getting darker? But it's the beginning of June, it can't be getting darker!'

'Relax, dear, it's just overcast all the time, we haven't had any sunshine since . . . Not once.'

He sat up and gripped her by the arm. 'Do you mean . . . like twilight or . . .?'

'No, I mean it's just overcast! Clouds, do you understand, clouds! Why do you have to make me so nervous?'

Far off in the town that siren started up again, it howled endlessly at long intervals, almost like a helpless wailing that always had Emily beside herself. Kristian had tried to calm her down by suggesting that perhaps there was a generator at the fire station that had somehow gone haywire but it didn't help, she just sobbed. And that is what she did this time too, she jumped up and blindly began organising her tins on the kitchen shelf. One of them fell, rolled along the floor and knocked over the candle. The flame went out.

'Look what you've done,' he said. 'How many matches do you think we've got left? What are we supposed to do when we run out, sit in the dark and wait for the end? We've got to open that window!'

'Oh you and your window!' shouted Emily. 'Why can't you just let me be happy, you like it when I'm happy, don't you? Aren't things just fine the way they are? I found a bar of soap yesterday, do you understand what that means? Soap!' She suddenly pulled herself together and continued: 'I try to make our home cosy. I go out and do the shopping. I find nice little surprises . . . Why do you frighten me, why do you have to be so gloomy about everything?'

'What do you . . . how do you think I feel, lying here like a cadaver and not being able to take responsibility for you? It's infernal.'

Emily replied: 'Are you proud? Are you? Did it ever occur to you that in my whole life I've never been able to take care of matters and make decisions about things that are important? Just let me be, don't take that away from me. The only thing you need do to help me is never to let me become frightened.' She found the matches and lit the candle, then she added: 'The only thing I care about is that they don't come here and take our food. Nothing else.'

One day Kristian forgot to wind up the clock. At first he did not dare mention it and told Emily only later that evening. She was standing at the sink; she froze and didn't say a word.

'I know,' he said. 'It's inexcusable. I don't have anything else to take care of and then I go and do something like this. Emily? Say something.'

'They've all stopped,' she said in a very low voice. 'Every single clock. Now I'll never know when it's time to go for the shopping.'

Again he said: 'It's inexcusable.'

After this they no longer discussed the matter. But the incident with the clock changed something, established an uncertainty, a timidity between them. It wasn't very often Emily went out with all her shopping bags; what need was there, after all? The grocers' shops were all empty and sitting at Eriksson's only made her wistful. In any case, on her last visit she had rescued a large Spanish silk shawl that she had found draped across the piano – it would bring a little colour to the barricaded window. On her way home Emily saw a dog. She beckoned to it but it ran away.

As she stepped into the kitchen she said: 'I saw a dog.'

Kristian became visibly excited. 'Where was it? What did it look like?'

'A brown and white setter. In the park. I called out to it but it was frightened and ran off. The rats are never afraid like that.'

'Where did it run?'

'Oh, it just ran away. Strange that nobody's eaten it. I daren't even think what the poor dog has had to eat. It certainly didn't look very thin.'

Kristian lay down on his mattress once again. 'Sometimes,' he said. 'Sometimes you surprise me. Women surprise me.'

Emily and Kristian continued like this for some time. Kristian's leg was slowly healing, sometimes he could even sit up at the kitchen table. He would sit counting out matches into piles, so and so many for such and such a time. Every time Emily had gone out to fetch water he would ask her if she had seen the others. One morning she had seen them.

'Were they men or women?'

'I don't know. They were too far away across the park.'

'You didn't see whether they were young or old?'

'No.'

'I wonder . . .' said Kristian. 'I wonder if they've also noticed how it's getting darker all the time. What must they be thinking? Do they try to talk to one another, make plans? Or are they simply scared? Why haven't they gone like everyone else? Do they think they're completely alone, that there's not a single person left, not one . . .?'

'Kristian, dear, I don't know. I try not to think about them.'

'But we have to think about them!' he exclaimed. 'Maybe it's just them and us left. We could meet them.'

'You don't know what you're saying.'

'Yes I do, and I mean it. We could talk to them, work out what can be done – together. Share things.'

'Not our food!' Emily cried.

'Keep your tins,' Kristian scoffed. 'We could share what has happened, what you never want to talk about. What happened, why it happened, how we can carry on, if there's anything to carry on for.'

'I've got to empty out the dish-water,' she replied.

'No you don't, you'll listen to what I have to say. It's important.' And with that Kristian continued talking, trying to express the ideas that had formed in his head over the last days and weeks cooped up in the darkness; he offered Emily his respect for her sense of judgement asking only for the trust and loyalty he felt his wife should show in return. He was in fact trying to tell her how much he loved her, though she did not understand this and left without a word so she would not have to listen.

Once Emily had left, Kristian was gripped by an all-consuming rage. He made his way over to the window and tore down her Spanish shawl, dislodged first one timber, then another; he attacked the window in a fury of frustration until his leg finally gave way and he collapsed to his knees. Through a small opening on one side of the window daylight finally shone into the room.

Emily had returned, she stood on the threshold and screamed: 'You've ripped my Spanish shawl!'

'Yes, I've ripped your shawl. The world is fast disappearing and someone has ripped little Emily's shawl. How terrible! Bring me the axe, quickly!'

Kristian lunged at the barricade. Time and again he fell to the floor and dropped the axe, then tried again.

'Let me,' Emily whispered.

'No. You have nothing whatsoever to do with this.'

With that she went forward and steadied him so that he could carry on. Once the window was finally free she began to clear up the mess Kristian had made. He waited, but his wife said nothing. Their kitchen looked strange in the grey light shining in: a room exposed, unorganised in its shabbiness and teeming with useless paraphernalia.

Emily said: 'They're on their way.' Without looking at him she continued: 'Your leg seems fine. You're so difficult nowadays that I can hardly put up with you. Come on, we're going out.' She threw open the kitchen door.

'Do you trust me?' asked Kristian. 'Do you believe me?'

'Don't make a spectacle of yourself,' she replied. 'Of course I trust you. Take your coat, it's a bit chilly.' She helped him put on the coat and took his arm.

Outside it was becoming darker as evening drew in. The others had moved closer. Very slowly Emily and Kristian began to walk towards them.

# *Congress*

## Erno Paasilinna

*Erno Paasilinna (1935–2000) was nicknamed the official dissident of Finnish literature in the second half of the 20th century. He was an aphorist, essayist and satirist who refused to fit into any given mould or to submit to the expectations of others. He became a fervent defender of freedom of speech and opposed bureaucracy, totalitarian societies and the herd mentality. His writing is always sharp and hard-hitting, and he has been called the only true satirist in Finnish literature. Erno Paasilinna won the Finlandia Prize in 1984 for his collection of essays* Yksinäisyys ja uhma *('Loneliness and Defiance'). The short story 'Congress' was first published in a collection of essays and satirical texts entitled* Alamaisen kyyneleet *('Tears of an Underdog', 1970).*

Doctor Smith said he believed that an attack from outer space would not be imminent for a long time yet. He stated that current observations did not support the claim that any preparations for such an attack had as yet been laid. Technologically speaking they are more advanced than we are, but this does not give grounds for any kind of panic. He described as inane the general assumption that an encounter with visitors from outer space would in some way automatically lead to war. Rather, he claimed that humans have proved a far greater threat to themselves. He asked members of the congress to ensure that steps were taken in all countries towards peace not war. He said he did not wish to sound sarcastic, but pointed out that those who prepare themselves for a war generally always end up fighting one.

Dr. Smith commented that the visitors from outer space

have in fact behaved very moderately and have actively avoided any aggressive confrontation with humans. Referring to the often cited Barcelona Case, in which a motorist was killed, Dr. Smith claimed that this was a matter of pure self-defence, the type to which any pilot would resort in an emergency situation. The belligerent motorist had approached the unknown pilot, pointed a weapon at him and asked him to "put his hands up". The fate of three hikers allegedly kidnapped in Dublin could be understood as arising merely from a keen intellectual interest. There is no evidence to support claims that the hikers were tortured or that any other attack was made against their persons. According to eye-witness accounts they were simply shown into the ship, after which the ship rose into the air. Dr. Smith explained that he had the impression from witness statements that the hikers had in fact boarded the ship of their own accord. One of them had even "laughed and waved his hand". In view of the current political climate on Earth, the experiences of these hikers appeared to speak in favour of the visitors. He said it was natural that our guests from outer space should wish to examine the behaviour and physiology of human beings. This honourable congress should strive at all costs to understand this side of the argument too, he said.

The representative from the United States said he found such a notion unacceptable. He believed establishing needless trust in this manner was something which could well be left to the press, as it appeared so many governments had compromised their national security to such a degree. The speaker argued that the possibility of a military invasion was supported by the number of sightings recorded in the vicinity of research institutes and military targets. Surely the honourable Dr. Smith was not unaware of these sightings. Based on material collected in the West, it would appear that even projects of the most remote interest were well documented in outer space. We can even say that the submarine Tornado, lost last summer during a military operation in the Pacific, was literally snatched from beneath our eyes. I hazard to suggest to Dr. Smith that many of the military experts present at this very congress are awaiting the return of this submarine with great interest – if, that is, he can arrange for its return. We cannot afford to reject as fancy the disappearance of our most valuable submarine, after three admirals in the United States Navy and a host of lower-ranked officers witnessed how, in mid-operation, the submarine was raised out of the water into an enormous flying ship which then disappeared forthwith. I do not wish to rebuff Dr. Smith for his generosity of spirit, but I would prefer this provocation towards the United States to be seen as stemming from a primarily scientific interest.

Dr. Smith replied that in no way did he deny the truth of the events in question. However, he urged those present to assess whether representatives from outer space may simply consider our machines a curiosity. This argument is substantiated by the fact that the visitors have not destroyed these machines, but have in fact striven to acquire a representative cross-section. In this they seem to have succeeded, he added.

A general from the Soviet Union said that perhaps he had not understood the irony of Dr. Smith's words. He asked whether Dr. Smith represented a particular government. Dr. Smith replied in the negative. The general then asked who or what exactly Dr. Smith did represent at this congress, if not the visitors from outer space themselves. Dr. Smith stated that he was speaking as an expert at the invitation of the conference organisers. The representatives from outer space do not need anyone to defend them – quite the contrary, it seems to me, he replied.

The general then turned and addressed the organisers, asking whether delegates might now consider Dr. Smith's expert opinions heard and continue the discussion of questions of a more military nature. He said he felt it would have been preferable, concerning the functioning of this congress as a whole, if Dr. Smith's expertise had better addressed the facts.

After Dr. Smith had left the lecturn, the general expressed his condolences for the losses experienced by the United States delegation and admitted that the Soviet Union had been aware of this. He said he considered it symptomatic of the age that the interest of those from outer space seemed to focus so strongly on our military operations. We may have to accept the fact that all our new inventions are widely known about and that the possibility of keeping future developments secret was very small indeed. He felt it harmful to the military status quo that the developments and material powers of those in outer space were so sparsely documented here on Earth. He also revealed the acquisition of a number of metallic objects, but reported that the process of examining them was significantly slowed due to the peculiarity of the metal. Analysis has been hindered by the almost complete lack of similarity to other known elements. This, however, is only one side of the matter, said the general. If the argument for the decommissioning of weapons achieves a foothold amongst delegates, the chances of winning any potential conflict will be lost. Here he made reference to the previous conversation and stated that the Soviet Union had already asserted its position on the matter. He also pointed out that this was a position shared by the United States and hoped that other governments would soon follow suit. What is at stake is ultimately the fate of the human race, said the general.

A speaker from the floor asked delegates to consider a situation in which the visitors from outer space may feel it necessary to invade the Earth. He said that this was not a question which could be assessed from the standpoint of traditional military objectives. He proposed, speaking only for himself, that one such objective may be that of sustenance. If we assume that the Earth has something to offer them, a military invasion of this nature may not be out of the question after all.

A Kenyan biologist pointed out that, being himself familiar with the food crisis on Earth, it would be strange to assume that the visitors would settle for the meagre benefits of such an invasion. In a scenario like this, the benefits would not be ample compensation for the sacrifices an invasion of this scale would undoubtedly require. He said he would be pessimistic about the future of the human race in the event that the visitors sought merely to improve their food stocks. In his assessment he said that biodiversity on Earth may indeed be well suited to the visitors' nourishment requirements, but that it was equally possible that they were interested in humans themselves. The Kenyan representative did, however, ask delegates not to misunderstand his words as condoning the use of humans as a foodstuff.

The Belgian representative said that the proposed scenario was undoubtedly a highly interesting one and could indeed prove correct. He hazarded that it would be worth considering the scale on which humans, harvested and refined, could serve as a foodstuff for the visitors. Then we would find out precisely what benefits they would be yielding. He did not suggest that it would be wise to predict development of this nature, but was keen to point out that, in the event that such action proved unavoidable, people would have to prepare themselves well in advance. He asked that the revulsion widely felt towards this type of system not prevent delegates from debating the matter on a theoretical basis. Personally he believed that it might be possible to achieve very high production levels indeed. This would, of course, require the majority of the human race to be confined to zoos, nourished entirely by the Earth's own food stocks, and this in turn would raise the overall volume of humans considerably. He calculated that steady feeding, if it were properly regulated, could guarantee the production of at least 16–18 billion people. These were the sort of projected figures, he said, which one could assume would be of great interest to the visitors. These days it is common for food to be distributed very disproportionally indeed, something which, he pointed out, had come in for much criticism of late.

The Norwegian representative asked whether this turn in the conversation meant that the congress was now to concentrate on debating these newly proposed solutions as opposed to the possibility of military intervention. He stated that he was not vested with the authority of his government to take part in a debate of that kind. If he had understood the conversation correctly, he said, he felt this would in effect amount to the surrender of the human race.

The American delegation replied by pointing out that these problems cannot be viewed separately, rather they should be seen as intrinsically bound up with the wider question of military strategy. In ascertaining the objectives of the visitors we are simultaneously ascertaining the challenges we will face in the event of a possible military defeat. In this sense we believe the new proposals are firmly linked to our fundamental question, something which does not necessarily involve surrendering. To put the matter discreetly what we are looking at is some kind of compromise.

A Swiss researcher said that, as a scientist, he was of course not the right person to pass judgement on a matter of military strategy. But it seems that this debate is assuming that human meat is somehow more valuable than that of animals as a source of nourishment. Naturally this is partly a matter of individual taste, but even if we were to leave this point for a moment, it is undoubtedly true that humans would be far easier to mass produce than animals. The speaker argued that a small number of human beings could, due to their superior levels of intelligence, be trained to oversee the production of those raised for meat; naturally this solution would require fewer of the visitors than for, say, raising animals in bulk. Of course, there would be nothing to prevent them from raising animals in addition to humans. These are merely practical considerations, the speaker added.

The French representative confirmed that it would be possible to refine humans so that carcass weight could be increased, thus making the whole operation more cost-effective, and that specific improvements could be made in the quality of the meat itself. He added that speculation of this nature may seem macabre, but that these were nonetheless the biological facts. The speaker suggested that those trained to oversee production could also serve as quality controllers and experts with a firm grounding of the conditions on Earth. He said that these were perfect conditions for such cooperation. He declined to comment on the ethical questions raised. That would clearly require the opinion of an expert.

At this point the comment was made that the debate had not yet considered the implications of transporting slaughtered meat or how human meat should be preserved, as the quantities involved would be so vast. The speaker said he was convinced of the benefits of mass-producing meat on Earth, but said that the possibility of marketing human meat in interplanetary commerce was wholly speculative. He said he believed that turning the Earth into some kind of food supplier in space would involve ironing out many details yet, though theoretically he considered the idea entirely viable.

A West-German professor said he agreed whole-heartedly with the other speakers, as he felt the voluntary organisation and coordination of meat production may be precisely the kind of positive gesture the occupying forces would no doubt expect from responsible leaders on Earth. The suggestion of a system of quality control he said was "spot on". He said he believed that, in establishing meat production of this kind, the aim will presumably be firstly to save on production costs and secondly to minimize the number of staff tied up on Earth. The professor said that, in the event of an invasion, the question would arise as to whether there are people on Earth with the skills required to undertake leading positions in product development. As much as he did not wish to seem overly patriotic, he said, he felt his countrymen have experiences which may be of great use in this matter. He suggested that a committee be established without delay to take care of any preliminary organisational matters and to prepare for ongoing contact with the representatives from outer space. The speaker said he was happy to leave open any questions regarding the details of the action required for such a change, but that he considered making initial preparations a matter of the greatest urgency.

# *Good Heavens!*

Arto Paasilinna

*Arto Paasilinna (born 1942) is one of Finland's most popular writers and his novels have been translated into 35 languages. Paasilinna's writing is direct, approachable, humourous and often overtly picaresque. A recurring theme is that of freeing oneself from the shackles of society and his texts often take a comical and parodic view of myth and religion. He is the brother of Erno Paasilinna, also featured in this anthology. Arto Paasilinna's breakthrough came in 1975 with the novel* The Year of the Hare *('Jäniksen vuosi'). The extract featured here comes from the novel* Herranen aika *('Good Heavens!', 1980).*

## *Chapter One*

My death came to me as a complete surprise.

It was an August afternoon and I was walking along Kaisaniemenkatu on my way home from work at the editorial office of a local newspaper. I was in a particularly good mood and felt decidedly full of life. At the time I was only thirty years old. Throughout my lifetime I had never seriously considered the idea that I might die in the middle of everything; that it would be sudden and final.

But that's exactly what happened.

Kaisaniemenkatu in August was a hubbub of happy, carefree life. The street attracts all kinds of city women, the vainest and the prettiest, who stroll around department stores picking out that autumn's most fashionable clothes; all the airheads, still proudly sporting their summer tan, whose mere presence has the power to catch men's eyes. Watching them is a great deal of fun, examining their thighs and their hips. At this time of year the exhaust fumes of Kaisaniemenkatu smell of cosmetics – Madame Rochas, Dior, Max Factor.

Perhaps I was watching the bustling life on the streets a little too intently. For a few metres I decided to walk along the road to get a better view of a lovely pair of legs at the edge of the crowd on the pavement. Their firm calf muscles were showing nicely. I quickened my step so I could catch a glimpse of her face. I'm a thorough man, I don't settle for seeing only a woman's legs, I want to see her expression too. After all, it's the overall impression that counts.

As it turned out I didn't live to see her face as all of a sudden I was hit by a car, and that was that.

The impact sent me flying back on to the pavement, where I struck the ground and lay motionless looking well and truly beaten up. The knock was terribly painful, I heard my head crack open. The pain stopped immediately.

For a short while everything went black.

Then I saw what had happened. My body was lying on the pavement and the traffic had come to a standstill. The woman I had been following had heard the sound of the crash and had come back to take a nosy look at what had happened. Now I saw her face. Nothing to write home about. I was rather upset: a man in his prime had been run over all for *this*?

The car in question had pulled over by the side of the road. The driver was examining the front of his bonnet, in which there were now a few dents. One of the front headlights had cracked. The man took a hankerchief and wiped blood from the splintered glass. From the direction of the railway station came the wail of an ambulance.

A crowd of people surrounded my body. Somebody rolled me on to my back and held a compact mirror in front of my mouth. Somebody else loosened the tie around my neck. In shock I knelt down next to my body to see if any vapours rose up to the mirror.

The surface of the mirror remained crystal clear. I looked myself in the eyes: my expression was lifeless, my pupils were growing smaller: apparently I was dead.

A moment later the ambulance arrived. The paramedics quickly checked my pulse and shook their heads. They lifted me on to a stretcher and placed me in the back of the van. They were no longer in any hurry, I was dead as dead could be. With that the ambulance drove off to take my body to the hospital. This time, however, the sirens weren't blaring.

A few minutes later the police arrived on the scene and set about taking notes. The group of onlookers began to disperse, the most interesting part of the incident was over. A security guard from the department store came out to sweep broken glass off the street. A caretaker appeared with a hose to rinse off the few blood stains on the pavement. The man who had run me over was explaining to the police that it was entirely my fault. Distraught, he surveyed the damage done to his car.

So I was dead.

It seemed impossible. Death had decided to claim *me*, of all people . . . the idea was very hard to take in.

Where was the sense in dying like that, by sheer accident? The triviality and pointlessness of it all began to infuriate me. Who benefitted from a death like this? Would it have been too much to have been allowed to live for even another ten years? Then I would have had enough time to prove that I was still a decent person and not just a good-for-nothing.

Couldn't some needless person have died on my behalf? Now everything was left up in the air. Come to think of it, I hadn't really done anything important or noteworthy, anything permanent in my life. I felt cheated: was an end like this the reason I had lived for over thirty years?

I thought hard about what I had to do next. Perhaps it would be best simply to let things take their natural course. I stood on the street, unsure and still in shock. It crossed my mind that this was something no living person would ever experience. I smirked at my own stupidity: of course the living know nothing about death. If they did, they would no longer be alive.

Was I now supposed to continue on my way home, as if nothing had happened, as if I weren't dead after all? That certainly seemed the logical thing to do. Before the accident I had been planning to stop by a small pub on Liisankatu and have a few pints before going home to my wife. Now after my sudden death, the idea of going to the pub somehow didn't appeal quite as much. People might even have thought it slightly inappropriate: a man gets himself killed and the first thing he does is head for the pub. In any case I wasn't the least bit thirsty any more. The desire for a cold beer had obviously remained in my dead body, which was at that very moment being driven to the hospital.

Suddenly I panicked: I could lose my body for good if I didn't find out where it was being taken. It was probably best to follow the ambulance, which had driven off along Unioninkatu in the direction of Hakaniemi. I dashed off in pursuit and noticed at once that I could move at the speed of thought. In a flash I was in Hakaniemi, the Zoo and finally Alppila, where I caught up with the ambulance, which was travelling far slower than I was.

Through the ambulance's darkened windows I saw a body lying inside, its face covered with a sheet. I recognised myself from the suit I was wearing and the briefcase which had been placed on my stomach. I was wearing a light brown summer suit and new brown shoes that I had only bought two days ago. Now buying those shoes felt rather pointless, because they had been expensive and my old shoes would have done perfectly well for the last two days of my life. But how is a person supposed to know? Still, when I thought about buying the shoes a little longer I began to feel a certain satisfation – after all, I was wearing a nicely fitted suit and had a sharp pair of new shoes on my feet. Thankfully I had washed my hair in the morning, making me all in all a rather stylish corpse indeed.

The ambulance drove to the hospital in Meilahti. My body was stretchered inside. On arrival the duty surgeon gave me a quick examination. He pronounced me dead. They opened up my briefcase. There was nothing out of the ordinary inside: some newspapers, notes for forthcoming articles, a few books, a jar of pickled onions.

I had always liked pickled onions. My wife never bought

them, so I was in the habit of getting hold of them myself. I began to think about how we – my wife and I – had never really had much in common throughout our married life. We shared a bed, an address, but nothing much else. That is something, of course. Now I had made my wife a widow. She was finally free of me and my pickled onions.

The surgeon confirmed that I had died of serious head injuries. I thought as much when the car struck me. You could hear the impact on the skull. The surgeon rolled me on to my side. A small amount of blood dribbled out of my mouth on to the stretcher. It wasn't a pleasant sight.

My wallet was inspected. I was ashamed to be present whilst they were counting out my money; there was so little of it, just short of eighty marks. In all respects I was quite a diminutive body. If I'd known that I was going to be run over this very day I would have handed in my notice at the newspaper first thing in the morning. My wallet would have been bulging with my enormous pay-off and at least then nobody would have been able to call me poor. Perhaps the caretaker or the surgeon might even have pinched a few notes from my pocket. Things like that have happened before: pathologists have been known to take rings, watches and even gold teeth from their patients. As crimes go, stealing from the dead is a fairly safe bet, as the victim is very unlikely to file a complaint.

My details were taken from my passport and logged in the usual hospital paperwork. I read the form over the secretary's shoulder. It occurred to me that people can't even die nowadays without someone filling out forms about them.

Once she had filled in the form with my particulars, the receptionist walked over to the surgeon and asked him whether to inform the deceased's next of kin, in this case my wife, about what had happened. We didn't have any children – thankfully.

The surgeon told her not to call anyone for the time being. He said that the body would have to be cleaned up first before informing my wife.

'We'll get him dolled up a bit first, then take him down

to the refrigerator. Call his wife in about half an hour,' he instructed her.

I had to hurry. I would have to leave straight away so that I could be at home when the news of my death was announced. On my way home I wondered how my wife would take the shocking news. Would she burst into tears? Tear her clothes to shreds in a fit of agony? Or would she be too shocked and slip into a desperate state of apathy?

Hardly . . . but that would all soon become clear. Perhaps she might cry just a little bit. I had been her husband after all. Surely that meant something.

## *Chapter Three*

The first few days after my death were filled with ever stranger surprises. Even the fact that I could move unhindered and at the speed of thought continually managed to astound me. More than once I was forced to accept that even after death you still learn something new every day.

Had I been sent to heaven or hell, or was I stuck in purgatory? Matters like this didn't particularly bother me. The main thing was that I could carry on living – or existing, whatever that meant.

I was nonetheless somewhat puzzled by the question of where I actually was. Why hadn't I just died once and for all? Why had I been allowed to hang around as some sort of spirit? For the time being these questions simply remained unanswered.

I sometimes wondered who ran things on this side. Who or what was the top dog round here? What was my place in the new hierarchy, or was existence beyond death not ordered in the slightest?

When a person is born into the world they appear as a small child, a helpless baby. Newborn babies don't understand anything of the world around them, they don't ask questions, they're not afraid of their new lives and they don't find it strange in the least. All that matters to them is that they get to suck on their mother's tits and sleep all day long. Only years later do children gradually begin to understand their environment and ask questions about things going on in the world.

Birth and death are actually very similar events in that death is the beginning of a new life too – I'd just experienced it for myself. Still, death is rather more of a trauma than birth, because when people die they generally have all their wits about them and they are forced to face this new world completely cold and unprepared. There are an enormous number of questions buzzing through the minds of the newly dead. It takes a lot less than that to make a dead man's head spin.

If people were born into the world as fully grown adults, instead of as babies as is normally the way, the world would be fairly chaotic, what with all the new arrivals immediately having to acquire the skills and knowledge of other adults. Maternity wards would be overrun with clumsy newborn adults lining the corridors, wailing impatiently at the reasons for their incomprehensible entry into the world. If people were born as adults, mothers would have to be far bigger than they are nowadays. A woman about to give birth to a full-sized human being would weigh at least three hundred kilos and would be over four metres tall. Her waist-line would have to measure at least a metre and a half. At the sight of a woman like that an average sized man would quake in his boots, for better or for worse.

A few days after my death I went down to the reading room at the city library to see what kind of announcement my colleagues had placed about my death in the newspaper. I had to go to the reading room because I could no longer just buy the newspaper at the kiosk, the penniless, bodiless man that I was, and I couldn't flick through it either. At the reading room people turn pages for the dead too. All I had to do was hang around behind one of the living people using the room and read the paper along with them. I've never liked people reading the newspaper over my shoulder, but now I too was forced to lower myself to such a faux pas.

There were twenty or so people sitting around the room

reading their papers. But something took me quite by surprise: behind each and every one of them stood one or more other persons reading the same paper with them. I realised that all in all there were about a hundred people in the room. In perfect silence all of them were going through the day's papers, some sitting, most of them standing.

I noticed that the majority of those standing reading over someone's shoulder were dressed in slightly old-fashioned clothes. Their attire seemed to stem from many different eras: most people were dressed in clothes from the 1950s, but there were some whose style dated from before the war, right back to the turn of the century. To my surprise I saw amongst their number two poor soldiers, who had both clearly served at the front during the last war. One was a sergeant, the other a private. Both of them looked as if they had walked into the reading room straight from the battlefield.

This mixed bunch stood silently reading the day's news along with those sitting at the tables.

A shocking thought suddenly occurred to me: what if these people were all dead just like me? What if there were other beings in this afterlife and I wasn't alone after all?

This was indeed the case. How could I not have thought of such a possibility before? Even the dead want to know what's going on in the world and the library was the obvious place to come and follow the news. I realised that the role of the city libraries as sources of information was not limited merely to providing a service for the living, but that it was used daily by crowds of dead people too. In this respect it was only right that library funding be significantly increased, as providing the dead with a way of keeping up their reading skills was by no means without its value. If only the political powers that be knew how many people actually used these libraries every day the funding bodies would soon find some extra cash and libraries everywhere would be able to order far more newspapers than at present.

I could feel myself blushing. I had leisurely strolled into the reading room in the belief that I would be alone, only to discover that we spirits far outnumbered the living in the room! I tried to concentrate on reading the paper, whilst out of the corner of my eye shiftily looking around at the other dead folk standing about, who didn't seem to pay me the least bit of attention.

I didn't know quite what to do. Should I say hello to all of these strange beings, or would it be better to keep away from them and try to look as if coming to the library was an everyday activity? It all felt slightly awkward: it's always a pain to end up with a group of strangers when you're not quite sure how to behave.

Reading the paper with me – over the shoulder of a living person sitting at the table – was a fat, ruddy, oldish looking man. He was a short, unkempt, burly man with swollen cheeks. His clothes were dirty, his hair tangled, strands sticking up here and there, and a few day's worth of stubble had grown across his face, which had clearly seen better days. The man glanced over at me and said in a low voice:

'Are you new then?'

I was so taken aback by this man's none too subtle question that I hurriedly shook my head. Ignoring me, the man didn't give in and said:

'No use making a fuss, I saw your picture in the paper this morning. Aren't you the same bloke that got himself run over on Kaisaniemenkatu the other day?'

I admitted that he was right. Our conversation caused some consternation amongst the other dead people, it must have disturbed their reading. Most of them knitted their brows and looked over at us disapprovingly. Even the dead have to be quiet in the library, I learnt.

The scruffy man whispered to me, suggesting we go outside and have a chat, and as he did so he stepped through the window on to the street and beckoned for me to follow him.

Again I learnt something new: people like us could walk through a pane of glass without smashing the window. Stepping through the glass I did have difficulty breathing for a moment, but the effects weren't lasting. My eyes didn't even sting, though the glass shimmered as I walked through it.

Once we were out on the street the bloke and I walked off down the Esplanade. My new acquaintance began to explain how things worked round here. He told me that both the living and the dead walk about the streets in one big crowd. I would have to take a close look at people in order to learn to distinguish us from them. The man started pointing at people walking past:

'Living, living, dead, living, dead, dead, living . . . you see how easily I can tell one from the other?'

I noticed that dead people's dress sense was drearier and less fashionable than that of the living. You could tell Finland was going through the boom years. But even the expressions of people walking past said a lot about whether they were alive or 'one of us'. Living Finns often have a distressed, tense expression on their faces; they are agitated and nervous. The dead on the other hand were, with a few exceptions, calm and looked very content. They don't rush anywhere, they have time to look around, take in the sights in the park and listen to the chirping of the birds.

The man greeted a few dead people as they walked past, and they gave him a muffled reply: you could tell my new acquaintance didn't have many close friends.

'Your eyes will learn how to tell the difference soon enough. See that man standing by the old ministry of education building?'

I looked in the direction he was pointing. There stood a stylish old gentleman in a bowler hat, a silver-plated stick in his hand, shining patent leather shoes on his feet and a pair of gaiters.

'That's Cajander. He used to be the prime minister, you know.'

He was right, it was indeed Cajander strolling about over there. He walked past without paying us the slightest attention; we lowered our voices as he approached us. It appeared that even in this world the haves and the have-nots were clearly in different classes. I mentioned this to my companion and he retorted:

'Well, Cajander is just the way he is.'

The man began to tell me about himself. He explained that he had died many years ago.

'My miserable body has long since rotted away to dust . . . I was a business man whilst I was alive, a speculator, a swindler, a smuggler, the lot – you name it. I lived quite a colourful, wicked life, you can tell just by looking at me.'

I had to agree that he did look a bit the worse for wear.

'I was a hardened man, a real bruiser. I amassed a fortune through a succession of bad deeds, I swindled people, drank a lot, got into fights, did all kinds of nasty things. I suppose it was in my nature, even as a child I was a right little devil, to put it mildly. The drink finally finished me off and it served me right.'

I pointed out that whether he'd died of the demon drink or not he wasn't doing too badly nowadays, sauntering down the Esplanade with the likes of Cajander himself. Neither of them seemed to be the least bit distressed.

'You haven't got a clue how hard life is for me here. I'm in hiding most of the time. Every now and then somebody else that I cheated out of money dies and for the life of me – if you'll pardon the expression – I'm in no hurry to bump into them. It's not exactly a barrel of laughs trying to make amends for all your petty crimes with everyone listening in. I've gone to the ends of the earth to try and escape people who have just died, but as I imagine you've noticed we can all move at the speed of thought round here, so it's impossible to escape . . . The only thing you can do is hide out in a cave somewhere, go into voluntary imprisonment, that's what my life here is like.'

I asked him what exactly he had been doing in the library.

'I'm not fussed about the news. Never did whilst I was alive either, if you don't count the stock exchange. Nowadays all I read are the obituaries to see if anyone I knew has just snuffed it. Last spring I read that an upstanding bloke had taken ill – I'd managed to con him out of an entire estate! I'm worried he's about to kick the bucket too, then there'll be hell to pay.'

The man sighed. He was having a rough time, I could see that now. Was this the way justice worked after death?

With a heavy heart the sinful man waved and went upon his way. As he was leaving he added:

'Welcome to the club . . . if you haven't got much on your conscience it can be fun round here. It all depends how you take things: how you take them here and how you took them in your former life.'

When he had almost reached the end of the street he turned and shouted:

'I almost forgot, that obituary of yours was in today's Demari on page 10! It could well be in some of the other papers too.'

I waved him goodbye and returned to the reading room. I was eager to see what they had said about me in the paper. I wondered whether they had put a photo with it . . .

# *The Slave Breeder*

Juhani Peltonen

*Juhani Peltonen (1941–1998) has said: "Life is full of disparate details arbitrarily joined together by dreams, pain and yearning. I do not long for sense, but I call for emotion and imagination amidst this chaos." In many ways this sums up the main thrust of Peltonen's entire output. In his poetry, plays, radio plays and novels alike the absurd is linked to melancholy, and humour to pain and sorrow. Surrealism and a sense of estrangement are always present in Peltonen's works, whether comic or tragic – indeed, often both are present at once. His works have been translated into 16 languages and have received numerous prizes. The short story here is from the collection* Vedenalainen melodia *('Underwater Melody', 1965).*

Werner Reiss gave speeches at board meetings, sat reading the daily paper in parks and on café terraces, rode horses during his summer break and was given every now and then to a spot of philately. But when – by something of a twist of fate – he began breeding slaves, his life changed completely: familiar daily routines suddenly seemed strange to him and he rapidly became distanced from them and withdrawn beyond reach. He was purely the slave breeder.

As the rays of evening sunlight turned red and cool, he would whip his slaves and sing out loud. He slept peacefully at night, though he had previously suffered from insomnia (the heart of winter had always been the worst time in this respect; as often as once a week he might remain awake for several days at a stretch), he did not wake to the moans of his slaves, to the riots which erupted every once in a while, nor even to the death cries of the weakest and most worthless of his slaves;

cries which lashed through the darkness. And in the mornings he was fresh, resolute and cheerful as he went to greet them with his whip. He relished reading their one unshakeable thought: they wanted to kill him. This knowledge was sweet, it was like stepping into a cold bath on a lazy morning to wash the fatigue from his limbs. And with this Werner Reiss knew that the unabating sense of rebellion which surrounded him was the only blessing he needed.

He would visit his slaves whenever the fancy took him, and would generously deal out blows, kicking those nearest him with his steel-capped shoes, shoving them in the face with his fist, and if he ever saw one of them breathing his last, he would mercifully put him out of his misery with a large, jagged stone. The slaves would tremble and their eyes flicker. They would throw themselves at their master's feet and stain his trouser legs with blood dripping from their eyes. This disgusted Werner Reiss, even though naturally he experienced a certain satisfaction. He would shake himself free, raise his whip in the air and begin his bombastic singing once again. 'I am your king,' he would cry, often to himself, out loud, sometimes almost bellowing. After all, he did command a realm which he could rule as he saw fit. He was the slave breeder and he rejoiced as his trusty whip curled round their disfigured faces and necks, as it sunk into their malformed bodies and spliced open the veins in their laughable, grotesque limbs. He was calm and content, whilst an unappeasing hatred and danger built up behind the gate.

The climbing plants were wild and gnarled, the stone was flaking, the wooden fixings ramshackle; one of the railings had collapsed at several points, parts of it still visible in a deep pit in the courtyard. Noisy crows flew in and out of an opening in the gable. Nearby the sea churned against the striated rocks. Its roar and the mysterious sounds from the shore greatly stirred the imagination of one unaccustomed to such phenomena. Werner Reiss was ecstatic; he had bought a castle and a hundred acres of land in a renowned area for which most people did not care. A moustached, presumably English gentleman (who refused to give any clear information on his origins, though Werner discreetly enquired several times) peered sternly over the rim of his spectacles as Werner counted the banknotes into his hand. Werner could well afford to pay in cash. He had sold his entire stamp collection, his apartment, his share in a grand schooner and four thoroughbred stallions, all of which had galloped around numerous hippodromes to great success.

'And now I shall return to the family grave in the county of my ancestors,' said the gentleman and waited expectantly for some reaction from Werner, but when none was forthcoming he handed Werner a set of crenelated keys and strode off, his satchel full of money in one hand and a cane in the other.

Werner could see that the castle's previous owner was in something of a hurry: only once did he look behind him, then quickened his pace and disappeared amongst the trees and bracken.

The forest surrounding the castle was thick and neglected. The path leading up to the gate was overgrown, peaty and full of stones. An enormous fir tree had fallen across the path and Werner spent the best part of a day doggedly clearing the path, sawing up the trunk, rolling away the blocks and such like, before the path was finally in reasonable condition; branches and thick chunks of bark had been cast out over a large area on both sides of the path.

Werner reversed his car into a vault in the cellar, which he had discovered after an extensive search. He had an old Mercedes; admittedly it consumed far too much fuel, but was nonetheless sufficiently fast and spacious. He was a bad driver, he knew virtually nothing about cars; in fact, he hated cars and the sound of engines, but "one would have to be an idiot to go on foot", he had once thought. He left his Mercedes in the vault, despite the fact that it hardly made a suitable garage: water dripped from the walls and ceiling, and the car's front wheels sloshed through deep, dirty puddles.

The castle was filled with small windows, thick walls, staircases both wide and narrow, corridors, closets, cupboards, chambers; it was cheerless, vast and impractical. A great balcony ran the length of the grand hall. The hall was furnished with heavy, tasteless fixtures; some of the smaller rooms felt cosier (one boasted a delicate brig hanging from the ceiling; another contained an array of oriental cushions, of whose authenticity Werner was not entirely convinced). He decided to sleep on the upper balcony on top of a large chest next to the railings. In a closet standing between two doors he found two fringed quilts, one of which he folded to form a pillow. He was rather tired, made himself a hot drink, smoked and examined four canvasses hanging one above the other depicting (from the top downwards): a group of dogs and fowlers; a voluptuous woman bathing – all chest, hips and thighs; a funeral cortège against a winter backdrop; and a still life containing a bowl of pears (some half-eaten), the plaster bust of a young boy and a long knife with flies sitting on its blade; after which he retired for the night to his unusual sleeping place. His sleep was hesitant, he imagined he could hear all manner of noises, and eventually awoke, propping himself up on his elbows. Periodically the door opened and shut, there was breathing in the hall, faint murmuring. He could see movement, people congregating on the floor below, tottering about here and there. Werner forced himself to his feet, leant on the railing and looked down. Their faces were staring up at him. Who were they? The moustached, presumably English gentleman had not said a word about anything like this. Did they come with the castle? Gardeners, butlers, guards? Werner did not move. He decided it would be futile trying to ask these people anything (though they did seem timid and harmless), people who in the middle of the night had forced their way into the grand hall of his castle, his home; what difference would it have made to him if one of them had responded by expanding at length on their predictably bitter, bleak past? And at that moment an idea occurred to him. He came down the staircase and walked through the bizarre crowd, which obediently made way for him. He went outside, double-locked the door behind him, drove his car out of the vaults, turned on to the path and headed for town. He was in an excellent mood, put his foot on the accelerator and sat listening to a foreign radio station broadcasting meditative piano fantasies through the night. He had to wait several hours for the shops to open. He then rushed in and ordered a considerable quantity of steel rods the width of a thumb. That afternoon a lorry filled to capacity pulled up outside the castle. Werner also contacted a team of professional welders; the next morning these men appeared and unloaded a selection of soldering irons, blow torches, gas cylinders and other indispensible tools at the designated spot. Werner was particularly pleased with his creation. He treated himself to a hearty meal (including peppered steak, which he adored) and drove back to the castle. A grand architectural plan was developing in his mind, as was his new occupation and conviction. And all the time these unknown people, his slaves, remained standing in the hall; no doubt they were completely unaware of being his prisoners.

The welders listened morosely to Werner's instructions, asked a few routine questions and set to work. That evening there stood beside the castle a vast roofed cage. The holes in the grating were minimal, barely the size of an eye; the floor of the cage was partly rock, partly trampled lawn. For the long rainy season Werner had acquired a protective sheet which could be drawn across the roof; of course the sheet would also have its uses during merciless heatwaves. He decided to think about how to deal with the harsh winter conditions later on, and naturally much depended on the endurance and resilience of the slaves themselves.

The sun shone red against the curved steel, the final joins still glowed warmly from the welding; the whole complex resembled a feverish vascular system. Werner was overjoyed and extolled the welders' craftsmanship; they spat on the floor, wiped their mouths on their shirt sleeves and pushed their caps back on their foreheads. Werner paid them well in excess of what had been agreed and gave them a brotherly wave as they were leaving. He then entered the cage and strolled back and forth. It was very orthodox indeed: spacious yet stiflingly cramped. He had bought a hefty lock for the cage door. And thus overwhelmed by waves of wonderful, unprecedented emotion he ran into the hall and stood before his slaves.

'Follow me,' he bellowed and showed them the way.

The slaves humbly followed him and the crooked procession slowly approached the cage. Werner held the door open as one after the other they crouched down and made their way inside. Once all of them were inside Werner turned the lock and hung the key around his neck.

'You are now my slaves,' he shouted as he lept around the cage admiring them from all angles.

The sound of their petrified silence almost made him want to clap his hands.

That night Werner did not sleep a wink: he was preparing his whip. To make this he used a length of flexible steel rope. He sat working for hours in a draughty woodshed in the bowels of the castle. The lantern was smoking; it fell over and went out. Werner was freezing, fumbling as he looked for some matches; but he did not allow this to upset him, for his intention was so simple and calming. He spliced the head of the whip into three prongs, used tweezers to prise apart the strands of wire, twisted them upright and supported them at the base with several layers of steel thread; he then attached a number of staples to the head of each prong. In addition he busied himself with the whip's handle, wrapping it in soft leather and thin cotton thread. And with that the whip was ready. Werner's hair was tousled, his head ached and his eyes were bloodshot. The draught had numbed him. As he was walking back upstairs he stumbled and hurt his knee. He then made himself a hot drink, smoked a great deal and looked once again at the four canvasses hung one above the other, focussing in particular on the lowest of the four featuring the plaster bust of a young boy next to the bowl of pears and the long knife with flies sitting on its blade. But no sooner had morning broken than he took hold of his whip and ceremoniously stepped out to address his slaves. Each blow was liberating, it was like unshaking proof of the great lie of God's existence. He lashed them around the shoulders in a blind frenzy and herded them together; some of them writhed on the floor in agony, and he thrashed their quivering limbs all the more. Women, children and the elderly, men and young boys, and each and every one of them was his slave. And he roared this at them repeatedly so that they would know it and so that they would learn to respect and love him. When he left them he was happier and more satisfied than he had ever been. Goodness only knows how long he stared through the grating at their wounded cheeks, their contorted foreheads and lips; and he was particularly fond of their eyes, which were without exception deep-set and moist, yet which all seemed ablaze. Eventually he left them and went to attend to his whip. He washed and oiled it and placed it on a stand which he had made especially. This done, he made himself a hot drink, smoked and wondered what exactly the artist had meant by placing the plaster bust of a young boy and the long knife with flies frozen on its blade in the same painting. In the evening he gave the slaves another thrashing and repeated almost exactly the same steps; before going to bed he skipped joyfully around the cage, and the air he breathed was like thick, sweet smoke.

That same winter, during which Werner destroyed all his papers, there was not a flake of snow to be seen. By Easter heavy rainfall had set in. The slaves were cowering in a field tent which Werner had mercifully erected inside the cage. Another example of his incredible generosity was a small stove, which in favourable winds did not smoke a great deal and which gave off a faint warmth. The pile of logs, considerably diminished after the winter months, was covered with a rainsheet next to the tent; a saw, an axe, a trestle and a chopping block were all under temporary cover near the logs.

Werner spent a lot of time wandering near his castle. He enjoyed the rain and, besides, his rain clothes were second to none. He would stop on the shores, eaten away by the ageless sea; everywhere he looked there were hollows, caves, strange cracks and fissures; water bubbled inside the rock; floating logs battered against the nearby cliffs. The rain was unabating. Ugly wet birds circled overhead; the hillside was thick with willows; miserable cats roamed. On the first day after the Easter holiday Werner received a visitor. He had been busy stuffing an owl he had found dead on the steps. He rinsed his hands clean of feathers, innards and preserving fluid and went to the door. The visitor was driving a car with a two-stroke engine and indicators that were so stiff they often had to be moved by hand. Werner recognised his visitor through the rain trickling down the front window: he was an old friend with whom Werner had often gone hiking. The friend jumped out of his car and gave Werner a curt, loud greeting; he had a ruddy face, thin fair hair and a newspaper protruding from his coat pocket, just as it always had done before.

'I see you've bought a castle,' said the friend.

'Indeed I have,' said Werner. 'Where did you hear about it?'

'I follow matters like this, it's part of my job,' the friend replied.

'Well, do come in out of the rain,' said Werner and attempted a smile.

Werner gave his old friend a tour of the castle. The friend was very polite and appeared interested in every little curio and detail. They walked around many rooms and talked either about the castle, salmon fishing or rifles. The friend was startled at the sight of the owl lying on Werner's desk with its stomach slit open; at this Werner laughed and covered the bird with a white sheet. On their return to the grand hall Werner implored his guest to take a seat and went off to find something to serve up. They drank coffee and cognac and Werner was pleased to note that his guest paid due attention to the noteworthy vintage. They sat smoking and Werner suggested a game of cards, though he knew it would bore them both. They played together for many hours. Finally Werner introduced his guest to the cage and his slaves. He ordered them out of the tent. The wind was particularly unfavourable, so the tent was filled with smoke and the slaves rushed out spluttering, staggering; some fell flat on their faces. Werner recounted several witty anecdotes about his slaves and illustrated these stories by whipping them.

'Watch,' Werner beamed and nodded towards the ground: a thin, dishevelled boy was coughing up phlegm and gripping his stomach with both hands.

'Is he . . . are they ill?' the friend asked in shock.

'No, on the contrary!' Werner replied. 'They are my slaves, my marvellous slaves, and I am their breeder.'

Some of them slid around the boy, trying to drag themselves towards the wall and haul themselves upright. Werner's face lit up like a settler surveying his bountiful harvest. Yet his friend was frozen to the spot staring blankly ahead. Werner nudged him lightly. The friend gave a start and muttered something.

'Aren't they a fine slaviary?' Werner asked proudly.

'. . . a fine slaviary,' whispered his friend, barely moving his lips.

Suddenly Werner thought his friend particularly unpleasant. Why is he behaving like this? Why can't he be happy for me and enjoy it? Werner looked at him out of the corner of his eye and thought: he's just standing there like a stupid statue.

'You might want to take a closer look and point out any flaws or deficiencies,' Werner suggested opening the cage door to his friend and showing him the way. In a dreamlike trance the friend stepped inside the cage and Werner slammed the door shut behind him, turned his back and hurried away. He drove his friend's car with the two-stroke engine and the protruding indicators off the cliff and into the sea, then hurried back home to make himself a hot drink, smoke and think hard about the plaster bust of the young man and the flies on the blade of the knife in the lowest of the paintings. After this he dashed back to his desk, where the owl awaited him under a white sheet with its stomach open.

The following morning Werner graced his friend with a thrashing of the whip; the friend hardly flinched, Werner could barely draw blood from his body; this infuriated Werner considerably.

And so Werner's life merrily continued. He worked vigorously during the day. The owl was all but ready, all he needed now was a suitable branch on which to display it. Many an hour he spent walking around the forest, but still he could not find one that pleased him. The owl had therefore temporarily to settle for lying on Werner's desk; he bought it an expensive pair of glass eyes and it looked wise. All he required from his slaves was continual subservience at the meticulous blows of his whip – he tried to teach them how to accept these blows like well-deserved gifts. And morning and night the sound of singing pealed out from the cage: Werner sang and thrashed away to his heart's content.

Every few years Werner would wake up in the middle of the night, next to his tacky whip (each night he took it from the stand he had made especially), as the wind rattled the grating on the roof of the cage and the vines of the climbing plants battered against the gutter and the window of the room in which he slept (alternately the room with the delicate brig hanging from the ceiling and the room with the array of oriental cushions, the authenticity of which was still unconfirmed). On nights like these he could never get back to sleep, so would go instead to make himself a hot drink, smoke vast amounts and walk back and forth around the grand hall considering where he should display the owl once he found an appropriate branch.

As time went by the cage filled with slaves, none of whom remotely resembled ordinary humans. 'No matter,' thought Werner. 'A slave's a slave's a slave.' As he whipped them he would often comment wittily to himself on their appearance. Some of them were even missing essential body parts; their sensory organs had arbitrarily swapped places with each other; they all expressed themselves in terms of grim individual ailments (one warbled like a broken unmelodious flute, another hissed like a stove); and one of them (whose most striking feature was a set of dead, sunken eyes) had a hand on the end of its leg; another had a pencil-thin tail metres long. Any attempt to classify their gender was pure guesswork. Werner split them at random into two groups and lashed them together, so that the number of slaves would not drop. New slaves were born (some of the strangest looking creatures), yet the death rate was also considerable. In addition to this a virulent epidemic broke out (a fever of some description causing pearl-like boils to appear on the skin) and this took its toll on the slave population on four consecutive autumns. The first year this happened Werner too became ill and was forced to lie in bed in pain for over a month with a high fever until providence, in her immeasurable clemency, gave him back his health. During his recuperation Werner managed to turn one of the corridors in the cellar into a shooting range and spent day after day shooting his saloon rifle standing, kneeling and lying on the floor. The owl still lay on his desk. Its feathers and glass eyes were covered in dust. He no longer had the strength to roam the forest in search of a decent branch; he was approaching old age and needed all his strength to whip the slaves; still, once a week he would undertake a longer trip to the forest and scrutinise potential trees. He noticed that he was not quite himself after the illness. He made himself a hot drink, smoked and thought hard: the owl simply cannot lie on my desk for ever and a day, it's almost finished.

Shortly after this he began to lose his authority over the slaves. They had become aggressive, primitive like animals; on one occasion he had been forced to save himself by darting out of the door midway through their morning thrashing and his left jacket sleeve had been ripped off in the struggle. He immediately contacted the team of welders. After only a few hours they glumly appeared, dragging their gas cylinders behind them, unlit hand-rolled cigarettes and empty cigarette holders drooping from the sides of their mouths, their loose overalls covered in metallic dust. They welded the door shut, climbed on top of the cage and cut a hatch in the roof. At Werner's request one of them felled two young spruces and fashioned a step ladder to give him unhindered access to the hatch. That day the sun was shining intensely; everyone was puffing with exertion and the air was stifling. Werner was forced to go to the garage on countless occasions to cool off. Only later that evening did he tar the step ladder.

Since, after this turn of events, Werner could no longer – indeed, he *dared* no longer venture into the cage, he could also no longer whip them. This made him very unhappy. He did however gain some amount of pleasure from a sturdy, thin staff, one end of which he had filed to a point. And thus maintaining his familiar routine he would climb up to the hatch to stab and poke his slaves. Putting out their eyes was in fact a particularly challenging sport, requiring both accuracy and a steady hand. Despite this he was highly frustrated at being unable to blind a single eye on one of the slaves who had five in a row on its forehead. It always dodged out of the way just as Werner was about to stab it. He was starting to lose his temper, and was on the verge of leaping on top of the thing to be able to gouge out just one of those five eyes.

Exhausted and furious, Werner would often trudge back to his castle and fall asleep in the first available place. All he ever dreamt about was cracked plaster busts, fresh knives and flies; waking in a cold sweat, he would rush down to the shooting range in an attempt to drown out the terrible beating of his heart. His general state of health had suffered dramatically due to the unforeseen changes to his routine with the slaves.

And so it was that these difficult nights gradually began to occur with increasing frequency: the wind howled, the climbing plants rattled at the window and long-clawed shadows scraped along the wallpaper in his bedroom (alternately the room with the delicate brig hanging from the ceiling, and the room with the oriental cushions or reproductions thereof). On one such night Werner felt rather weak and could not sleep. He made himself a hot drink, smoked profusely and marched around the grand hall with heavy, deafening steps. The owl still lay on his desk (he had moved his desk into the hall) and he stopped to examine it. As he looked at it he saw a dark little insect crawl across one of the owl's glass eyes, leaving behind it a thin trail through the dust. And as he took a closer look at the feathers around its head and wings propped up with steel wire he noticed these creatures everywhere. This made him very sad indeed, and he decided to acquire some strong chemicals to destroy the infestation straight after his morning duties, and to stay in the woods as long as was necessary to find a suitable branch.

Early that morning (it was in fact still night-time) he climbed up on to the roof of the cage, opened the hatch and began hurling down buckets full of rotten meat. He managed to herd the slaves into a group so he could scratch and cut as many of them as possible with one blow. He lay on his stomach staring inside, shouting, battering them in a frenzy; they all seemed so limp and lifeless. But suddenly the five-eyed slave gave some sort of signal, and all at once a dozen or so slaves, all resembling monkeys, formed a carefully planned pyramid, and the two at the top grabbed Werner by the head. Werner clasped the grating as hard as he could but the force of the slaves was overwhelming. He was wrenched inside the cage. The slaves helped each other up the pyramid, pulling the last of their group up by the hands and jumping down to the ground. The five-eyed, former slave remained by the hatch; a moment passed and he was handed a large, jagged stone. He hurled it with all his might at Werner's face, knocking him to the ground beside the pile of rotten meat. And before he finally lost consciousness Werner's thoughts turned once again to the poor owl, which was at that moment being consumed by pests and which would never have its branch or be placed proudly on display after all.

# *Transit*

Johanna Sinisalo

*Johanna Sinisalo (born 1958) has written novels, short stories, essays and comic strips in addition to pursuing a career as a screenwriter. Her novel* Not Before Sundown *('Ennen päivänlaskua ei voi', published in North America under the title* Troll – A Love Story*) was awarded the Finlandia Prize in 2000 and has since been translated into many different languages. In addition to this her short stories have seven times won the Atorox Prize for best science fiction or fantasy short story of the year. Sinisalo's works often deal with themes such as the struggle between humanity and nature, the problems of otherness, power structures within society and the subjective nature of reality. 'Transit' was first published in the short story anthology* Ensimmäinen yhteys *('First Contact', 1988).*

*Handler: Lamminmäki / pk*
*Subject: Transcript of dictated confession of Klaus Antero Viksten, arrived in custody 14.7; awaiting trial.*

(Heavy breathing. Thud. Deep breaths.)

Alright. Alright. (Pause.) Okay. Doesn't matter, I'll still be locked up for the rest of my life, so it won't make any difference if I talk now – is this thing recording? Sounds like it's running. (Nervous chuckle.) I don't know what they're going to try and pin on me, but the only thing I can be charged with is destroying public property or something, not manslaughter. I'm not a murderer; definitely not that kind of murderer. I know you can't make head nor tail of what I'm saying, so there's no reason I should start talking now either, but I've got to get it into your thick skulls that I'm not a fucking murderer. Everything was sweet right up to the end, every second of it.

I was with these guys Kaarina and Hepe, we'd just left their place – we'd been doing a few tabs and drinking lager all evening and by this point we were having a really good time, knocking each other about on the grass and laughing like lunatics, it was fantastic, we were tripping out of our heads on gear and the night air, and so they wanted to go somewhere and have another few drinks but I was out of cash and I really wanted some action, something more that just sitting cooped up inside all night knocking back the pints. I thought I might go over to the Square and hang out and see if any of my mates were about. I knew Kapa and Remmi had been let out of the nick and they might have some plans, a bit of gear or a party or some job on the go – I was skint, did I say that? Anyway, I swung down into town, still kind of floating, and just by the station hill these three big blokes came up to me, fancy Lacoste shirts, white trousers, the lot; the air was really warm, it was probably still about twenty-five degrees even though it was eleven o'clock or something. So these Lacoste guys started looking at me like I'm a piece of shit, but I was having such a blast I went up to them and asked them if they'd got a problem. One of them said something like keep it shut mate, and it was just what I'd been waiting for, so I smacked one of them right in the face and he flew arse over tit and got grey scuff marks on the backside of his trousers, heh heh. The other two were on top of me right away, but I was really quick 'cause I'd taken some speed and I started legging it down the hill towards the station and I was sure they wouldn't bother chasing me, but then one of them came after me like a sprinter. Jesus, I've never run that fast, it was a close thing he didn't catch me, followed me through the underpass too, I could hear him breathing behind me and then I saw a police car turn into the tunnel at the other end and the bloke started shouting and trying to flag down the old bill, so I thought I'd better get the fuck out of there; I ran out in front of a car, jumped across the road and headed off towards Stockmann's, and just as I came out there was a bus, the number sixteen, it was there at the bus stop just about to pull away and I managed to slip in the doors just before they closed. I've got a season ticket, so I dug it out of my pocket, showed it to the driver and the bus drove off, and I knew the bloke hadn't made it.

I sat down, I was totally out of breath, and wondered where I should get off so they wouldn't be able to follow me, some place soon, and so when the bus turned round by the old swimming pool I jumped off and stood in the bus shelter for a minute. My head was still spinning, my heart was going like the clappers and I wandered off towards Amuri as if nothing had happened, I thought no one'll be able to link me to the fight if I just walk off like normal. I soon got down to the railway tracks and thought I might walk carefully back into town, down to Raatsa maybe, so I made a left and thought I'd go just to be on the safe side and sit in the park at Näsinpuisto for a minute until the pigs had given up looking for me. I walked up the hill and went and sat under a tree, a bit hidden away, and looked down towards the harbour and the amusement park at Särkänniemi, where there were still lights flashing and things going on – it was like watching a giant anthill in the distance.

I'd just lit up when the girl appeared. At first all I could see was a figure against the darkening sky, thin with short hair, walking right towards me. I was convinced she must have thought I was someone else, the way she was walking up to me, but then she came up under the tree and sat down next to me. She didn't say anything, she just looked me right in the eyes. And I've never, *never* seen anyone look at me like that before, I looked back into her eyes and it was like looking down two tunnels with light flickering at the end, but still they were normal eyes – the way she looked at me, it was like someone had punched me in the stomach. And at that same moment I was sure as hell she was the most amazing bird I'd ever seen. The woman of my dreams. I mean, she was sort of . . . (unclear; voice falters) I could never have done something like that to her, I couldn't have . . . (unclear). And then she started talking. (Thud. Heavy breathing. Long silence.)

*Handler(s): Lamminmäki and Eerola / pk*
*Subject: Transcript of interview with care worker Airi Kurkinen*

Q: Can you expand, in your own words, on Nina Salminen's diagnosis?
A: She is autistic.
Q: Could you please explain the term?
A: An autistic child shuts off any contact with the outside world. In other respects they develop normally, but at a given age we notice that they have stopped developing mentally. Or rather, it's difficult to assess the stage of a child's mental development, because the child will stop all communication with his or her surroundings. Physical symptoms, such as spasms, are often linked to this. What's decisive, however, is the fact that the child stops learning, stops being able to master new skills, and often stops speaking.
Q: What exactly causes these symptoms?
A: Can you tell me what this is all about? What has happened?
Q: I'm sorry, Miss Kurkinen, but could you please answer a few more questions?
A: . . .
Q: How did Nina Salminen develop this . . . this autism?
A: At the age of two Nina stopped learning to speak. For a while she regressed to the nappy stage, but thankfully we've managed to toilet-train her again – it's an exceptional achievement. She then became completely shut off in her own world. She no longer recognised her parents. Most autistic children never reach Nina's age. Essentially they stop living altogether.
Q: Do we know why this happens?
A: It's very unclear. People have tried to isolate certain physical factors or psychological triggers, but there's no simple answer. Sometimes we wonder whether the child makes a conscious decision to sever all ties with the rest of the world, to be on the outside and not to function according to 'normal' rules. Some autistic children speak

a language of their own which no one else can understand. They often behave in a self-destructive manner. They can be violent. There are no fixed rules except for the unassailable gap between them and us.

Q: You look after Nina Salminen. What does caring for her entail?

A: Nina is neither violent nor self-destructive. She cannot speak. She spends most of her time lying on her side staring into space. She won't make contact with anyone, but doesn't try to resist being fed or taken to the toilet. I've been caring for her since she was four years old, so for about the last ten years. Her parents cover all the costs.

Q: You said that Nina cannot speak. Are you quite sure of this?

A: Are you suggesting that after ten years of caring for her such a minor detail might have gone unnoticed?

Q: You said that autistic children sever all ties with the outside world. Would it still be possible for a child like this to carry on learning things, but simply not to make use of their learning or to reveal it in any way?

A: Are you completely . . . ? Mmm, what an odd question. No, I don't think so. No. Of course, all their senses function normally, and of course it's possible that they register something of the world around them, but they do this entirely on their own terms. It has never been observed of autistic children that they merely pretend not to learn. I find this quite an offensive way to consider such a serious psychological defect.

Q: So Nina Salminen could not function in any way without the constant supervision of a professional carer?

A: No.

Q: How would you describe the level of her mental development?

A: She has the abilities of approximately a two-year-old child. She can walk, she doesn't wet herself as long as she is taken to the toilet regularly. She could say a few words before she became ill; now all she can produce is gurgling throat noises and screams. They don't have any communicative value, they are merely a form of . . . self-expression. She has to be fed.

A: So, in effect, it would be impossible for her to survive by herself?

Q: Think how well a sick toddler would survive! Not at all. Of course, Nina is the size of a fourteen-year-old and is physically much stronger than she is mentally, but the situation is still serious, very serious indeed. So could you please bring this farce to an end and tell me what's going on?

A: If you would bear with us, Miss Kurkinen. What time was it when you discovered she was missing?

*Handler: Lamminmäki / pk*
*Subject: Transcript of dictated confession of Klaus Antero Viksten, arrived in custody 14.7; awaiting trial.*

(Breathing, crackling in microphone.)

She said her name was Nina. Right from the start I was sure she was out of it too, and I wondered what it was she'd been taking; I decided she must have been smoking pot or something. Whatever it was she'd had quite a bit 'cause her speech was really slow and deliberate, like she really had to think about every word, how to say it and what it meant – I know what it feels like, I've knocked myself out like that plenty of times.

She had a short blond plait and a face like an angel: I don't mean pretty, I mean it was just as if none of the world's shit had ever touched her. And her clothes were fairly odd, too: this was no trend-setting young lady, she was bare-foot in a pink tracksuit. I could still feel the tabs whirring round my head; I put my arm around her and thought I'd try my luck, but she just kept staring at me and smiling and then having another look, and she was talking well out of line. I watched her lips as she struggled to speak, then she said if I help her out with something she'll be my friend forever. Friend, Jesus Christ, friend! She was quite some bird for someone who looked that innocent. First she said we'd need a car, a big car, and that I should go and find us one.

I started thinking this was just the sort of action I'd been looking for that night, doing something completely mental with a fantastic girl with real fire in her eyes – we could do anything, something totally hardcore. A car, of course we'd need a car, a big car. It must have been just after midnight by this point and things were quietening down, and I knew a few little places where we'd find ourselves a car – I've done enough car jobs to know what I'm doing.

The girl said she'd wait in the park and I didn't really want to leave her, but then again I did believe she'd wait, so I ran off to find us a motor. It only took me fifteen minutes to find a big, extended Transit van, ten to pick the lock and another ten to attach the jump leads. It had a full tank and the back was empty apart from a few sheets of veneer and a tarpaulin. I sped out of the carpark on two wheels and started driving like a nutter back to Näsinpuisto, and sure enough the girl was still there: I can't remember ever feeling so excited as when I saw that figure sitting exactly where I'd left her under the tree.

She jumped in and told me what she needed next. It was so mental I slapped my thighs and laughed out loud. Christ, she wanted boxes. Big boxes and superlon mattresses. I thought to myself this is some fucking girl; she didn't say a word about what she was going to do with them, she just told me what to do and that was that. She seemed like she was really in her element. I drove over to some warehouse belonging to a removal company my mate Remmi used to work for, I knew they'd have big wooden chests and things, a couple of cubic metres deep inside, iron reinforcements down the edges. Probably normally used for packing smaller items in polystyrene or something. I parked the van right outside the gate; it's a good job it was Saturday and there was no one on a late shift. The warehouse was like a barn, we might as well have crawled under the door, it was so easy to get in. I had to pick an old lock they had, but after that the path was clear. There were no guards or cameras, but there wasn't anything of any real value either. I asked Nina how many chests she wanted and she said five – straight up. Okay, so we slipped inside and carried five of these chests back into the Transit. They just about filled the back of the van. I was laughing so hard the heavy boxes almost fell on her toes. She must have been pretty strong, I mean, she looked thin and that, but she carried those chests like you wouldn't believe.

We picked up the mattresses from the loading bay of some old junk shop, there were loads of them piled up under a plastic cover. Again, all we had to do was basically walk in, I managed to get the wire fence open just by sticking my hand through the mesh, although I did have to fiddle with the lock a bit first. Who can be bothered watching a place like that, I mean, who'd want to pinch a load of fertiliser? We took shed loads of thick, ready-cut superlon. Nina made sure it all fitted in the chests. It was quite a good size, mattress-sized stuff. We must have taken about twenty of them. Loads of the stuff, at least four per box.

When she told me what was next on her list I started wondering if there was any sense in the whole thing; still it was a pretty smart address, but the worst one yet. I tried to think which chemists' the lads used to do over and which ones had alarms fitted. Finally we drove away from the city centre out towards Messukylä where there's a chemist's in a small old house by the side of a busy road, nicely tucked away in the bushes. We didn't waste any time: brick through the window, door open and inside. I had a quick look round for some speed, or dex or whatever, while Nina went and picked up two enormous buckets full of some vaseline ointment. It was bloody funny, like someone had broken into the off-licence and only nicked the carrier bags. We were in and out in less than a minute.

After we'd been on the road for a while, we turned and drove off through Nekala so we wouldn't be spotted, Nina saw an old bin outside a shop – it was probably just for sweet papers. She wanted that too. We picked it up and then she told me to drive back where we'd come from, so back to the bottom of the rocks near Näsinpuisto. By the time we got back there it must have been about two in the morning, and when she told me what we needed to do next, I swear I've never laughed so hard in my life.

*Handler(s): Lamminmäki and Eerola / pk*
*Subject: Transcript of interview with care worker Airi Kurkinen*

A: It was six o'clock in the morning. Nina normally wakes up very early indeed, and now I woke up because she didn't start whimpering as usual. Waking up is clearly distressing for her and she tends to react very strongly in the mornings. So I awoke to an unusual calm and went to her room to check on her. The bed was empty. I quickly searched the flat – Nina lives with me around the clock, except during my holidays; her parents didn't want to put her into an institution – and I realised that she was nowhere else either. I checked through all the cupboards as well.

Q: This is slightly off the subject, but isn't being at work around the clock extremely taxing?

A: Nina is in fact no trouble whatsoever and her parents pay me very well. Are you implying that I haven't taken good enough care of her, that I'm too exhausted to watch her carefully? Now listen here, Officer, I am . . .

Q: Miss Kurkinen, the fact of the matter is that Nina disappeared without her carer's noticing it. These are the facts.

A: Another fact is whether you would expect your own two-year-old to run away from home. The place they feel the safest – if they feel anything at all that is. This is someone who is so uninterested in the world around her that she can't even open the front door. There's no way I could have seen this coming.

Q: You mentioned that she opened the door – something, clearly, that she could not previously do.

A: Yes, unless someone opened it for her from the outside. I strongly believe that is what must have happened, but why would someone have done a thing like that? From the inside the door opens almost silently. The only possible explanation is that she opened it herself from the inside because any other noises would have woken me up straight away.

Q: Is there any way of explaining why she could suddenly do things she had not been able to do before?

A: I'm as baffled as you are; more so probably, you're not very familiar with the subject.

Q: Miss Kurkinen, this sounds strange, and you reacted rather strongly a moment ago when we touched on the matter, but is it at all possible that a child with these symptoms could suddenly acquire new strengths, skills which were blocked and then released?

A: So what you're suggesting is that all this time, without my knowledge, she has been taking in information about the world around her and then, abracadabra, she decides to start making use of it?

Q: You could put it like that.

A: Officer. (Pause.) Let me see. Do you think autism is merely some kind of outward block? That children like this learn and develop and have an awareness of things, but are simply unable to show anyone what they can do – and we think they are simply withdrawn? It's a very far-fetched hypothesis and I have to say I've never thought of the matter from such an angle. Just a minute – are you seriously suggesting that Nina has managed to break down this so-called block and started using her skills by opening the door and running off into town in the middle of the night?

Q: Or that some external factor may have caused the block to subside?

A: I can't imagine it.

Q: All we know so far is that she left your apartment between 11pm and 6am last night. Can you tell us, Miss Kurkinen, everything you and she did the previous day . . .

*Handler: Lamminmäki / pk*
*Subject: Transcript of dictated confession of Klaus Antero Viksten, arrived in custody 14.7; awaiting trial.*

Once I'd pulled myself together I looked at her and said: are you off your nut? She just stared back at me with that mysterious look in her eyes, and that's when I realised that maybe she'd been right all along, maybe that's exactly what we had to do. I took a handful of the tabs I'd nicked from the chemist's and that was it: after that everything felt okay and sensible.

I'd never been to a dolphinarium before. It was in Särkänniemi, just down from the planetarium, in amongst the spruces. I knew there would be guards about at night, and I knew something would have to be done about them.

Nina stepped out of the van and I parked it a little way off round the back. She stood there looking helpless, shifting her feet and peering around. It was about half an hour before the guards turned up. There were two of them and they both had walkie-talkies, but thank God there were no dogs. Perhaps they couldn't have a dog 'cause of the little zoo right next door, the smells probably get them all excited, or maybe their mutts were on sick leave. Anyway, the blokes went up to Nina and asked her something, they could obviously see she was having some difficulties, she was talking funny, and one of them was about to say something into his radio when she fell on the ground and lay there limp. The guards dithered for a split second, and that's all it took. I smacked one of them above the ear with a wrench and he fell to the ground. The other one turned round and I booted him in the stomach – I did a lot of karate the last time I was inside. He was staggering there winded and was just straightening himself up when the pink panther grabbed him round the neck: Nina grappled him to the ground and all I had to do was clobber him again.

I took the radios off them and threw them as far as I could into the bushes. I didn't know how long they would be out for, but I didn't dare hit them again. I didn't have to: Nina picked up that bloody wrench and smacked them both round the head. I hope she didn't fucking split their skulls open. I'm not a murderer. You've got to understand, I'm not a murderer, I might be a right old bastard, but I'm not a murderer. I'm not.

We then drove the van down to a set of glass double doors and reversed it right up close. I don't know how you'd open a lock like that and I didn't have any equipment with me. In any case the glass might be alarmed. But then something happened that I still don't understand. Nina walked up there and opened the door – it wasn't even locked. I still don't get it, for some reason someone had just cocked up big time, the way to get yourself the sack pretty quickly. But why did it happen just then, and how did Nina know about it, for Christ's sake? As if she'd arranged it, or she had a mate who worked there and they'd either left it open themselves or distracted someone else so they forgot to double check it. Something like that. However it happened, we were there inside and you could smell the sea. The smell of salt water was amazing, just like being on the beach. Benches rose up on the left, in front there was a tiled trench or some sort of walkway, and on the right hand side there was a glass wall and, behind that, water; an enormous pool with steps going up its side coming out of the walkway. Nina ran up the steps to the edge of the pool, fiddled with some buttons and then a net separating the pool into two parts rose up and, with the sound of water rushing, five beautiful, dark-backed animals came bounding across.

Their snouts bobbed just above the water and the noise they made was really strange, like a ping-pong ball being smacked against a surface really fast, krrrrr, krrrrr. Nina backed off slightly and they leapt out of the water and landed on their stomachs at the side of the pool. It was amazing to watch. Then Nina said: now.

I was standing next to the glass wall, or acrylic or whatever. I'd taken one of the reinforced chests out of the Transit van and I threw it corner first as hard as I could towards the wall.

I knew it was strong stuff, but I knew how much pressure there must have been behind it as well. That's why there was a trench between the pool and the arena; the couple of metres of water above the actual pool could run down there if anything funny happened – there's drains and everything. And something funny was about to happen. The chest hit the glass full on. It created a little star-shaped pattern in the glass, nothing too serious. But then, as I watched it in a kind of trance, the cracks stretched out really slowly. Then they started to move quicker and quicker until a huge section of the glass looked like it an enormous spider's web. And then it collapsed.

The box flew back at me with the rush of water and an entire piece of the glass wall was in smithereens. The dolphins must have jumped out of the water so they wouldn't get caught in the first wave. The trench was already almost half full and water was splashing against the double doors.

The dolphins jumped back into the pool and allowed the current to carry them gently out of the hole one at a time and into the shallow water at the bottom of the trench. The whole thing lasted about two minutes. Soon they were bloody lining up at the door.

We opened the doors and the water flooded out down the hill towards the road. They were really big animals, a couple of hundred kilos each. Nina said they weren't even fully grown yet. We placed a sheet of the veneer slanting down towards the van and a piece of tarpaulin which we'd found in the back – I wondered whether Nina would have asked me to get some of that too if it hadn't been there already. We put the tarpaulin on the ground and lay the dolphins on it one at a time. It seemed almost like they were wriggling along to make it easier. And they weren't a bit afraid. Then the two of us took hold of the rails at the corners of the tarpaulin and pulled like hell. Totally mental; we only just managed it. The boxes were stacked neatly by the van, one at a time we turned them on their side right next to the boot. Mattresses at the bottom; dolphin inside. It took all our strength to heave them upright and push them to the back of the boot. Then straight on to the next patient. We slogged away for about half an hour. It was already starting to get light and I kept thinking we'd soon hear police sirens coming over the hill. Finally we filled some buckets with water and poured it into the boxes. That's when I understood: the wet mattresses were to carry the dolphins' weight and keep them damp. Finally we filled the bucket again, put it in the boot and set off for the motorway like there was no tomorrow.

*Handler(s): Lamminmäki and Eerola / pk*
*Subject: Transcript of interview with care worker Airi Kurkinen*

Q: Then what happened after lunch?
A: We went on a stimulus outing. My contract stipulates an excursion like this at least once a week.
Q: And where did you go?
A: The dolphinarium at Särkänniemi.
Q: Miss Kurkinen, now this is extremely important. Try and tell us as precisely as possible what happened. Everything, the slightest detail.
A: We bought the tickets and went inside. Nina was being rather phlegmatic; she walks like a machine, but this time she wasn't reacting to anything. It's quite rare, in fact. These stimulus outings are just a formality really. I remember she almost stumbled as we were walking down the steps into the arena. Our seats were on the fourth row, I think . . . is there any point to this?
Q: Please, continue.
A: Well, the dolphins came in through something like a corridor and into the pool. There were a couple of young girls guiding them, commanding them to do all sorts of tricks; to jump into the air, to swim up to the edge of the pool, to hop along on their tails. These girls appeared slightly on edge. As they were talking us through the various tricks, they kept explaining that things hadn't gone quite as they should have. Apparently the dolphins were having difficulty concentrating, what with it being the holiday season – they must have hundreds of shows. Still, it was as if Nina lit up during the performance, even though the show itself wasn't up to much. But this is typical of autistic children; they may not react in the slightest if a bomb exploded next to

them, but they can go frantic at the sound of a fly buzzing around in the next room.

Q: How was she behaving?

A: She was looking fixedly at the pool and she seemed to understand something of what was going on. The performance was full of stimuli: the trainers' voices, the sound of the whistle, the rush of the water, the splashing, the salty smell. There was a time when Nina was so afraid of the amusement park that she would almost have a catatonic fit; now she was clearly consciously reacting to what was happening. Typically children with Nina's symptoms often get funny notions into their heads. I haven't noticed it in Nina, but this time she must have made real contact with that environment and was reacting accordingly.

Q: And how did this reaction manifest itself?

A: At the end of the show she didn't want to leave. Nina has never had violent or destructive outbursts before, but when I started guiding her towards the exit – the glass double doors leading into a tiled trench along the side of the pool – she started struggling and resisting me. It was probably because the dolphins happened to have stopped at precisely that spot and their snouts were all pointing towards her, as if they were watching her. And then Nina went wild. She was jumping up and down, trying to climb up to the dolphins and when I tried to calm her down she started lashing out blindly, punching and kicking and screaming at the top of her voice. This went on for some time and I remember the other people who had been at the performance staring at us in shock and distaste. Outwardly, after all, Nina looks perfectly normal, so for an outsider this must have looked almost grotesque, a teenage girl shrieking like an animal, biting and kicking. I remember thinking that the sudden appearance of new symptoms can often signify a turn for the worse. Nina's condition has been quite stable of late. Then all of a sudden she stopped. The dolphins were still there behind the glass. Nina stared at them in silence for a long time, very intensely. This was another new reaction: she appeared to see them and perceive them perfectly clearly, even though she is rarely aware of external impulses. It was almost as if she was listening to them and watching them, her head tilted to one side. And when I gently nudged her as a sign that it was time to go, she stood there in perfect silence and didn't move a muscle. It must have taken about five minutes before she let me guide her away.

Q: What happened next?

A: Nina had gone back to her phlegmatic state; we got in my car and drove home. She went straight to bed and for all I could see she fell asleep. Nothing out of the ordinary happened that evening – she dozed off, I fed her, she lay on her bed again. I watched television. She went to bed rather early, about nine o'clock. That's all.

Q: So absolutely nothing else untoward happened that evening?

A: No, not that I can think of. Well, there was one thing: she was lying on her bed with her eyes shut, in a foetal position as usual, and I noticed she was purring gently to herself. Very quietly, and I wouldn't have noticed it at all, but it was such a strange sound. I remember thinking it was new to her range of sounds: it was odd and sharp, krrrrr . . . krrrrr . . .

*Handler: Lamminmäki / pk*
*Subject: Transcript of dictated confession of Klaus Antero Viksten, arrived in custody 14.7; awaiting trial.*

We were on the motorway driving out towards Pori; me, Nina and the dolphins. Nina was in the back – there was hardly enough room for her to walk between the boxes, so she was walking along their edges. She had those enormous pots of vaseline and she was rubbing it into the dolphins' backs. The Transit van was chugging along with the extra weight, but we were moving smoothly enough and I even tried to drive carefully so the ride wouldn't be too bumpy. The dolphins looked exhausted and pained, even though I know they breathe air and that, so they couldn't have been in too much trouble, but it must have been a bummer to be out of the water all of a sudden. That's why Nina was rubbing their sides and backs with vaseline, so their skin wouldn't dry out. Then they would have been in serious trouble.

Nina said their names were Joona, Veera, Näsi, Niki and Delfi. Apparently Joona and Delfi were boys and the others were girls. In dolphin years they were teenagers, still kids really. I don't know where she got all of this from, she must have gone to the dolphinarium a lot and got this crazy idea that someone ought to set them free.

We drove on and on through the summer night. There wasn't much traffic, everyone was probably on their summer holiday. We passed Pori and turned off towards Luvia, then on to a small road heading out to Laitakari and Nina said I should look for a spot where we could drive the van into the sea.

That's when it struck me for the first time that dolphins don't live this far north – would they survive in the Baltic Sea? It had been unusually hot across the whole of Scandinavia for the last three weeks, but would the water temperature be warm enough for them, and would there be anything for them to eat? They normally live down in the Med. My head was starting to clear and suddenly I was sick with worry and the beginnings of a nasty hangover.

This is what they want, Nina said. Even if they don't survive, at least they'll die free.

How can you tell that, I asked and the Transit shuddered in my hands as my teeth chattered and sweat started pouring down my forehead.

They've told me, she said.

My head was throbbing something rotten. It was like being in a dream when we found a shallow cove with a sandy beach; I turned the van round and reversed it far enough into the water that the waves were beating against the rear doors.

We opened it up, pushed the boxes one at a time towards the edge and tipped them on their side. Splash. Joona. Splash.

Delfi. Splash, Näsi, splash, Niki, splash, Veera. The water was still a bit too shallow for them, but they struggled forward until it was deep enough. Then they disappeared; five wet, dark backs.

The sun had risen and it was already getting bright.

It all felt completely surreal. A Transit van backed into the water, five cushioned chests. A girl shivering in a pink track-suit. Heart-breaking birdsong. (Pause. Long, heavy breaths. Sniff.)

And that's when it happened. I looked at Nina and thought about the stupid, mad things we'd just done together and how after an experience like that nothing in the world could separate us again; we'd been brought together, it was as if we'd been doing this sort of thing for years, and I knew she was the woman for me, for me and nobody else. And I was going to take her in my arms, carry her back to the front seat of the van and make love to her slowly, gently . . . then something about her face changed. It happened in an instant, like she'd taken off a mask and what was underneath was strange and empty. I saw that flame in her eyes dwindle until it was just a spark, then die away altogether, until all of a sudden in front of me there was a little brat whimpering and sobbing, and I could see she was scared, scared, scared!

A helpless fear came over me, I was sure she . . . she'd taken so much gear that she'd gone kind of schizo, so I tried to drag her on to the front seat so I could start up the van and take her somewhere, somewhere she could get some help or medicine, but she struggled loose and jumped out the back of the van into the sea and started thrashing about. I jumped in after her, I tried to talk to her, drag her back, but she couldn't see or hear me, she didn't recognise me, for Christ's sake, she didn't even recognise me; the water was up to our waists and she just kept on wading further and further out.

The next thing I remember was trying to start up the van and get help, but my hands were shaking too much and the motor wouldn't start, so I left it there with the doors wide open and ran like a lunatic, like an animal, and I remember battering on the door at that house and shouting for them to bring a boat and call an ambulance, and then the old bill turned up and nothing's made any difference since then, do you hear, nothing makes any difference. And what Nina did she did by herself, she died free just like those dolphins, and even though I still don't know why she did it or what happened to her, I'm not a murderer! (Voice breaks. Thud. Silence.)

# *The Monster*

Satu Waltari

*Throughout her career as a writer Satu Waltari (born 1932) has played with reality and its various meanings. A theme particularly close to her is the boundless imagination of young people and their joy in trying new things. At times she may take inspiration from the art of Hieronymus Bosch, at others from a little girl's love of horses or the deep schisms within families, but the result is always unexpected, absurd and uplifting. She is the daughter of Mika Waltari, also represented in this anthology. 'The Monster', the extract in this collection, is from the work* Hämärän matkamiehet *('Twilight Travellers', 1964).*

It was a wonderful night. Almost full, the moon was shining against the black sky like a toddler's self-portrait. They were infuriating – little children's self-portraits – they were everywhere. On the walls, on book covers, on every piece of paper imaginable; always entirely misshapen. The one in front of her now was rather more successful; it had been drawn with a good orange crayon and this time its eyes and mouth even fitted inside the outer edges of its face and didn't bulge outside as in the majority of Romi Nut Bunny's drawings. At least Stumpy's drawings were slightly more skilful, even though she only ever drew crown princesses, which, from a distance, looked like nothing but big triangular tents. She gave a sigh and looked away from the sky. There really was no time to lose, sometimes the nights seemed to fly past in the blink of an eye.

The open bed yawned white in the darkened room. On the pillow there was a large black hole: it was brown spittle. It's never really a good idea to fall asleep with a piece of chocolate in your mouth. Out in the hall there stood a tall white ghost.

Her own reflection in the hall mirror: a girl dressed in a white night gown stretching all the way down to the floor. Viivian. At first she had been furious upon noticing the name on the covers of her school books. Every single book contained that same name written out in her own handwriting. If she was not allowed to keep her own name then she might at least have been called Helena or Leif or Boy, anything else remotely tolerable. Never in her whole life had she heard of anyone called Viivian. Still, people eventually get used to all sorts of things. But on that first night it had made her very cross indeed.

Even so, Stumpy was a very silly name. Stumpy was fast asleep with her beloved spotted blanket pulled up over her lips, snoring softly and dreaming with her brow knotted, her bare feet hanging out of the bed like a chariot driver fallen on his back. Viivian giggled quietly to herself. Outside beneath the window a horse whinnied faintly in reply. Truly. But first she thought she had better do a little check before getting dressed; sometimes Father would sit up in bed reading almost until daybreak.

Everywhere was quiet and dark. A rasping sound came from the kitchen. The small door on the cuckoo clock creaked open and the cuckoo popped out. "Cuckoo, look at you, how time flew," it said. How infuriating! You never knew whether it meant the strike of three o'clock or a quarter to without going up close and squinting. It was 33 o'clock. Romi Nut Bunny was asleep curled up beneath his red silken quilt with one dummy in his mouth and another clasped in his fist. Asleep he simply looked like a chubby baby. No one could have imagined how he hit, kicked, ripped, scratched and tore at everyone and everything and dashed about like a bundle of bones and muscles let loose, just like the real White Rabbit, who always feared he would be late and miss out on something exciting. Whilst he was asleep you could even stroke his cheek.

The faint smell of roast chicken hung around Mother, as

always when she had started another one of her endless dieting regimes and was dreaming of good food. She was snoring too.

Father's clothes were strewn all over the floor; he was sleeping with two foreign books under his head and another open across his face with a mountain of blankets covering him, and on top of the mountain sat the middle cat who narrowed its eyes, raised its head and winked. The coast was clear.

Viivian ran with silent, rapid steps back into the hall, tying her plait around her head as she went – hanging loose it would only get in the way beneath her helmet and would catch in the trees and bushes. She tore off her nightgown and quick as a flash slipped on a long-sleeved grey vest and tights, an iron chain mail suit, leather knee pads and spats, bent down to attach spurs to her shoes. She got rather flustered with the awkward straps and buckles of her plated armour bearing an Airedale terrier crest, tied a sword belt around her waist, a dagger hanging from one hip, a sword from the other, pulled first a grey hood then a helmet complete with plumes and Airedale terrier motifs over her head, checked that the visor moved freely up and down, slipped on a pair of long-sleeved leather gloves with metal knuckle protectors, picked up her bow and arrows from the coat rack in the hall and threw them over her shoulder, and with only a few swift leaps she was at the window again and jumped out straight on to the back of the black horse waiting beneath. The horse gave a contented snort and set off at a furious pace.

The fresh night air brushed her face like soft, moist fern leaves; the air whistled through the helmet's raised visor and its plumes, through the feathers of the arrows and the horse's thick mane. Tired of waiting, the horse galloped joyously with all his strength; he did not care for the bridge beneath which silent bats swirled on their rapid hunting flights, oh no, but he raised his shod hooves in a great leap, stretched his entire body and together they flew across the babbling brook as easily as the night hawks. In a blur they scaled the hillside, then rushed down into the meadow. At the edge of the forest Viivian pressed her face against the horse's fragrant mane so that the low-hanging branches would not whisk her from the saddle. She gently stroked her steed's silken neck, a shudder ran through the horse's body and he burst into an even more dizzying gallop. Startled red deer ran crashing from where they slept; squealing frantically, a family of wild boars dispersed across the dark pathway; Viivian laughed with joy. A large bird all but lost its footing on its branch, dived to just above the forest floor, then with a fluttering of its great wings disappeared into the shelter of the trees.

Deep inside the forest it was pitch dark. Every now and then the horse's hoof would strike a stone amongst the moss and give off a bright spark. Viivian slowed the horse a jot. It would be dreadful if the horse should suddenly stumble on some of the tree roots creeping out across the path and she were to be thrown to the ground. Though in fact riding a horse was no more difficult than sitting on a hay sack lain across the cottage doorway.

'Oh no! Don't change,' she shouted anxiously. 'My dear, dear horse, don't ever change,' she said in fright taking hold of the horse's hot, muscular neck. The horse gave a snort, bounded onwards, and in only a few leaps they had crossed a small swamp. The water splashed up to the her knees; it smelt of mud and of the night. Only for a split second had her steed resembled the old hay sack, that horrible limp old thing with two dried thistles sticking through as ears. At the other side of the swamp they paused for a moment in a moonlit copse. Viivian thanked the horse with a gentle stroke along its quivering neck from the silken skin beneath the ears right down to the saddle's breast strap, and at this the horse turned its head and very carefully touched her foot with his lips.

'You *are* real,' she said softly consumed with a silent joy. She patted the horse's shanks and gently hopped down from the saddle. Only once she was standing with both feet firmly on the ground again did she realise that she was shaking through and through, as though they had just been saved from a terrible danger. She rested her head against the horse's neck, stroking its powerful breast and filling her nostrils with its wonderful, warm scent.

The horse belonged to her, it was entirely up to her whether she kept it or not and whether she could breed it into the fastest and bravest horse in the world. A single unhappy thought could destroy it all. Nonetheless, not even two happy thoughts were enough to grow the horse a pair of wings, because such things simply don't exist. Viivian gave a wistful sigh. Then she shook herself from her daydreaming, checked the horse from the tip of its muzzle to the hairs on its tail, pulled its bridle straps, tightened its saddle belt, lifted each and every one of its legs to make sure no sharp stones had caught in its hooves, ran her fingers through the horse's wavy mane and tail, and with a fragrant bundle of ferns she brushed away the sweat on the horse's sides.

Once the horse had taken a few sips of water from a spring, their reflections dancing with the stars across the surface, she led her steed over to a suitable rock and hopped once again into the saddle.

'What now?' she said to herself. They could easily have stayed there forever, like the Red Knight who, at the ford in the river, sat night after night upon his horse thinking and waiting for imaginary enemies. In amongst a clump of mountain currant bushes sang a nightingale, the forest was filled with the scent of butterfly orchids and moss. The horse listened to something far in the distance with his ears pricked; the still and calm was like a restful dream.

Viivian let the reins dangle loose around the horse's neck and spread out a small map, etched on a soft, paper-thin piece of lamb's skin that she kept in her saddle bag.

In the dim light of the stars she did not even have to squint to examine the map, because it was very old indeed and therefore simple and as easy to read as a child's drawing.

'We're in the King's Wood, to the left of Badlucksberg, and here is the swamp,' she said; the horse stretched one of his ears back to listen to her. 'If we travel straight ahead for a while we'll cross the Black Hills and arrive at an uncharted area marked with three stars.'

She rolled up the map, picked up the reins and with her spurs touched the horse's side as gently as a feather. The steed rose up on his hind legs, excitedly snorting the slumber from his nostrils and galloped forward. A fanfare of horns could be heard in the distance.

'They're at the pond,' Viivian said to herself. 'The King is calling in the crayfishers, they are on their way home.'

At that moment they arrived at the Black Hills, but behind the row of hills a terrible surprise awaited them. Quicksand stretched through the darkness as far as the eye could see.

'Well, boy,' Viivian spoke to the horse, whose ears were twitching restlessly as they took in the sight before them. 'No wonder this territory has been left uncharted.'

Very cautiously the horse placed his hoof on the sand, only to draw it sharply back to the verge that same moment, as where his hoof had been the sand moved all by itself, its fine grains began to flow into the depths of the earth, into the emptiness beneath, like through an enormous hourglass, until a small stone blocked up the hole. Upon that, as if by magic, the surface of the sand was smooth once again. An unwitting traveller may not have feared it in the slightest.

'Huh!' exclaimed Viivian impatiently. 'Easy does it. Softly and quickly forwards,' she said guiding the horse on to the sand. And the horse moved sideways across the shimmering, whispering sand, as nimbly as a ballet dancer, as lightly as though he were dancing across freshly laid dove's eggs. They flew like the wind and after only a few minutes they had crossed the quicksand and were standing safely on the firm, heather-covered ground at the edge of a small wood. The stretch of sand surrounding this mysterious, unknown wood had not been as wide as it had looked from a distance. Laughing excitedly Viivian patted the horse's neck. But now the horse no longer paid any attention to these otherwise very pleasant displays of affection; he was listening out and sniffing the dark woods.

'What is it,' asked Viivian, though she too was listening carefully. Close by, from behind the trees, her own voice echoed back as if it had struck a wall. Above the trees the darkness was impenetrable, the stars were no longer visible. Viivian coughed warily. Her voice boomed as if they had been standing inside a great cavern with trees growing all around. Without her having to urge him, the horse began slowly walking forwards; through the trees there ran a winding path which seemed to be leading them down and down into a gorge. All around there grew tall ferns reaching as high as the horse's withers.

'Dead Man's Hands,' said Viivian in nothing but a whisper. She could feel her own whisper resound like a warm breath against her face. As she stretched her hand out in front of her she fumbled the black rock of the cliff face, which did not feel at all as cold as stone but was soft and warm, as if she had gently brushed a feather pillow. She brought the horse to a halt and pulled the dagger from its sheath.

'Just as I suspected, soapstone,' she said as she carved a thin piece out of the rock and let it drop to the soft moss on the forest floor. 'We must be in some sort of pass or cave,' she said to herself. The air was almost unpleasantly warm, humid and difficult to breath, her undershirt clung stickily to her back and she was too hot. All of a sudden the horse startled, took a great leap and they flew like a shot across a dizzyingly deep gorge. At once the air cleared. Viivian felt against her face a gust of fresh air, heavy with the fragrances of strange spices. The smell of cloves. It reminded her of the dentist. Onwards they travelled, down and down into the gorge. 'But how we find our way back is another matter altogether,' she said to herself giving the horse's neck a calming pat. The horse shook the reins and seemed clearly distressed.

'Let's have a little rest, my old friend,' she said dropping the reins and jumping down from the saddle. They had arrived at an opening in the trees, perfect for a rest, with a small, clear spring rippling out from the rock face.

'A little bite to eat would certainly not go amiss,' she said throwing herself down on a soft knoll. 'The next time we set off on a long journey like this we shall have to pack something small to eat,' she said as she rummaged in her saddle bag for a pen. This adventure would be of no use whatsoever unless she carefully marked the route they taken on the map. As always, she could not find a pen: she lived in house in which pens disappeared the minute they came through the door. She did however pull out of the bag a nice, white parcel. Very carefully she opened it up. Inside there was a smoked pig's knuckle.

She had seen this somewhere before. The previous day in Trotter's grocer's shop she had stared at it as she had queued to pay for her chewing gum.

'Oh my!' she shouted out loud. She would rather be anywhere in the world than in Trotter's grocer's staring at a pig's knuckle. She beat the air with her hand to banish the disturbing thought and realised to her relief that she was still sitting on the knoll at the bottom of the gorge. Beside her the horse was sipping water from the spring. 'Anyway, I don't particularly care for smoked meat,' she said, wrapping the knuckle up again.

All at once she heard a strange spluttering sound nearby; the spluttering stopped and she could clearly make out the wheeze of heavy breathing, as though someone nearby were having an asthma attack.

'To be or not to be,' came the hoarse, tense voice very close at hand. 'That is the question. What beautiful words. But the man who wrote them certainly didn't imagine what an enormous question this may actually be for some. It's as if those words were written about me,' said the voice. There then came the abrupt sound of someone blowing their nose.

The horse's ears twitched as he listened to this, but did not seem particularly afraid. Viivian stood up.

'Who's there?' she said to pluck up her courage as for safety's sake she gripped the handle of her sword. The voice sounded a touch unreal, as if someone had spoken with a pillow pressed against their mouth. She edged her way closer. The bearer of the voice had obviously not heard her and continued his monologue.

'Anyway, to be is only a verb. I am, you are, he is, she is. He is not really here, and neither are you, so I can't really be sure whether I am here either. What a curious thought! Like a circle.' Again someone blew their nose heartily.

Viivian was now standing right at the mouth of a small cave. Now and again, carried by the faint breeze, a horrid, stale smell wafted out of the cave and reached her nose. The smell of an unemptied rubbish bin. On the ground, scattered around her feet, lay various cutlet bones, all licked spotless, and old egg shells. Some of them were green with mould around the edges. Viivian stretched her neck to see as far as she could into the dark cave when there came a sudden clatter, as if someone had dropped a sewing box.

'Oh!' cried the startled voice. Viivian was also startled, took a step back and just to be safe drew her sword halfway out of its sheath. She then took several sharp steps backwards as a strange being came running out of the cave and very nearly stumbled on top of her. 'Huh, boo!' bellowed the creature in a terrifying voice.

The horse raised his head from the tussock where he had been nibbling at the short, fresh grass and looked absently and fearlessly towards the cave.

'Boo-oo!' the creature shouted right at Viivian's face and breathed out such a foul stench that she almost fell over dazed. The animal – assuming it *was* an animal – was just larger than the horse but a lot fatter. Its four short, bulky feet, all covered in fur, resembled a bear's paws, whilst its back, all apart from a perch's fin half a metre high, was covered in dark green lumps like a newborn pine cone. With its large buck ears pricked, it stretched its long, thick neck towards Viivian. Its dark eyes, shaded by long, velvet eyelids, were clearly more used to the squalid cave's darkness than to the dim half-light, for they were blinking as if the animal were trying to hold back tears. And as for the poor animal's nose, it resembled a trumpet – next to that, even a pig's snout looked almost like a rosebud about to burst into flower. It was not a nose at all, it was a trumpet. The animal's head was covered in lumps and bumps, scratches and sores, clumps of coarse hair and small horns. Its tail end disappeared far off into the cave, thinning like that of a lizard.

The creature looked over Viivian from head to toe, then blew a wet cloud of steam from its snout.

'That will be quite enough, thank you,' Viivian said in disgust. The creature stared at her, its eyes wide and round. 'Perhaps you should blow your nose more often,' she snapped.

'Boo!' the creature bellowed loudly.

'Boo-hoo, and good evening to you too,' replied Viivian. 'I overheard you talking to yourself, so I know full well that you can speak properly.' The creature looked at her, somewhat hurt.

'I'm sorry if I offended you, I'm not normally this uncouth unless it's absolutely necessary,' she said softly. 'It seemed there would be no end to all your booing,' she smiled.

'Why are you not afraid of me?' asked the creature in a hushed, curious voice.

'I don't know,' she said somewhat baffled. 'The horse isn't afraid of you either.' The creature looked the horse up and down.

'Is this your horse?' it asked pensively. 'It's very beautiful indeed. To me. My wife died recently. It's barely been two hundred years.'

Viivian anxiously thought of something appropriate to say. 'My condolences' or 'how terribly sad' or 'I'm sorry'.

'I'm sorry,' she said finally.

'How?' asked the creature, intrigued.

'In some way,' Viivian replied a little surprised. 'I share your sorrow.' The creature looked at her in delight.

'Listen,' he said in a friendly, familiar voice. It looked as though he had sat his rear end down, and Viivian thought it might be polite to sit with her legs crossed at the mouth of cave once she had cleared a spot amongst the bones. 'Tell me the truth: do I exist?'

Viivian thought for a moment. 'Yes, you do,' she said very seriously. 'Does life seem unreal to you?'

'What does that mean?' asked the creature raising his eyebrows.

'I don't know, but sometimes I feel as though I know that I exist, but I don't know exactly where,' she said.

The creature pondered this, then burst into happy laughter.

'That's what I feel too,' he said with a chuckle. Together they laughed long and hard.

'Sometimes when you meet a complete stranger, it suddenly feels like you have known them forever,' Viivian said wiping tears of laughter from the corners of her eyes.

'Indeed it does,' said the creature sniffing horridly.

'Couldn't you blow your nose every now and then?' she suggested, but the creature was pretending not to listen.

'Do you know what I am?' he asked, still laughing.

'No,' replied Viivian somewhat taken aback. She had not given the matter a second thought.

'Guess.'

'A brontosaurus or some other sort of dinosaur,' she hazarded.

The creature giggled excitedly. 'No.'

'A bugbear.'

'Ehem, no,' he chortled amusedly.

'A nightmare.'

'No.'

'You are . . . a very large pangolin,' Viivian decided after a lengthy guessing game.

'That must be it,' cried the creature. But when he noticed that Viivian was becoming rather annoyed at always guessing wrongly, he bent down towards her ear.

'If you promise on scout's honour to keep it to yourself, then I'll tell you what I really am,' he whispered. Viivian gave a serious nod.

'A dragon,' said the creature, no louder than a breath. At this, Viivian stood bolt upright, as if she had been stung by a bee, slapped her hands against her knees, jumped up and down, fell to the floor holding her stomach and swayed back and forth unable to breathe.

'Now I've frightened you to death! I'm sorry,' said the creature helplessly. Viivian managed to take a deep breath, hooted loudly, wooh, she shouted, tears streaming down her cheeks.

'Don't shout, my friend, I won't harm you,' he said trying to calm her down.

'Huh, huh,' said Viivian, who could speak once again. 'I

wasn't shouting. A dragon!' she laughed so hard her sides almost burst. The creature looked at her disapprovingly.

'What's so funny about that?'

'If you'll forgive me, you really are the most badly drawn dragon in the world!' she said, then added sceptically: 'Or else you're pulling my leg.'

'I'll bet you I'm not lying,' the dragon said firmly. 'I have papers and documents to prove it.' With that he scurried into the cave and soon afterwards came the sound of scratching, digging and the rumbling of stones. A moment later he returned, slightly out of breath, bringing with him a foul gust of wind like that of a bedroom which had not been aired or cleaned for a hundred years, a smell so strong that anyone less hardened to such things than a nine-year-old girl would surely have fainted on the spot.

'This is a document dated August 1123,' said the dragon as he thrust an old parchment into her hands. 'And this is a sketch for my portrait,' he said proudly displaying a quickly drawn, smudged charcoal sketch from which she could barely make out the dragon's essential features.

'Several hundred years ago an artist came here and drew my picture. It was meant to be part of a larger work of art, so it's not a proper character study. Still, quite a resemblance, isn't it? He gave me this by way of thanking me for posing as his model. Since then, technically speaking, I have been by myself down here,' said the dragon and pressed the shabby picture lovingly to his chest. Looking very serious and businesslike, Viivian carefully unrolled the parchment.

Once she had spread it out she read through the parchment, Viivian took a long, hard look at the dragon from the tip of his trumpeted snout to the point where he disappeared into the darkness and read through the document one more time, and all the while the dragon stood waiting intently. Finally Viivian raised her head and stared the dragon solemnly in the eyes.

'It says here that in August of the year 1123 a young woman by the name of Klaara, the sweetest and most beautiful young woman in Genoa that year, was sacrificed to appease the dragon so he could maul and eat her.' The dragon seemed somewhat embarrassed and began to fidget nervously.

'Yes, that was rather an unfortunate incident,' he said. The dragon then raised his head and looked Viivian fearlessly in the eyes. 'But in actual fact it wasn't my fault at all.'

'It says here: to appease the dragon. You must have done something,' she retorted.

'Look, it's like this,' said the dragon taking a deep breath. 'Some time around the year 1100 finding a bite to eat round these parts was a bit of a problem, given the amount I used to put away as a youth. That, and of course the fact that humans had begun intruding into the forests too. So one evening I had just left my home, when . . .' The dragon's story came to an abrupt halt and he raised his paws up to cover his snout.

Viivian cleared her throat. 'When . . .?'

'As shameful as this is to admit, I find all kinds of eggs quite delicious. Sea birds' eggs, chickens' eggs, even small birds' eggs. Tortoise eggs are especially good, have you ever tried them?'

'You're trying to change the subject,' Viivian pointed out angrily.

'No,' shouted the dragon. 'On the contrary. Because it was that same year, when people realised I actually existed and that I lived here in this very forest, I went out at night – what a fool I was! – like a thief I went out to the edge of the town to steal eggs from people's chicken coops. I decided, once and for all, to eat as many eggs as I could find and have my fill of them for some time. But of course, the clumsy thing that I am, I trampled on the chickens and the coops, a few pigs, water barrels and everything else under my feet. Smashed everything to smithereens, if you see what I mean. To this day I still feel very sorry about this, but back then I was considerably larger than I am today; age and the shortage of food have shrunk me beyond recognition. Sometimes when I look at myself in the spring, I can hardly . . .'

'Get to the point,' said Viivian firmly.

'Well, people simply made up their minds – as I had destroyed their possessions – a dragon, they thought, it must want to eat people. They had scriptures claiming that dragons eat people. So the good townfolk assumed that, despite all my efforts, I had been unable to find a single tasty human on my egg excursion and would certainly come back again and again unless they did something about it. And so the only logical idea that occurred to them was to find the tastiest, tenderest young lady in the town and deliver her, as it were, straight into my bed, so that I would never again destroy their houses.'

'You do rave on. So what, my good friend, happened to the girl?' asked Viivian, assuming the dragon's tone of voice.

'It's a very sad story. She was brought all the way out here, she was standing where you are sitting now, at precisely the same spot, nine and a half centuries ago, crying and wailing, and I had been thinking so hard – my head ached with all the thinking – trying to think where I could put her and what I would feed her, because as I said provisions were so hard to come by back then, but when I walked out here to say hello and bid her welcome to my humble abode, she looked at me and fell to the ground, pale and silent. She didn't make a sound. I rushed over to the brook to collect some water and tried to revive her, but when I returned and touched her I realised that her heart had stopped – forever.'

'How terrible,' said Viivian sorrily. 'What did you do then?'

'Then I ate her,' said the dragon nonchalantly. 'But things didn't stop there.'

'I think perhaps we should be on our way,' said Viivian. The horse raised his head, rattling the bit. 'Goodness only knows what the time is,' she said squinting at her watch, which often showed all sorts of times, especially if she forgot to wind it up.

'Oh, please don't go yet,' the dragon said sadly. 'It's so rare that anyone ever stops and listens to me.'

'We really ought to be off,' said Viivian and glanced again at her watch; she had a feeling it looked somehow strange. Instead of numbers, twelve little ant faces stared back at her. They were looking at her boldly, almost grinning. Their small hands gripped the clock's hands and spun them furiously, first clockwise then anti-clockwise. Then, like soldiers performing a drill, the little creatures lined up in twos at the centre of the clockface, handing the hands of the clock back and forth, carrying them first up towards the top, then heave-ho, about turn, and marched back towards the base.

'Ding-dong,' said the clock. The little ants turned their heads and gazed up contentedly at Viivian.

'Hm,' she sniffed removing the watch and putting it in her pocket.

'In any case you can't continue your journey, as you've come to a dead end. This is the centre of a labyrinth, the only way you can go is backwards,' said the dragon apologetically. 'Sit down for a moment, though I'm afraid I have nothing to offer you,' he implored.

'Very well then,' said Viivian graciously. 'Carry on your story.' Somewhat bewildered, the dragon scratched his head.

'Where was I?' he asked. 'I talk to myself so often that it doesn't matter where I leave off.'

'The first young woman you ate,' said Viivian. 'But there's one thing still puzzling me,' she continued pensively. 'The purpose of a labyrinth puzzle is generally to find hidden treasures, not a dragon.'

'Indeed, but the purpose of this puzzle is precisely to find a dragon,' he said with a smirk, but regretted it immediately.

'Not at all. Please don't think I'm awfully vain, I was only joking,' he quickly added. 'Let me tell you quite how overjoyed I was when I saw you.' His face suddenly turned a deep purple colour. 'There is of course treasure to be found here, but it's certainly nothing to write home about. Are you interested in it?'

'Absolutely,' replied Viivian. 'Of course, if it's too much trouble for you . . .' she added politely, not wanting to seem overly eager.

'Wait here a moment,' said the dragon and with that he disappeared once again into his cave, from which after a few moments there came a crash and a clatter as though someone had knocked over a cupboard full of china. Viivian stood up and walked over to the horse.

'You're not bored, are you, my old friend?' she asked stroking the horse's black neck. The steed gave her cheek a friendly nibble with its soft velvet lips and lay down near the brook. Viivian untied the bridle straps, removed the stirrup from the horse's head, wound the reins round her arms, opened the buckles around the chest and stomach and lifted the whole saddle from the horse's back. Awkwardly the horse rolled over and with all four hooves in the air he began excitedly rubbing his sweaty back on the soft green moss. Then he jumped upright with a snort and shook off all the dust and dried leaves. Viivian hung the bridle and the light saddle on a thick willow branch nearby, reached into the saddle bag for a curry-comb and with only a few long strokes the horse's sides gleamed like freshly smoothed ice. The horse was chewing away at a few willow leaves when the dragon reappeared huffing and puffing at the mouth of the cave, covered in dust, cobwebs and all manner of dirt.

'The chest is stuck fast in the ground and I can't move it,' gasped the dragon. 'It hasn't been moved since it was brought here and even then I had no reason to lay a finger on it. Mmm, back then I was only a child, nothing but a small basilisk less than two feet long. At first, you can well imagine, I got terribly lonely in here all by myself,' he said wistfully and sat down to think more clearly. But as he sat down he gave a terrifying roar. Viivian jumped and the horse startled and rolling its eyes it stared at the dragon, its ears pricked.

'I must have twisted my back, or else this is a case of lumbago,' groaned the dragon.

'You wouldn't last a minute with my mother. She's always moving the furniture around. She only lifts the piano enough to put a rug under one end, then she drags the rug and the piano around the room,' said Viivian.

'Why?' the dragon asked and Viivian simply shrugged her shoulders.

'It cheers her up,' she replied. The dragon looked her up and down somewhat perplexed.

'It's a good job your mother hasn't found her way out here,' he retorted finally. 'Or St. George for that matter. At one time there were lots of stories written about how he went about slaying dragons. It took a lot of time and energy to block the gorge with boulders so he would be unable to get here.'

'That was a long time ago,' she said cautiously.

'Very long indeed,' the dragon enthused. 'Nowadays he can be found in Heaven and in church paintings. And since then the mountains have collapsed and the boulders I had piled up have all rolled down into the ravine. It's been several hundred years since any other Tom, Dick or Harry has turned up here trying to poke me with spears and swords. My beloved wife came and went. She was always on the move, she was what they call a flying dragon, a real beauty. Her wings were like the fin on my back but far, far greater. I always told her all that flying around and gallivanting would be the ruin of her, and just as I predicted, one day she perished in a flying accident. I waited for her, I waited and hoped with all my heart, but it was only many decades later that I heard how, on a stormy night, she had plummeted into the sea in a ball of flames near a Phoenician fishing boat. At that moment the storm abated and the sea calmed, and you can imagine all the stories those fishermen told until the end of their days.' Viivian nodded in sympathy. She could feel her eyelids becoming gradually heavier and heavier.

'Times went from bad to worse and gradually people stopped bringing young maidens out here, and to be perfectly honest it was a great relief. They tasted awful, I can tell you. And on top of this I realised I was in fact allergic to young women. Before I had ever met a young woman my head was beautiful and smooth like other lizards, but I soon came out in a rash, and became covered in scabs and warts – the itching was unbearable, I would scratch my head night and day. And look at me now, there are almost horns on my head. Not once did anyone ever think to bring me a tender, young piglet or a well-done veal cutlet, just maiden upon maiden.'

'You shouldn't scratch your head,' said Viivian sleepily. 'Anyway, how do you know what pork and veal taste like if no one has ever brought you pigs or calfs?'

'I have many cookery books, I very much enjoy leafing through them. In fact I have quite an extensive library. I would invite you in to look at it, but I'm afraid I wasn't expecting company. I haven't tidied up . . .' said the dragon, a touch embarrassed, and scratched his ear.

'Don't scratch!' said Viivian sharply, then burst out laughing as she realised that she too was thinking about scratching her head. Other people's bad habits catch on without our noticing. 'Tidying up isn't so terribly important. If only you could see our bedroom on a Sunday morning.'

The dragon looked at her suspiciously. 'I can't help scratching. Just thinking about young maidens makes me itchy. You can't imagine what they are like, some bits are full of fat, others chewy and sinewy, ugh!' At this he shuddered from top to toe.

'You must stop thinking about it,' she said comfortingly. 'You need to learn to concentrate. Just keep thinking: I must not scratch, I will not scratch. And if the itching gets so bad that you can no longer control yourself, then pick a spot and scratch it very softly, just one spot, though, not your whole head. That's what I do, and gradually you'll stop doing it altogether.'

'Aha!' exclaimed the dragon excitedly.

'Still, it's your own fault,' she continued. 'As far as I can see you could have hidden or stayed in your room and let the maidens run away and go about their business.'

'I tried, I swear, I tried my best,' the dragon shouted sadly. 'Some of them ran off and sunk into the quicksand. There's still a lot of quicksand on the path, isn't there? Others couldn't escape at all. Their only thought was that now they had been sacrificed to the dragon and so they came into the cave and searched for me amongst the rocks. Once, when I had gone out for a walk especially so that the day's victim could leave in peace, what should I do but bump into her in the gorge and she died of fright. They all eventually found me and died of shock. Tell me, do I really look so frightening?' the dragon asked, his voice full of a profound sadness.

Viivian took a close look at him.

'No,' she said finally. 'I'd say you're – to put it mildly – rather untidy looking.'

'Am I not repulsive?' asked the dragon eagerly.

'Not in that way,' she replied after careful consideration.

'Am I not terribly ugly?' the dragon asked in all but a whisper.

'No, you're not,' she laughed. 'You are rather strange looking, but not at all ugly. You're a very nice colour . . .' Viivian looked very closely at the dragon, and the dragon looked back. 'In fact, you're rather beautiful,' she said, somewhat surprised herself at the statement. 'Allow me to clean you up a little,' she decided. 'I don't suppose you have any soap.'

A little embarrassed, the dragon shook his head.

'Well, I'm sure a basinful of water and a curry-comb will do wonders.'

'I do have a bottle brush somewhere,' the dragon informed her.

'Excellent!'

So whilst the dragon clattering and throwing things around rummaged for the bottle brush Viivian took a battered old basin and collected water from the brook and brought it to the mouth of the cave. Then with the help of a few ferns she swept a large area clear of ancient, dried leftovers.

'Right,' she said firmly as the dragon stepped hesitantly out of the cave. He sat down and Viivian began cleaning him up. She began with the dragon's spiky back, which after a thorough wash and a scrub gradually looked less and less like a broken umbrella and began to shine in all the colours of the rainbow. Viivian brushed, scrubbed, scraped and polished. Using the curry-comb and some sand she made the dragon's armoured back change colour and it soon began to gleam a light shade of green. Viivian scrubbed and brushed the dragon from the tips of his ears right down to the end of his tail; every now and then she ran over to the brook to fetch more fresh water, by now dripping with sweat. The dragon sat up on his hind legs and Viivian brushed his stomach, covered in soft downy hair, until it shone as white as snow.

'The twenty-third basinful,' she said quite out of breath. 'After this I'll fetch some rinsing water. But I don't know how to wash your hair. My mother always washes our hair.'

'Surely it can't be all that dangerous, let's get it done too now that we've started,' said the dragon who was also gasping for breath.

'Very well then, but you mustn't start crying,' she said and, clenching her teeth, poured a basin of water over the dragon's head.

'The water's going in my eyes,' he shouted in dismay.

'It'll soon come out again. That's what Mother always says,' she explained rubbing the dragon's head with sand as hard as she could. Once she had rinsed his head she cleaned the dragon's ears and his trumpet-shaped snout, a task for which the bottle brush was the perfect tool. And once she had fetched twenty basins of rinsing water she finally stopped and admired the dragon with her arms folded.

'How sad that you can't see yourself,' she said, satisfied. 'You look altogether different.'

The dragon turned his neck and examined himself as much as he could, and looked very pleased at what he saw.

'I feel suddenly very hungry,' he said somewhat surprised.

'I normally become very thirsty after washing myself,' Viivian replied quickly. 'But I certainly could eat something too. What do you normally eat at this time?'

The dragon looked her up and down, then back again, and a mischievous grin spread across his face. Viivian sensed the warmth suddenly drain from her cheeks and she felt very cold. All at once her hands and feet seemed numb. But then the dragon could not help but burst into laughter.

'Mushrooms. Nowadays I eat nothing but mushrooms,' he said with a giggle. 'I grow them in the cave where my bed used to be. But there are very few of them and they grow very slowly indeed.'

'You frightened me,' Viivian said very quietly.

'I don't have a single tooth left,' he chuckled.

'That's true, we didn't brush your teeth,' she thought. 'You should be glad you don't have any teeth, there is nothing worse than visiting the dentist,' she said casually. 'I could cook you some porridge and other soft food instead.'

'You thought I was going to eat you,' the dragon smirked.

'But first of all I'll cook you some oat porridge,' she said. At this the dragon grimaced. 'Oat porridge is very good for you. And even though you don't have any teeth, you still ought to gurgle and clean your mouth every day. Breath out,' she said sternly and the dragon breathed out.

'Hhhhaaaah.' Viivian felt herself lifted from the ground; there she floated high, high up above the treetops.

'Huh,' she said to herself, the dragon's breath smelt truly rancid and revolting. The watch in her pocket seemed to be moving, its little hands pulling at her and tickling her hips.

'But how can I make porridge and light a fire when I don't have any matches?' she asked.

'Psst, psst! It's seven o'clock!' hissed the little ants. Their whispers were becoming louder and louder.

'Oh, I have to go now,' she shouted in a panic. 'Take care of yourself,' she said holding with both hands as tightly as she could to the hay sack as it flew above the trees, over small houses, across the town the dragon had spoken about.

'I'll bring some matches next time,' she said. She flew further and further away, as if carried upon a great gust of wind, first into the darkness, then into a grey light gradually becoming brighter and almost blinding.

'That's all I need, I've fallen into the sea,' she said to herself. 'And now I'm coming up to the surface. Those Phoenician fishermen will have something to talk about again.'

'It's a good thing I remembered to unsaddle the horse,' she said just as her head burst through the surface of the water and she was finally able to take a deep breath.

Mother was standing leaning over her. The smell of the dragon's breath still hung in the air around her. Hopefully Mother would not notice. What a stroke of luck that she had returned to her bed before morning. She must have lost consciousness and the kind fishermen must have brought her home.

'Good morning, it's seven o'clock,' said Mother quietly.

'Time to go to school. Bath, breakfast, books and bus – the four B's,' she said as if it were some kind of joke.

In the next bed Stumpy stretched her arms and legs and opened her eyes, looking dazed as if the dawning of a new day were a miracle. Then she gave Viivian a broad smile.

'And what do you think you're staring at?' Viivian shouted grumpily.

# *A Diseased Man*

Boris Hurtta

*Boris Hurtta (born 1946) is a pseudonym. He is a prolific writer, whose areas of particular interest are history, mythology and horror fantasy. In addition to his numerous novels he has published over 70 short stories. He has a very distinctive style, drawing upon both an archaic narrative tradition and the rich dialects of Finnish, and his voice is as much at home in the realistic depiction of the everyday life of a bygone age as it is in entirely imaginary milieux. The short story in the present volume, 'A Diseased Man', was first published in the magazine Portti.*

As a man, Kaarlo Huovinen was like a slab of concrete discarded on a building site: strong and unyielding, but by now crumbling around the edges and riddled with hairline cracks. Was his core really as rotten as it felt? Would it take only one smack of a crowbar to reduce the whole block to a pile of cement dust and a mesh of rusty supporting irons? Or was there life in the old boy yet? Another five years? Three even? Surely a person can never be in such bad shape that they don't expect to make it through the next twelve months.

At the last count Huovinen had turned sixty-eight, but only last autumn had he finally traded in his ten-wheeled Volvo with all its trailers and MOT licences and started thinking about things besides shifting whole gravel piles from one place to another for wiser men to refine and sell. He had been a carefree man, without a debt to his name, for two whole weeks, but he still didn't know what to do with this sudden spare time; he began to feel bored. He didn't feel like going out hunting, the idea of a long holiday didn't take his fancy, and neither did sitting in the pub all day. The missus had left him over a quarter of a century ago, bitter after years of fourteen-hour days and seven-day weeks. It would have been a bit pathetic to look her up now and see if they could patch things up. The paper and the television, those were his only friends, and now he could allow himself to get cheesed off with them in a different way from before, when he could only spend an hour or so in their company before dozing off for the night.

His idle body decided to start playing up and soon Huovinen noticed that even a trip to the supermarket and carrying the slightest bags of shopping up to the front door felt as much like hard work as shovelling gravel on to the back of a lorry as a young man. Still, not to bother the doctor. No wonder he was tired, he hadn't had a holiday in donkey's years.

The winter passed and Kaarlo Huovinen gradually became as brittle and smelly as an October mushroom. He suffered his joints and swollen feet like a man, along with the chest pains and the dizziness, but it gave him a real fright when his stomach, which over the years had put up with rich, fatty foods at any hour of the day, finally threw in the towel. It felt like he was shitting juniper bushes, though all that came out was a thin reddish brown sludge splashing down the sides of the toilet bowl and dirtying his backside in the process.

It was another few months before Huovinen eventually decided to pick up the yellow pages. There were very few doctors and lots of patients, all more urgent, more impatient and more demanding than he was. If you can hold on a while, Sir, let's see . . . there's a slot with the doctor in five weeks' time at 15.15, that should be easy to remember. Until then drink lots of water and eat only gruel, porridge and vegetables. If the trouble goes away, as it probably will, then you should call and cancel the appointment, so as not to waste the doctor's precious time.

There can't be anywhere quite as depressing as the waiting room at the local surgery. Certainly not for someone whose body and soul had held a private meeting and passed a pretty grim sentence. Deep down you know it's not worth it, you miserable creature. You left it too late. You should have taken the initial signs more seriously; you could have tried to get an earlier appointment; you could have gone to a private clinic with fast, experienced, efficient staff, assuming you've got the cash – and you had plenty.

The room was wide with a low ceiling and lots of pillars and dark corners filled with all kinds of people killing time, all of them probably very ill, but some appearing sicker than others. Whining children, drunks herded about by the police, looking in astonishment at their makeshift bandages, and a tribe of gypsies were all in need of help before anybody else.

The doctor proffered his hand as merrily as any freshly graduated engineer and politely tried to chivvy along Huovinen's lengthy explanation of events. Tests and photographs would have to be taken and a new appointment was quickly scheduled. Had this been giving him trouble for long? All through last winter, Huovinen replied. Though, in fact, hadn't he actually seen this coming for a while, by giving up his job driving the gravel truck, sorting out the work he had promised his friends and finding a decent buyer for the lorry? All told, the process had taken about three years.

And so eventually it turned out to be cancer looming above him, and the prognosis wasn't good. If only he had reacted three or even two years earlier his chances would have been far better, explained a different, greyer and altogether more serious doctor. It'll require an operation, he said and cleared a slot for the following week.

Kaarlo Huovinen didn't feel like dying just yet, especially since he had been taking part in the ice-fishing competitions on the sunny lake at Pyhäjärvi – albeit with a cold sweat on his brow and his legs quivering. He had caught such a whopper of a pike that even the experienced fishermen were left green with envy and for the first time since his retirement he had felt human again. It had weighed over six kilos and, as if to taunt him, it had had a nasty growth on its tail, like lots of pikes nowadays. Huovinen gulped down a large cup of black coffee – but no cake – in the surgery cafeteria and with a heavy heart he decided that he would never return to this building again. This was going to be nothing but an open and shut case, an exercise to make the staff feel that they had done everything they could, then send him off to an early grave with a nice, specific diagnosis. Now was the time to see Aatami Määttä again.

By the end of the Continuation War Kaarlo Huovinen had finally become a man. As a conscript he had served in the forest garrison where discipline had been strict and the conditions harsh. Back then leave was like gold dust. Transport services were poor and conscripts never had cars of their own. It was best to forget about evenings off and other such luxuries and just sit in the canteen, or the mess as all the boys called it back then, listening to the radio and playing billiards.

Esko Huttunen, the son of a wealthy farmer, slept on the upper bunk. Lady Luck had certainly been shining on him as, after careful consideration, he had been granted three days' leave to go home. But everything was about to go pear-shaped when he fell ill at the last minute, and the sergeant major of the company never sent home soldiers who were not in tip-top condition, not even those who had been relieved of outdoor duties, let alone those with a high fever. And Huttunen had a rising temperature, his cheeks were as red as a cider apple, his speech was quicker and his movements more fidgety than usual. Without a shadow of a doubt this was going to be one for the reception and the infirmary, and maybe even a transfer to the field hospital. But for Esko Huttunen, this leave was of the highest importance: he had the matter of his inheritance and some woman problems to attend to, and as it turned out he did come back to the unit with an engagement ring on his finger.

But before that something strange happened. Back then the boys in the company knew a good few ways of bringing up a fever and quickly creating visible symptoms, but as for the other way round . . .

Someone told Huttunen that there was a Private Määttä in the infirmary who might be able to help. His name was

Aatami and compared to the other 1928 boys he looked as old as his name; he'd been through the war, done his fair share of probation, been in prison more times than anyone could remember, and was the most infamous skiver in the brigade. Despite all this Aatami Määttä should have been sent home a long time ago, but the corporals wanted to get their own back on him: the medical officer had refused to give a man festering in the infirmary the all-clear, and so Määttä had stayed put.

The man winked and told Huttunen to go and have a chat with Old Aatami, 'and don't forget to take all the fags and daily allowance you've got,' he added. Esko Huttunen bribed the duty officer with coffee and buns, went down to the infirmary after lights out and didn't return until just before morning muster.

Huttunen seemed perfectly strong and healthy, he was like a new man. The corporals and the head of the division, a vindictive old bastard by the name of Sergeant Kilpinen, had got wind of Huttunen's illness and ordered a ferocious workout for the whole company, thinking Huttunen would collapse from exhaustion. But no: he took the onslaught of mock formation exercises with a smirk and afterwards went up to the sergeant major to report for leave; he later claimed he'd shown how fit he was by doing thirty press-ups. In any case he was allowed home and returned three days later with a smug, exaggerated grin on his face and a ring on his finger. In amazement Huovinen asked him about what had gone on in the infirmary, to which Huttunen replied simply that this Määttä had bought his illness. But quite how it had happened or how much he had paid for it and to whom, he was not at liberty to say.

It was soon afterwards that their training session came to an end and the boys were sent elsewhere, and Huovinen saw neither Huttunen nor Aatami Määttä again before he was finally relieved of his duties.

A few years later Huovinen found himself involved in logging work at the forest extremity north of Kitinen. As one of the stronger men he had agreed to carry the post to a logging site way out at Jätkälompolo. There was a phenomenal amount of snow and no certainty of how much weight the drifts would hold. On arrival, amidst a heavy snowstorm, he staggered into a cabin in which a group of men were midway through a very serious game of cards. Such things were expressly forbidden on all of Gutzeit's premises, but here even the boss was sitting around the table alongside a dark-eyed Lapp and a long-necked stud poker shark from the south with quick and smooth, unchaffed hands. They were all knocking back the yeast ale and the table was covered in piles of four-figure banknotes. The Lapp had even gathered a few gold nuggets on the joker card in front of him. That was the reason Huovinen had come to Lapland in the first place. The gold rush to Lemmenjoki was still in full swing, though in the end he never actually made it that far. One of the players was an elderly bloke with a terrible cough. The pale, bleary-eyed old man was wrapped up in a turtle-necked jumper and a leather waistcoat, even though the air in the room was so hot and heavy that most of the other blokes were sweating in shirt sleeves.

Huovinen was still so young and naive that no one would even have him as a kibitzer. He found himself a free bunk at the back end of the cabin and lay down. He somehow managed to keep up with things, as this was clearly no ordinary card game. Jurmu was firing on all cylinders. He was raking up banknotes like there was no tomorrow. Jurmu was the shrivelled old guy with the cough; tuberculosis, said a lad in the next bed. It'll have him in the grave before the ground's thawed.

Huovinen had drifted off but woke up as the game came to an end. The Lapp had lost face and money, and slipped quietly out into the dark snowstorm. The shark had pulled a bottle of liquor from his bag and begun drowning his sorrows, but Jurmu slapped a crumpled note on the table and bought the bottle right from his lips. Jurmu had amassed a fine bunch of pocket watches and started scooping his gold nuggets into a clip-topped water bottle by the handful. He was coughing so much that most of them would have ended up on the floor – but of course there were plenty of people happy to lend him a helping hand.

His voice squeaking with excitement, the young lad said that Jurmu now had enough money. What does a dying man want with so much money? You'll never believe it, but there's a bloke in there who'll carry his illness for that amount of money.

'You mean Old Aatami, Määttä's son?' asked Huovinen casually.

The boy gave a start and asked whether Huovinen was here to collect Määttä. Huovinen assured him he had only come to bring the post and was travelling on skis.

'He's over there in the boss's room,' the lad whispered and pointed towards the far end of the cabin, the realm of the managers and the kitchen staff and a place the loggers only went when they were told. 'They brought him here by horse from Tornionjokilaakso last week. They say he was on a black sleigh drawn by a black stallion frothing yellow spittle. Never in my life have I seen a man as sick as this Määttä.'

'How did he know to come all the way out here?' asked Huovinen, but never got an answer.

Jurmu had gathered together his winnings, picked up his bag and the bottle of liquor and went up to the boss's door. He knocked gingerly. Everyone kept an eye on him, but from a good distance, as if they were scouting at a bear's den. Huovinen got up, joined the other men and stood up on tiptoes.

'He hasn't gone and died, has he?' the lad whispered beside him.

Jurmu knocked again. Was that a faint grunt? Jurmu certainly heard it, whatever it was, as he pushed the door ajar and slipped inside. Aatami Määttä was sitting on the edge of the bed; at first he looked almost angelic in his knee-length nightgown with his straw-blond hair. But angels don't smoke pipes, nor do they have sunken, fox-like features streaked with a devilish smirk. Määttä eminated the strong stench of sickness, so strong that it wafted into the main cabin making the men back off instinctively.

The door closed. The boss lay down on the bed nearest the door and told everyone to get some sleep. Gradually the whispering escalated into a chatter, and eventually the foreman got up and snuffed out the lamps, saying that there was a hard day's work ahead tomorrow and anyone who didn't settle down would be given their marching orders.

Not a sound could be heard from the room at the far end of the cabin. Outside a terrible storm raged and howled, and Huovinen, exhausted from skiing such a distance, soon fell asleep to the sound of the wind.

He finally awoke just as the men were about to leave for the logging site. Through the kitchen hatch he was given some of the remaining oat porridge and strong tea. As he ate, coughing could be heard coming from the boss's room. Before long Jurmu appeared and walked right up to the hatch for some breakfast. He wolfed it down; he looked starving, but now he seemed more like a convalescent than a sick man. He finished his breakfast before Huovinen, to whom he then turned his back and started vigorously sharpening his saw. Every now and then a rasping cough could be heard from behind the door.

Kaarlo Huovinen made all the usual enquiries, but would a man like Aatami Määttä even have a permanent address, let alone a telephone? That is, of course, if he were still alive.

He wondered whether Esko Huttunen might be of any help and concluded that he probably would not. Instead he went to the police station. Over the years his run-ins with Superintendent Martikainen had cost him an arm and a leg, but he had no reason to be bitter. All down to his own stupidity or the excessive zeal of a young police officer. 'Do you want some coffee?' Martikainen asked and started talking about the good old days – from his hairline and the size of his belly you could tell he had more good old days behind him than he had still to come. It took a while before he finally asked:

'Huovinen, what do you want?'

'I need to find Aatami Määttä,' he said and vaguely estimated the man's age.

The policeman went over to an old filing cabinet, found some papers, puffed and gave his neck a scratch. He then started tapping his computer keyboard as if working with a volatile, dangerous piece of machinery.

'He's still alive,' came Martikainen's interim report; he then dug a thick instruction manual from his desk drawer and continued grappling with the computer, working up a sweat in the process.

This all took a good half hour. Coffee was Martikainen's fuel as smoking had been banned indoors. He was clearly pleased with what he eventually uncovered.

'I'll go and check in the records, but I can tell you now, you won't get a penny out of him.'

'He'll be on the receiving end,' replied Huovinen.

So the man was alive after all, but even Martikainen couldn't find out where he was. He said he didn't understand why a no-gooder like Huovinen was bothering himself over the whereabouts of someone like Aatami Määttä.

But he was. And it was urgent. 'Is there no other way?'

Martikainen hesitated for a moment. He did have some old friends from the academy, blokes who had nimbly scaled their way up the career ladder. They might know about certain registers to which the police shouldn't technically have access.

The following day Huovinen was once again sitting opposite Martikainen with a mug of coffee in his hand. The superintendent seemed ill at ease, absent-mindedly rubbing his chin and hiding his mouth behind his mug.

'Why did you have to come and plague me with this bloody Määttä?'

'Out of pure friendship; you've always been such a fair bloke.'

'Police officers don't have friends. You can't have any in this job,' Martikainen retorted and angrily stared Huovinen in the eyes from behind his coffee mug. Huovinen stared back until the policeman finally lowered his gaze.

'Alright. But I hope you know what you're getting yourself into,' he said.

'Yes and no, but I don't have any choice.'

Huovinen had heard somewhere that the skeleton of an adult male weighs only fifteen kilos. He had to believe it when he saw Aatami Määttä writhing in pain, strapped in between the raised sides of a hospital bed. A network of tubes and cables travelled between his tortured body and the various contraptions keeping him alive. A monitor showed his erratic pulse struggling in vain.

The man didn't look wicked, but there was certainly nothing of the heavenly angel about him. His angular skull was covered in short, bristly hair. His toothless mouth gaped wide open, his lower jaw sagging down towards his chest. His breath came in rasping wheezes. All his fading energy was concentrated on slowly killing him. The eight-bed ward was full of similar patients, older but hardly weaker than Määttä, all off in their own clouded worlds. Huovinen tried to attract Määttä's attention. He didn't respond to speech, but when Huovinen gently shook the man's shoulder and clasped his cold hand in a greeting, he came to.

In the glare which shone from deep within the man's skull, Huovinen thought he could see a glimmer of that same cruel malevolence, a way of warding off people looking for help.

'I won't buy anything again. I've got enough troubles of my own. How did you find me?'

'Our path's have crossed before.'

Huovinen began talking about his days in the army. At this Määttä seemed to perk up like any ex-serviceman; you could even see it on the monitor. He started rattling on about them soon having to close the division for the holidays and send home the fitter men like him; he'd get to spend the summer months gallivanting around the countryside like when he was younger.

'Alright then. What have you got for me?'

Huovinen whispered that his insides were riddled with cancer.

'I could see that straight away, ha-hah-hah!'

Määttä seemed prepared to make a deal, though he

admitted such a serious illness might prolong his own return to health. Then, he said, he'd buy himself a train season ticket, live it up in cheap hostels and relive old memories at the harvest fairs.

'I want a decent price, mind. You know that,' the old man spluttered.

'How much?'

'As much as you can afford.'

'That's quite a lot.'

'For some people maybe, not for others. It's your cancer.'

After a spot of car dealing Huovinen had scraped together a hundred thousand marks in the bank. He'd withdrawn the lot in cash. It was quite a tidy sum for a dying old man who, according to Martikainen, had spent most of his life in squalour living as a vagrant. Hundreds of times he had spent the night in the police lock-up, in prison wagons and countless different institutions. He was continuously being taken to hospitals and emergency rooms within an inch of his life. The internet had yielded numerous doctors' statements, all manner of death sentences, which Providence had then decided not to carry out. Määttä had never had a home or an address, though his pockets were often bulging with cash. This would have to be enough for him, as he would never again be able to walk out of this hospital on his own two feet.

Huovinen had also brought a deed, drawn up and signed in advance, in which he signed over his house to Määttä. He was hardly going to need it.

The old man had dozed off again without agreeing the exact sum. Huovinen woke him and asked how long the operation would last and where it could be carried out.

'Huh, it'll only take a minute. Right here's fine.'

'So what took all night back in the army, or at that logging cabin at Jätkälompolo?'

'They were fretting over the second condition. Didn't I say? You should pay as much as you can afford, but not so much that you'll come to regret it once you've recovered. If you regret it, the sickness will come back.'

Thinking like that'll send you round the twist, thought

Huovinen. Right then he felt a searing pain wrenching at the bottom of his stomach. He handed over the cash and the envelope containing the deeds to the house.

Määttä didn't bother counting them; he told Huovinen to put them in the drawer by the bed so he could take them when he left. Then for the operation. It was a fairly blunt procedure, no prayers or healing rituals. The old man asked whether the other patients were conscious and as they were not he asked Huovinen to turn around and drop his trousers.

Kaarlo Huovinen felt a hand fumbling around his anus and a bony finger boring its way deep into his rectum. An instinctive shudder turned his knees to jelly. Nothing any worse than that happened. He heard a slurp. Was that him licking his finger clean? Huovinen felt sick.

'Have you already been to the quack about this?' asked Määttä. Huovinen explained the situation.

'Then you'd better let them operate, just to keep them happy. So you won't run into any problems with them later on.'

'Is that right?'

'That is right.'

Kaarlo Huovinen was amongst the first to go out ice-fishing that winter. Martikainen had retired and he was a keen fisherman too. They walked out on to the ice together, though Martikainen was somewhat taken aback by Huovinen's recklessness.

'Look how the ice is shaking! You may have got through that operation, Kaarlo, but you're not immortal.'

'Yeah, pretty embarrassing for the stomach doctors. It wasn't cancer, after all their promises. Well, good to know things can turn out that way too for once.'

'A clean bill of health, just like a baby. No worries, no house. How's a free spirit like you getting used to life in a high-rise?'

'It's easy enough.'

'How did you do it? Only a minute ago you had cars, a house and the lot. And now you're renting a bedsit and living off the odd fish.'

'I had a load of old debts and what have you. It's a burden off my shoulders.'

'Come on, you old fox. You must have a fortune stashed away somewhere. You'll regret selling that house, especially now you've got your health back. I can hardly keep up with you!'

'I won't regret anything, not a thing,' said Kaarlo Huovinen as he looked out across the lake at the dazzling ice stretching beyond the horizon.

# *Chronicles of a State*

Olli Jalonen

*One of the trademarks of Olli Jalonen's (born 1954) work as a prose writer is his desire to bring together his earlier works to form part of new, larger entities, thus making his texts comment upon one another. His writing shows a delight in playing with the nature of reality, be it in an analysis of the power relationships between humans or dark, dystopian visions. Jalonen was awarded the Finlandia Prize in 1990 for his novel* Isäksi ja tyttäreksi *('Becoming Father and Daughter'). In addition to his highly respected, pioneering, large-scale novels Jalonen's output also includes a significant body of short fiction: the story 'Chronicles of a State' is from the collection* Värjättyä rakkautta *('Dyed Love', 2003).*

I have no reason to lie. There has never been a reason for me not to give my name.

But if someone here were to ask me who I am, then perhaps I should answer, quite simply, the man who wrote the history of the State of K. A book so well known that I need not say my name or give myself any greater introduction.

An abridged version was made for schoolchildren as soon as the book was ready to be published as a full-length history book. That complete version was eventually never published; it was shortened instead and given the same name as the abridged version. It had to be changed quite a lot and large sections of the manuscript were omitted so that the book would fit better into the schools' Know Your Neighbours series. The Modern Age. A Short Course for Intermediate Students.

Work books were produced, along with supplementary

texts and interactive learning material, everything necessary was done, audio material was compiled and illustrations added to the text to form a single, gleaming package. It was very well received in schools. Over fifty thousand schoolchildren have had to read extracts from The History of K, or at least look at the pictures or take part in the activities.

And so I have never had to introduce myself further because people simply know who I am. They wouldn't know my name in any case, because the publisher thought it wise, for reasons of layout and marketing, not to print the author's name on the front cover or in any advertising, and eventually it was omitted altogether.

It doesn't bother me. It isn't lying.

You had to do something, there was no way of finding work in a foreign country. There are no benefits here for defectors from neighbouring countries. Neither should there be. Some get by and some don't, and those who don't only have themselves to blame.

When I first arrived here, if you managed to get across the border – back then the checkpoints were still heavily guarded and the borders were secure – you were locked up in a special centres for the duration of your interrogation and background checks. In my case this took only three months, as I had been in such a high position previously. I had to turn every stone the authorities thought of. No matter, interrogation doesn't bother me. Everyone has a job to do and is simply stationed where they are told.

During these investigations we were given food and one set of clothes: a pair of straight trousers, a flannel shirt, underwear and brown walking shoes. In the first few years I used them rather a lot, as I was collecting material for the history book and had to live from hand to mouth with the savings I'd brought when I left.

When I started putting the history together, at first I began very far back in time. That's the way to write a history, if it's done well that is, building up piece by piece from the foundations right to the top, the way people used to build strong brick houses back in the olden days.

Writing about events a very long time ago simply isn't very interesting, I was advised when I showed the publisher my first version of the manuscript – no more than a synopsis in fact. No, I said and immediately tore out almost ten thousand years from the beginning.

I concentrated instead on what I myself knew and what I had experienced in my own life and what I felt was otherwise important. This made sitting around in archives a far easier task, as familiar decades, names and images were already in some sort of mental order and there was no need to double check everything or qualify information with footnotes or references.

Many excellent photographs still existed from those decades. All the most important events had been documented impeccably. Back then every photography studio and agency had had plenty of resources and enthusiasm. In retrospect, even the landscape looks slightly more lush. Buildings were smaller and there was no need for thoroughfares as wide as a runway, not even on the main roads coming into the capital. There were charming little parks and long, empty beaches for which the State of K was renowned abroad. Tourists still flocked there, and there was no need to restrict people's coming and going due to any exceptional circumstances.

That was perhaps the golden era. It was as though the country had grown year upon year, the number of people and factories and almost everything else besides increased steadily, the State became richer, its power around the world grew and as a nation it grew from the inside until finally it was worthy of its name. Why shouldn't I have concentrated more on those golden years?

The publisher only wished to leave this period in the manuscript by way of contrast, so that previous times could serve as something of a colourful background to the bleakness of later events. We have to shepherd the younger generation very carefully indeed; a disaster or an attack of this scale is not at all possible here, but it is a healthy and chilling reminder to see it happen as close to home as in our neighbouring country – perhaps this can be an important lesson for our youngsters today, I was told at a meeting of a committee whose function it was to unify teaching material as I was presenting the outline of my book.

By way of contrast all the good of those years was condensed into five minutes and three double page spreads after which, without any explanation of the various factors leading up to the events which followed, that whole peaceful era of growth and development was cut short with a documentary report:

'Thus far there is no more specific information about the chain of events in the north-eastern reactor zone. A crisis group, established alongside the research committee, does not rule out any possible explanation. The fusion silos may have been the target of a large-scale enemy strike or a contained attack. Technical protective structures around the reactors may have collapsed. The accident may have been triggered by the sudden destruction of data in the operating systems. At worst this may be a case of an uncontrolled release of accumulated gas inside the fusion reactors themselves, otherwise known as helium cancer. The State news service stresses that citizens have no need to fear for their lives or their health. The accident is localised and has been contained entirely within the north-eastern reactor zone.'

I was probably the best person to write The History of K, or at least the sections dealing with these particular stages in its history, as I watched events unfold both inside and outside the north-eastern zone. When the accident occurred – or the attack or whatever they eventually decided to call it – I was working as a journalist for channel two and had just come back from the reactor zone. I had been carrying out a series of interviews for an item about farming entitled Pure Food.

A number of farmers had been relocated in sectors within a given radius of each of the seven fusion reactors in order to put the waste land to use and to capitalise on the excess heat given off. People were so sceptical about the food originating from these farms – over 70 in number – that details of the origin of any produce had to be changed before it was distributed to the shops.

When people at channel two started asking for volunteers

to investigate the accident at the reactor, I simply felt I was the most suitable to go. I had just returned from the zone, I knew my way around and had many contacts there. In the last few years visas were seldom granted, and permanent residents were not permitted to travel outside the zone.

I finally convinced the channel's director and my superiors. I signed a voluntary consent form and a confidentiality agreement, checked a car out of the depot, took an array of broadcasting equipment and set off through the State towards the north-east.

There was very little traffic. The closer I came to the zone the fewer cars I passed, while travelling in my direction there was no traffic at all. At the beginning of August, when I had first gone there to interview the farmers, I had passed a steady flow of lorries from the aluminium and steel factories near the border. Now even service stations were shut, though luckily I had taken a full canister of fuel with me.

Not once did I have to go through routine inspections on the north-eastern motorway. On the slip road there were only a handful of deserted checkpoints with security cameras hidden in black boxes high up on the lamp-posts.

It had been a week and a day since the events in the reactor zone. Problems in energy distribution had begun to emerge, power cuts and heating failures. At the darkest time of night people said they could see a faint glow on the horizon in the north and the north-east, like a cold, gossamer fire. If fire can be cold, that is; I remember pondering this question whilst on the road.

Autumn seemed to have arrived sooner than normal. It was as if there were more brown leaves on the trees than the previous year, and fewer yellow ones. Who can say which leaves are right and which are wrong? The grass is still growing but winter will come eventually. Snow claims the grass, and it is no more. But then grass reclaims the snow, and winter is no more. Or is it? I remember thinking like this as I drove onwards. Of course, with many years of hindsight all this seems like an omen of what was to come, but back then they were nothing but scattered fragments of thoughts, and it felt somewhat overwhelming to see the forests and verges turn more autumnal by the hour.

Someone so much bigger than man can't hide his handiwork, Father would say when things happened which were utterly beyond anyone's control. Just like in April every year when the stream would flood the garden. My younger sister and I would take the red plastic sledges left by the front steps and try to row across to the flagpole at the other end of the garden. Above the yard the water was always the greyish colour of clay, its surface speckled with shining colourful patches where naphtha and petrol for the aggregate unit had spilled from their tanks during the winter.

Bigger than you and me, Father used to say about his cancer and went on to live with it for another ten years, at least; he was always moving the deadline forward slightly. First it was when Eeva started school, then when Eeva had turned twelve so that Mother wouldn't have to take on such a burden. Then when I had finished school, though he didn't quite make it that far.

I drove along the motorway lost in thought. Everywhere around me dusk began to fall, even though according to the given sunset time it should have been light for a good few hours yet. A thin mist had formed across the sky but the sun could still be seen clearly through it, a dim orange glimmer nowhere near the horizon.

The sky was not darkening, it was becoming dusky. As if a matt gauze had been drawn before the sunlight.

I could heard a distant humming, and above the horizon there appeared a pale, shimmering patch of light, a glow. I couldn't quite make it out, but it no longer dispersed in the north-east.

A lorry with a trailer sped past back towards the cities. Its cab was concealed with a darkened windscreen and on its left side all the lettering and paintwork seemed to have been burnt off, leaving the metal plating scarred and rusted.

Soon after this I was forced to slam on the brakes. The road appeared to be blocked. An enormous pile of scrap metal was spread across both carriageways. I tried to drive around it and along the embankment. An electrical current ran through the body of the car. Outside there was a crackling sound and the smell of burning.

I drove past without stopping. A delivery van had fallen on its side. It seemed to have been caught inside an electric field. Sparks flew forth and struck the road. Nothing but a heap of metal, charred and burnt, fire-damaged pieces of platform and cargo, and probably several bodies too.

When I switched on the radio I heard a crisis council bulletin on the news claiming that human casualities had been avoided altogether in the reactor zone, collateral damage was minimal, and life within the immediate proximity of the so-called accident site had gone back to normal. The so-called accident site, said the newsreader. I was puzzled by that expression. By now I was so close to the zone border that there was no mistaking the dimmed sky and the strange gusting wind; it was clear that across the border something on a very large scale had taken place, something irreversible. And as for the lorry with its side burnt off and the delivery van lying across the road, they weren't simply 'nothing'.

Throughout the rest of the journey I had to drive through those electric fields, the car motor kept choking and cutting out, but it would always start again. Once I had arrived at the edge of the zone I stepped out of the car and tried to listen for any sounds beyond the ridge.

A high ridge surrounded the entire reactor zone. Before construction of the reactors had begun, an additional protective layer had been built on top of this ridge. Evidence of trucks transporting earth could still be seen – a clear line cutting through the terrain below – though these churned patches of soil already nurtured a covering of small plants and bushes. Above the shifted soil the colour of the ground was different too: lighter stone and gravel, as if the coast of the Yoldia Sea had been moved and transplanted into the middle of the forest. On either side of the north-eastern motorway stunted forest plants covered the ground until about ten or so metres from the ridge.

There at the top you could look down into the zone.

For I long time I stood on the spot, unable to do anything but stare, as I hadn't prepared myself for such widespread devastation.

From the bottom of the ridge farming plains stretched out towards the first three of the reactor's silos – or what was left of them. The outer walls of the silos had all collapsed. The enormous external pipes of the spiral-shaped cooling system had been ripped apart and the water cisterns and deuterium tanks lay in piles of shredded and twisted steel, aluminium and titanium. A dirty mist hung in the air, everywhere except directly above the defunct silos, which still glowed like bright orange furnaces. The light was so bright that you couldn't look at it directly.

Nowhere was there the slightest sign of life. Both the roads leading to the reactors and those to the farms were empty and everything on the surrounding plains was quiet and motionless.

Something like this had never been predicted. Risk analysis and calculations based on theoretical scenarios had consistently shown almost negligible probability of any accident. In all the material I found whilst sifting through piles of literature and archive sources for my history book, I never once came across a statement to the contrary. Presumably other ways of handling the same data did exist, but only select statistics were ever made public.

Standing at the top of the ridge, looking down on the destruction below, I was a different person from the one I am now, it was so long ago. Now I understand more – or so it seems – but back then I thought I knew exactly what was right and what task then awaited me.

I was the first reporter allowed access to the zone after the events of the previous week and I had the necessary equipment in the car to broadcast reports. Because all official communication was striving to downgrade the scale of the damage to keep the public calm, I felt it was my duty to tell the truth, the whole unvarnished truth.

I continued on my way deeper into the zone. I got back in the car and drove down the ridge to the checkpoint on the north-eastern motorway. On my previous visit in August the checkpoint had been fully manned, complete with security police and stringent border control. Now the entire station was deserted, the gate had been left open and all the steel latches unlocked. The security cameras on the walls of the building looked broken and their lenses had all been turned upwards to face the sky.

I drove to the transport and maintenance centre where either a great gust of wind or a pressure wave had smashed the windows and toppled waste bins. There was no one in sight, not even bodies. Across from the centre stood the zone's one and only school; it too stood empty, like on those deserted evenings during a public holiday. All manner of paper, plastic rubbish and chaff blew about the yard driven by the wind. Veils of smog had darkened the daylight into a premature evening and the raging fires above the fusion silos could now be seen more clearly blazing against the sky.

It was from there that I immediately sent the first of my live broadcasts from the scene of the accident. Reception figures soon reached a level unprecedented on channel two. Because of this widespread support I was allowed to continue my broadcasts almost every day, even though there had been plans afoot amongst the board of directors to put an end to them altogether. There was a great deal of pressure from above, because the State communication strategy was based firmly on keeping a low profile, and it had been decided to keep the situation in the reactor zone as quiet as possible, so as not to cause mass panic. Of course nowadays I realise that this is one way of going about things, but at the time I had only one option and so I worked tirelessly to make public as much news from the zone as I could. Given the situation, anything less wouldn't have felt right.

The worst of it was that the hundreds of people who lived in the reactor zone had, perhaps even deliberately, been forgotten about altogether. From my previous correspondence in the area I knew that, beneath all the central buildings and cellars, a variety of bunkers had been dug out and equipped to be used in the event of an accident or heavy radiation. I went out in search of anyone hidden there, despite the fact that the channel had told me not to go any further into the zone and I was informed by the office of the Secretary General himself that any weakening of State security with images of corpses or the serious wounded was expressly forbidden.

I couldn't understand such an edict and I did not uphold it; it was only due to the mass support for my live broadcasts that the channel and the State communication office allowed me to continue reporting at all.

Within a matter of days I had become renowned throughout the State of K and I realised at once the opportunities this presented for me. I made the kind of programmes I thought were just and right, and I began calling them The Truth Show. I started and finished every broadcast with the words: 'This is A.C. Hahl for The Truth.'

I could no longer be sidelined or kept quiet. I made sure the fate of the reactor zone remained current news, and once the problems in energy distribution grew and the effects of the reactors, all the while blazing and churning out radiation, began to be felt elsewhere throughout the State my words had increasingly more clout.

From the north-east everything will spread elsewhere. It's like a cancer. It can be quiet for a long time then flare up all at once. I've seen the signs up close. Sometimes the wind whips up, then blows on past and is forgotten. But it doesn't go anywhere, it's bigger than you or me. Through my broadcasts I tried to tell people that the seeds of devastation were already spread throughout the State, you no longer needed to travel out to the reactor zone to see it.

I managed to implement so many changes and improvements that I can no longer remember them all. Few people in their lives can ever raise an entire mountain range, but I did. Using earth brought from elsewhere the protective ridge around the reactor zone was built hundreds of metres higher. That was my doing. As a result of this someone on a debate programme at channel two suggested that the new mountain range be named the Hahl Mountains after me, because they would never have been built higher if I hadn't used The Truth

Show every day to demand it and to show people that the collapsed silos and blazing reactors must be shut off in their own stone box behind the mountains. Protecting the rest of the State cannot be dependent upon the sum of a mere few dozen billion.

This is how best to effect change. If you reiterate the same fears and the same sensible measures with proper argumentation enough times, even difficult decisions will begin to seem like the only justifiable solutions. No one in their lifetime can make mountains grow, the person suggesting the naming of the mountains had said. No one can move thirty kilometres of mountains by themselves, I commented in a later broadcast. As a backdrop to this item we used a newly drawn map with the words 'The Hahl Heights' printed above the mountains.

The Secretary General called me at the studio straight after the news broadcast and said that, from the State's point of view, words like this were absolutely right given the current situation. I thanked him like an imbecile. But as soon as that short and one-sided conversation ended, I knew that things could no longer be like this. I mustn't, mustn't thank people, mustn't do favours for which other people can take the credit, and all in the name of the State.

I simply knew this for a fact. From that day onwards my path was marked out. You can't see the future, but you can look far ahead.

As the situation throughout the State worsened by the day, eventually the Secretary General had to be changed. Things all happened the way they should. The head of channel two became the new Secretary General. This of course suited me fine, because such a decision would never have been made without the reflected light of The Truth Show, and I knew very well that the new Secretary General would remember this as long as he was in office.

I was promoted first to the position of head of programming at channel two and later to a position directly beneath the Secretary General, where I was to control all State broadcasting and all channels.

The situation was such back then that we couldn't afford to

risk a thing. We had to establish a body to unify the content of all scheduled programmes, and I was that body.

I kept my own programme, but now it only ran once a week. I began prerecording sections in the office studio and storing them ready in the archive, suitable for a variety of different occasions but so that they looked like live broadcasts. It isn't lying, because you don't always have to visit a place personally when you already know exactly what is happening.

Rather, knowledge is when at any given moment you know what is right or good. Or at the very least what is appropriate.

When I received the promotion and was moved into the Secretary General's office as chief controller I had to learn to know far more. In such a position, as the head of all State channels, you simply can't be ignorant of anything. You must be able to respond quickly and say what is right or at the very least what is good for the State. Of course, this all varies depending on the particular instance in question and the constantly changing circumstances. So if, say, the given circumstance is the climate, then the instance in question will be that day's weather. Then of course you also have to dress accordingly. If the suit fits, then it is right.

For anyone to talk to me of change would have been pointless. In a new position like this the need for change was natural, because you had to learn to know more. You won't find summer roses blossoming in the snows of January. There's no use floating around in the past relying on your imagination.

I'm no longer in contact with those who saw fit to talk to me of change. In fact, it's for the best. In my new position I certainly couldn't have been seen to take a personal interest in my former friends' business over other people's. I finally removed The Truth Show from channel two and ordered it to be shown once a week on all channels simultaneously. This way programming became far more balanced. Staff at the Secretary General's office thought this a very sensible solution too, because it helped ensure the wide reception of certain important decrees.

Despite this, there were some people who saw fit to criticise me for such rational thinking. I just let them talk and listened patiently. It's a good way to treat your staff; let them vent their anger, then they'll be humble again for a while once they realise that they ought to be ashamed of what they said. And if they are not humble, there are other means.

In difficult situations like this you need to take decisive action, and the situation throughout the State was far from good. The air temperature was cooling because of the clouds of smog and soot particles drifting across the striped sky. The entire energy system had to be reorganised by regulating and rationing consumption and by collecting red hot earth from the reactor area and packing it around heat-retaining units.

So even though everything was getting worse all the time, we had to give the impression that things were in fact improving. This was part of my new job. I had to play the State optimist, even though I was aware of so much.

When I was transferred to the position beneath the Secretary General my workplace moved into the head office building. The Secretary General's offices were on the eleventh floor. At that time my office was four floors lower, on the seventh floor. Even from my window you could see the sky in the north and the north-east, and how the reactor zone was marching closer by the week.

Nothing was done about it and no one seemed to take responsibility for anything. I began to talk about these matters very discreetly amongst a small group of trusted friends. Whenever appropriate, I reminded people that I would remain loyal and faithful to the Secretary General, even though I had no faith whatsoever that he would be able to turn things in the State around.

All these plans were merely talk within small, closed circles, and none of it was meant to get out in any way, but, of course, eventually it did. That very day, when I first heard the rumours of calls for reform amongst the leading factions of the security police and the army, I went up to the Secretary General's office on the eleventh floor and told him of the rumours I had heard, and a little more besides. The Secretary

General looked concerned and, for the very first time in a matter of such importance, he asked my advice.

I had already developed an appropriate proposal. I suggested creating a new, more expansive task force, one with a far greater mandate. If we take the initiative ourselves and place an axe on the table, it'll knock the wind out of the sails of anyone grumbling, I said. The Secretary General then asked me to lead this task force. Naturally I agreed because of the benefits this would bring the State, but I suggested that alongside this new assignment I might also continue as chief controller of the television and broadcasting network. The Secretary General thought this a very sensible idea indeed.

I moved my office up to the tenth floor. From the windows you could see even more clearly the blazing skies, the governmental district and far out across the State.

From the very first days everything became crystal clear to me. A constant flow of issues and decisions made their way up to the head of the task force, and I had great confidence in myself; I knew which direction to steer the State in order to get through the present adverse situation with as few casualties and sacrifices as possible.

I increased inspection and surveillance at every level to ensure that dissent and opposition were not allowed to gain a foothold. In exceptional circumstances such as these, basic rights have to be compromised for the general good. Only once people have accepted this fundamental principle can they become fully integrated members of society, but if they won't accept it they'll be left on the outside, in opposition to everyone else.

All manner of trouble-makers and revolutionaries were moved out of the cities and resettled near or inside the reactor zone. There was plenty of work available measuring pollution and fallout, or in various purification and clearing up operations. And of course much of the workforce was sent to harvest foodstuffs and transport them back to the cities. The fields had died back and the soil left barren after the farmers had gone and the weather had turned cold so suddenly, and so this workforce had to be instructed in how to gather food in new ways, harvesting year-old self-germinated wheat, mushrooms which grew in the cold, potatoes left in the ground, mutated crops and lots of other items people weren't used to gathering or eating – or certainly not for the last hundred years.

Because organising mass food distribution in these changed circumstances required a great deal of work, we had to find a suitable workforce. In a relatively short time, life in the State became much calmer and less crowded, as the worst of the grumblers and doubters and the entire antisocial, undesirable part of society was sent to do useful labour near or inside the reactor zone.

From within my small conversation circles I got rid of anyone I felt I couldn't trust one hundred percent. Several people's careers possibly came to an abrupt end over nothing, but as the head of a task force like this you just can't be too careful. The security forces have to be unified behind you like a bar of pure steel.

At the same time I watched my back and announced new decrees and orders, all formally in the name of the task force, and I was constantly using the State channels and broadcasting network to help me convince people that I alone was behind all these new measures.

My orders were all good. They were firm. People couldn't possibly have been unclear about the fact that things were not going well, but now at least they had the assurance that matters were being dealt with and that people weren't afraid to talk openly and frankly. And once life in the cities began to calm down and the streets became quieter, it was impossible not to notice that something positive was finally happening.

For three weeks I appeared in all news and current affairs programmes on every channel talking about the present situation and defending the new restrictions and orders. I left legislation about all citizens' compulsory security service up to the citizens themselves. In due course an opinion poll was conducted via all channels.

Over 98 percent of people voted for the option Yes: I wish to be involved in protecting the general good.

When I was named the new Secretary General the following week, by this point it was nothing but a formality. The former Secretary General had been on negotiations abroad and had decided to stay there. I transferred a suitable amount of money to cover his pension and sent him one of the embassy staff, whose job was not only to help him write his memoirs but to ensure that no potentially damaging claims or columns about the State of K began spreading through our neighbouring countries.

The very day I became Secretary General I gave a speech to the citizens on all channels. The speech features in my history book too, or rather the most important parts can be found in the supplementary material. After all, I couldn't very well censor myself out of the Chronicles of K altogether.

'Almighty God, who art in Heaven, give this nation the strength to bear its suffering, give the fully integrated members of the State of K the courage to endure this strife, give us a common will and an unselfish mind. Let us find strength in unity, though ordeals be sent to test us. God of Heaven and Earth, give me the strength to lead this State through the trials and tribulations beyond our control set upon our path.'

This is how I began my first speech as Secretary General. I had isolated two ways in which I could establish my power quickly and effectively. It was important to speak directly to the citizens and to focus on strengthening morale.

There is no nation as weak as one which is empty within. As Secretary General I wished to impose meaning on people's lives.

I decided to give religion an important role in leading the State. Both cults and the church were given more air time, but their message was unified. Preachers had speeches written for them at the Secretary General's office. A few of the cults didn't accept this as the only sensible method of ensuring the general good of the State, but they were eventually banned, their preachers prosecuted or exiled without charge, and members of their congregations separated from one another in small communities in the north, far away from the cities.

I gave the security organisations increased powers of

authority, though naturally I still had a perfectly realistic idea of their work. Their job within society is not to protect, it is to guard. Plucking out weeds, that's how I defined the job of the investigative police, whilst giving new orders about the role of the security services in these changing circumstances.

Whenever a new law or a regulation was qualified with the phrase 'changing circumstances', it was like trying to float in a rocky waterfall. There was already chaos everywhere, and I was in the middle of it all. The striped horizon was blazing furiously day and night. All State information was brought up to the Secretary General's office, but from the eleventh floor windows you could see just as well and just as clearly that the horizon was ablaze. Every week the north-east and the north edged their way closer. You didn't need statistics filtered through numerous different bureaus to tell you that. From such a height you could see that, behind the stained sun, a chill was marching forward; deep frost and a white aridity.

It was sent by God to rape the earth. That was the message a prophet of the Ash Cross cult tried to spread as a broadcasting preacher. I was forced to do something about it because no one else would. There's no need to frighten people like that. For humility to flourish there need only be an appropriate level of fear. If there's too much, what will flourish instead is anger and repression. Anger is difficult to control. It's like boiling earth, a quagmire. A society built upon anger cannot make any moves. Anger has to be dealt with early enough in order to channel it properly. It can be used effectively, but it has to be kept at a manageable level, dominated by fear.

The eleventh floor is over thirty metres from the ground. From up there everyday things on the ground look very small. Unity Square down below would sometimes fill with swarms of people – despite the fact that this was supposed to be one of the most closely guarded government districts in the State – but from a height of thirty metres it makes no difference whether there are a hundred people down there or a thousand.

Often I would draw a chair up to the corner of the large windows and gaze out, down into the square at support rallies organised by the army and the investigative police or out to the north-east and the striped, glowing sky, which by now had spread and already engulfed both the north and all of the east.

If people aren't willing to see, they won't see anything. In a new place everything looks perfectly clear at first. You know exactly what has to be done. Then your eyes grow accustomed and your mind goes numb. You're at once awake and asleep, and whilst you're awake you're making sure that no one disturbs you whilst you're asleep.

If I made a mistake, then it was this. When you no longer have the will to see, then you certainly won't see a thing. There's no mention of this mistake in my history book, or anything else about the final stages of my reign, for that matter.

I'm not a saint, and I'm not stupid. Omitting things isn't lying. I have no reason to lie. I've never had a reason to lie, neither in the State in K nor here. But then again, who would be mad enough to nail themselves up for nothing?

Someone so much bigger than man can't hide his handiwork, Father would say when things happened that were almost beyond his control. Or was it that some things are bigger than you and me?

Every April without fail the stream would flood the garden and my sister and I would try to row across the yard. She was so light that she could row a plastic sledge all the way to the flagpole at the other end of the garden, but it took a couple of planks and some styrofoam to carry me. The water was a grey colour from the clay in the garden and shone, it was like a mirror in which you could see your face and behind that the great clouds in the sky.

I don't suppose I would ever have gone to the zone to report on events if Eeva and Aspi hadn't been settled there. Young couples were asked to go there to farm the wasteland in between the reactors, so-called Pure Food Farms were established more to help create a positive image than because they reaped any great economic benefits. That was over twenty years ago now. Eeva and Aspi's two daughters were born there.

I first went there to do a report on farming, then after the reactors had been destroyed I volunteered to go back and report on the news. Eeva and Aspi's younger daughter Taira had died. No one who had been living in the zone was allowed across the border back into the State. I would go and visit Eeva, Aspi and Ireina whenever I was up there reporting, and take them food and money. This could have got me into a lot of trouble, as any form of contact with the zone was forbidden, but I still visited and took them money every now and then.

Aspi was employed as a dirt transporter when hot earth began being moved from the reactors to the areas surrounding the heat-retaining units. By replenishing the hot soil, energy could be transferred to other areas of the State. Aspi was put to work with others who had lived in the zone and those sent across from prisons. Transporting dirt required a large workforce: work was conducted in three shifts a day, seven days a week.

Eeva joined the Ash Crosses and on the command of some prophet cremated all those who had died in the reactor explosions, dug up those already buried and burnt them, committing their bodies to fire and air.

I can't be held responsible for what happened to Eeva and Aspi's family. How could anyone have helped them when even keeping in contact was forbidden and strictly controlled? Of course, reporters are even more closely guarded than others, and once I took on a more powerful position I could hardly be seen to favour my own relatives. The law is the same for everyone, and I couldn't be responsible for bringing a shadow like that upon the Secretary General's office, let alone upon myself.

You can't do everything you want. People who had lived in the zone were simply not granted permission to leave, it was nothing to do with me, it was a question of general order and security. Eeva and Aspi didn't understand anything beyond themselves and with their constant letters and requests they put me in a very awkward position. As if it was all my fault, or as if I alone could have decided their fate. In fact, this couldn't have been further from the truth.

After the devastation, the zone wouldn't even have existed for the rest of the State without me and The Truth Show. There would have been nothing but emptiness. The wind would have howled behind the border, but there would have been no one there; there are never people on the other side, just disturbance and problems. As long as people continue talking about something, at least it exists. But when people don't talk about it, the wind just howls and the north-eastern sky is aglow day and night with aurora borealis, and even that is explained away as protuberances of the sun, and the power cuts and the lack of heating are what they are: nothing but terrorism or the work of the enemy. Without State publicity the north-eastern zone would have disappeared altogether.

I didn't allow the zone to be forgotten. Something removed from the mind doesn't exist. In my reports I etched out an image of the zone so many times that it stayed put. Without The Truth Show the people living in the zone would have had nothing. There was no point in Eeva and Aspi sending me their letters, first to me personally, then to the channel and finally to the Secretary General's office when I was promoted; keeping such contact caused me a lot of trouble.

When I first visited the zone everything was well and good. Eeva and Aspi were farming their land, Taira and Ireina were little. I was filming my report and interviewing people. At night you could see a glow burning in the sky above the reactor silos, like seven bright moons in a line.

Once the silos' several metre thick outer walls had collapsed in the explosions, the reactors became little suns. The protective structures around the silos fell to pieces and the ceramic mass melted. Everything in the vicinity was burnt to a crisp and the light could be seen for hundreds of kilometres, filtered into radiant beams. When the light had gone, all that was left was the heat. When the heat began to disperse, the sky was left striped with soot and smog. Light is colder when there are parts of it missing. Under this constant shadow the zone was plunged into a grey twilight, which at first was contained and limited to the zone itself, but then began to spread its chill to the rest of the State. First the weather changed, then the climate. From my panoramic windows at the Secretary General's office I had to acknowledge it as it moved closer week by week. There was nothing anyone could do about something like that advancing.

In The History of K, I included an extract from the prophecy of the Ash Crosses, because after all these years it seemed to encapsulate something very true about those times.

'And the sky disappeared, like a parchment rolled up, and all the mountains and the islands and the plains were uprooted and moved towards the north, from which night was cast upon the earth; from which the rapist of the earth arises, sent by God. The end of ends is nearer than near, no verdant plants shall grow on earth, bushes shall stand barren, fruit shall fall to the ground unripe, the ground shall be covered with hoar frost, frost shall be covered with ice, ice shall be covered with snow.'

Back then these words spread a message of fear, and there was no need to increase fear throughout the State. There need only be appropriate level of fear, then humility will flourish. If there is too much, there is only paralysis or anger and cornered rage. These are dangerous matters – all anger and activity must be turned as swiftly as possible against either the external or the internal enemy, thus reaping benefit from them too. All tumult which reigns within the human soul can be used to govern.

I was good as Secretary General, skilled, but at a time like that nothing is quite sufficient. A cold era had arrived. The sun was striped with sheets of radiation and soot belching from the collapsed reactors and could no longer warm us.

Like a crooked Venetian blind it covered the State halfway across the sky, from the horizon up at a forty-five degree angle. Hundreds of thousands of square kilometres had been caught in a dry, snowless winter, and every month when I received new readings and results, winter had indeed come closer. Statistics no longer spoke of winter but of winters at varying definable stages. The coldest was the dead zone at the middle of winter, on either side of this were autumnal winters and before them vernal winters or dead summers; month by month they approached like a great beast.

As Secretary General I ought to have been able to prevent such a thing from advancing, but nobody had that kind of power – no amount of knowledge or technology can regulate the weather or the climate. Nobody mentioned the A.C. Hahl Mountains any more, raised to protect the State; in fact, they had been deleted from most newer maps.

Even despite the fact that all State information right down to the thoughts of our citizens was brought up to my office carefully collected and screened, I still couldn't prevent it. I couldn't make out the whole, just disconnected pieces, like sailing through rocky rapids, all you can see is what you can make out through the spray and the boulders as you rush forward headlong.

One of my mistakes was that I became too caught up with the details, when what I should have done was simply concentrate and try simply to see. I didn't trust other people, after the first few months I no longer trusted anyone at all, and so I tried to make as many decisions as possible myself, and it was this which eventually ruined what was left of my ability to see. Those who opposed me were isolated from society, unity was the priority – my priority, everybody's common priority. Thus unified, the State was to grow to a new level of greatness, until it was true to its name, the State of K, but by then it had already outgrown itself. A cancer had grown within it, born of itself, fanning its own flames.

I restructured the voluntary security service organisations, as both around me and directly below me I needed easily manoeuverable forces. There's nothing on my conscience about what happened back then. If unity is the democratically accepted goal of the majority, then it is everyone's common aim. There is no acceptible justification for working against the State.

Those who opposed this were convicted of treason. I wasn't the one who made these decisions, but I did give the State courts clear instructions. Anyone even remotely suspect was interrogated, because interrogation is by far the most effective method of speedily banishing inappropriate thoughts from the mind.

The office research department kept a close eye on changes in public opinion and in people's reactions. Very often I gave speeches on all channels directly to the people. I had to try and convince our citizens that perhaps this cold era would never come, or that it would never reach us, or that it would be so far in the future – and not during our lifetimes – that we would never have to prepare ourselves for all those winters. Autumns would not become winters, but every year winter would blossom into spring and June would not be merely the beginning of the dead summer.

My position required me to speak with an air of hope: that everything would change for the better as long as the State had the strength of character necessary and remained unified. Given the situation I either had to increase trust and faith amongst the people or frighten and threaten them with the internal or the external enemy. This was my job, but no matter how much fear or hope the leaders of a mighty State can compress into their words, no matter how much they tell people to turn a blind eye, they can never purge the mind of every single citizen. Of course I knew that the State would never become a single pure block of steel, not even if you melt it down and forge it again, for inside there will always be unmelted grains of sand and grit.

People swimming through those rapids haven't made the river flow. There's nothing on my conscience about what happened back then, because all power had to be concentrated on what was good for the State. No one can prevent the future from coming. I tried hard, but my time in the rapids was wearing thin.

When I began to uncover conspiracies and resistance, at first I tried to deal with it gently. The final six months alone were a very dark time indeed. The security service organisations were faithful to the last and I had to use them like a stone in my hand.

At first you try to swim, just swim, then you try to stay afloat and dodge the rocks. Then you stop caring. If you took a knock, then so be it. In a tight spot people always have to cut their losses. Ultimately all you can do is look out for yourself.

There's nothing on my conscience whatsoever about what happened back then. Things simply happened the way they did. Of course there were some small matters I could have dealt with differently. When it was time to leave, I moved to the nearest neighbouring country. Here I have never had to lie or deny my name.

Here I can live in peace. No one comes up nosily asking who I am. Here I am nameless. Or rather, not nameless, but the nameless person who wrote The History of K. That is my name here and the previous one I have given up.

# *A Zoo from the Heavens*

Pasi Jääskeläinen

*Pasi Jääskeläinen (born 1966) has three times been awarded the Atorox Prize for the best science fiction or fantasy short story of the year and has won a number of prizes for his writings in different genres. One of the principal characteristics of his writing is the exploration of children's worlds and his ability to fuse together the everyday and the fantastical in an elegant, almost imperceptible way. In 2000 Jääskeläinen published the collection of short fiction* Missä junat kääntyvät *('Where the Trains Turn'), which was awarded a prize by Star Rover magazine for the year's best work of Finnish science fiction. The present text 'A Zoo from the Heavens' is from this collection.*

Marmot's father has never been a particularly talkative father, at least he never is in front of Marmot. Indeed, there is a very good reason for this: there is a peculiar problem with his father's mouth. Marmot once heard his mother telling Aunt Violet that Father finds it very hard to talk about painful subjects, or about anything at all, in fact, and that to get him to express an opinion about something you have to pull the words out of his mouth with tongs.

Because Father is so quiet, it's easy to forget he is there at all. Rather like an old leather armchair. He often looks like he is sleeping or daydreaming, even though his eyes could hardly be more open and his body is doing all sorts of things: flicking through the newspaper at the breakfast table, sitting on the sofa playing with the television remote control, rolling cigarettes or repairing the car engine.

Marmot's father is very good indeed at repairing engines.

He says he enjoys tinkering with them because at least you can understand machines, and even when there is something wrong with them, fixing them and putting them back together again is relatively simple.

Father never ever reads books. Whenever Marmot asks him to read him a story, *The Moomins* or *Paddington Bear*, Father closes his eyes and shivers as if an invisible flurry of snow has blown through him, shakes his head and says that reading books is far too nerve-wracking.

Marmot will sometimes go up to his father when he's like this, at once awake and asleep, and say something to him. Father will turn around and stare at him silently and strangely, and for a moment Marmot will feel as if this is not Father at all, but someone else, Father's double. And that double is very cheerless and frightening, almost nothing but a shell, hollow and hardened, just like those horrid stuffed animals hunched in the museum, and this is why Marmot doesn't often like disturbing him when he is dreaming with his eyes open.

Father has always been a very quiet father indeed, but for some reason over the last few days he has been chatting to Marmot far more than usual, in fact probably more than every time before put together. This may be because they have come out to the country to the house where Father grew up. Or maybe his mouth is getting better at last.

It is a warm afternoon and Marmot and his father have been sitting in the sun on the steps outside Grandma's old house, when Father suddenly starts talking again, telling Marmot what it used to be like a long time ago when he was a little boy. This feels very strange to Marmot, as he is not at all used to the sound of his father's voice. It sounds rather hoarse, as if he had a sore throat, and a bit gruff, the way fathers' voices often sound, but not nearly as gruff as Father Christmas.

Marmot hesitantly asks Father when exactly he was a little boy – the thought seems very odd and to be honest Marmot slightly suspects Father may be pulling his leg.

Father says that, at a rough estimate, it is about three thousand years and five long days since he was a little boy. Marmot thinks that sounds about right, in three thousand years all sorts of things can happen.

As a child Father lived here at Warren's End in this very same white house which Marmot knows as Grandma's and where he and his mother and father have been for the last three days. Grandma isn't here any longer though, because last year she got that thing called 'death' that most old people get.

When a person has 'death' they split into two parts: the body and the soul. Then their body stops working and they look as if they are sleeping, not moving a muscle and holding their breath, except that once the soul has left the body you can't wake them up any more, no matter how hard you try.

After 'death' the empty body is placed in a very narrow bed with a lid which is then carried up to the church in Warren's End and lowered into a deep hole called a 'grave'. Then people throw lots of flowers into the hole. This is all so that no one will try to wake up the empty body, which might very well happen if it was left sleeping in a normal bed.

Once freed from the body the soul then flies up to heaven where Marmot's Grandpa and a man called Jesus are waiting for it.

(All this was revealed to Marmot by a minister who performed at Grandma's funeral; he also assured Marmot that even though it was very windy on the day of the funeral, Grandma's soul was in no danger of being blown off course and ending up in Warren's Marsh or Portugal or the big ferris wheel at the amusement park instead of heaven and that Jesus man.)

Marmot remembered all this very well, the minister's explanations, the death and the funeral, but still he was half expecting Grandma to be waiting for them when they arrived at the house; fretting, straightening out her dress with the flower patterns and a bag of peppermints in the pocket, the way she had always been.

With a very serious expression on his face Father begins to tell Marmot that when he was a little boy (three thousand years ago) the men in the Soviet Union and the men in Finland became very angry with each other and went to war.

Like all the other fathers, Marmot's father's father had been sent to war too.

The rules of war go something like this: the men are all given rifles and cannons and ordered to shoot one another. If they want they can also throw little bombs at each other. Some of them fly up in aeroplanes and drop bigger bombs on the houses and the people down below, smashing their houses to smithereens and starting fires and blowing off people's arms and legs if they got in the way (and of course the tails and floppy ears of any dogs that happened to be there too, Father explains, confirming Marmot's worst fears).

Wars can last for a very long time, for many years even, and for all that time the men have to live in dugouts in the forest and eat rations. And sometimes one of the men would be shot by a rifle or a cannon or hit by a bomb and his body would be broken so that his soul would leave the body and fly off to heaven.

Still, sometimes only a part of their bodies would be lost, a hand or a leg or an eye, and this often meant that their soul would still be attached to their bodies. After that the man would be able to come home, after he'd been to the hospital where he would be given a glass eye or a wooden leg and a pair of crutches and any sleeves or trouser legs left dangling loose would be snipped off.

The war carries on until everyone has been shot or until the leader of one of the sides gets bored and orders his side to stop shooting so that everyone can go home and do something else for a change. No one ever managed to shoot Grandpa though, so when the war finished he was allowed to come home to Grandma and Marmot's father.

Marmot says that Father must have been very glad when Grandpa finally came home in one piece, still with all his hands and legs and eyes and his soul still firmly inside his body.

Father nods, but at the same time he looks as if he is thinking about something else entirely. Then he says: 'It just so happened that he wasn't the same when he came back from the war. You could say that, although his body was still in one piece, something was still out of order.'

Marmot asks how this is possible and his father explains: 'You see, at war all the men have to be very angry at the men from the other country, so they can aim their rifles at each other better. At the same time they have to be on their guard so they can dodge all the bullets and cannon balls and bombs fired at them. And so when someone has been angry and on their guard like that for so long, they sometimes don't know how to stop being angry and on their guard.' (This is the same as pulling a face: if you keep your face screwed up for even a second too long it won't straighten out again without very complicated surgery.)

And this is precisely what happened to Father's father. When he came home he was still angry and constantly on his guard, even though he didn't have to shoot at the Soviet men any more or dodge the bullets flying around in the air. He would try to smile but nothing ever came of it because he was so angry that even a smile looked like a grimace. He tried to sleep but he was too nervous to drift off. He didn't like having to be with women and children either, because at war he was used to spending time solely in the company of other angry men.

And so after coming home Marmot's father's father began to spend more and more time alone in his workroom, and his wife and little son were expressly forbidden from ever going in there.

A little worried, Marmot asks his father if someone could start a war now where all the fathers would have to take part.

Father says he doesn't think it is very likely nowadays, especially not in their part of Europe. According to him, times were very different back then.

'How were things different?' asks Marmot.

'Well, you've seen old films and photographs, haven't you? You've probably noticed how the world wasn't very colourful back then. All those colourless landscapes made people very unhappy and that caused a lot of terrible things to happen like the years of oppression, revolutions and wars. Nowadays only very remote places are still black and white and there are very few of them left. You might find the odd colourless little nook or cranny over by Warren's Marsh if you look very carefully. And of course in those days people used to move faster and more jerkily than they do now, and this was one of the reasons there were so many wars, because people couldn't stand looking at each other for very long at all.'

Marmot's father carries on explaining how people's jerky movements were probably the result of a different diet. Back then no one had invented vitamins or even bananas. So because there wasn't enough normal food people often ate tree bark and lingonberries (which of course were more grey than red, and this made them very hard to find on the forest floor) and they made coffee from dandelions.

'So how did they make hot chocolate?' asks Marmot in bewilderment.

His father thinks for a moment. 'Generally by boiling potato peelings, or sometimes from dried beetroot. Of course, there was no sugar back then, so the hot chocolate was very bitter, but it wasn't all that bad once you got used to the taste.'

Marmot thinks this over for a moment then returns to Grandpa's homecoming. 'So what was Grandpa doing all alone in his workroom?'

'I wondered about that myself. Sometimes you could hear muttering and swearing coming from inside, so I decided he must have been concentrating on being angry. I would have gone in to see him, but the door was always locked. Grandma wasn't allowed in there either, though sometimes she would knock on the door and try to coax Grandpa to open up. And that door was as dark and thick and heavy as midnight in December. It was so thick and strong that the knocking never reached the other side. And so I finally gave up and decided to let him hide there in his workroom and forget all about him and get on with my own chores.

'I would help Grandma with the housework, I collected water from the well and logs from the woodshed and took out the dish-water, and during that time Grandma taught me to read. Sometimes Grandpa would come out of his workroom, but I would pretend I hadn't seen him. He didn't want people to see him either. I tried not to think about him and I tried to be happy, even though Grandpa couldn't smile any more; after all, I was a child and children are supposed to be happy. Nowadays there's even a law about it, or at least a parliamentary act, from 1962 if I remember correctly, but even back then people generally agreed that children should always be happy. But how should I put it – it's hard to be a carefree little butterfly when the saddest elephant in the world is sitting nearby.'

Marmot is astonished. 'An elephant? In your garden?'

Father looks at Marmot for a long time.

They are still sitting on the steps. A cigarette is burning away in Father's fingers; invisible insects hover, poking inquisitively at the thin trail of smoke rising up to the sky. A pair of dragonflies buzzes low across the garden as if they are looking for something in the grass. They dart out from behind the sauna towards the garden swing, then onwards circling through the currant bushes to the drinking water pump. (That morning, when they had gone to collect water for the coffee, Father had allowed Marmot to operate the green iron pump by himself.)

Through the sun-spotted foliage in the forest the frantic twittering of birds comes rolling in towards the house – a swell of sounds, whistling, chattering, squawking, warbling and chirping, almost drowning out the gallant buzzing of the crickets in the garden. Marmot rubs his eyebrows and strives to imagine a great grey elephant walking through the spruce trees and into the garden, its tusks outstretched and its trunk swaying lazily from side to side. Was Father really talking about a real elephant?

'What did you say?' asks Father, dazed, as if he has just woken up. His face brightens and he chuckles and shakes his head and slips back into that state of sleeping awake that means it's not a good idea to disturb him.

Listening to his father's stories, Marmot has always imagined that these ancient events happened far, far away, in another country even. But now in a flash it dawns on him that things took place in this very house, on these same steps – and here they are now, sitting in peace.

Marmot leaves his father and runs round the house excitedly to take a look at the thick, heavy door of Grandpa's workroom, something he realises he has never paid any attention to before.

But to his great disappointment he sees that instead of the old thick door that Father has been talking about there is a flimsy, modern door, which is not black in the slightest but white, and all in all very plain and boring. He recalls that Grandpa's workroom has not even been a workroom for a long time; now it is only a dusty old storage room full of cardboard boxes and newspapers and stuffy old clothes. Grandma put things in there when she still lived here, as she couldn't take them up the stairs to the attic because of her bad legs. In fact Marmot often helped her carry heavy things into the workroom and not once had he thought of the tiny little room as in any way special or noteworthy.

Father shuffles behind Marmot into the workroom. Marmot asks him pointedly why the door has been changed.

Father still looks like he is half asleep, his eyes glancing up and down the room. 'We had to break down the old door with an axe,' he says in a strange voice.

'Why?'

'Grandpa brought a Russian pistol with him when he came back from the war and he kept it in his workroom. He showed it to me once and told me to keep well away from the pistol and the workroom so that nothing terrible would happen.

'I smelt the pistol, it gave off the iron smell of war, it went in through my nostrils and lingered heavy in my sinuses. I hated that pistol and decided not to think about it, to forget it existed. And so for a long time I shut the pistol and Grandpa and his constant anger and nervousness out of my mind, just like he had shut me and Grandma on the other side of the workroom door.

'But one winter's day, when Grandma had gone to the doctor's about her sore hand and I was sitting in the kitchen reading Runeberg's *The Tales of Ensign Ståhl*, I heard a loud bang from the workroom. And that's when I remembered Grandpa and the pistol that smelt of war. I ran out here, stood behind the locked door and started battering it with my fists and shouting for Grandpa so much that my throat hurt.

'But now there wasn't a sound from the workroom, and that same smell was hanging in the air, the smell of hunters who have just shot an elk or a hare. And I smelt the smell of that pistol and I knew that something terrible had happened after all.

'Shouting at the top of my lungs I ran to the woodshed to fetch an axe and started breaking down the door. I wasn't very old, in fact I wasn't much older that you, and I was scrawny and had thin little hands, and normally I wouldn't even have been able to lift the axe, but I battered that door with a terrible strength and force. Splinters of wood flew from the door until finally it gave way and I knocked a hole in the middle, I threw the axe to one side and looked inside and there I saw . . .'

Father blinks and seems to notice Marmot's presence again. For a moment Marmot has the silly feeling that he has been caught eavesdropping.

'So what did you see?' Marmot demands to know, whilst at the same time dreading the answer.

Father looks pale and tired and a little frightened.

Everything is perfectly still, like in winter after a heavy snowfall when nothing moves. Marmot realises that now is not the right time to chivvy Father along, but finally plucks up the courage to ask him whether the sad elephant in the garden might possibly have had something to do with it.

Father takes a deep breath, nods his head and says yes, yes, the elephant had rather a lot to do with it. He sits down on Grandma's old sofa, one of those old-fashioned ones that looks like it's made of pug skin, with curved sides like the thighs of an animal that can run very fast. He thinks for a moment and then begins to tell Marmot the story of the zoo that fell from the heavens.

After the war things were a bit topsy-turvy, Father explains, and it so happened that one day an enormous Soviet cargo plane came crashing out of the sky and landed right next to Grandpa's house.

The plane's mission was to carry a large collection of animals from a Soviet zoo to some other destination. No one knew for sure where exactly it had come from or where it was going or, indeed, why those animals had been herded on to the plane in the first place. In any case it somehow strayed from its course and one Sunday afternoon, a few weeks after the war had ended and the men had started returning to their homes, the plane appeared in the sky above the forest and plummeted to the ground with smoke billowing out of its choking engines.

The plane most probably landed on the enormous swamp at Warren's Marsh, several dozen kilometres from Grandma's house, right in the middle of the tangled woodlands of Warren's Wood, a forest so thick that to this day no path has been cleared through it. If the pilot had survived he must have escaped through the forest and found his way home, because nobody ever reported seeing him. (However he most probably died in the crash and sank with the plane deep into the swamp – the aircraft was never found either, though some people did go and look for it after the first snowfall that year.)

As if by a miracle some of the animals had survived the crash and managed to make their way out of the plane in time. Most of them soon disappeared and went their separate ways. But some of them wandered the area for a while trying to get their bearings; some ended up very close to Marmot's father's childhood home and sometimes, he says, you could even catch a glimpse of them from the garden.

'It must have been a big story in the newspapers,' says Marmot, but Father shakes his head.

'On the contrary. The authorities covered up the whole incident. They claimed that there had never been an aircraft carrying animals, and so no one was allowed to write about it in the papers. You see, whenever something strange like that happens, it's the authorities' job to tell everyone that it's just a rumour or a simple misunderstanding. And of course back then it was perfectly understandable: the war had just finished and the political situation was very strained, because a lot of people were still very angry.'

'Grandpa was angry too. And then the elephant appeared in the garden,' Marmot sighed in amazement.

'The greyest, largest, saddest elephant in the world,' says Father. 'It was such a sorry sight. You could tell straight away that it had lost something very important.

'Perhaps it had lost its wife and child in the crash. Or perhaps it was sad because it really didn't have a home any more. Imagine: elephants belong in Africa, but because this one was probably born in a Soviet zoo it had never even visited its homeland and didn't know how to be an African elephant properly. And it was only in the Soviet zoo because it had never had any other choice.

'It certainly didn't feel at home round our way. Autumn was getting colder day by day and the African elephant probably caught a chill as the temperature reached zero. Maybe in the aeroplane it thought it was finally on its way home, wherever that happened to be, but instead its journey came to an end here in our barren lands. The elephant must have been terribly disappointed. And there was nothing else it could do but stand at the edge of the forest, its grey hide soaking in the grey autumn rain, and its mournful eyes would stare at our white house.

'Perhaps it was comforted by the presence of other living creatures. Nobody dared shoo it away, because sad or not it was still an enormous, frightening animal, and when they get angry elephants can do a lot of damage.'

Marmot takes a breath, spellbound. 'And the big grey elephant was staring at your house!'

His father fidgets nervously with his trousers. 'For many days and nights it stood there looking at us. You couldn't see it all the time, but I knew it was there somewhere.

'After a time I found I could no longer enjoy life because of that elephant. It was as if I had become ill and would not recover, even though Grandma would make me beetroot hot chocolate and bake an entire batch of bark cakes just for me. I felt so sorry for the elephant that my stomach hurt. I kept thinking what I could do to help it, but I was so small and it was so big that there was nothing I could have done. All

I could do was watch it suffer, and let me tell you, of all the animals in the world none of them suffers quite like an elephant.

'Did you know that the word 'suffering' comes originally from the African word for an elephant's trunk? Some missionaries began using the word at the end of the last century, when they saw an elephant that had lost its son; its trunk was drooping in grief. No one can remember what the word for 'suffering' was before that. Well, at night I used to hear the elephant plodding back and forth across the lawn, and how sad it looked as it dragged its legs along like great pillars. Thump, thump, thump, scuff. You can't understand it unless you've heard it for yourself.'

'Poor elephant! What about the other animals in the aeroplane? Did you see them too?'

'Once, one autumn day when it was far warmer than usual, a flock of weird and wonderful birds flew overhead; they were clearly from a far off, exotic land. Another reason I remember that day is because Grandpa came out of his workroom whilst Grandma and I were having breakfast. He drank a cup of dandelion coffee and said how nice it was and patted me on the head, something he hadn't done for years. I was so surprised that I couldn't finish my porridge and instead ran out into the garden.

'And that's when I saw the birds. One of them had a very big beak indeed, I think it was a toucan. And there were parrots too, and then I saw one of those birds with long pink legs flashing past. But the very next night there came a frost and after that we never saw them again. They probably never survived the cold weather.'

'I know! The pink bird must have been a flamingo!' Marmot shouts out in excitement, whilst at the same time feeling a great sense of sorrow at the birds' tragic death in the freezing cold. Father agrees on the flamingosity of the pink bird and continues his story, this time in a far more serious tone. 'Of course there were other strange creatures in the forest too, but for the most part they remained well hidden. Shortly after the arrival of the elephant a large predator appeared. It was probably a lion. I never actually saw it, but I could sense its presence. It was there, pacing around our house, enraged by the cold autumn rain. Did you know we used to have a dog back then, a hunting dog called Mannerheim. After the beast arrived, the dog chewed its way through its leash and ran away and we never saw it again.

'Perhaps the animals from the zoo ate it. The heavy odour of a large, wet wild cat hung in the air, and so did the threat of that great predator. The elephant had made me very sad indeed, but the knowledge that the beast was so close frightened me so much that I couldn't concentrate on a thing. You could say I was on my guard, a bit like Grandpa, and that in itself is quite tiring.'

Marmot gives his father a puzzled look. 'But couldn't Grandpa have shot the lion with his pistol?' he asks.

Father stares at his shoes and frowns. 'I suppose so, but he never came out of his workroom, and I don't think he even knew about the zoo animals at that point, I don't suppose anyone had told him about the plane crash. Even Grandma didn't do anything about it, though I knew she had noticed the animals too. She went from day to day pretending they weren't there; she must have imagined that this would make them go away. But I could still see that she was just as frightened and worried about them as I was.

'All I could do was wait for something terrible to happen and finally something did happen, as always when you wait so intensely for something awful like that. One cold, rainy night the lion came into the house and attacked Grandma.'

Marmot takes a loud gasp. Father looks at him and for a moment he too looks like a frightened little boy, not at all like a grown man. Marmot starts to shiver, even though the hot and humid weather has finally made its way into the room, like a bygone age clinging fast to the old furniture.

'The lion came in *here*? Into this house, your house?' Marmot asks in a faint voice.

'That's right. It must have been too hungry and cold and angry to wait out in the forest any longer. Back then I used to sleep in the attic. I thought it was the safest place in the house, even though it could get quite chilly sometimes and there was a wasps' nest in the far corner. Grandma used to sleep on the bed in the kitchen and Grandpa slept out in his workroom, though I don't know whether he actually ever slept a wink after returning from the war. Anyway, one night I awoke to a terrible noise, it was November, if I remember correctly. Loud banging could be heard coming from downstairs, things falling over, doors slamming and Grandma screaming, the whole house was shaking as the lion snarled and bellowed and roared. At once I realised that the beast from the forest was now inside the house.'

Marmot gives a small, terrified peep. 'Of course I wanted to go and help Grandma, but I simply couldn't move – a weakling like me wouldn't have been much use against the lion, it would have gobbled me up like a potato chip.

'Finally, when it seemed like the noise would never stop, everything went very quiet and little by little I began to feel my cold legs again. Shivering, I tiptoed downstairs. The kitchen had been turned upside down. Things thrown all over the place, the curtains had been torn down, chairs smashed to pieces, and in the middle of all this devastation was Grandma lying on the floor crying.

'The lion had ripped her clothes to shreds and mauled her badly. She was still alive, which made me very happy, though I was somewhat surprised – I had been convinced that the lion would eat her. Of course, all this time Grandpa had been in his workroom. He seemed to be blissfully unaware that a lion from a Soviet zoo had just sneaked into his house and tried to eat his wife.

'I wanted to go and fetch him – after all, the lion attack was quite an exceptional situation, something which I felt required his presence too, but Grandma screamed and grabbed hold of my leg and told me not to disturb him under any circumstances.

'And then I understood why: Grandpa was already very angry and on his guard, and if he had to be on his guard because of the lion and all the other animals which had escaped from the wreck of the plane, his condition would get worse and worse and he would never be able to work again and we would all end up begging.

'I was ashamed of how thoughtless I had been – I had almost condemned us all to ruin. And so to preserve Grandpa's peace of mind we never spoke about it again. Except once, some time afterwards, when I tried to ask Grandma what the lion had looked like and how she had managed to drive it out of the house, but Grandma got very angry and told me to be quiet – what's done is done, she said, there's no need to go on about it.'

Marmot is quietly fidgeting. 'So had the lion left for good?' he asks gravely.

Father shakes his head. 'I'm afraid not. It couldn't bring itself to leave us alone. All the time I could still feel its presence close by. Sometimes it would disappear for a few days at a time and I would hope that it had finally gone or frozen stiff in the forest, but it would always come back to stalk us. It was always careful to stay hidden, but sometimes the wind would carry its scent into the garden. It was there somewhere, pacing round the house watching us.

'It was waiting, just like the elephant. By now the cold weather had killed or driven away all the other animals that had survived the crash, but the lion and the elephant were tough. They stayed put, even though winter was well on its way. The elephant longed for our company just as the lion craved our flesh – their motives were that simple.

'And then came the night when the lion tried to eat *me*. It was too cold at night now to sleep in the attic so I had started sleeping in the kitchen next to Grandma. And imagine: in the middle of the night I awoke to a heavy odour, to the lion's strong, fusty breath, which went in through my nostrils, filled my lungs and my head and almost choked me.

'When I opened my eyes, there it was. It was very dark and I couldn't really see anything, but it was there, no doubt about it, the same lion that had been circling the house. Its eyes were glowing menacingly through the dark and little by little I could make out its shape: its dirty mane and its damp muzzle, every last piece of the enormous, long-suffering creature. It was standing right next to me, its yellow eyes watching me, as if it were wondering which bit of me might taste the nicest. There was a low, thunderous rumbling sound coming from its stomach. And its breath smelt so bad that all at once I was about to throw up and faint, and I knew it had come to get me, to tear me to pieces and kill me and gobble me up.

'I decided to lie perfectly still and pretend to be asleep. I remember thinking like a coward that if I lay still enough it might eat *Grandma* instead and leave *me* in peace.

'Then suddenly there came a piercing scream. I don't know whether it was me or Grandma who screamed, but the lion began to roar so loudly that the plates shook in the cupboard and I wet myself, and then it leapt up on to the bed and the bed creaked so much I thought it would collapse under the weight of the beast, and then, before I even had time to be afraid, it hit me round the head with its great big paw.

'Even though it was dark I could see bright lights and red, black and green spots and all the noise sounded as if it was coming from far away and I could feel myself being dragged somewhere dark and wet. I remember faintly thinking that now it had finally happened: I was dead and the lion was dragging my lifeless body into the forest to eat it.'

Father looks at Marmot and suddenly realises how pale the boy has turned. 'You're not afraid, are you?' he says somewhat taken aback. 'You know the lion didn't kill me or gobble me up – here I am!'

'I know,' mumbles Marmot, though he does not seem at all convinced; he finds it difficult to believe that the boy in the story could have survived a situation as desperate as being trapped in the lion's jaws. 'You mean the lion didn't eat you after all? What happened?'

'When I finally came to, it was already light. It was day. I realised I was in bed. My face hurt and when Grandma brought me a mirror I saw that it was all bruised and swollen. Still, I was pretty much alive. When I asked her about the lion, she wiped my face with a cool cloth and said that there had never been any lion and that everything was all right, everything would be fine and I would never have to worry again.

'Then I asked her about Grandpa. Grandma said that he was in his workroom, but that she had told him all about what had happened, and he had been very stern indeed and promised that something like this would never happen again. I asked her whether the lion had gone for good and she stroked my forehead and told me once again that there was nothing for me to worry about, that everything would be just fine.

'And then Grandma made me some beetroot hot chocolate and I decided that Grandpa must have gone and told the lion to be on its way now that he knew it existed. I wanted to ask Grandma whether that meant the elephant had gone too, but decided not to say anything, because I could tell she didn't like talking about all the animals.'

'Well, had the lion and the elephant finally gone?' Marmot asks excitedly.

'The lion appeared to have gone, but I wasn't sure about the elephant. I wondered whether the elephant had been frightened by the noise that night and retreated deeper into the forest, but I was sure that it would come back again some day. Nonetheless after a few weeks I began to accept that both animals had probably moved on. Maybe the elephant had tired of staring at our house and had gone off in search of a better place to spend the winter.

'Little by little life began to seem normal again. Of course, Grandpa still spent every day and night in his workroom, but, as I said, I didn't give him a second thought. Grandma got on with things in the house and tried to keep us afloat; she would go into town and do little sewing jobs for people and she earned just enough so that we didn't starve. She often went to the home of a school mistress and this lady very kindly gave me the first and last book I ever owned, *The Tales of Ensign Ståhl*.

'After all, in the odd spare moment Grandma had taught me to read and at the age of six I was already quite a good reader. So I would spend hours on end sitting in the kitchen with my nose buried in the book reading Runeberg's heroic stories. And I was just reading the tale of Sven Dufva when I heard a bang come from the workroom.

'The book fell from my hands and since then I have never read a book again.'

Marmot gulps loudly. 'And then you ran up to Grandpa's workroom and battered a hole in the door with an axe and looked through the hole and saw . . .'

Marmot's father picks him up and sits him on his knee, something which does not happen very often, strokes his head and looks him deep in the eyes. He takes a moment, then he finishes telling the story.

'Somehow the lion had managed to get inside Grandpa's workroom, probably through an open window. Maybe it had been trying to get into the house that way so that it could eat me or Grandma.

'But when it got into the workroom it met Grandpa, who as we know was always on his guard and was already very angry. And so Grandpa fought furiously with the beast. The workroom was covered in blood and there were tufts of the lion's fur on the walls. Grandpa had shot the lion and wounded it fatally, but before it had died it had managed to bite a large chunk out of Grandpa. And there they lay, dead in each other's grip, Grandpa and the starved lion.

'When Grandma came home we dragged the lion's carcass into the forest and buried it there and we agreed never to talk about it again – the lion had become so thin that it hardly weighed anything at all. And Grandpa was buried in the churchyard, the same place where Grandma was buried last summer. We told everyone that Grandpa had been cleaning his pistol when it had gone off by accident with tragic consequences.

'After the funeral I noticed that the elephant had returned: it was standing once again at the edge of the forest, grieving, staring sadly at our house. It must have been frightfully cold because there had been lots of snow and the weather was getting colder by the day. It stood there for about two or three weeks, then finally went on its way and I never saw it again. Perhaps it died of the cold, or maybe its hide thickened and it grew used to the cold weather, I don't know.

'But sometimes I get the feeling that it's still around here somewhere, that it's living somewhere close by, perhaps in one of those black and white areas around Warren's Marsh. Because even though I never saw the elephant again, there were times when I thought I could feel something very big and very sad watching our house from the safety of the forest.'

Marmot is about to ask something, when his father's eyes close like someone drawing the curtains and turning off the lights. He stands up and Marmot remains seated, watching him as he dozily walks into the kitchen.

Something makes Marmot sense that Father's talkative period is now over, perhaps forever. Marmot sits down on Grandma's old sofa and stares out of the window. He sees his mother coming in from the forest. She looks very tired indeed.

When Mother walks into the house her lips form a smile. Father is making coffee in the other room, not dandelion coffee this time but real Costa Rica from the shop. The old grandfather clock is rattling in the corner of the room. During the day you hardly notice it at all, but at night it makes a ghostly sound that makes Marmot pull his covers over his head and hate the stupid clock with all his heart.

It is very hot and Marmot does not have the energy to do anything special, so he just sits there thinking things over until evening comes and it is time to go to sleep. There isn't even a television at Grandma's house, which is strange. There is a radio, but who on earth listens to the radio?

That night Marmot sleeps on the fold-out bed in the kitchen. Or rather, he does not really sleep: instead he lies listening to Mother and Father talking in the next room. The words they use are different from before; they are no longer tense and angry, but somehow softer and sad. Like when someone's dog has been run over. Mother and Father are talking about something which is 'awfully final', as he hears his mother say several times.

Just before Marmot finally dozes off to sleep, words from the other room floating around his ears like dark night butterflies, he can almost hear the sound of a great, heavy animal plodding across the garden. The sound of its footsteps is very sorrowful indeed, thump, thump, thump, scuff, it stops for a moment to look at the house, then returns with slow, heavy steps back to the forest.

The following morning Marmot and his mother drive back into town by themselves. Father does not come with them; he remains sitting on the steps outside the house as Mother steers the car out of the driveway. For a moment Marmot wonders whether she has simply forgotten to take Father with them, since it is just as easy not to notice when he is missing as when he is there, but decides not to get involved in something that doesn't really concern him.

When Marmot waves out of the rear window, Father does not respond; instead he just stares blankly out into the forest. He must be dreaming with his eyes open again.

# *Datura* and *Pereat Mundus* (extracts)

Leena Krohn

*Leena Krohn (born 1947) began her career as an author of children's fiction. Her works for adults are highly original, often sarcastic explorations of strange realities and the nature of awareness. In 1992 Krohn was awarded the Finlandia Prize for her work* Matemaattisia olioita tai jaettuja unia *('Mathematical Beings or Divided Dreams'). Other works available in English are* Tainaron *(1985; 'Tainaron: Mail from Another City', trans. 2004) and* Doña Quijote ja muita kaupunkilaisia *(1983; 'Doña Quixote and Other Citizens', trans. 1995). The first three extracts in this anthology are from her novel* Datura *(2001), while 'The Ice Cream Man' is from* Pereat Mundus *(1998).*

### *The Lord of Sounds*

'There are sounds all around us, everywhere you might not think mummummum. We cannot hear them, but they exist nonetheless – there in the most silent of silences.'

The same colour tinged the silver sky, the Lord of Sounds' suit and his level voice.

'I'm sorry, could you tell me more about this alternative audiotechnology?' I asked, a touch impatient. 'I've only been at the editorial office for a few weeks. Of course, there are lots of important matters in this job that I've never heard of.'

'Alternative audiotechnology is a way of revealing sounds which the human ear cannot normally mummum.' The Lord of Sounds explained things in a friendly but rather hushed voice.

I felt frustrated. It seemed that I needed some of this

alternative audiotechnology myself just to understand what he was saying.

'But everyday life would be very unsettling if we could hear every possible sound,' I said. 'It's surely only practical and fortunate that the human ear only discerns as much as it can.'

'Of course, the function of the brain is mummum,' he agreed. 'It cannot process absolutely everything. But the mummummum of our hearing tricks us into believing that there is nothing else to be heard. The same goes for our other senses naturally, even our mummummum.'

His voice became so inaudible that I had to cut him short once again. 'I'm sorry, I didn't hear.'

'. . . even our common sense and our intelligence, our rationale,' he repeated. 'After all, how can we know what we do not know! We cannot even guess at it!'

'You're right there,' I said. Despite its apparent simplicity, this notion was in fact quite new to me.

'And still we are convinced that we know something fundamental about mummummum mum mummummum.'

'Excuse me?' He was beginning to try my patience.

'. . . something fundamental about the laws and regularities of the universe,' he said.

'Well don't we?'

'This and that; that goes without saying. But reality is not confined merely to our empirical world. And sometimes it would be mummum, or at the very least mummum, to be able to hear more than we normally can,' he continued. 'It really broadens people's mummummum. It is with this in mind that I have developed the mummummum mummum mummummum.'

'The what?'

'The Silent Sound Detector.'

'What's that?' I asked.

'It is a very simple device,' he explained. 'I use a cassette recorder, which is triggered by the faintest sound and begins to record. I place it in an empty room when I go to work. There are no mummummum to the room.'

'It didn't catch that.'

'. . . no keys to the room except the ones I have. Last year I mummummum the walls in the room. When I get back from work I listen to the tape.'

'Every day?'

'Every day. It has become something of a mummummum.'

'Pardon?'

'. . . a habit. Of course, sometimes there is nothing to hear.'

'But does that mean that sometimes you *can* hear noises? Sounds in a locked, empty room?'

'Oh absolutely, very often in fact. Sometimes it sounds like the buzzing of a mummum nest; at other times you might think a high-powered machine had been switched on. Then sometimes it sounds like some form of mummum.'

'Sorry?'

'. . . like a vehicle slowing down, then accelerating again.'

'Well,' I said. 'Hmm. How fascinating. Have you thought of writing an article about this phenomenon for the New Anomalist?'

'Yes, why not indeed!' said the Lord of Sounds. 'That was my intention. But that is no reason to mummummum about this phenomenon alone. Of course, alternative mummummum encompasses much more besides. It can reveal previously unknown mummum about the universe and humanity itself.'

'Is that so?'

'Perhaps you have heard of instrumental mummummum?'

'I'm sorry?'

'. . . instrumental transcommunication.'

'I'm afraid I haven't.'

'Or Dr. Konstantin Raudive and his mummummum?'

'Pardon?'

'. . . and his goniometer.'

'Sadly not.'

He looked displeased.

'Well what about EVP?'

'I'm not familiar with that either, I'm afraid,' I replied, somewhat embarrassed at my ignorance of the subject.

'EVP stands for electronic voice phenomena,' he explained patiently.

'It seems one learns new things every day in this business.'

'EVP sounds last typically only a few mummum and are extremely difficult to hear. One generally has to use a good set of mummummum and train one's mummummum in order to make them out properly.'

At some point – out of tiredness and frustration – I gave up trying to listen to him. It was very hard work indeed having to strain my ears constantly, even though there was no doubt that what he was saying was strange and entirely new to me, and as such highly interesting.

'Very well,' I said, rudely interrupting his mumbling. 'That's splendid. If you'd kindly agree to write a short article on this subject. We'll have a look at it. Unfortunately we can't guarantee that it will be published. What about the next issue? The deadline would be the beginning of March.'

'Mummum!' he exclaimed, clearly satisfied with matters, and disappeared into the winter paleness.

## *The Trepanist*

If I was asked which of the subscribers to the New Anomalist should be put in the Raving Mad category, after slight hesitation I would certainly choose the man we refer to as the Earl of Cork. The hesitation is due to the fact that I once met, albeit only by e-mail, a woman who believed in what she called Inverted Speech. This young woman was convinced that if we record the speech of any given person, then listen to the recording backwards, we will then discover what that person truly means. As far as I understood, she shared this conviction with a substantial number of people, if not an entire cult. Even if the recorded person were to lie, the young woman had written, his or her hidden agenda would nonetheless be revealed for all to hear. Inverted Speech thus exposes lies and tells us what people take such pains to conceal.

This aside, The Cork was a far more serious case. He was volatile and focused in a way that made me shudder. It is at least for legal reasons, therefore, that his identity shall remain undisclosed.

The Cork sent the editorial office an expansive article under the heading: 'Enlightment Through Trepanation!'

'What is trepanation?' I asked the Marquess, who happened to be in the office as I opened the letter, but even he had never heard of such a term. After reading the article we never wanted to hear of it again. For once we were in agreement. We decided not to publish the article, because even the Marquess thought it went well beyond the bounds of decency.

The Cork's article outraged me so much that, against normal practice, I did not even deign to reply to him with the usual formulaic letter of refusal: "Thank you for your submission to our magazine. Unfortunately . . ."

Soon after the publication of the next issue a stocky, gargantuan man appeared at the editorial office sporting an ugly yellow baseball cap bearing an advertisement for a DIY shop. He introduced himself as the author of the article on trepanation and demanded to know why it had not been published. I thought it was odd and rather rude that he did not remove his cap, though the reason for this was soon to become apparent.

I decided not to mince my words.

'Because we will not encourage our readers to do anything quite as mindless,' I said. 'We'd probably end up being taken to court if we did so. And so would you.'

'That's a risk you simply have to take,' he said, his stern jaw jutting forwards. 'We have to fly in the face of convention and the law; we're talking about something which could benefit the entire human race! Trepanation exposes the human mind to glorious visions. It is a practice which opens a new path to the spirit. It offers us a chance to escape from the bony material prison that is our closed skull.'

'I'm not at all convinced by your theories,' I replied sharply, turned my back to him and began to go through my papers. I had hoped he would take the hint and leave.

'Then you clearly haven't considered the matter thoroughly,' said the man accusingly. 'Did you even bother reading my article right the way through?'

I was beginning to get angry.

'I've considered it quite enough. You are encouraging people to bore a hole in their own skulls. To me, that is entirely irresponsible. Performing lobotomies is punishable these days – thousands of patients regressed and became idiots as a result. The poor people that suffered such abuse are awarded a fortune in compensation. You even advise people what kind of drill to buy, so they can pierce their own skulls.'

'Of course,' said the man. 'Advice like this is of the utmost importance. Black & Decker is highly recommendable.'

I continued: 'You've even drawn comic-strip diagrams explaining how best to bore the skull open. This is an inappropriate and shocking thing to suggest.'

'Listen, you clearly have no idea that trepanation has been practised for thousands of years with great success. It is a fine, noble art. The ancient Greeks, the Romans, the Egyptians and the Native Americans all had a mastery of the secrets of trepanation. Having said that it was generally carried out on slaves and other lower castes.'

'I don't doubt it,' I said. 'The history of civilisation is a litany of shameful acts.'

'During the Middle Ages, the skull was opened to let out demons. There is proof that those who survived the operation acquired new, even supernatural spiritual dimensions.'

'Oh, and exactly how many of them survived?'

'As we grow, we lose the intuition and the sense of perception we had as babies,' The Cork continued, ignoring my question. 'The flow of blood to the brain is reduced, our perception and senses diminish. It has been scientifically proven that trepanation restores the vitality of our senses and strength of our emotions.'

'Very scientific indeed,' I muttered.

He did not allow me to disturb his lecture.

'As you know, new-born babies have an opening in their skull, the fontanel, and this gradually closes over. With time our skulls harden and the flow of blood to our skulls is reduced. Trepanation is one of the most effective methods of permanently restoring our original resilience and our state of happiness. I happen to know a doctor, a surgeon no less, who bored a hole in his skull using an electric drill. He's never felt better! Would you like his name and address? You can ask him for the finer details yourself.'

'No thank you, that'll be all right,' I said remaining cold as before. He seemed to be searching for pen and paper nonetheless.

'I believe you have a duty to your readers to tell them about this practice!'

His voice was becoming sharper. He leant on my desk with both hands – and what enormous hands they were – and brought his head so close that the brim of his cap brushed my forehead. The situation was becoming strained, even threatening. I pushed my chair away from the desk and wondered whether I should alert the Marquess.

'I'm sure my conscience will cope if I don't tell a soul about your methods,' I tried to assure him, but my voice sounded frail and wavering.

'Don't you want to hear about my experiences?' he asked.

'Thank you, I'd rather not,' I replied.

He decided not to respect my wishes, swiftly removed his cap from his head and turned his back to me. I was stunned. There in front of my eyes, right in the middle of his crown, amidst his thinning, greyish hair, stood a cork; a perfectly normal cork from a wine, or possibly even a champagne, bottle.

What would have happened if someone had yanked it out? I shuddered at the thought of the cork popping out, and the murky contents of his head spraying out across the room like a fountain.

'I managed to get my hands on various bandages and some local anaesthetic by the name of benzocain,' he continued, replacing the cap on his head. 'Of course I needed some iodine to sterilise the open hole. I went to the DIY shop and bought a good quality, light hand drill and some adjustable drill heads used for ceramics. The assistant was hardly an expert. I asked him what kind of drill he would recommend for opening up the skull. Imagine, he said he couldn't recommend anything at all. What badly educated staff! Still I was very happy with my choice, though I'm sure metal drills would be just as suitable. I would highly recommend the double-handed Black & Decker.'

I truly wished he would stop and began pointedly underlining parts of Voynich's manuscript. But The Cork leant over my desk again sending waves of heavy, sickly air wafting in my direction. I jumped back in my chair. Perhaps this was the stench of his brain fluid.

'It's best to use a chair with a head rest. A decent work chair or a sturdy armchair would be fine too. If you could get your hands on a dentist's chair, it would be your lucky day. You'll need to build some kind of support so the head stays firmly in position. And a safety belt, you'd better not forget that! It would be rather unfortunate if the drill started cutting out the odd chunk here and there.'

'If you don't mind, I'm actually rather busy,' I sighed wearily.

'I started drilling slowly and calmly, assisted by a friend who is an expert on the subject,' he continued. 'In fact, I've promised him I'll return the favour. After watching the procedure he's all the more convinced of the benefits and can hardly wait his turn.'

I groaned. I was feeling weak.

'We proceeded little by little, the dent in my skull became deeper and deeper until after about an hour I heard a new, strange sound; a bubbling, fizzing sound. Then I understood: the air bubbles in the skull were being released from their bony imprisonment. What joy! My friend then carefully removed the drill from the fresh hole.'

'I really don't want to hear any more,' I said. I was afraid I might throw up.

Paying no attention to my expression of disgust the man continued remorselessly: 'Using two mirrors I could see the blood in the hole rising and falling with my heartbeat. I was euphoric, I had never experienced such joy, such peace of mind. And I have felt like that ever since. How fervently I wish others could experience it too! You too, my friend!'

He patted my hand.

'It's not even expensive. I've given talks at many clubs and societies on the bliss these methods can offer. I implore you to seize this opportunity and publish my article. It could bring well-being and a new quality of life to so many poor people. If enough people finally realise the benefits of this practice, it could alter the fate of the human race! In fact, I think even political parties ought to adopt this issue.'

I pulled myself together and tried to muster some authority in my voice: 'We are not going to publish your article. It's out of the question! That's final. You can publish it at your own expense, if you really want to end up in court.'

'I'm shocked and disappointed. I would have expected a more open-minded and unbiased approach from the editors of the New Anomalist,' he said, disgruntled.

'Sorry.'

To my great surprise he finally seemed to have given up hope of making me understand. Relieved, I escorted him to the door and I did not like the look on his face as he bade me farewell. To me this seemed far from euphoric.

'You'll regret this, you know,' he said. 'You really are in need of trepanation. We'll be in touch.'

I wondered whether a double-handed Black & Decker would fit into The Cork's coat pocket. After this incident, at my request, the Marquess had the door fitted with a spyhole.

## *A Finger to the Lips*

I had arranged an early morning meeting in the library café and took a short cut through Dufva park. As I was slightly early, as happens quite often nowadays, and the weather was glorious, I decided to sit down on a bench in the sun, picked up a free newspaper someone had left behind and started flicking through it to kill some time. A few hundred metres away was the main road heading east out of the city and the morning rush hour was just beginning. The incessant boom of traffic was mixed with the joyous twittering of starlings and larks.

I read an article about the government's artificial rain experiments, in which hundreds of people had died, and it occurred to me that not even the most paranoid readers of the New Anomalist would have imagined such a thing could happen. I felt a sudden thud in my ears. I gave a start and looked up from the newspaper. The shadows of the trees were moving across the dusty path through the park just as before. A little girl sped past me on a scooter, her hair flapping in the wind. On another path a mother bent down to tie her child's shoe laces. A balloon sailed past the newly gilded dome of the cathedral, whilst up above a jet aeroplane left a foaming trail across the sky.

But something had changed. A moment or so later I understood what had happened. The disturbance was a gaping silence. The familiar sound world had been wiped away. The scooter turned and the little girl glided past in the other direction, but she travelled through the grit without making a sound. The jet plane passed silently across the city. It was as if the everyday bustle of the city had been sucked into a great invisible vacuum.

The surrounding world soon began to resemble a silent film. Perturbed by this I stood up to stretch my legs and stuffed the newspaper into the bin without it rustling in the slightest. I peered through the rows of blossoming trees out towards the street, where people were hurrying to the shops, to work or school. The traffic lights turned green and an endless stream of cars jolted forwards. But I could hear nothing: neither tyres, motors nor footsteps.

This was oppressive. I shook my head, brought my hands up to my ears and tapped them. Had something happened to both my ears? Can someone go deaf in a flash?

A sudden movement made me glance over my shoulder. There on the bench sat a man in a grey suit with a old rucksack on his lap. Where had he appeared from so suddenly? There was something familiar about him. He raised his hand to greet me and gave me a nod. Or was he greeting me? I looked around, but as there was no one else in the immediate vicinity I gave him an unsure and barely perceptible nod back.

My shortsightedness meant that I did not immediately recognise him.

I gingerly walked up to the bench. The man stood up and indicated for me to follow him. Now I realised who it was: the Lord of Sounds, the mumbling man, just as grey as ever. I noticed I was pleased to see him after so many years.

The Lord of Sounds strode purposefully ahead carrying his backpack, I did not ask anything and followed him as if in a dream. In the middle of the park there is a glass-roofed stage used by orchestras on public holidays. From the stage you could see far, through the park, to the market square, the boulevards, even out to the harbour. He spoke to me as we stood there on the stage, or perhaps he whispered, but I could not hear a word of it, not even mumbling this time. I pointed to my ears and said, apparently rather loudly: 'I can't hear anything!'

I could not even hear my own voice. At this I became very disheartened.

The Lord of Sounds then raised a finger to his lips and gave a mysterious smile. He gestured to me to come closer. He obviously had something to show me. He began rummaging through his backpack.

His mouth opened once again. I watched the movement of his lips and thought I could read the word 'Voilà!'

The Lord of Sounds produced a jar, the same as the one he had shown me in the editorial office but much bigger. Then I realised: it was a new model of the Sound Swallower he had promised to demonstrate to me a long time ago. So now it was ready. Now it worked. And you did not even have to bring it up to your ear, its effects could be felt from far away. The Sound Swallower had sucked up the sound of the city. Perhaps everyone in the city was now experiencing the same silence.

A mixture of disbelief and surprise spread across my face. Gesticulating beautifully the Lord of Sounds explained that he had something else in his bag to show me. He delved inside once again and produced a rectangular object wrapped in crêpe paper.

'Another new contraption?' I tried to ask.

The Lord of Sounds either heard my question or read my lips, and nodded. Moving his lips very slowly he ennunciated two new words, as far as I could make out: 'Im-age Swal-low-er.'

Once he had unwrapped the package I was taken aback. It was not a contraption at all, it was a flower.

He was holding my very own flower, the first one I had ever been unable to identify. I was convinced that this was not just another of the same species but the very same flower. It glowed in exactly the same light, every leopard spot was in place, every speck of pollen precisely where it had been. How had he managed to acquire that flower after all these years? How had it remained so fresh for decades?

I tried to ask him about this, but he raised his finger to his lips once again. He then gestured, encompassing the panorama opening out in front of us, and pointed to the flower from my childhood. He raised it up level with my eyes so that all I could see was the deep chasm inside.

What light erupted from the flower! It filled my eyes, my head, spread in a resplendent cloud throughout the park, banishing all shadows and contours, even the colours of the flower itself. It devoured the trees in the park, the streams of cars and the throngs of people; houses, department stores, factories and cathedrals, even the sea and the spring, sparing nothing.

Now I was both deaf and blind, but something touched my hands and led me forwards through the milky silence, perhaps down the same steps I had climbed up to the stage. Although I had lost my most important senses I did not mourn for them, and I was not afraid. It felt as if I were being led not by the Lord of Sounds but by the flower. Resting in my palm its leaves were like another hand leading me towards the fundamental mystery of being. For that I was willing to exchange all that went before.

My trance was shattered by a scream which opened up my ears with a thump. Someone was crying, a child, nearby. That pure, shrill cry brought back the lost city, its sounds flooding loose; once again I could hear life's counterpoint. The fog dispersed around me. It was the same little girl who had earlier sailed back and forth along the path. She had fallen right beside me and hurt her knee on the grit. A thin trickle of blood ran down her tanned shin.

I felt I ought to help the whimpering girl to her feet and ask: 'Did you hurt yourself?' I was about to do so, but hesitated for a moment and missed the chance. She had already stopped her tears, got back on her scooter and bravely continued on her way. I was redundant.

I peered around, turned, looked for the hand leading me and the Lord of Sounds. I wanted an explanation, I wanted the flower, but it was too late. The Lord of Sounds had taken it with him.

## *The Ice Cream Man*

'Where's that noise coming from?' Elsa asked somewhat bewildered.

'What noise?'

'Sounds like someone typing.'

'Who would be typing on the beach?' said her mother. 'It's probably just a lawnmower or a boat.'

'But it's coming from the ice cream van!' Elsa exclaimed. 'Let's go and take a look.'

On the empty beach there stood a small white hut. Why was the beach deserted even though it was a sweltering day, wondered Elsa and her mother. On cloudless days like this it was usually impossible to find a space for your towel and there was always a long queue to the ice cream van. But today there was not a soul to be seen. It was uncanny. Still, this way they had the entire beach to themselves.

As they approached the ice cream van the sound of frantic typing could be heard all the more clearly. Elsa glanced at her mother and said: 'It's not a motor.'

'No, you were right,' her mother replied.

Inside the ice cream van sat Håkan tapping away at a small

portable typewriter. Håkan was wearing a black suit, a white shirt and a dark blue silk tie. His typing was very concentrated and solemn, his back straight. Every now and then his eyes would absent-mindedly glance at the horizon and the empty beach.

'It's a new ice cream man!' said Elsa.

'Looks like it,' said her mother. 'What an outfit.'

'How odd,' said Elsa. 'He's sitting in the van typing. Whatever for?'

'You get the ice cream,' said her mother, languidly closing her eyes again. 'I'll wait in the shade. I'm sure he'll be able to leave his writing to sell you a cone or two. At least you won't have to queue like normal.'

'Aren't you having one?'

'Yes, I'll have the mango if they've got any,' her mother said.

Elsa looked at the ice cream van. A faint haze was shimmering above the sand. The van looked like it was inside a cloud, a cloud of words.

As Elsa approached the van Håkan removed his fingers from the typewriter.

'And what's it to be?' he asked.

'Why are you writing?' asked Elsa.

'Because I have to.'

'Aha. What are you writing?'

'A will,' he replied. '. . . of sorts.'

'You mean where you say who gets your things when you die?'

'Another kind of will,' he said. 'And what would you like?'

'Mango. Two. Are you going to die soon?'

Håkan took two wafer cones and filled each one with two scoops of yellow mango ice cream.

'I have no intention of dying, but it might very well happen. And not just to me either. That'll be eighteen marks.'

Elsa looked in her purse and gave Håkan the exact change.

'Other people too, you mean?'

'Have you noticed,' he asked, 'how there seems to be no end to this heat wave?'

'I know,' said Elsa. 'It's great. I can come to the beach every day.'

'Well, great, I suppose, however you wish to understand it,' said Håkan. 'We must be prepared for all eventualities.'

'What do you mean?'

'Heat waves are not entirely harmless,' he said.

'Do you mean someone could die from the heat?' Elsa asked sceptically.

'And why not?' he replied. He had returned to his typing and no longer took any notice of Elsa.

By the time Elsa got back to the shade with the cones the ice cream was half melted.

'The ice cream man was saying funny things,' she told her mother. 'He frightened me.'

'Was he scaring you?'

'He said somebody might die. And he's writing a will.'

'He's just pulling your leg,' her mother said. She walked over towards the ice cream van. Håkan was typing so intensely that at first he did not notice the new customer. Elsa's mother tapped her nails on the desk, Håkan raised his head and stopped typing.

'I hope you're not frightening little children,' her mother said.

'I beg your pardon?' asked Håkan.

'Did you just tell my daughter that someone might die?'

'It's possible.'

'That you said that to her?'

'That someone might die.'

'Of course they might, but there's no need for an ice cream vendor to discuss such things with little children.'

'Not normally, no. But these are exceptional times. There are many things one should talk about, many things one should prepare for, especially those with a family.'

'What are you talking about? What times?'

'Consider the weather, for instance. And the birds.'

'The birds?'

Elsa's mother looked around her at the beach and the sea. She could not see any birds.

'There aren't any birds here.'

'No,' said Håkan. 'Nor are there any people. Strange, don't you think?'

She walked back and joined Elsa. 'Best not to pay any attention to what he says. I think he's a bit . . . a bit . . .'

'A bit of a weirdo.' Elsa suggested.

'That's right,' said her mother. 'He's very strange in any case.'

'Ugh!' Elsa shouted. She had found her bottle of suntan lotion.

'What's wrong?' asked her mother.

'The suntan lotion! It's leaked into the bag. The sunglasses, the comb, your book – they're all covered in it!'

'Isn't the lid on properly?'

'Yes, it is,' said Elsa.

'There must be a hole in it, then,' said her mother.

Elsa wiped the bottle and the lid and checked them both carefully.

'But there isn't,' she said. 'It's not damaged at all.'

'Show me.'

Her mother bent down and fished the bottle of suntan lotion out of the bag. The lid was indeed shut tight. Her fingers slid as she tried in vain to open it, but still everything in the bag was smeared with yellow oil.

'It's a mystery,' said Elsa contentedly. 'Maybe we'll never know what happened.'

'Maybe. Aren't you going swimming?' asked her mother.

'Yes, but I'd like another ice cream first,' she replied.

In fact she did not really want another ice cream. She wanted to carry on talking to Håkan.

'This will be your last one today,' said her mother. 'And don't hang around talking to that man.'

'More mango?' asked Håkan.

'No, something else this time.'

'We also have pistachio,' he told her. 'You can't get it everywhere. Did I scare you earlier? I didn't mean to do that, but facts are facts.'

'Not really. I'll have the pistachio then,' she said. 'Large.'

Her temples had begun to throb. Something like the faint smell of sulphur hung in the air.

'Are you a real ice cream man?' Elsa could not help but ask.

'No. I'm just a stand-in.'

'Do all stand-ins wear suits like that?'

'Not normally. Neither do the full-time employees.'

'So why are you wearing one?'

'To commemorate this special day.'

'Is it your birthday?'

'Quite the opposite,' replied Håkan.

'Oh.' Elsa had to start eating the ice cream, as it was already dripping through the cone.

'Do you know what the temperature is today?'

'Yes, I've got a thermometer,' he said cheerfully. 'It reads nine and thirty.'

'Wow!' exclaimed Elsa. 'Can you die from that?'

'Not really,' replied Håkan. 'If you're healthy, that is.'

'That's good,' she said. 'I'm perfectly healthy.'

'While it lasts,' he said.

'What?'

'Health. But now perhaps it's time to go.'

'Where?'

'Back home,' said Håkan. 'I'll be leaving shortly too.'

'Is the beach closing?' asked Elsa.

'It ought to be closed.'

Elsa rejoined her mother, who had wet a towel and placed it over her face.

'Mum?'

'Yes?'

'It's thirty-nine degrees. But the man said you can't die from that.'

Her mother sneered. 'Well, that's comforting. Why did you go and talk to him?'

'He said we'll have to leave.'

'Oh did he now! What a shameless man. The ice cream man doesn't decide how long we can and can't stay on the beach.'

'But he said the whole beach should be closed.'

'What on earth for? Don't go up to that van again. You never know with people like that. Who knows what they'll come up with next?'

'Do you know what,' said Elsa. 'It feels like I'm in an aeroplane. My ears have popped.'

'Try swallowing. Maybe it's the air pressure, it's probably dropped.'

Elsa thought for a moment as she swallowed and licked her ice cream. 'I wonder if the thing with the suntan lotion had something to do with that. Maybe there's a storm coming or something,' she said slightly worried.

'Maybe,' replied her mother. 'The weather's changing, that's for sure. It can't go on like this for long. I think a real storm is brewing. Maybe we really should go home, but not because of that ice cream man.'

'I want to go swimming first. That's why we came here.'

'Off you go then. Maybe I should go too,' said her mother. 'Though the water is probably boiling hot, it won't cool us down much.'

They lazily walked over to the water's edge, Elsa slightly ahead. Just before her toes touched the water she stopped in her tracks.

'What's wrong?' her mother asked.

'Let's not go,' she said. 'The water looks strange. There's something in it.'

'Fish!' exclaimed her mother.

'Look, they're all swimming upside down.'

'They're not swimming at all.'

There in the shallow waters floated many different kinds of fish of all shapes and sizes. Their white stomachs shone. They stank.

'Are they dead?' asked Elsa.

'It looks like it. Strange that the birds haven't noticed them yet,' said her mother. Elsa looked up at the hot, empty sky.

'The birds have left,' a voice said. The ice cream man was standing on the sand in his exquisite suit. His black shoes were gleaming. How ceremoniously quiet it was.

'They look like they've been cooked,' said Elsa as she stared at the fish.

'My dear, they are cooked,' replied Håkan fondly. 'Look.'

It was dead calm. The reeds stood regally like javelins. Further away amidst the rushes, where the mist hid everything from view, came the sound of bubbling. The water was rippling and babbling.

'Why is the water moving like that?' asked Elsa.

They looked in turn at the bubbling surface of the water and the thickening haze. It began to surge and swell, its density building. More fish were washing up on the beach, piling on top of each other. The humid, stinking fog swirled around them, dampening their hair.

'It's steam,' said Håkan. 'The sea is boiling.'

'What are you suggesting?' Elsa's mother exclaimed, flabberghasted. 'In front of children.'

'Run!' he shouted to Elsa. 'Who'll be first back to the car?' He turned and looked at her mother and said sharply: 'You too, madam.'

Elsa's mother grabbed her by the hand and they ran like never before. At one point Elsa almost tripped over and looked over her shoulder. There amongst the steam she could see the figure of the ice cream man, standing upright in his black suit. He was not running.

The ice cream man raised his hand in a wave and behind him, far out across the sea, loomed a great white bubble, round like a mother's breast. It bulged and swelled like a dream beneath a strange, incandescent sun.

# *Three Prose Poems*

Markku Paasonen

*Markku Paasonen (born 1967) is a poet whose style often approaches prose, and in particular the vignette. Paasonen's prose fragments play with the boundaries of reality, as with uninhibited imagination he conjures up images which could stem equally from horror films, film noir or a Dalí painting. Simultaneously he takes a very close look at the world around him, whilst regularly allowing the world of dreams to put in a satirical appearance. The three prose poems featured here were first published in the collection* Voittokulku *('The Triumphal March', 2001).*

### *Despilfar*

Despilfar is displayed in a great glass cabinet. We know it is Despilfar, because its name has been engraved on a small brass plaque. If there were no plaque, no one would be able to call it by that name. It has a pleated shell, or armour, beneath which curl eight tentacles. Their chelae turn inwards as if they were pointing to the weight dangling from the nerve of its heart. Each time the museum clock strikes eight, Despilfar jolts one degree. In a year it completes two full rotations around an invisible axis; the question as to whether this motion is endogenous or governed by the planets excites researchers who convene each year around Despilfar like a fraternity. They examine its circuits, attach probes to its gnarled back and return home, their sole prize a sense of collegial unanimity: a bygone science has offered them this being which is a stone, a machine or a fish. I believe that, one day, they too will surrender the contents of their studies to their successors like a dream beyond interpretation.

## *Punishment*

I have seen an author's head. I saw it in Paris at the natural history museum. On display were the skeletons of Siamese twins, cirrhotic livers and other examples of nature's playful scourges. They were stored in glass jars filled with formalin, but time had seeped through the glass and warped the tissues so that now they were grey. I would gladly have learnt what the liver looks like, what the spleen and the heart look like, but now all I can say is this: they all looked dull with white filament drifting around them, their tips swaying back and forth in the aquarium filled with formalin like the hair of the Medusa. The only exception was the author's head. His bloodless face was frozen in violent spasms and his white hair fumbled at the surrounding liquid as if fishing to recapture the escaped spirit of a novel. You could tell straight away that he had never achieved what he had longed for with those tens of thousands of pages now being nibbled away by mites in the basements of second-hand book shops. Though his pen had probed deeper and more purulent cavities than any other, though he had thrust his hand into the ragged gullies of the gullet and with his nails ripped bloody discords from the vocal cords, he had not dared to reach deep enough and had not pierced his readers' stomachs with hooks of pleasure. That is what it said on a label stuck to the side of the jar. His punishment was to spend the rest of eternity pickled in formalin with all his senses intact, and thus with frozen eyes he could do nothing but stare at the tourists whose secretly cherished feelings as they walked past were a mixture of satisfaction, shame and sympathy.

One more assignment to be carried through and I would be given the key to a room with space for a mattress and a roof that didn't leak, that's what the boss promised me when I went down to the office, dragging my foot down the endless staircase, down in amongst the labyrinth of boiler rooms and parking levels. He stared at me intensely from behind the sharp points of his shoes resting on the desk and made me give up any ideas I had had of leaving the case. Now at least I had an assignment and I felt the soles of my feet press into the same mud as those hurrying to work every morning tread with their shining shoes; I could make out individual pairs of eyes amidst the human pulp oozing from the mouth of the underground station, and I sensed that they could see the same as my eyes, their like, a pair of eyes with a small yet unyielding place amidst the scheme of moving parts throughout the city. The boss had explained exactly where I had to go, he had said I couldn't go wrong, and now I felt that the world was leaning in precisely the right direction. Water rinsing the streets rushed the same direction as me, a solitary bird shook loose its feathers and searched for a new direction, precisely where I was going. Once I reached the cranes I increased my pace, though this took its toll for someone dragging his foot. Then I saw him! The back of his coat was dark, as if at that spot all light had disappeared from the world. He was walking in front of me towards the furthest crane and didn't so much as jump at the blasts from the funnels of ships breaking loose from the quayside. When I think about it more carefully, I'm sure that the ships didn't make a sound, the fog was so thick that it caught around the tips of the birds' feathers, the air thick with tar groped at the collar of my jacket making it stand up rigid with fear. I clasped my fist tighter around a paper bag containing the last sandwich crumbs I had saved, stamped my healthy foot more purposefully against the surface of the road and thanked my luck, which I rarely had any recourse to address. Then I saw him! The back of his coat was dark, as if at that spot all light had disappeared from the world. He was walking much faster than me. I thrust my hands into my pockets and threw everything I found over the railings: orange peel which may yet have yielded a few drops, a coin which may have had some value in a neighbouring country, a thumb and a ring finger wrapped in paper which I kept as proof that I had carried out my previous assignment to the letter. Then I saw him! The back of his coat was dark, as if at that spot all light had disappeared from the world. He was walking so fast that I had to run. You can imagine, it wasn't easy. Dusk was falling and every time I saw him he was walking ahead much faster than me. I cast my hat aside and removed pieces of beard hanging stiff beneath my chin. Nothing made any difference. When night finally swallowed him up, I had come full circle to the neighbourhood from which I set out. I found my very own nook, lifted the grille aside and curled up to go to sleep thinking of how the following day would be the same. I curl up in my nook evening after evening, lighter and lighter, until one day all that is left is the back of a dark coat, as if at that spot all light had disappeared from the world.

# *The Golden Apple*

Sari Peltoniemi

*Sari Peltoniemi (born 1963) has published many books for children and young people, whilst her science fiction and fantasy short stories have been published in several magazines. Her novels have twice been shortlisted for the Finlandia Junior Prize. In addition to this she has written the lyrics to numerous rock songs. Peltoniemi's texts often deal with the weakest, most vulnerable members of society, people upon whose lives myth and fantasy begin to encroach. Finnish mythology is especially close to her writing. The short story 'The Golden Apple' was first published in the magazine Portti.*

Rea went running almost every evening. It was such a short journey into town that she could easily have carried on at the gym or an aerobic's class, but jogging felt much better. You could always take a slightly different route – along the saw tracks through the woods or out towards the main road and maybe pop into the pub. You would almost always meet other people jogging, walking dogs or simply out for a stroll. Sometimes Rea would bump into her pupils from the school, loitering about in front of the shop or at the bus stop. Chatting to people and seeing their homes made her feel like she was gradually running her way into the heart of the village.

Many times during her run Rea would stop to admire the beautiful gardens and wooden houses. The majority were well looked after older houses, but a lot of new houses had been built alongside them. The village was rapidly expanding towards the town on one side and the parish on the other – in a few years' time it would probably no longer be a village but a fully-fledged suburb. The nearby woods were fast disappearing and joggers had no need to worry about getting lost, even if they cut along the path. It always felt as if the nearest house was shouting distance away, and still the tall pine and spruce trees created the impression of being out in the countryside. Doubtless there would be mushrooms and berries for the taking, even though there were plenty of people to pick them. Gardens throughout the village were already littered with children's plastic buckets filled with unripe lingonberries.

Rea had found a babysitter close by. As a new addition to the village, she had been advised to contact a large local religious family, where she would find willing helpers for all kinds of jobs. Laura, one of the older girls in the family, was more than happy to earn a little pocket money, though she was not greedy. Besides, she had received a firm grounding in childcare at home.

Rea had placed some money on the kitchen cupboard.

'Could you stay a moment, just so I can have a shower in peace?' she asked.

'Of course.'

From the shower she could hear the telephone ring and Laura answered. Rea instinctively began to hurry. Perhaps it was the headmaster; perhaps she would have to do some extra preparation for tomorrow's classes. Perhaps one of the parents wanted to see her.

As Rea came out of the bathroom Laura was already putting on her trainers.

'Oh, you were in a hurry after all. Have you still got homework to do?'

Laura shook her head. As she turned round Rea noticed she was blushing.

'Who was it?'

'It was a prank.'

'What do you mean? What kind of prank?'

'He said rude things. I won't repeat them. I'm going home.'

'But I haven't paid you yet!'

'Just give me a little more next time.'

The door closed and Laura could be seen jumping on her bike. Tuisku was beginning to grumble with tiredness. Making him eat his supper, wash himself and go to sleep took so long that Rea only remembered the phone call as she was going to bed. It was those big boys. They would sit at somebody's house calling all the teachers one by one, seeing who could say the rudest thing, then cackle down the phone. That must be it.

Tuisku had taken to walking in his sleep. He had done it a few times before, but since they had moved he would get up every night and start wandering around the house. Rea would finally wake up as he walked past her bed. Sometimes Tuisku would try to go outside, but Rea would gently steer him away from the front door. Sometimes he would pull down his trousers and wee on the floor or go and sit on a stool by the kitchen window as though he were looking outside. In the mornings he would laugh when Rea told him what had happened. He thought she was only pulling his leg.

Rea had meant to ask the school nurse what could be done about it, but had decided against it. At their first meeting the school nurse had not seemed the sort of person to whom a single mother could pour her heart out without social services being alerted. Best just watch him, she thought, and see how he settles in. He would soon meet new friends and start to feel more at home. Even without the advice of the school nurse Rea knew that Tuisku's symptoms were not at all rare – in fact, they were probably to be expected, what with everything changing all at once.

Perhaps he also sensed that something was troubling his mother too.

For the first time in her life Rea had her very own reception class and a full-time job. So many children had started school in Närvä that autumn that a third class had been formed.

Some of the children did not seem ready to go to big school, even though they had all been to the nursery. Some could barely tie their shoelaces, let alone concentrate for a whole lesson at a time. On top of this the autumn had been exceptionally warm and the little ones found it hard to sit indoors all day.

'Miss! Can we go out and play yet?' Little Teemu would whine at the beginning of every lesson.

'First we're going to learn some numbers. We can go out tomorrow for PE.'

'But I can't do it, it's . . .'

'I'll show you. Let's let everyone else concentrate.'

Rea went over and looked at the boy's smudged papers. He had managed to write out a few wiggly threes and was angrily tearing his hair.

'I'll draw one and you can copy it.'

'No, do the whole line. I can't do it.'

'Of course you can't, yet.'

One of the girls put up her hand. This was still relatively rare.

'Yes, Ulla?'

'Miss, Eetu's lying on the floor!'

Rea walked over to the back of the classroom. Eetu was lying stretched out on the floor behind his desk.

'Come on, back to your desk.'

'He's asleep,' someone sniggered.

'No he isn't. Get up now,' said Rea and knelt down beside him. She gently shook him. The boy rolled on to his back and opened his eyes. From the bewildered look on his face Rea assumed he must indeed have been asleep.

'Didn't you get much sleep last night?'

Eetu dozily shook his head and crawled up to his desk.

'Were you playing computer games till late?'

'I haven't got a computer.'

'Give me your book. I'll write a note to your parents, you need to go to bed earlier.'

'I always go to sleep before nine,' he maintained. The others all nodded in agreement and someone said:

'Miss, you were asleep once.'

'No I wasn't. I just had my eyes shut.'

Rea had nodded off last week whilst the children had been drawing rowan branches with crayons. The sun had warmed her desk and the classroom had been unusually calm.

'You were snoring, Miss.'

'No I wasn't,' she chuckled.

After break someone would always come back in crying. The bigger children would throw balls at the little ones or shove them in the queue. This time fair-haired Mikael was howling in the corridor:

'Miss! Miss!'

From the amount of screaming Rea was expecting to see a bleeding wound in his knee, but all she saw was his tear-stained face.

'Did someone hit you?'

'No!'

'Well what's happened then?'

'Someone's nicked my phone! My mum's going to kill me, I'm not supposed to bring it to school.'

'Where was it?'

'In my coat pocket. I bet it was Little Teemu. Make him give it back, Miss!'

'We don't know who took it. Are you sure you had it with you?'

Mikael continued shouting.

'Yes, I was showing it to the girls at break time. Do something, Miss! Don't be so soft on him!'

Nothing seemed to calm him down, he just carried on screaming blue murder. The other children were starting to come back inside. They gathered behind Rea and listened to Mikael's tantrum.

'Has anyone else got a phone with them?'

Nobody had one; at least, nobody admitted to having one.

'You ought not to bring mobile phones to school. If for some reason you have to, then keep it in your desk. I'm going to take Mikael to the headmaster's office. Go back to the classroom and take out your exercise books. I'll be back in a minute.'

Rea took Mikael to the staff room and made him drink a glass of water. Then she reported the phone missing at the head's office.

The big boys had doubtless been at it again. They were probably hiding somewhere right now laughing and cackling in their breaking voices. That had to be it, because thieves did not hang around Närvä.

A pile of post was waiting for her when she got home. On top of the pile was a letter. Rea recognised the handwriting on the envelope and ripped it up straight away.

'Can I rip something up too?' asked Tuisku. Rea handed him some junkmail and he proceeded to tear it to pieces.

'Looks like a wolf did it!' he said proudly. Rea nodded.

She had not received any letters for a long time now. But where had he found Rea's new address?

That evening Rea went out jogging again. The rain was drizzling, but it did not bother her. Every now and then Rea shook her hair, as if all her worries would evaporate with the raindrops.

Whereas in other towns people put gnomes in their gardens, people in Närvä preferred bears. Round here they really seemed to fit in better. They stood in front of most houses in the village. The basic model was always the same: a bear carved with a chainsaw from a single block of wood. The features were rough, but still – or perhaps even because of this – the bears looked and seemed just right. Many people had varnished their statues black or a dark brown. Someone had put a bunch of dried flowers in their bear's paw, whilst someone else had draped their bear with the garish banner of a local sports club.

Some of the fancier houses also had garden statues, the usual angels, frogs and naked cherubs; there were even a few fountains, though at this time of year the water was turned off.

The smell of apples was heavy in the air. As if to tempt thieves the apple trees in many of the gardens grew right by the lane so that all you had to do was reach out and wait for one of the heavy branches to drop a ripe fruit into your palm.

'You've got a bear too, haven't you,' she asked Laura as she untied her wet shoelaces. 'Who makes them?'

'Some farmer, on the side. He sells them at craft fairs and he's got an advert in the paper. Apparently they're selling so well that soon he won't need another job. We got ours for free. My Dad helped him out with something and then one morning there it was in the garden. My little brother almost wet himself; it was dark and he was the first to leave for school and he found the statue right in front of the door.'

'Can we have a bear too?' asked Tuisku.

Rea laughed.

'We don't need one, there's one next door. You can go and see that one.'

'The man keeps bees too. No one round here buys honey in the shops any more because his is so much better – and cheaper,' Laura explained.

'That's good to know.'

After Laura had left, Rea turned on the television.

'The children's programmes have finished,' moaned Tuisku. 'What can I do?'

'You don't need to do anything. It'll soon be time for supper. Just let me watch the news.'

Tuisku mumbled away to himself for a while longer, but quietened down eventually. Rea soon noticed that it was too quiet.

'Tuisku, where are you?'

He did not reply.

'You haven't fallen asleep, have you?'

Rea found him in the kitchen. The floor was covered in shreds of paper.

'What are you doing?'

'I'm just tearing up these letters. I'm a shredder!'

Rea had opened her mouth and was about to shout at him when she noticed something. Pieces of a letter were strewn in amongst the rubbish.

'You could join in. You like tearing things up,' Tuisku

suggested as Rea sat on the floor and picked up the corner of an envelope. There was no stamp in sight. Had there been one that morning? Had the stamp been loose and fallen off? Rea rummaged through the strips of paper, although she already knew the answer.

Outside it was already dark.

'Let's close the curtains and lock the door,' she whispered.

'There aren't any curtains in the living room,' laughed Tuisku.

Though she was tired Rea could not get to sleep. She sat listening to sounds from outside and felt glad that she lived in a terrace. The neighbours were always close by. When Tuisku got up for his nightly sleepwalk, Rea glanced at the clock. It was just past two. This time Tuisku went straight up to the front door and tried to open it. He could not undo the lock, but he was trying so hard that Rea sat down on the floor and waited. She cautiously glanced out of the living room windows and looked down into the garden. She could see movement in the glare of the outside light. There was some-one in the garden. Rea gasped. Tuisku was still fiddling at the door and muttering quietly to himself.

Rea peered outside. She took care not to be seen as she approached the window. The people outside were not hiding, however, and Rea could soon make out who they were. She exhaled, relieved, and raised her trembling hands to her cheeks. Just children, she thought, and in their pyjamas. Each one was carrying a little bucket, and one by one they slowly disappeared round the corner. No wonder the kids were so tired at school, if their parents allowed them to roam around outside all night. For all she knew their parents might be at the pub or on night shift. Rea wondered whether she should go out and order them back to bed, but when Tuisku started wandering back towards the bedroom she decided to go after him.

The following week the headmaster's wallet was stolen from the staffroom. People suspected the boys in class six, who had been up to no good all through the summer and autumn. But when a Toyota belonging to one of the teachers disappeared from the carpark, Rea knew exactly what to expect. She felt she may as well give up straight away. What else could she do?

She had already told the ladies at the pre-school that Tuisku was not to go home with anyone else. She had asked them to keep a close eye on him when the children were out playing, and lied that he had a habit of running away. But what was she supposed to do? Should she and Tuisku sit at home behind locked doors every evening?

The telephone rang constantly, and whenever Rea answered it she could hear nothing. She knew it would not be long before something happened; something which would blow her new home, her job and her peaceful village to smithereens. Soon they would be nothing but a memory. But until then all she could do was go on as normal and try to be strong.

On her runs Rea was sure she was being watched and followed. She no longer went through the woods but stuck to larger roads with houses nearby. Still she would often stop to watch a squirrel munching away by the side of the road and leaping from tree to tree beside her, or to collect bright crimson maple leaves to occupy Tuisku.

And she could barely hide her excitement when she discovered Tuisku's favourite plastic bucket full of chantarelles on the step.

'Wow!' she exclaimed from the door. 'What wonderful mushrooms you've been picking! Let's fry them right away, so Laura can have some too. Where did you find them? Maybe there'll be enough to freeze . . .'

'No,' Tuisku snapped.

'What do you mean, no?'

Laura appeared behind Tuisku, smiling unsurely.

'He said they're not to be eaten.'

'Why not? They look delicious!'

'They're for my game,' he said firmly.

Rea gave a laugh. 'We don't play with food. Why don't you collect pebbles instead? Or leaves maybe.'

The discussion was cut short. Tuisku flew into such a tantrum that Rea had to carry him to bed.

'He's at that age,' she said to Laura holding the bedroom door shut. 'You can come out when you've calmed down,' she shouted through the door.

'I hadn't noticed he was especially disobedient. He's generally very calm and seems mature for his age,' said Laura, and Rea had to admit she was right. Had Tuisku really picked up on Rea's fears, even thought she tried so hard to conceal them? Had he become worried too?

Tuisku had fallen asleep on his bed before Laura left. Rea decided to let him sleep, even though this meant an early start the next morning – and surely a long night-time walk as well. Rea too fell asleep almost immediately.

Ever since Tuisku was born Rea had been a light sleeper. Even when she was exhausted she would still wake up at the slightest sound or movement. This made it all the more difficult to fathom why this time things were different.

She woke up the next morning as the alarm went off. Tuisku raised his head from the pillow and said, baffled:

'I'm already dressed.'

'That's because you went to sleep like that,' Rea reminded him. He seemed once again to be his old cheerful self.

'Come on, let's have some breakfast,' she called. Sunlight was shining in through the curtains. It would be another beautiful day, even though it was now the middle of September. In her sleep Rea thought she had heard the sound of rain during the night, but now the skies had cleared again.

Rea put on her slippers. As she raised her head she noticed footsteps on the bedroom floor. The muddy patches led to the foot of Tuisku's bed, and next to the bed lay his wellington boots. Rea jumped up and followed the footsteps up to the front door. The door was ajar.

'Did you go out last night?' she asked.

'No, I was asleep.'

'Your wellies are by the bed.'

'Why did you put them there?'

Rea gave her head a shake and closed the door. She noticed Tuisku's bucket was on the step, empty.

'Your chantarelles,' she said, though she knew this might spark off another tantrum. The mushrooms seemed very important to him.

'What about them?'

'Someone's taken them.'

Tuisku seemed perfectly calm. 'No, I was playing with them.'

'So you were outside last night?'

The contradiction dawned on him and he said, somewhat bemused: 'That's funny. I was playing with them in my dream. It felt almost real.'

It had been a good time to move house. Rea would soon have been kicked out of her student flat and Tuisku was still young enough not to worry about leaving his friends behind. Their terraced house in Närvä was close to the primary school and only a few hundred metres from the pre-school. She did not need a car, as the bus into town stopped almost right in front of the door.

But now all that trouble seemed to have been for nothing. Rea had thought of taking part in next summer's marathon once her stamina built up. She had even started going jogging in the mornings before class, once she had dropped Tuisku off at pre-school; but now her thoughts were far from the marathon. She would be glad just to see next summer.

Running was the only way of calming down for a while, even though it always felt as if she was not alone. It truly touched her to think of all the village had given her; it had accepted her, showed her its beautiful sides, both its people and the countryside. Of course Rea did not imagine for a moment that she was living in a perfect world, but she knew she would never forget the warmth she had encountered that autumn; how Laura would often bring round some of her mother's home-made buns or how the woman next door had raked the leaves from Rea's garden as she had been raking her own garden anyway.

Or how one foggy morning she found herself on the bear carver's land. First she noticed the beehives in the meadow. Past them she saw a group of figures standing next to a muddy track in the field. Through the fog she expected to see people going about their morning business, but then realised that the figures were standing still. These were the bear sculptures facing out towards the road. Most of them were complete, but some were still only taking shape. They were all fresh and unvarnished. At least seven wooden bear brothers, new born or still in creation, were each awaiting the journey to a garden of their own.

Rea had never seen an exhibition quite like it, and she was not sure whether these sculptures represented true art or were simply glorified garden gnomes. Nonetheless, the bears on the meadow looked like a squadron of guards; they seemed to be saying: 'Don't give in! This is your village now, and our village too. We won't let any harm come to you.'

'I'm more childish than my first-years,' Rea whispered to herself and for a moment she felt at peace.

Rea began seeing other things she knew she would remember for the rest of her life.

Tuisku was still sleepwalking, and this time Rea woke up. Now she realised she had not forgotten to lock the door. Tuisku had learnt how to open the lock and left the door ajar as he went outside. He even put on his wellington boots, though otherwise he was only in his pyjamas.

Rea snatched a hooded jacket from the rail. It was so chilly outside that soon she would have to wake Tuisku up, or at least guide him back indoors. The boy picked up his bucket and walked off with such determination that Rea could not help but follow him – her curiosity shutting out the cold and the fear. This she had to see. She chuckled to herself; Tuisku would probably laugh too when he heard what he had been getting up to during the night.

She was startled and instinctively stood still when she realised that there were others outside too. Children, all different ages; some toddlers like Tuisku, others she might have called youngsters. They were all walking in the same direction, and none of them seemed to notice Rea, though she was standing in full view.

There were at least several dozen children, so many that Rea could not help but wonder: was she really the only adult watching this? Was everyone else fast asleep?

The group finally gathered at the end of the path, in a garden Rea had often stopped to admire. In between the trimmed hedges and flower beds stood a wooden bear. Rea was not the least surprised to see the children congregating around the sculpture. They emptied their buckets in front of it – she could not make out the contents of the buckets, but could well guess – and sat down on the wet ground. Rea had to control her desire to shoo them all home. They would most probably all have a sore throat the next day. Some of the older children hugged the younger ones. Tuisku sat on the knee of one of the older boys; precisely the kind of big boy that would be the prime suspect when someone steals the headmaster's wallet.

The children sat in silence. Rea did not have a watch on, but she sensed that a long time passed; an hour at least, possibly more. Then the children stood up and picked up their buckets.

The sky was clear and full of stars. Beneath the constellation of the Great Bear the little figures toddled back to their beds and Rea followed her own son home.

No one in class the next morning was coughing, but many of the children were hopelessly sleepy. This time Little Teemu fell asleep during morning assembly. The others giggled but Rea let him sleep.

Tuisku had not reacted in the slightest when Rea had walked him past his night-time meeting place that morning. Nor was there any sign of the berries, mushrooms or honey left around the bear – not even little footsteps.

It never occurred to her to discuss this matter with the headmaster. Although common sense said otherwise, Rea was convinced everything was as it should be. It was not her place to get involved and, besides, she had no desire to do so. There had been such a sense of calm and safety at the children's nocturnal meeting that she had no need to worry about Tuisku. On the contrary, Rea herself felt much more at ease, more prepared for what was to come.

Several more incidents occurred in the village; the police were called to investigate and began interviewing people. Everything took place close to the school, so even the children were asked all kinds of questions, but Rea saw no use in kidding herself any longer. He was taunting her; it was a reminder of all that could happen. This was just the beginning, but the petty theft, the graffiti and the crow left hanged on the school door were all just a game – a cat playing with a mouse.

Rea would always pop home during the lunch breaks, even when she had nothing in particular to do there. She would check the post, have a cup of coffee or put on a clean T-shirt if she had had a PE lesson that morning. Often she would wash up the morning dishes or make the beds.

This time something warned her before she even opened the front door. Something was different. As she opened the door she could see and smell the cigarette smoke. She wanted to run back to the school, hide behind the headmaster and call the police.

Arttu was sitting at the kitchen table. He had been using Tuisku's porridge bowl as an ashtray.

If Rea had bumped into Arttu anywhere else she would hardly have recognised him. He had put on at least twenty kilos and and had cut his long hair.

'Hello,' said Arttu in contrived friendship.

'When did you get out?'

'A while ago. Why didn't you come and meet me?'

'I didn't know.'

'Of course you knew. I told you in all my letters. You did read them, didn't you?'

Rea nodded.

Arttu had taken some milk out of the fridge and drank straight from the carton.

'Never mind. I'm here now. Nice place you've got.'

'What do you want?'

'I want to see my son. And then we can carry on where we left off, eh?'

Again Rea felt the impulse to run away and hide behind someone.

'I can bring my stuff round this evening,' Arttu continued. 'And don't look so frightened. I'm a changed man.'

The last sentence was presumably one he felt he had to say. Coming from Arttu's mouth it didn't sound very convincing; this didn't even seem to be the point.

'You can't move in,' she said flatly.

'I can, and you know that very well. Don't you remember all the good times we used to have?'

Rea could not really remember, she did not want to remember. It had taken a lot of effort to get over the blur of the past, and she did not need anyone to remind her of that or tell other people.

'Listen, I'm in a bit of a tight spot right now. I need some support, surely you understand that?'

Rea had half expected him to explain that a boy needs his father, that their love wasn't dead and so on.

'I've got to get back to school. Don't be here when we get back.'

Arttu shrugged his shoulders and lit another cigarette.

'Have you got anything to eat? The fridge is almost empty.'

'I'm going now.'

'Haven't you got time to pop into the bedroom? I've missed you, you know.'

Rea turned and almost ran out of the door.

'Didn't you get my message?' Arttu shouted after her and gave a throaty laugh.

The morning paper remained untouched on the floor, but everyone at school was talking in shock. They had probably all been talking about it that morning, but Rea had been so busy she had gone straight to her classroom and had not spoken to anyone.

'How is this going to affect the children?' sighed one of the teachers. 'I hope they catch him soon, otherwise we'll have to organise transport for the children.'

'What we need is a Neighbourhood Watch, I've said it before,' said another.

'Nothing like this has ever happened here before. Never.'

'Well, until now. I suppose you've got to expect it, we're so close to the town . . .'

'What's happened?' asked Rea.

The other teachers could not believe that she had not heard.

'Old Mrs. Koistinen . . . you know, the lady in the yellow house with the apple trees and a wooden bear in the garden.'

'Everyone round here has apple trees and a bear in their garden.' Rea was trying to sound calm but her jaws were trembling.

'The house is just where the saw track starts – not even hidden away. With the paint peeling. Why are you shaking?'

Rea remembered. She had seen a very old lady with a walking stick in the garden trying to pick berries on one of the bushes.

'No one knows how long she'd been there. The neighbours started worrying because no one had seen her and she wasn't collecting her post.'

'He was certainly barking up the wrong tree if he thought she had any money stashed away.'

'And the way he . . . who'd have thought? And to mutilate the cat like that as well.'

'There was a letter,' someone said.

'What kind of letter? Who to?'

'Hulmala didn't say, but he'll let us know soon enough. All he said was that the message was left to crown it all off . . .'

The headmaster raised his finger.

'Remember, we cannot talk about the details. We're not supposed to know anything, but please don't say anything to the press. Hulmala should learn to keep his mouth shut. And we mustn't let any of this slip in front of the pupils. Otherwise before we know it we'll have a swarm of terrified, restless kids on our hands, then we'll really be in trouble.'

'No, of course we mustn't talk, but still we have to warn the families. You never know with people like that.'

'Parents will take precautions once they've read the papers and watched the news. They'll have quite enough information. But they don't need to know everything.'

'Ignorance is bliss, I suppose,' somebody tried to be witty and the headmaster agreed:

'In this case it most certainly is.'

Rea did not want to know any more either. This was the day everything started to collapse. The perfect timing was probably unintentional on Arttu's part, but he had succeeded more than he could imagine. The full horror hit Rea at once, casting everything else in its shadow.

In the yard a slaughter van was waiting for a calf which had spent all summer happily hopping about the meadow, fooling itself into believing that the sun would shine forever.

By the afternoon the house was empty. Tuisku could smell the cigarette smoke, though the butts had been cleared away.

'Let's have a little rest,' Rea suggested. 'Come and sit on my knee and I'll read to you.'

Tuisku did not want to sit down.

'Why does it smell of smoke?'

'It's probably the ventilation. Don't worry about it. Come and sit next to me.'

'No. Let's play with the lego.'

'Or we could go to the shop. I could get you some ice cream.'

'Yes! We can go on your bike.' Tuisku was getting too big to sit in the child seat.

'Next summer we'll get you a bike of your own. One with two wheels,' said Rea and immediately realised that this may be a difficult promise to keep. Thankfully Tuisku could not see her face.

'Look, Mum, Laura's got two bears now. Cool!'

Next to the dark bear sculpture on Laura's garden there had appeared another, light-golden coloured bear.

The golden apple, she recalled, that's what people used to

call bears long ago. 'The forest's Golden Apple' people would say, because the word 'bear' was too frightening and sacred.

'Why can't we have one of our own?'

'Because we can't afford it right now. I've got to buy us some clothes for the winter first; then there's skis and ice skates and everything.'

'Don't you know?' snorted Tuisku.

'Don't I know what?'

'They don't cost anything.'

'What, the bears? Of course they do.'

'No they don't. You just have to go and ask that old man, then we'd have one of our own. Laura got them for free.'

'And Laura's father helped him . . .'

'Then you can help him too. A bear would be *so* nice. I could give it a hat and a scarf for the winter.'

'We'll see.'

Old Mrs. Koistinen's house was cordoned off with yellow tape, but Tuisku seemed not to notice. He was too busy debating whether to have strawberry or pear ice cream.

That night Tuisku went out wandering with the other children again and Rea followed him. Everything happened precisely as it had the night before, the only difference was Rea's disquiet. What if Arttu appeared out of the darkness? What if he harmed the children, wandering around as happy and innocent as lambs? Just waking them up would be terrifying enough.

But no one appeared. The next day Rea decided to spend the lunch break at school and even offered to do extra playground duty.

Upon coming home that afternoon she was greeted with another cloud of tobacco smoke and cigarettes stubbed out in the sink. She quickly cleared them away. For weeks she had fretted about how to warn Tuisku. How could she warn him so he wouldn't start living in fear, but would still be on his guard? Many times she had started to tell him but never quite finished. Now it could be put off no longer.

Tuisku had never asked about his father. Whenever the

subject had come up, Rea had lied and said that his father was dead. After all, to Rea he was dead. In no way had he been any kind of father to Tuisku.

She gave Tuisku a sandwich and a pot of yoghurt.

'Listen. Has anyone told you that something very bad has happened in the village?'

'No,' he said, stuffing the sandwich into his mouth.

'An old lady had some money stolen and . . . something terrible happened to her.'

'Who did it?' Tuisku's usual curiosity began to awaken as his hunger abated.

'No one knows, but . . .'

'They should hire a detective.'

'Yes. Still, I don't want you to go into the garden by yourself any more, only with me. And stay close to the teachers when you're out at school.'

Tuisku promised he would. But what could the ladies at the pre-school do if Arttu decided to get serious?

That night Rea lay awake once Tuisku had gone to bed. She was sure he would soon get up and pick up his little bucket, which this time had some honey in it. She had had to buy a big jar of it for his 'game'. For Tuisku this was so obvious that he didn't see why he had to explain it to Rea. You filled the bucket in the evening, and by morning it was empty again.

Before Tuisku awoke, Rea heard someone fumbling at the door. She confronted Arttu as he stepped inside. The telephone was on the hall table, but Rea did not have time to try and call for help.

'Hi. I would have come earlier, but I had some business to attend to.'

'Be quiet. Tuisku's asleep.'

'I'm bloody hungry. I hope you've got some grub this time.' Arttu's eyes gleamed in the dark. His speech was slurring just enough for Rea to notice. 'But first things first.'

'Let's talk.'

'No talking. I know you've probably been shagging around all these years, but I've been missing out. Bed!'

'No! Don't go in there!'

'Same difference, get your clothes off.'

When Rea did not start undressing Arttu tore off her nightdress. She lay perfectly still as he panted on top of her. It was over quickly.

'You're like a fish. You used to be a lot friskier. Got any beer?'

From the kitchen Rea could hear Tuisku getting up. She tried to divert Arttu's attention by rattling a pot, but he had already noticed Tuisku in the hallway.

'Well well!' he bellowed.

'Be quiet, he's sleep-walking.'

'He's going outside, the little devil!' laughed Arttu.

'Let him go, he does this every night. He walks about a bit, then he comes home.'

Arttu gave Rea a sceptical look. 'What are you on about? What is this? You're up to something!' He stood up quickly. Rea grabbed hold of him.

'Let him go! You'll see, he'll be back soon.'

Arttu shook himself loose and knocked Rea to the floor. Then he went off after Tuisku.

'Wait!' Rea shouted, but he had already shoved open the door.

Tuisku was already at the end of the path and the other children were walking beside him.

'Leave them alone,' Rea pleaded with him, but Arttu continued striding towards them.

The children had almost reached the garden when Arttu caught up with them and began shouting and ranting. A few of the children woke up from being knocked to the ground and started screaming in terror. The others carried on walking and seemed not to see or hear a thing. At the foot of the sculpture they laid down their buckets, though Arttu continued to run about pulling at their pyjamas. They sat down on the grass, and Arttu succeeded in waking up a few more. He pulled the hair of one of the older girls and she started shrieking. The lights in the house went on.

Rea was curled up on the ground. She was shaking and

moaning quietly and was unable to do anything. She could hear Arttu bellowing.

'What the hell's going on?'

The woods were some distance away. Here there was not even the slightest strip of trees; only a few fruit trees and the odd birch in people's gardens. Afterwards Rea could not say where exactly the bear had come from. It had just appeared from behind her, crawled past her on all fours, then stood up on its hind legs.

Arttu was standing with his back to the bear and was dragging a little boy by the shirt. The blow must have come as a complete surprise. He did not have time to be startled or fear for his life as the giant paw struck him in the back and seemed to split him in two.

Even the children who had woken up now stopped shouting. They all watched in silence as the bear mauled its victim. Not one of them screamed or even cried out in fear. Rea noticed that a man had appeared at the door of the house, but even he did not shout or run into the garden; he simply watched what was happening, then went back inside. The lights went out. One by one the children stood up and set off on their way home.

Rea was sure that the next morning the garden would be as it had always been. No little plastic buckets, no piles of berries. No male body ripped to pieces.

It started snowing. Soon the ground was covered in a thin, white sheet. Tuisku had wrapped a scarf round the neck of their very own bear. It looked very gaudy against the bear's wooden surface, but still it seemed just right.

Rea knew that the children would be wide awake the next morning, and every morning from then until spring.

# *Desk*

Jouko Sirola

*Jouko Sirola (born 1963) is a writer of short fiction and essays. In his writing elements of the mundane and the surreal collide in a fascinating and highly idiosyncratic way, all the while heightened by a style at once economical and objective, and yet always powerfully expressive. The short story featured here, 'Desk', is from the collection* Käveltävä takaperin *('Walking Backwards', 2003).*

For a long time it had stood still. At times it had changed position in the room, but even then someone else had moved it. There it stood on four legs, expressionless, as if there were no life left in it whatsoever. No external impulses could penetrate its indifference, something which with time had become its essential characteristic.

However, the step which it now took was indisputable. No one saw it stir and start moving, but that was because of the time of day. Morning light filtered through three panes of glass on to its surface as it arched its back and awkwardly stretched its front and back legs; it was no more or less difficult to walk in either direction. The wood creaked and rasped, groaning as if a hard frost were wreaking untold damage to its brown, rectangular form, but there was no one to hear this, and the people downstairs – an elderly couple who otherwise paid particular attention to any noise reaching their ears – had popped out to the shops.

The desk raised its front leg – some papers and an alarm clock fell to the floor – and, trembling slightly, slowly inched it forwards. After this it moved the other leg at the same end, putting the worktop under considerable strain. With a creak it flexed like a cat stretching its back, and its hind legs screeched across the floor. It had been a long time since it had last moved of its own accord.

It stopped for a moment, as if to gather its thoughts, leant slightly towards the radiator (probably trying to prevent its doors from swinging open) and shunted both legs on its longer side forward at once. This made walking far easier. Two feet at a time, waddling along like an overweight human being, it stepped up to the living room door. Scratches appeared in the door jamb as it dragged itself over the threshold. It continued out into the hallway.

Perhaps it had never seen people opening doors. Perhaps its knowledge of locks was limited to the inner sensation of a key turning in its own locks. Either way it now stopped and stood still for a long time.

It felt as if dusk was descending, as if upon a moment suspended in time, air thickening around anything motionless. The metre and a half long, nut-brown, waist-high desk stood behind the door darkening and darkening. Only once a click came from the stairwell – a door was pulled shut – did the desk rise up, lean over, shuffle briskly backwards and stop. It then carefully rose on to its hind legs, propelled itself forwards with surprising vigour and crashed into the door. The door gave a crack, wood splintered and the desk staggered and dropped down against its front edge like a bull falling to its knees. The computer monitor with its enormous cranium slid off the worktop and came crashing to the floor.

The lock held, the hinges did not give way, but as far as wood was concerned, the desk now knew it was the stronger of the two. Only a small piece from the rim of the worktop, overhanging each end like a thin eave, had been chipped away in the collision.

Had the couple downstairs really been at the shops this long? Or could their ears no longer distinguish the banging coming from above from the everyday family noises, the shouting and sounds of objects being thrown around, noises which they had suffered for years to the point of almost moving out? In any case, no one was standing there watching when the front door finally gave way and the desk came crashing through and collided with the railings at the top of the stairs. It was a good job the railings didn't break, or the desk would have plummeted down the stairwell and smashed. To pieces, to its constituent parts, blocks of wood and scatterings of nails, the darkness of its drawers suddenly illuminated and united with the air of the corridor.

It took a moment for the desk to get back on its feet, one end leaning against the metal grille of the railings and the surging depths beyond, rising majestically like a pillar up to the roof. An angular floor leading downwards stretched out in front of the desk with three or even four more landings before it would be at the bottom. But did it think of stopping? No, not any more. Like a bovid bred to malformation it gingerly placed a foot on the top stair and began its descent. It fell over on to its chest and slid down along the edges of the stairs, but stood upright again, as if it had felt some kind of pain, something quite different to what it had felt breaking down the door, which was also made of wood. It knocked against a number of letter boxes, but no one appeared from behind them to observe its dogged progress. All the adults were at work, the children in daycare, the house was empty and listened in silence. And even if a lonely eye had happened to glance out through a peephole, its impatient companion across the nose momentarily shut, at that moment the desk may have been standing perfectly still, as if the people carrying it had tired halfway down the stairs.

Finally the desk lowered its hind leg from the last step to the ground and stared at the front door through which it could see a thick green bush swaying in the wind. Perhaps in some way it understood that it was akin to the bush, though they belonged to different worlds. It tiptoed across a rough fibred mat and out towards the light.

The desk's legs had become suppler in the stairwell and its progress now seemed far less cumbersome as it approached the door and tried to ram its way through the glass. As it pushed with all its might at the hard, invisible air the door gave way and opened as if to show it the way. Soon the desk was standing on the tarmac outside letting the breeze soothe its back, now free of all other objects. The bush caressed its side first with one branch, then another. All around there was grass; insects and cars behind which there stood a row of enormous trees. Otherwise the yard was empty.

Empty of people and yet not empty after all. But because people are the only beings who may lend an ear to this story, we should say: empty. An old man standing on his balcony in the opposite house saw the desk. He saw it by the bushes, then at the corner of the house, and later on the lawn behind the cars. Every time he looked down the desk was standing motionless, as if someone had moved it from one side of the yard to the other, moving house most likely. And time went by, it went by so quickly nowadays that the man had years ago given up paying it any attention. Changes could only be discerned once they had already taken place. That's the way of the world.

Nor did the man on his balcony see the desk skipping around the lawn behind the house, throwing its front legs in the air, creaking and twisting like a kitten chasing its tail, until it returned to the path which at this point was covered in gravel. The small stones scratched its legs as it hobbled towards the bins and stopped at the base of a tall tree. Its hind legs knelt backwards and it crouched there, its front legs straight, as if trying to gaze up into the treetop swaying freely.

But was the treetop truly free? It was part of the trunk, rooted fast in the ground, though it could sway with the wind without severing its roots or losing its connection to the past, building up layer upon layer around the trunk in different sized rings according to how well the year had gone.

Perhaps the desk felt a certain melancholy. For it, however, there was no return to being a simple tree. It was now fundamentally different, it had evolved to be like this and all it could do was simply carry on.

The desk straightened its legs and staggered past the tree. It clambered on top of a pile of sand in the middle of a field opening up at the side of the lawn and turned around, as if to look back at the house it had just left. It then came down the other side of the sand pile and walked across the field towards a small wood with a path running through it. The path had been tarmacked, which suited the desk's legs very well. Sand scratched the wood, and on the damp lawn its legs sunk in too deep, almost up to its base. After all, its legs were only ten centimetres long. It was not a particularly modern desk.

Long cracks ran through the tarmac, a testament to the power of the earth. If for a few years the town remained as quiet and deserted as at this moment, in this small wood, weeds would soon take over the streets. Hawks would return to church towers as if they had never left. But the woods were quiet only for a moment. From far off the whine of an underground train could be heard as it braked. Cars accelerated away from the traffic lights and drove along a street which looked into the woods, though from the street things inside the woods always looked mysterious. That is the nature of the forest. The desk stopped beside a park bench painted a mud brown colour, leant to one side and waved one of its front legs in the air.

Years of motionlessness had not prepared it for journeys like this. It leant against the bench for a moment. Painted wood touched varnished wood, both of them brown, yet still so different. The bench was anchored to the ground. Heavy concrete blocks had been placed underneath the soil, now covered in thick grass. The bench could not follow the desk, wherever it was travelling. But perhaps the desk revealed its destination to the bench. Even the thought, the mere possibility of it brightened the moment and the desk turned to face the direction it had come and rested its other pair of legs.

Who could have dumped a desk like that all the way out here? There's all sorts goes on after dark, an old woman sighed. There was barely a sound as the woman shuffled along on her zimmer frame to the other side of the woods, where a luxurious old folks' home gently purred in the sunlight. Walking past you could make out its sound, like a giant conveyor belt humming deep within.

Beside the bench there stood a green, metal rubbish bin on one leg: rubbish strewn at its foot, a black bin liner inside. The desk straightened itself and carried on walking. The ground gradually began to slope downwards, but a cyclist battling against the wind at the bottom of the hill didn't so much as turn his head and didn't see the dark rectangular figure through the tunnel of trees slowly growing bigger and bigger, which now, if seen from the front, all but blocked the path and eventually turned on to the pavement.

As it sauntered down the pavement the desk passed a window covered in garish stickers behind which pizzas were made to order. The shadow which passed across the window was nonetheless faint and barely discernible, and insignificant compared to the shadows cast over the mind of the pizzeria's Moroccan owner. His curiosity was not aroused in the slightest. He turned his eyes back to the comics in the evening paper. Reading them in a strange language was a nuisance and did little to alleviate the other, unknown troubles gnawing at his mind. What had once happened to him was something that couldn't be divined from his pizzas and didn't show through the foreign colour on his face.

The desk wobbled across the street and turned to follow a low hedge bordering the car park. It stopped for a moment and before long a sparrow landed on top of it. A red bicycle was visible through the hedge. All sorts really did go on at night. Who had left the bicycle there after stealing it on a whim? The bicycle had no owner, no next of kin. It had no history of its own, it didn't belong to anyone, and a stranger picking it up, riding it through the suburbs and casting it aside into the hedge, had not really changed a thing.

The desk preferred not to think of the bicycle's owner. It hardly noticed the bicycle. After all, it didn't have eyes, it was only a desk. If it had been able to look around, what would it have thought? Would the darkness of its drawers have thought on its behalf, interpreted the light seeping in between the worktop and the sides, single-mindedly and matter-of-fact, without even the most basic sensory faculties?

The sparrow fluttered into the air and the desk was on the move once again. A buggy and a young mother with a revealing slit in her skirt came careering round the corner from behind the hedge. Nothing's lost yet, that's what the slit was trying to say. A cyclist, an elderly man, who very nearly collided with the desk, seemed for a moment to be chasing the woman. As he approached her he slowed down, as if the sudden incline in the road had appeared simply to help them fulfil their desires; so that for a single, ecstatic moment life could be nothing but the flesh disappearing beneath that skirt, the thrill of revealing it and being the lonely object of its revelation. The cyclist made his way past the buggy, slowly, reluctantly.

The sight of bare flesh didn't excite the desk. It crossed the road again and walked past a building with a kiosk on the ground floor, an old shopping centre that looked more like a bunker, its windows decorated in short combinations of letters and numbers, exclamation marks, colourful advertising slogans and several grey plastic lumps with glass screens covering their front. The desk made its way over the crossing and disappeared into the park. At the edges of the path around the suburb the park was wild and covered in thicket, but nearer the shore the lawn had been mown neatly.

Square footprints zigzagged their way along the sand path to a sign forbidding dogs on the shore. At the foot of the signpost the desk leant over so its doors flew open and its drawer slid out, vomiting out its contents. It shook its body, then turned sharply on its other side. The doors slammed shut. It continued walking with its drawer open, but only as far as the rubbish bin, then leant against the bin to push the drawer back inside. Now it was completely empty and much lighter, so much so that its footprints could barely be seen in the sand. Why hadn't it emptied itself earlier?

A messy sight was left behind it. Papers, envelopes, staplers, discs, invoices, a camera, an old computer mouse and a few magazines lay scattered around the pole. It was the sort of pile that those passing by later wouldn't dare bend down and rummage through – certainly not if anyone was watching – not even to pick up the camera which looked quite new. Not that they were in any way bound by an inner respect for other people's property, but simply because going through rubbish aroused other suspicions. Everyone with an ounce of self-respect already owned a camera like that, and what would someone want with two?

Without a care in the world for humans' everyday worries the desk stared out to sea, its corners blunt, the smell of the ocean between its boards. It was a clear day, a ferry with flocks of passengers on its deck bobbed past on the waves. One of the passengers seemed to be waving at the desk, though this was hardly possible. Why would anyone have been waving at it? Only the people living in the house and perhaps the nearest pieces of furniture – if, that is, they knew anything at all – were aware of its existence. And its former owners of course, who had already passed away, and their other possessions, sold off or left rotting at the dump. The desk was no longer new, it had a past of its own, even though its drawers were now empty.

Wearily the desk dragged itself on to the lawn. The ground led down towards the sea and became rockier towards the shore. Four inquisitive ducks appeared from behind the rushes. They swam ashore, stood up, argued angrily amongst themselves, crossed their legs beneath them and lay down to rest. The dark, wooden figure crept up behind them obscuring the park bench from view. The birds hardly paid it any attention.

Was the desk thinking about its creator, the seed, the tree from which it had grown, its early years deep in the nut grove, the logger, the sawyer, the carpenter, all those who had been involved, who had gradually made it squarer and squarer, more practical for human use, so much so that there was barely a glimmer of its former nature left? Be that as it may, the nearby trees, which had grown in a tight clump at the edge of the lawn, gave a deep sigh, pressed their branches together and rustled against one another.

Was the desk still a tree, an untamed piece of nature blowing in the breeze; could it sense the sigh of the leaves shimmering through its non-existent boughs like a ghost pain? Or was it ultimately humanised, a civilised onlooker; an object at which people could not help but sit and jot down a few numbers, memoes, or lazily open up the day's papers and stare out across the centrefold at the house opposite and the clouds appearing from behind the house, lilting in the sky and finally disappearing into the blue yonder behind the window frame?

There was no answer. The footprints stopped where the desk now stood, bird droppings and a few flies on its worktop, the evening sun warming its side, the sound of the water and the rumble of a far away truck deep within its boards. It leant over, took a long, carefully considered step and stopped at the water's edge. Was it thinking of going for a dip, of wading out into the water, or did it realise that it would sink straight away because it was heavy and unsealed? Nonetheless, it stopped at the water's edge and did not take another step.

As dusk began to fall the desk was still standing put. It seemed to have frozen to the spot, as if it were listening to something. It was surrounded by the scuffing of running shoes, first coming closer then disappearing again, and the sniffing of roaming dogs. The dogs would always mark their territory before leaving. 'Look, that's a nice looking desk,' exclaimed one female voice to another. The other answered – something.

Evening gradually darkened into night. Invisible laughter and the clinking of bottles, accompanied by loud swearing, could be heard approaching. A while later the voices burst through the hedgerow and on to the illuminated pathway along the shore.

'Fucking hell! Check this out!' A young man left the group and bounded down to the water's edge. He leant his head to one side, raised his leg up high as if he were aiming at something in the sky, kicked the air in front of him, turned, gave a shout and kicked out behind him. There was a thump and the desk crashed into the water.

The splash had frightened the ducks snoozing in amongst the rushes and they quacked in annoyance for a moment. They shortly calmed down, the clink of bottles faded away and all that was left was the lapping of the water and the distant growl of cars speeding along.

But, surprised at the weight of the desk, the young man had

stumbled and fallen into the water and got his trousers wet. Even after a few drinks things didn't always go as smoothly as they did in films, and the guffaws of his friends were merciless. If only he had been able to, he would have taken his kick back, he thought as, shivering, he trudged home where a light still glowed in the window.

# *Blueberries*
# *The Explorer*

Jyrki Vainonen

*Jyrki Vainonen (born 1963) is a writer, translator and teacher of creative writing. He has published fiction, radio plays and numerous articles. His work as a translator includes* A Tale of a Tub, *a selection of Irish pamphlets by Jonathan Swift and four anthologies of contemporary Irish poetry (including the works of Seamus Heaney, Paul Muldoon and Thomas Kinsella). In Vainonen's prose there is a vibrant sense of the strange and the dream-like, often resulting in decidedly kafkaesque visions, though surrealism is perhaps the most prominent feature of his writing. The short story 'The Explorer' is from the collection* Tutkimusmatkailija ja muita tarinoita *('The Explorer and other stories', 1999), whilst 'Blueberries' is from the collection* Luutarha *('Bone Garden', 2001).*

## *Blueberries*

August emptied his sixth pail of blueberries into a large vat by the sauna steps. Less than a kilometre from the house he had discovered a copse teeming with blueberries. Tucked in between the rocks surrounding the lake, the spot's entrance was guarded by two enormous boulders, sitting blankly on the rock, staring ahead like the blind eyes of a giant frog. Blueberry bushes spread evenly across the ground like a thick carpet, and the stalks growing at the sunny southern end of the patch sagged under the weight of their indigo fruit. August had spent the last two days there on his haunches, and as soon as his pail was full he made his way back up to the cottage to empty the berries into the battered tin vat. After only a few pails the base of the vat had all but disappeared from view, and after the fourth load it was almost half full.

August put the sauna door on the latch, picked up his bucket and began to make his way back into the forest. Once he had reached the hill he sat down in the shadow of the giant boulders for a rest. He took off his frayed cap, which by now was rimmed with sweat, wiped his brow on his shirt sleeve and licked his dry lips. The calm of a summer's afternoon lazed around him. Sunlight filtered through the trees, here and there revealing the cobwebs which laced the plants and trees. He looked out between the treetrunks, out across the open lake, the glint of the sun almost dazzling his eyes. Suddenly his thoughts turned to winter, to its short, cold, dark days. He could see the frozen, snow-covered lake in front of him and relished the thought of what those blueberries would taste like on winter mornings, how they would bring summer flooding back into his mouth. And what about the taste of the lingonberries, which he was to pick next? Or the mushrooms, which he would pick after the lingonberries? He cast his eyes over the abundant nature surrounding him, brimming with joy and thankful that it would provide for him amply through the winter, as it had done the previous four winters.

August put his cap back on and picked up his bucket by the handle. As he straightened his back he felt a nasty twinge between his shoulder blades. Perhaps he had overdone things the last couple of days . . . less crouching down than this would have been enough to make his muscles ache. The previous evening, after a hard day, he had collapsed exhausted on his bed, his back and arms aching, and fallen asleep like a stone dropped into a well.

He took a few steps and looked around. Once he had placed the bucket securely between two tussocks he carefully lowered himself on to his haunches. His back gave another twinge. August grimaced, grabbed a handful of blueberries from the nearest clump and popped them in his mouth. As he was chewing the berries he noticed that there was something odd about the tussock on which they grew. He bent down for a closer look: something white could be seen amongst the moss. His jaws stopped. He rested carefully on his left knee and poked at the earth around the root of the clump.

It took a moment before he realised that the shoot, from which he had just grabbed the blueberries in his mouth, was sprouting from the left eye socket of a skull buried in the ground.

August stuck his fingers down his throat. No matter how much he spluttered and coughed, despite the churning in his stomach and the sweat on his brow, he could not vomit; only the bitter taste of stomach acid rose to his mouth. He stood up, took a deep breath and instinctively looked around himself. He then knelt down on the tussock again and began frantically scraping away the rest of the moss streaming out through cracks in the bone. Through the skull's right eye socket grew another blueberry sprig, and a whole clump of berries was protruding from its mouth, just beneath two brown upper teeth. August could feel his mouth drying out and the hill seemed suddenly to be spinning around him, but he clenched his teeth and carried on digging. After much exertion he had managed to excavate a yellowed human skeleton from amongst the moss and plants. Its ribs and thigh bones were shrouded in the tattered remains of clothes.

August lifted the skull with both hands and carefully raised it up to his eyes. Using his fingers he wiped away damp grains of sand stuck to the bone. Sunlight shone through the skull; in its cranium there was a hole the size of a bottle top, through which the blueberries had stretched their roots. He placed the skull on the ground and wiped his brow. From the shore he could hear the squawk of a sandpiper skimming the water and suddenly, for a fleeting moment, August could see himself from the bird's perspective: lying on his back, his limbs outstretched in the shallow waters along the shore, his eyes and mouth wide open, and at regular intervals a blueberry appearing from his mouth like a blue air bubble.

When four years ago August had left his wife after fifteen years of childless marriage, resigned from his teaching position and moved to the old house in the middle of the forest, a cottage he had inherited from his uncle, his friends thought he had taken leave of his senses. The divorce had not come as a surprise, certainly not to August's close friends, but how would a shot gun, some fishing net and a hectare of land be enough to keep alive a man who had spent his entire life in the city? And how would someone who had worked as a teacher for decades grow accustomed to life in the wilderness, kilometres away from his nearest neighbour? Would the solitude not be too much?

August could no longer remember the anguish he had felt in the beginning, how he would sit on the steps up to the cottage for hours, battling with his feelings of guilt, surrounded by nothing but the calm of the wilderness. At first he had been unable to hear a thing, not even the silence, but gradually his ears had become a part of the forest and the surrounding nature had begun to speak to him. Even his guilt had eased over time. Nowadays he would spend his evenings sitting in a rocking chair in front of the tall old hearth, with his feet on a stool, staring at the blazing fire through the grate. With a single blow he had severed all ties with his former life; in four years, no one had set foot in the house but him, no friends or neighbours, no random passers-by. Not a single eye had observed August inside the house, watched him mending his fishing net, reading, washing the dishes or playing patience in the evenings by the light of an oil lamp. He had no siblings and both his parents were dead. August had never seen his father, who had died in the war only a few months before his son's birth. August's mother had often recounted how handsome his father had looked standing at the altar in his soldier's uniform. At this, tears had always welled in her eyes. August soon learned which subjects he was not allowed to bring up: the funeral, his father's body shot to pieces.

After his mother's death August had looked for a place on the bookshelf for his parents' wedding photograph. He had wanted to show his respect for the dark-eyed young man with the earnest expression, who had valiantly held his own against the enemy in the battle which was to be his last. At least this is what, one morning years later, in a grave and consolatory voice, an envoy from the army had informed his mother, with August clutching at her skirt.

August visited his parents' grave a few times a month, as he drove his old van the ten kilometres into the village to stock up on food and other supplies. He would often exchange a few words with whoever happened to be passing by, so as not to become completely isolated, but he never enjoyed being around other people for more than a couple of hours at a time.

It was shortly after moving to the woods that August had begun collecting bones. He could not remember how or when this hobby had started or where his interest in bones had originated, and by now he had stopped thinking there was anything remotely odd about it.

The first bones in his collection he had found deep in the forest only a few weeks after the move. A dead, half decomposed hazelhen had been lying on the ground at the foot of a spruce tree. August had poked at the corpse with a stick until the last feathers and lumps of flesh had loosened from around the bones, then placed the skeleton in his back-pack, which had fortunately contained a plastic carrier bag. Upon returning home he had sat cleaning the bones for hours by the light of the oil lamp, painstakingly trying not to break the most fragile bones, the bird's needle-thin and breath-takingly beautiful wing bones. As dusk approached on that late summer's evening he finally succeeded in piecing together the delicate lattice of bones. August could still rem-ember the joy which had blazed inside him as he had looked at his creation. He had dabbed a small, gleaming drop of glue at some of the skeleton's most important structural joins. He was particularly taken with the hazelhen's delicate skull, which tapered out into a delicate beak in front of its eye sockets.

That very night he had cleared a space for the bone-bird on a wooden shelf in the cellar. Later on, as he had begun amass-ing more bones from the surrounding forest, he had put up more shelves, until finally they covered every wall in the cellar. Nowadays the cellar walls were lined from floor to ceiling in bones: entire skeletons and individual bones, the skulls of various animals, fragments of bone. There were birds, foxes, squirrels, hares; there were elk bones and bear bones, a deer's torso; a long, flat bream.

Until now there had not been a single human bone to complete August's collection. As he carried the bag full of the bones of the unknown deceased, August knew there would not be room in the cellar for such a large skeleton. He decided to take his discovery and put it in the woodshed. He cleared a space along the wall just inside the door and piled the bones like logs on top of some empty sacks of fertilizer. At first he had thought of leaving the skull on the top of the pile, but after running his fingers over it for a moment, he could not bring himself to leave it in the woodshed and decided to take it inside. He placed the skull on one of the bookshelves between Sophocles' Oedipus and Shakespeare's Hamlet.

All evening August thought about the body; who it had been, how they had died and why. Every now and then he glanced over at the skull and wondered whether he should report his discovery to the local police. He sat down in his armchair, lost deep in thought, and battled with his conscience. Finally he decided to keep quiet about it. It was clear that many years had passed since the death; there was probably no one even looking for the deceased any longer. What point was there in digging up the past?

After coming to this decision August calmed down considerably. He browsed through his library and found a dusty old book on bone discoveries. Judging by the size of the skull he concluded that the body must have belonged to a man. The skull's empty eye sockets and its gaping mouth unnerved August, and he found himself wondering what colour eyes the unknown man had had, what kind of eyebrows, what sort of face. Several times through the course of the evening he felt a strange presence staring at his back and wondered whether he should have left the skull on top of the other bones in the woodshed after all. Perhaps even after death people still have the right to their own bones.

The following morning August continued with his blueberry picking, as he wanted something to take his mind off his discovery. Once he had filled the barrel, he packed the blueberries into containers and stacked them in flawless piles in the freezer. He left himself a bowlful of them to eat. The previous year August had bought three freezers at an auction: one for berries, one for mushrooms and one for other foodstuffs. He needed to keep a stock of food, because he did not own a tractor or a snow plough to keep the narrow lane leading up to the cottage clear. During the winter the only way he could get to the village shop was on skis.

Two days after discovering the skeleton August had once again sat down in his rocking chair, when he was suddenly consumed by the feeling that he was not alone in the house. He lowered his feet to the ground and listened, but could not hear a sound. He stood up, wandered around the room pretending to tidy things up, watered the flowers, walked from window to window. He finally plucked up the courage to inspect the entire house, checking upstairs, downstairs and in the cellar. Don't be ridiculous, he chided himself as he climbed down the stairs to the cellar. No one has found their way out here to the back of beyond in years. Once in the cellar he lit an oil lamp and stood in the middle of the room. There in the lamp's flickering light he looked over his collection and filled his lungs with the faint, lingering smell of the bones, a scent to which his nose had grown accustomed. How beautiful they were! He held his lamp up higher and walked from shelf to shelf, looking at them, touching them. He fingered the bones, held them in his hands, ran his fingers over their knots and indentations, along their smooth surfaces and jagged corners, and felt his body relax completely. It was as if the timelessness of the bones had flowed into him, stopped him in his tracks and calmed him. But as he climbed back up the stairs the restlessness returned. Eventually he grabbed the skull from the bookshelf and took it out to the woodshed, placed it on top of the pile of bones and turned its stark face towards the wall. That'll teach you, he thought as he closed the door to the shed and fastened the latch.

That night August dreamt for the first time in four years. Immediately after his divorce he had stopped dreaming altogether and had come to accept the idea that his subconscious was dead, that it was as calm and still as a summer lake and that never again would anything disturb its deep, dark waters.

The following morning he was still consumed by the dream. He woke up in a cold sweat, a strange metallic taste in his mouth. He thought it must have been the blueberries he had eaten just before going to bed and gulped down the glass of water he had placed by the bed. The man in his dream had had a familiar face – so familiar that August felt he ought to have recognised him. No doubt he had met this stranger back in the days when he had still lived around other people. What an odd sight the man had been: he had been wearing heavy, old-fashioned clothes and he was standing by himself on the platform of an unfamiliar railway station, which had been painted red, with an old cardboard suitcase at his feet, staring indifferently in the direction from which the train was to arrive. There was no one else on the platform and the station house looked deserted; not a soul peered out at the platform through its empty windows.

To put the dream behind him August first opened the window. The light and fragrance of summer flooded in. Birds busied themselves in the apple trees in the garden and a gentle breeze fanned the thin white curtains. After a breakfast of bread, porridge and blueberries August hurried down to the shore and into his boat, with its strong smell of tar, where he had left his fishing equipment the night before. He swiftly pushed the boat out on to the water and headed off towards the open lake, as calm as a mirror and draped with floating wisps of mist. The gleaming sun had already risen above the treetops on the nearby island. After rowing for a while August removed his jacket and rolled his shirt sleeves up to his elbows.

He steered the bow of the boat into a patch of rushes where he had set two fish traps. The first was empty, but as August lifted the second one, he could feel by its weight that here was a catch. He balanced a lever on the edge of the boat and wrenched at it, but the trap was so heavy that he was afraid the boat might start taking on water. He stood up, assumed a sturdy haunched position and grabbed the lever with both hands. The trap bounced and finally rose out of the water in a shower of sparkling droplets. August saw two sturdy, thrashing pikes; two broad, shining backs.

He saw something else. When the pikes stopped wriggling for a moment he could make out another, dead pike lying at the bottom of the trap. Its head had been gnawed away so much that its white jawbone shone and flashed in the sun. August lost his grip on the lever and the trap fell back into the water with a great splash. Once he had fished the trap out of the water again and tipped the pikes into the boat August was taken aback by the sheer size of the dead pike. It was almost a metre long and its exposed jawbone the size of a fox trap. What a fine addition to his collection that would make! The fish had already begun to decompose and the strong stench caught in August's nose as he rowed briskly back to the shore. He had never encountered anything like this before: the pikes in the trap had killed and eaten one of their own kind; they were predators, after all.

As he approached the shore August turned the boat around to back it in beside the jetty. Just then he thought he saw some movement by the corner of the house. He held the oars in the air, gleaming drops of water dripping from them. The oars protruded like a giant wingspan, the boat bobbed on the spot and August carefully examined the shore, but saw nothing out of the ordinary. Finally he returned the oars to the water and calmly rowed back to the jetty. Not once did he lower his eyes from the house and the garden. After climbing on to the jetty with the red bucket of fish in his hand he quickened his step. He placed the bucket just in front of the door and bolted round the side of the house. Nothing, no one. August felt his heart relax and he was angry at himself for letting his imagination get the better of him.

Later that evening August heated up the sauna. He went to the woodshed to collect some logs. The bones were stacked in a neat pile precisely where he had left them: shins, ribs, hips, wrist bones, thigh bones, ankle bones. On top of the pile sat the skull, a hole in its cranium, staring with empty eyes towards the doorway.

That evening August went to bed early after drinking half a bottle of home brewed beer and eating a handful of fresh blueberries for supper. Again he lay dreaming all night. A giant pike with glorious feathered wings soared through the clouds. In flight it opened its mouth, an enormous contraption, then its jaws would snap shut. The creature flew down and landed on a spruce tree, opened its mouth wide, revealing its teeth – and began to sing. Standing at the base of the tree, August gazed up at the strange creature; even the birds had fallen silent to listen. Then, all of a sudden, the man from the previous night's dream appeared again. He was running through the forest, leaping across the tufts of blueberries, weaving in and out between the tree trunks. August could hear the man gasping for breath, he could see sweat pouring down his young face, plastering his hair to his forehead. The man was dressed in a soldier's uniform, the buttons on his jacket were dangling open, his vest was soaked with sweat. He ran stumbling up the gentle hillside, resting every now and then against a pine tree. The man did not appear to see or hear the pike, the giant fish singing its heart out at the top of the spruce, nor did he see August staring silently from the base of the tree. August could see that the soldier was afraid, terrified, every time he looked over his shoulder.

August awoke with the taste of lead in his mouth, sat up in bed and listened. The silence of the summer's night hissed around him. August was convinced something had disturbed that calm; a sound, just now, only a moment ago, and wrenched him from his dream world. He sat there listening, his ears pricked, barely daring to breathe. He gradually calmed down, got out of bed and plodded barefoot towards the window. It was already light outside, the dark branches of the apple trees were glimmering, dewdrops sparkled on the spiders' webs. The lake was utterly calm, thin threads of mist hung here and there amongst the rushes.

August gave an exhausted yawn, but did not go back to bed. That afternoon, as he was weeding the vegetable patch, he discovered a dead mole. He had always thought of moles as big-boned coulters, but there it lay on the palm of his hand, small and cold as the thick of a chisel. He raised the mole up to eye level and blew back the fur on its head until two small dark points appeared: the mole's eyes. He lay the animal down and continued weeding. After half an hour he had found a selection of small bones buried in the soil, and two hours later he had discovered the skeletons of eight common moles. Using a watercolour brush he carefully dusted them clean of soil and laid them out on sheets of newspaper. With a few skilful swipes of his knife he quickly skinned the dead mole and looked for a place to display it alongside the other mole skeletons. As he stretched his back the thought occurred to him that he had been growing his vegetables in the moles' graveyard. Looking out across the lake he imagined himself standing on top of the moles' catacombs. Their tiny burial chambers extended several metres down, on top of each other, next to each other, and at the foot of each one; deep down, hidden by the black earth, lay a delicate collection of shining white bones.

Before going to bed that evening August ate a slice of the blueberry pie he had baked. He fell asleep almost as soon as he had lain down and pulled the covers over himself. He could feel the effects of a day in the vegetable patch in his limbs, and the final thought in his head before he fell asleep was the knowledge that he was slowly growing old.

This night too his dream was lively and vivid. The pike was still sitting up in the tree singing, this time it had piercing mole eyes, and the spruce's grey bark smelt of dried resin. The soldier had stopped running and was now crouching by the side of a giant boulder, his back against the rock, holding his breath and listening. This time, August too could hear the footsteps approaching over the hillside. He could see the fear in the soldier's eyes, the throbbing veins in his neck and forehead, the teeth biting into his lower lip, the ribs rising up and down beneath his shirt and rough cotton jacket. As the soldier turned his head to look back in the direction of the footsteps, something at his neck flashed. An identification tag, thought August and suddenly realised that it must have been the clink of the tag hitting the rock that had woken him the night before. He could hear two people approaching, they were marching up the hill side by side. At this the soldier dashed out from behind the rock and darted to the left, straight towards the other giant boulder. August could already see his two pursuers; two soldiers each carrying a rifle. He saw their uniforms, their collar badges. One of them knelt down, cocked his rifle and took aim. August did not hear the shot, but he saw the flash, and imagined the bullet shooting through the air until it pierced the back of the soldier's head and sent him flying face first in amongst the heather. At this point August began to shout: Don't shoot, he's one of your own, for God's sake don't shoot your own! But in the dream not a sound passed his lips. The only sound to be heard was the pike's song pealing out from the top of the tree: there it sat singing, a pike with the eyes of a mole, snapping its gigantic jaws, silencing every bird.

The following morning August climbed back up the hillside to the place where he had found the skeleton. He got down on his knees and bent over to examine the spot where the skull had lain. He sifted through the cold sand, carefully scrutinising every handful, and discarded the sand in a pile beside him. After digging for a short while he finally found what he was looking for: a small, flat aluminium tag. It could easily have been broken in two, but both halves were still intact. August carefully wiped the tag, rubbing away the sand. He tried to decipher the numbers on the tag, but some of them were so worn away that he could not be sure whether they were in fact zeroes or eights.

August rushed back to the house, changed into his town

clothes, put the tag in his battered brown leather satchel and got into his car. He was gone for two days. On his arrival he parked the car in its usual place in front of the house, went inside, changed into his everyday clothes and reappeared carrying a black bin liner. He walked straight up to the wood-shed, placed the skeleton he had found in the forest piece by piece into the bag and lifted it on to his shoulders. He then headed out to the forest, up the hill to the place he had originally discovered the bones, found the place where they had lain and knelt down. He dug for a quarter of an hour, moving the grit and sand with his fingers, lifting it to the side of the hole in his bare, cupped hands. Then he proceeded to empty the contents of the bag, placing the bones one at a time in the freshly dug hole. On top he carefully lay the skull.

Crouching there on his knees, looking at the hole in the back of the skull, he remembered the clip-clop of footsteps on the lacquered stone floor in the hallway of the archive building: he remembered the somewhat curious expression on the round face of the archivist as he had introduced himself, handed the man the identification tag and asked that he would like to know to whom it had belonged.

The archivist had soon recovered from his surprise. When he had asked where August had found the tag, August had to explain as precisely as possible the time and place. He decided not to say anything about the skeleton; he simply said he had found it whilst out picking berries.

'This is a tag lost in the war,' the archivist had explained. 'It hasn't even been broken in two.' Then he told August to go and have a coffee in town whilst he investigated the matter. 'Come back in an hour.'

An hour had been more than enough, because when August returned to the archive the assistant was already able to tell him who had originally carried the tag.

'But . . . don't you have the same surname?' he exclaimed after telling August the name of the owner, as the truth had dawned on him.

August could no longer remember what he had replied to that friendly, unknown person standing in front of him with a mixture of surprise and shock on his face, a small aluminium tag dangling from his right hand; a tag which during the war had dangled around the neck of August's father. But he did remember that no sooner had he stepped out on to the street than he had decided never even to attempt to find out who was buried in his father's grave; who was lying there next to his mother.

## *The Explorer*

Dr. Klaus Nagel, the director of a remote meteorological station, went missing in the early hours of April 6th. The station was situated on top of a small hill on the outskirts of town. It was a windy night, low clouds drifted across the sky above the houses and the treetops. Between four and six o'clock in the morning it had rained, furrowing small trenches along the dirt track leading up to the station. Behind the station streams of rain water curled their way down the hillside.

On night shift that evening, the meteorologist Johannes Dagny was waiting to go home. He was sitting drowsily at his desk and staring out into the yard by the light of a small table lamp. Every now and then his head bobbed down to his chest waking him with a start. Trying to stay awake he stood up, stretched his legs and peered outside. Puddles gleamed on the uneven yard and vapour rose from the sand. Raindrops sparkled on the branches of a birch tree growing behind the window. Dagny was waiting for Dr. Nagel, waiting for the headlights of his red Honda to caress the hillside and for his car to splash through the puddles, the crunch of sand beneath its tyres.

An alarm clock ticked on the table. When the doctor had not appeared by seven o'clock Dagny assumed his colleague had overslept and decided to wake him.

The telephone rang five times before a sleepy voice answered. It took him a moment to explain the situation to the doctor's young wife Marianne, who had risen from a deep sleep to answer the telephone. 'Just a moment,' she sighed into his ear.

Some time passed. The morning news could be heard on the radio. Dagny took a spoon and stirred the cold, stagnant coffee in his cup. Birds were chirping in the woods behind the station. He imagined Marianne rousing her husband, handing him the receiver, yawning, stretching her arms, running her fingers through her dark hair. Dagny had only met Marianne once at a reception at the doctor's house. He would gladly have swapped roles with Nagel and woken up every morning next to a woman like that.

'Hello?' It was Marianne's voice. 'He's not here, he must be on his way.'

But Dr. Nagel was not on his way to work. He was not sitting behind the wheel of his Honda, nor was he driving past the town hall nor steering his car on to the main road leading out of the city. After the telephone call Marianne noticed the pile of clothes her husband had laid out for work lying carefully folded on the back of a chair. She slunk out from underneath the warm blankets and pattered barefoot into the kitchen. No one. No one in the hall or in the toilet. Once she had returned to the bedroom and tightened the belt on her dressing gown she noticed a piece of paper propped on her husband's bedside table. She switched on the small lamp. The note contained a single sentence written in Dr. Nagel's sharp, angular handwriting: 'My dear Marianne! I have disappeared from your life in order to get inside your life. Klaus.'

A few hours later a police constable with a serious expression upon his face was standing in the Nagels' kitchen asking Marianne if she had the slightest idea what the note might mean. Marianne shook her head. Together they listened to the sounds of policemen searching the apartment: furniture being moved around upstairs, a bookcase being emptied in the living room. Someone coughed in the bathroom. The young constable was visibly uncomfortable. 'There's no need to worry, Mrs. Nagel,' he said trying to comfort the woman standing in front of him and raised his eyes from her brown hair to an unspecified point on the ceiling. 'We'll find him.'

But there the constable was wrong. Dr. Nagel was never

found even though the investigation was conducted with great care and a notice of the disappearance was given out to the local media. It seemed that the last confirmed sightings of Dr. Nagel were on April 5th. In the morning he had been at the meteorological station, then at three o'clock the staff on evening shift relieved him and he went home. Nothing out of the ordinary had happened that evening either, Marianne told the police. At eleven o'clock the doctor had kissed her good night, whilst he had stayed in his office reading a book about conquering the North Pole, in which he had been immersed for the past few days. The following morning Mrs. Nagel had woken up to find herself alone in their large double bed.

For a while the doctor's disappearance fundamentally shook the lives of those it had affected. Daily routines at the weather station were in upheaval and the normally peaceful working conditions had been shattered. Amongst the maps, monitors, bookshelves and computers swarmed groups of reporters, photographers and newshounds. With powder puffs the police searched the station for fingerprints, of which there were plenty. Time and again Johannes Dagny was required to go over the events of his shift to the press. He saw himself on television and could not stop thinking whether this was what he really looked like in the eyes of other people. Even telling people about the case upturned the life of the generally very conscientious Dagny. He enjoyed a certain sensation of power as he sat in front of journalists thirsting for what he had to say. Each time he recounted it he became more and more excited by his story and soon began to colour it with some choice details: the overnight rain became 'the flood of the century', the streams swelled into 'great currents' and his boredom and fatigue were a 'hibernation plagued with strange dreams'.

The media furore surrounding the case also seemed to affect Marianne. Soon after the disappearance she confined herself to the house and refused to speak to any reporters. The only person she allowed inside was the young constable. His journey home appeared very often to take him past the doctor's house, rising up on a pine-covered hillside on the outskirts of the city. Almost every day the constable's car could be seen standing next to Nagel's red Honda – even late into the evenings, when the blinds had been shut and the moon spilled light down upon the grass.

The secretiveness of the doctor's young wife only added fuel to the tabloids' fire. Information about the Nagels' failed marriage was leaked to the press. Marianne was painted as a fickle, neglectful woman with an insatiable hunger for men, even after she had married Dr. Nagel – for money, the papers claimed – a man twenty years her senior, killed him and hidden the body.

Amidst all the fuss, the police investigation was going nowhere. Marianne later noticed that her husband's rucksack and fishing equipment were missing, as well as a change of clothes he used to take on hiking expeditions. For some reason the police guessed that the doctor must have gone off on a night-time ramble. Some even suspected him of sleepwalking, but Marianne assured them that the doctor was not in the habit of wandering around at night; he always slept soundly. The woods around the city were searched thoroughly but to no avail: there was not a trace of Dr. Nagel.

Several weeks had elapsed since the disappearance before the commotion began to die down. The newspapers were finally forced to think up some new headlines and uncover new revelations. The folder containing all the information on the doctor's disappearance was moved into a tall metal cupboard in the police archives with the words 'Unsolved Disappearances' on the door. No one paid any attention to the fact that the young constable's car still stood in the Nagels' driveway every evening. No one seemed interested in the fact that Marianne, who still only rarely left the house, did not look the slightest bit devastated or grief-stricken, but was as radiant as any newly wed bride.

There was however one person with knowledge of this matter: Dr. Nagel himself. He was only missing inasmuch as he had not yet been found. He was not hiding out in the woods around his house, peering through his binoculars as the silhouettes of his wife and the young constable merged behind the blinds in the light of the window, when dark had fallen outside. Neither was he lurking in the basement or in the garage in amongst sacks of potatoes, jam jars, tool boxes and piles of studded winter tyres, let alone creeping about inside the house at night, dodging furniture in the dark, listening silently from behind the bedroom door.

Dr. Nagel had done precisely what he had said: he had left his wife's life in order to get inside her life. If his note had been interpreted correctly he would undoubtedly have been found. For in the early hours of April 6th Dr. Klaus Nagel had in fact moved inside his wife Marianne's right thigh.

Everything had been meticulously planned in advance. The decision to embark on this research trip had matured during the long, silent nights spent at the meteorological station, as had all the details. He saw this expedition as his final chance to nurture a closer relationship with Marianne. No more turning her back on him, no more headaches and tiredness in the evenings.

The doctor chose Wednesday April 6th as his departure date. Once Marianne had gone to her aerobic's class, as she did every Wednesday, Dr. Nagel was able to make the necessary preparations in peace. He decided to take only what was absolutely essential – after all, he was on his way to a place where the climate was similar to that at the Equator. So he packed his rucksack with a few changes of clothes, some tinned food, a book entitled Family Medicine Vol. 8 (dealing with the human circulatory system) and all the equipment needed for his research: thermometer, anemometer, barometer and a plastic test tube for measuring rainfall.

The doctor stashed his rucksack under the bed. After this he sat down to read and contentedly waited for his wife's return. He knew that, after returning home, his wife would say: 'What a tough programme, I'm absolutely exhausted', and that later on she would hint: 'Gosh I'm tired, I'm sure I'll fall asleep the minute my head touches the pillow'. And this is precisely what happened: Marianne dozed off whilst her husband was reading about the adventures of polar explorers; as he trekked across the expanses of snow, his breath in clouds around his head, picking icicles from his moustache. If it had only been on Wednesdays that the doctor had had to console himself with the company of polar bears and seals, the problem would not have been quite as serious, but sadly the temperature in their bedroom had been dropping evening upon evening, night upon night.

On this occasion Dr. Nagel wanted to ensure that his wife slept soundly. He dissolved a few sleeping pills in the canister of juice from which he knew his wife would drink when she got home. He wrote his wife a succinct note which he would place on the dressing table before his departure.

Once Marianne had curled up beneath the blankets Dr. Nagel lay next to her perfectly still and listened closely to her steady breathing. Silence hissed in the corners of the bedroom. The doctor waited. Shortly after four o'clock it started to rain. Dr. Nagel went into the kitchen and washed up the juice canister and the glass, so as not to leave any evidence behind him. He listened to the raindrops pattering against the window ledge and was afraid that his wife might wake up. This fear was however futile: his wife was wondering through the valley of sleep. It was time to get to work.

As he stepped inside the thigh the doctor noticed his hands sweating and his heart racing. Inside it was dark, moist and warm. There was an echo. He felt constant pressure in his ears and the rush of blood through the veins was like the distant hum of a motorway or the quiet purring of power cables above a field.

The doctor dug a torch out of his rucksack. He was standing up to his ankles in red water. It must have been the outlet of a lake, bringing blood from the heart to the furthest outreaches of the circulatory system. He turned and walked against the current. He was no longer Dr. Nagel but Dr. Livingstone. The source of the river was waiting to be discovered. In the quiet tunnel of the vein he could hear the squealing of monkeys, the squawking of parrots, the roar of lions and the clatter of delicate hooves as a group of antelopes galloped for cover. He looked at the world around him with the eyes of a true scientist, alert and his senses heightened. He was thrilled by the thought that he was stepping where no man had stepped before, he was seeing and hearing what no eye had seen and what no ear had heard.

He made notes, took readings and checked his position with a compass. Using these observations he would be able to tell others about his voyage. Walking against the current was hard work and breathing was rather difficult. Dr. Nagel realised that his clothes were far too warm. When he came to the first narrow tributary in the river he stopped for a moment to catch his breath and checked his position. He sat down on the river bank and removed his cotton shirt which was soaked in sweat on the back and around the armpits.

After folding the shirt into his rucksack the doctor set off once again. He noticed that his eyes had grown accustomed to the darkness. He switched off the torch by whose beams he had been guided until now. The current in the river was becoming stronger. At that same moment, in another world, in a house on the hillside, in the half-light of the bedroom, Marianne was waking up to the sound of the telephone ringing.

While the police turned over the house in search of clues, and while Marianne and the police constable were exchanging glances in the kitchen wondering what the doctor meant in his note, Dr. Nagel was wading through the red torrent inside his wife's thigh. Walking was now even more of a challenge, because since Marianne had awoken the current was stronger and pushed hard against the doctor's bare calves. Save for the makeshift loin cloth he had made out of his trousers Dr. Nagel was now naked.

For the first time in his life he felt that he was alive – not merely as a theoretical entity but as real tendons, veins and layers of skin. He was drenched in sweat and could feel his muscles, unaccustomed to such physical exertion, shrinking and relaxing, contracting and slackening again. He felt his lungs gasping for breath, his joints cracking and booming, yet still moving to the will of his muscles. The beauty of it all was how much he was enjoying it. It was as though the body, which for so long he had considered a necessary evil, put together simply to support the head, was in this new environment finally coming into its own. He thought how the joy he was experiencing was the same as an adder wriggling along the ground in the sunshine, dust and pine needles catching against its body, moist after shedding its skin. Or perhaps he was an ancient Celtic sorcerer, who winding an eel skin around his arm can feel the electricity pulsing through his limb.

In the evening of April 7th the exhausted Dr. Nagel finally arrived at his destination. During those long sleepness nights at the weather station he had selected the precise spot to set up camp, a place where for the first time he would be able to set eyes upon two dim stars. He knew they would be dangling in the dark sky like a pair of copper coins. In the world which he had left behind, they were not stars but vaccination scars on Marianne's thigh. The sight of them reminded the doctor of their first night together. He had caressed them, kissed them, pressed his groin against them. Touching those scars Dr. Nagel had felt the years dropping from around him and had placed the palms of his hands on Marianne's warm breasts.

When the stars came into view, his scientist's nature overpowered the vagrant within him. The time had come to set up base. Over the next few days the doctor did anything but save his strength. First of all he dug out a cave in the thickest part of his wife's thigh bone (throughout that time Marianne experienced such an agonising pain in her right thigh that she was forced to seek comfort in the arms of the young police constable) and kitted it out with the few items he had brought. After this he explored the area immediately surrounding the cave. It seemed safe and was well-suited to his research. The region was dominated with high plains covered in rocks and patches of grass. No trees grew there, but the rocky terrain was dotted here and there with miniature red-leaved bushes.

The river cut right through the area. There was no need for the doctor to fear starving to death. During his trek he had noticed that the river was seething with fish eager to bite into the worms squirming on the end of the doctor's line. There were two species of fish: small red ones and large white ones. Dr. Nagel recorded them in his notebook as simply reds and whites. The flesh of the red fish was very nutritious, though it left a strong aftertaste of iron. The white fish did not have an aftertaste, but had no other taste either. In no way did the two species live in the river in peace and harmony. The whites were constantly attacking the reds. The doctor was astonished at the fury with which they sunk their razor sharp teeth into the scaly sides of the reds. After conflicts like these the surface of the river was awash with the reds' mauled bodies or heads from which the body had been gnawed off.

Gradually Dr. Nagel's life began to settle down. He began his scientific work, transferring the surrounding world on to paper. Before his departure he had written out his motto on the first page of his notebook: 'Dive again and again into the river of uncertainty. Create in the dark, only then can you recognise the light.' In the quiet darkness of the thigh his pen brought light and order to the world. Page after page the world began to form a story. He was like a blind rune singer from whose lips tales of the beginning of time poured forth, of the light and the darkness, of the first human being.

His tale was nonetheless based on results. Three times each day the doctor picked up the equipment he had brought, measured the weather conditions and recorded the results in his notebook. Aside from his work he spent his time fishing, reading the family medicine book and hiking across the nearby rocks, between which there lay mist in the mornings. In the evenings he gazed at the sky in search of new stars.

The more he learnt about the world around him, the more the doctor noticed a change in himself. He was no longer the same Dr. Nagel as at the outset of his expedition. The muscles in his arms and legs had strengthened. The skin on the soles of his feet had toughened with clambering around the rocks. His hair, beard and nails had grown. A month after his arrival he had happened to catch a glimpse of his reflection in the river and could hardly believe his eyes: who was that dirty, dishevelled, wild man floating on his back watching him from the water?

His research became rather monotonous, because the weather conditions hardly ever changed. It never rained, leading the doctor to take a greater interest in changes of temperature. Once he knew the effect, he had to search for the cause. Of particular interest to him was a series of repeated heatwaves during which moisture would stream down the walls of the cave and the river's current became so strong that it almost flooded over the banks. If during one of these heatwaves he stood at the mouth of the cave, he often saw the air shimmering above the ledges. The air was electric. He would always get a headache. After the third week he finally worked out the logic behind these sudden changes in temperature.

There were two types of heatwave. At times the temperature would rise slowly and steadily whilst at others the air seemed to become charged in a matter of minutes. The doctor's notes revealed that the slow heatwaves always occurred on Wednesdays and it was this which eventually put him on the right track. The explanation came from the other world. It was on Wednesday evenings that Marianne stood with her legs apart waving her arms in the air listening to the instructor's rhythmical interjections at her aerobic's class. The more frantically Marianne waved her arms, the faster she brought her knees up and down and stamped her feet on the floor, the warmer conditions became for her husband hiding inside her thigh.

As the doctor searched for shelter from the heat, as he lay on the pile of clothes forming his makeshift bed, as he fanned his face with the branch of a red-leaved bush, the memory of Marianne began to disturb him. He thought back to the world he had left behind. As clearly as if he had peered out of a hole in the thigh, he saw the aerobic's hall and a few dozen women clad in leotards. The thought excited him. He tried to look up at the ceiling, count floor planks, analyse the pictures hanging on the wall, but his eyes always returned to the spots where yearning and absence turn into flesh: the buttocks, the thighs and the breasts.

When the class was over and Marianne stopped jumping up and down, stretching and dancing, the doctor sighed with relief. But he knew it was merely the calm before the storm. He would still have to suffer once more before the temperature would drop again: Marianne rushed into the shower. As the mirrors in the bathroom steamed up, the cave walls began to drip with moisture. The doctor's fingertips tingled as if he had scalded them in the water pouring over Marianne's body, flowing to the floor and running down the drain. Eyes appeared on the doctor's fingertips, eyes with which he devoured Marianne's body.

Dr. Nagel disliked these Wednesday heatwaves. As he sat in the loneliness of his cave, bathing in sweat, he imagined himself searching for a light blue flower growing at the edge of the spring which touched him with its resplendent leaves. Within the broad ring of blue petals was the spectre of Marianne's face. It disturbed his concentration on the absolute truth of numbers, on that which can be measured, that which is permanent and sure.

Even more of a trial, however, were the sudden heatwaves. In unlocking their mystery Dr. Nagel relied on logic and numbers and their incorruptible truth. He counted, added and subtracted, multiplied to the power of x. Yet time after time he found himself at a dead end. By far the most difficult matter to explain was why these heatwaves only occurred at night. The doctor was on the verge of accepting this as an inexplicable factor in the equation, when the answer finally dawned on him. He was sitting on the riverbank fishing and he became so excited that he dropped his fishing rod into the water and the fish got away. The explanation was all too obvious, if unpleasant: the doctor realised that Marianne had a lover. Nothing else could explain the sudden heatwaves at night. His joy at finding the solution to the conundrum was bittersweet due to the uncertainty of who this unknown lover could be. Who was arousing Marianne so much that the doctor all but roasted alive in his cave?

The doctor had to be content with using his imagination. Drawing on the depths of his jealousy he composed a story about Marianne's lover. There were two characters in his story: Romeo and Juliet. Romeo was a young, broad-shouldered police constable, who was investigating the disappearance of Juliet's husband and fell head over heels in love with her beautiful brown eyes. Every evening he would drive his car to the gates of Juliet's castle. Swarms of mosquitoes danced by the light of the lanterns in the garden and further off the currant bushes looked like people crouching in the darkness. The drawbridge, which Romeo had to cross to reach the castle door, strongly resembled a slab of concrete. The door which he knocked greatly resembled the door of Dr. Nagel's house. Juliet, clasped in Romeo's arms, was clearly Marianne's twin sister. Juliet was thrilled by her lover's kisses. She could feel inquisitive fingers lifting the hem of her skirt, caressing her bare thigh. She surrendered to her lover on the thick pile rug in the hallway. They made love twice in the wide double bed. Three times the air inside her thigh boiled, blood rushed in hot waves against the walls of her veins. Three times the heat woke Dr. Nagel as he lay sticky with sweat.

Life could have gone on like this indefinitely: in two worlds and in two stories. The doctor could have spent the rest of his life in his cave with the knowledge that not even death could separate him from his unfaithful wife. He could have taken comfort in the thought that they would share the same coffin, just as they had once shared the same bed. Marianne could have married her young constable, borne him a son and a daughter and later found herself another young lover once her bald, middle-aged husband no longer interested her. And no one would have remembered Dr. Klaus Nagel, the director of a remote meteorological station, who one day had disappeared without trace.

But the two stories were to cross each other one last time. It was exactly two years since Dr. Nagel had gone missing. Marianne had spent the weekend at her mother's house and was sitting in her car driving home. She was driving very fast along the dark motorway. She was tired and her eyelids kept drooping shut as she stared at the empty road ahead.

By the time Marianne saw the elk it was already too late. Its eyes shone like diamonds in the glare of the headlights. Marianne should have tried to swerve on to the verge and go around the animal, but she wrenched the steering wheel in the wrong direction and slammed on the brakes. Everything happened in a second. The car hit the elk and the windscreen smashed into thousands of shards, slashing open the animal's side. Marianne had forgotten to fasten her seat belt. She flew head first through the windscreen. The car went off the road and the elk's body was hurled from the bonnet into the bushes at the side of the road. Then a great silence descended upon the empty road. The car was lying on its side, two of its wheels still spinning. Steam rose from beneath the crushed bonnet. Shards of glass were strewn across the road, they shone in the light of the street lamps. A black skid mark could be seen across the tarmac.

Three minutes later a lorry happened along the road and the driver found three bodies at the crash site. The woman driving had been crushed beneath her car. Broken glass had cut up her face. Her right thigh had been severed at the knee. Next to the car lay the body of the dead elk. Its stomach had spilled out on to the road. Its innards steamed. The third body was lying in front of the car. Only once he came closer did the lorry driver notice that the man was naked. His skin was covered in a thick layer of dirt and his face with a bushy beard. His tangled hair reached down to his shoulder blades. His nails were ten centimetres long. The lorry driver recoiled and hurried back to his vehicle. He called for help on his car phone.

By the time he put down the telephone, more people had arrived at the spot. They parked their cars behind the lorry and peered down the bank to see what had happened. The lorry driver stood warning signs at both sides of the road.

The police arrived along with an ambulance, although the lorry driver had already told them that there were no survivors. Everyone was perplexed by the naked man. Had he been in the woman's car? Why was he naked? Paramedics carried the bodies into the ambulance on stretchers. The accident even made headline news. Identifying the woman did not present any problems: the police found a handbag in the car containing a driving licence in the name of Marianne Nagel. But who was the mysterious naked man?

The police went back to their missing persons' files. They found a folder boasting the name Klaus Nagel on the spine. This aroused some suspicion, but a final identification could only be made once the deceased's beard had been shaved and his hair cut. The man's identity was then confirmed when his shaved face was compared to a photograph of Klaus Nagel several weeks before his disappearance. The director of the meteorological station had finally been found.

# *Black Train*
# *Basement, Man and Wife*

Maarit Verronen

*Maarit Verronen (born 1965) began her career as a writer of short fiction and her early work is very clearly rooted in science fiction. Although her more recent output has come closer to the realist tradition, the strange and the mysterious, the mythical and the inexplicable are all still central themes. Her novels have twice been shortlisted for the Finlandia Prize. She has also written a number of radio plays. Both of Verronen's short stories in the present volume were first published in the collection* Kulkureita ja unohtajia *('Tramps and Forgettors', 1996).*

## *Black Train*

At the station in Zubotica stood a black train.

In front of a run-down station house eight passengers were waiting for permission to board that train and continue their journey south. None of them looked in any way dangerous or suspicious, but despite this they were surrounded by a dozen or so border guards, their weapons at the ready.

Zubotica had once been an important junction, a vibrant border town complete with beautiful old houses and churches. Now it was simply a border town; a town from which seven out of ten inhabitants had fled across the border to be with their relatives. From hundreds of kilometres away refugees had been brought in to replace them, but they did not enjoy being there either. The refugees longed for the ruins of their homeland, a place which Zubotica, their new home, did not resemble in the slightest.

A single train came across the border from the north each day, almost always empty. It returned immediately, only this time it was full of passengers grateful to be given permission to leave the country. Any people travelling in the other direction, like the eight in question, were grilled about their reasons for entering the country, and those reasons needed to be good.

The eight passengers answered the same questions in turn. The grandmother of a family of four had died and the family was travelling to her funeral. An old man was returning to his birthplace to die: cancer, two months to live, he said. A middle-aged man had arrived to collect his pregnant wife and their child and take them back to their homeland. A young man had come here in search of work.

The eighth passenger was only travelling through. As always before. Everywhere.

This eighth passenger was cleared through the border formalities much more easily than any of the others. No one rooted through any luggage, no extra questions were asked, all the relevant paperwork was stamped after only a quick glance. The chief of the uniformed staff remained expressionless, but two of the clerks beamed at the passing traveller as if they were trying to light up the station platform with their smiles. The eighth passenger looked them up and down and thought how they would have seemed equally appropriate marching in parades, standing at the border or taking care of staff entertainment. Humiliating people in one's mind was an old way of overcoming those who appeared threatening.

Guards escorted the passengers to their carriage. As they chatted, getting to know one another, there was an almost wild sense of relief in the voices, gestures and expressions of the youngster and the middle-aged man. The elderly man just stared blankly ahead, not saying a word. The family of four quietly, cosily, went about their business in their own compartment; the sound of conversation rising and falling could be heard through the wall; bags being opened, the rustling of sandwich papers.

The train did not move for half an hour. It gradually filled up with dozens of locals – those who had not moved away from Zubotica and whose people were in the majority in the country. Laughter could be heard, high-spirited jokes, lots of chatter and small disagreements about everyday matters.

At the first stop, a handsome young man sat down opposite the eighth passenger. He had acquired some gel on the black market and had rubbed it into his hair, which had been cut with care. The sunglasses on top of his head kept his coiffure in place. He was wearing a white T-shirt, jeans, trainers and had narrow hips. The eighth passenger was still so caught up thinking about the guards at the station that it was impossible to look beyond the exterior of a person. All one could do was try one's best, particularly once the young man began to talk about his home country – and to a foreigner, no less.

The man pointed out of the window: that's such and such a town, where there's such and such a famous building and where such and such a world famous poet was born. In daylight you can see how beautiful and peaceful it is all around; how refined and cultured, how thriving the countryside; how clean the towns are, with no need to worry about thieves or violence. I'm glad that you've come, he said, you can tell everyone what it's really like here. The world has turned its back on us, people only believe the mendacious propaganda bandied about by our enemies.

The eighth passenger was well aware of how peaceful it was in both the towns and the countryside, and reassured the man of this; there had been peace in that country throughout the long conflict. The neighbouring countries were at war with each other, but that was another matter entirely.

The young man began to talk passionately about the neighbouring countries and their peoples. He spoke of ignorant, bloodthirsty, uncivilised barbarians who were trying to force his fellow countrymen to leave their homeland and give up their rights. The man asserted that his country had not been involved in any of the troubles. He and his compatriots were peace-loving people, but still they were being punished for the problems across the border.

Throughout their three hour acquaintance, the eighth passenger could not decide whether the man was deliberately being economical with the truth or whether he was simply a gullible fool. Perhaps the young man really did not know that his own government had in fact instigated the conflict in the neighbouring country and had openly been involved from the start, providing arms and moral support, until their losses had become too great. Perhaps – or maybe he just did not want to know the truth.

The middle-aged man, travelling to join his wife and child, moved closer to the eighth passenger as soon as the self-proclaimed propagandist had left the carriage shortly before the terminus. The man first made some insignificant comment, and when the eighth passenger gave a friendly reply he began talking about his family. As the train was about to stop he finally got to the point: his wife may be in need of some help. Would it be at all possible for a foreign traveller like yourself to stay with us? The man explained that there were very few people left in the country that he could trust. He had always been an outsider, even before the conflict, though back then he had had nothing to fear. No one had directly threatened his life, but people had stopped keeping their promises; thieves and con-men were rife.

The eighth passenger agreed to go with him, for want of a better place to spend the night. Knowing where to find a reasonably priced hostel was all but impossible, and it would have been plain foolhardy to take a cab. The price of a taxi ride had shot up as a result of the fuel embargo and only the greediest and the most unscrupulous drivers were still in business.

A dozen or so people, two or three families, had turned up to meet the family travelling in the adjacent carriage. They all stood on the platform hugging, crying and lifting up each other's babies. The young man, who had said he was coming here to work, walked past them and slipped quickly through the crowds of people and out towards the main entrance. He skipped down the steps, his bag on his shoulder, and strode off confidently into the street.

The old man with cancer, returning to his homeland to die, did not leave the station. He stood on the platform for a moment clutching his few possessions and looking around. He then slowly trudged up towards the wall and into the doorway of a closed bar. There he lay down to sleep with a bundle of clothes as a makeshift pillow.

The eighth passenger followed the middle-aged man out of the station and across a broad boulevard. They walked up to a tram stop, waited for five minutes, then boarded a half-empty tram. The man paid for both their tickets and began talking again; about his wife and their first born, now three years old, throughout the entire journey.

He lived in a slightly dilapidated, dirty six-storey apartment block. There was no lift, and so they ran up the stairs to the fourth floor. The man bounded half a flight of stairs in front and could not even bring himself to wait at the door. As the eighth passenger arrived in the hallway, the man had already gone through every room in the flat and appeared from the bedroom scratching his head, looking rather confused.

There was no one in the flat. Some of the furniture was missing, as were his wife's personal possessions. What was left was old and in bad condition.

The door to the neighbouring flat opened and a woman with rollers in her hair knocked on the door frame. She gave both of them a long and heartfelt hand shake and explained that there had been a robbery the previous night. It was only after this that she mustered the courage to tell the man that two days earlier his wife and child had suddenly taken ill and died.

The man stood motionless for a moment.

The neighbour quietly backed off into her apartment, as the man turned and dashed into the kitchen. The sound of clattering could be heard for a short while, after which the man reappeared carrying a pistol.

He placed the gun in his pocket and said that he would rather not talk about the matter right now, but would take his guest to a hotel and go into town and drink himself to oblivion. There was a decent, cheap hotel right by the railway station. The man insisted on paying the costs for his guest.

They said goodbye to one another at the reception desk.

The man wished a happy life to the eighth passenger, who in turn appealed to the man to take care of himself.

Walking up the staircase, the eighth passenger never once looked back, but upon reaching the third floor rushed up to a window at the end of the corridor looking down on to the intersection below.

The man was standing on the street. Hesitantly, as if he were already drunk, he staggered across the lanes of traffic into the middle of the crossroads, stopped, turned slowly and took the pistol from his pocket. Then he shot himself.

The eighth passenger backed away from the window and crept slowly into the room. The man had never even fully introduced himself – what a thought. What had just taken place had been beyond anyone's control. Surely people couldn't expect someone to keep an unknown, erractic, armed man company!

The eighth passenger locked the door, switched on the television, laid out some clean clothes, undressed, took a shower and climbed into bed. There was still some food in the suitcase, but it no longer seemed appealing, even after eating nothing but a light breakfast all day. Eating in the restaurant downstairs was also out of the question. Best not to meet or talk to anyone, and not to leave any currency in this country whatsoever, not a single coin. Trying to get some sleep would have been something, but even that was difficult.

Crime was on the rise around the capital city, said the newsreader. Although there were lots of police officers, there were still too few and they could not get to the right places quickly enough. The newsreader insinuated that a large number of police officers may be corrupt. Gangs of criminals were more organised than ever before and shootings had become more and more commonplace. One such incident had just occurred and, exceptionally, the suspect had been successfully apprehended.

On the television screen a young man lay on the ground, lit by spotlights, his head in a pool of blood, his eyes staring blankly into emptiness. The same young man who at the border station had said he was entering the country in search of work; the one who had zigzagged his way out of the station, on to the street, disappearing in amongst the throngs of people.

To the side stood a young man of the same age, held in handcuffs between two policemen, his hair dishevelled, his white T-shirt soiled. He no longer had his sunglasses, and hissed at the camera something about defectors and traitors of the state. He looked and sounded panicked, as if he had been crying, as if all he wanted to do was throw himself into someone's arms and sob, and tell them that he had not meant any harm.

The eighth passenger turned off the television. Perhaps no one would ever know why the gunned down young man had really entered the country. He had talked about a job, but in this country official jobs paid money that would never have been accepted anywhere else. That money could buy people less and less of anything that had a price. Even honest work could no longer make young men move to a country where living and being successful was almost impossible.

The eighth passenger slept badly, woke early in the morning and realised that it would be possible to catch a train earlier than planned. What a stroke of luck: there was certainly nothing in this city to entice travellers to stay for very long.

According to the morning news the previous night had once again been restless on the streets. The police had been pursuing a group of criminals suspected of money laundering. They had been cornered into a hiding place under an old chapel, which by coincidence had also contained a store of smuggled petrol – and this had then caught fire. The criminals had all died, as had a family of four who had come to the chapel to mourn their late grandmother.

Four familiar faces appeared on the television screen: a man, a woman and their two children. In the photographs they looked almost as nervous as they had the previous evening at the station in Zubotica.

The eighth passenger reasserted that the goings-on in that country were of no concern to anyone else. It would have been naive to imagine that anything could be done about the situation. No one would be able to put an end to the mindless brutalities with simple, sensible measures, whilst mindlessness seemed to maintain the upper hand.

There was only a handful of people at the railway station as the eighth passenger arrived. Just as the train came into view, the same old man stumbled out of the waiting room. A cleaner was prodding him with a broom stick and threw his bundles of clothes out after him: on your way, you lay-about.

Climbing on board the train the eighth passenger wondered whether it had been worth coming back here for that. Looking out of the window, the man could no longer be seen on the platform.

The train left on time but came to an abrupt halt almost immediately amid a screeching of brakes and stood still. There was no announcement to explain the reason for this delay, but the old man's bundles of clothes had been scattered across the tracks in front of the train and the station staff were not allowing nosey passengers anywhere near them. The police quickly arrived on the scene – and promptly left again – followed shortly by a dark car, which was not an ambulance.

The eighth passenger looked beyond the car and saw the black train on a distant track, standing waiting for evening to come, for its return journey to Zubotica. It was a perfectly average train, but it had to be defied; everything had to be defied by doing something mindlessly rebellious.

The eighth passenger stepped off the train and watched it pull out of the platform; sat, stood, wandered back and forth across the station and its surroundings; watching that black train, this quiet city and its people, until everything became familiar and no longer seemed particularly special or threatening.

Three hours later they boarded the train on which their journey had originally been intended.

The man often stood in the boiler room, perfectly still, listening to the electric hum of the water tank, the crackle of flames in the firebox, and enjoying his freedom.

That room was his refuge. It was small and bare, and whoever had built it had made a number of mistakes, but over the years the man had managed to fix most of them. There was only one flaw he had left unrepaired, because his wife had thought the job would be far too difficult and expensive. Something approaching tearful hysteria crept into his wife's voice, and indeed her entire body, every time they spoke about the matter and by now the man had become wary of even mentioning it indirectly. Naturally it was a bit of a bind that the drain in the boiler room was situated at the highest point on the floor, but it would have been stupid to upset his wife over something so insignificant.

When the man had first seen the house he had barely even noticed the boiler room, because the woodwork room had grabbed his attention. Initially he had thought he could have that room all to himself: there was a carpenter's bench, there were shelves and hooks to hang all manner of tools and equipment which even his wife thought suitable for a man. In fact the man's hobbies had never really included woodwork or joinery – unlike the previous owner, who had built the house – but he had always done the odd bit here and there whenever necessity had demanded it. At his wife's parents' cottage, where they had lived until only recently, there had always been a constant flow of things in need of repair.

Now he had told his wife that he wanted to dedicate more time to woodwork. He led her to believe that making things from wood had always been his secret passion. The truth of the matter was that he wanted to do something in which the very act of doing it is more important than the eventual result, but he certainly couldn't tell any of this to his wife, who dismissed such things as 'useless pottering'.

It was of course rather risky to reserve himself a room like this for made-up reasons. When someone noticed that the room wasn't being used for its given purpose, that someone might very well assume that no one was using it at all. That particular person might even have had some other use for it.

The man had been swiftly forced out of the woodwork room, when his wife had set up her loom in there and started weaving rugs, wall tapestries and tablecloths to be used around the house. At the same time she had also moved a freezer and a mangle into the room, because anywhere else they would have got in the way of her other chores. The vast majority of the man's tools had been placed in a cardboard box in the corner of the room, whilst making one's way to the carpenter's bench was now all but impossible.

Learning from his mistakes, the man had never mentioned that the boiler room was in any way important to him, though his visits there were steadily becoming all the more frequent. He had in fact offered her the use of the room for some of her dirtier jobs, if they were such that she could choose freely where to perform them. This tactic had worked a treat: after a while his wife barely went to the boiler room at all. However she had clearly sensed that she had been tricked and jealously began keeping tabs on her husband's visits to the basement.

Over the years the man had developed a routine for his visits downstairs and always remembered to explain precisely what he was doing beforehand. Sometimes his wife would ask him accusingly what exactly he was up to when the man didn't have a particularly good explanation. At times like this the man felt as though his mother had caught him with his hands beneath the blankets.

He often thought of his wife in much the same way as he thought of his mother and didn't see anything strange about this. He had accepted the fact that there were a lot of similarities between them. His mother had always been at home and so was his wife. His wife had given up working whilst she was expecting their first child and had never gone back to work, because her husband's wage had been large enough to support the entire family.

Money had never been a problem in their family, the way it

is for so many families. They were neither rich nor poor; things were far more complicated than that.

Particularly when it came to her own needs and wants his wife always wanted to spend as little money as possible. She felt uncomfortable if she or her husband had to use large amounts at once or if he spent something, however little, on something she felt was unnecessary. If the previous day they had decided to buy a new appliance, the man would generally buy the first one that he saw. The following week his wife would then find an offer in the newspaper for a similar machine – one not quite as well equipped but perfectly adequate nonetheless – which would have cost less. After this she would suddenly become helpless with the new appliance: so expensive and complicated; I don't know how to use it; come and push these dials, you're the one that bought the wretched thing.

Scenes like this made the man seem like a squanderer and his wife a penny-pincher, but this impression was largely false. The man was in fact very frugal: he greatly enjoyed thinking up new, clever ways of saving money on, say, the car or the heating bills. His wife had noticed this tendency at the beginning of their marriage and had made a subconscious decision to be every bit as virtuous and thrifty as her husband. In this she had certainly succeeded. Now she alternated between reproaching her husband for excessive spending and telling him he was too much of a skinflint.

Their battle over money took many forms, one of which was that his wife didn't want a bank card or a credit card. Her normal argument was that then she would start wasting money, if she could no longer see how much actual money she had to give away for what she was buying. At other times she would turn the argument around: she didn't dare use the card for fear of overdrawing on her account.

She also never drew cash out of their joint account, where her husband's wages were credited, and she never asked him to do it for her or told him how much money she needed. Her husband therefore had to withdraw the money and guess how much his wife required. She would get offended if he openly handed her a bundle of notes, so they had to slip the money from hand to hand like a microfilm in old detective movies – even when they were alone in their own house.

Neither of them had any hobbies to speak of outside the house – or inside, for that matter. From time to time they would spend a few days travelling around the countryside, though neither of them particularly enjoyed it. Because his wife didn't have a driver's licence, the man had to do all the driving every day so that in the evenings he was always tired. Their day trips were always very long, so as not to waste any time, and they would trail around churches, war memorials and other sights that were all rather sombre and plain.

Normally however they would sit at home watching television and taking care of the house and the garden. They rarely had any visitors, and went even more rarely to visit other people, because they had no close friends whatsoever and only a few acquaintances.

Every other week the man would go on domestic business trips for a day and a half at a time. Although these trips had over the years become more and more routine, he still enjoyed them as much as he had at the beginning of his career. Perhaps even more so, because now everything was familiar to him, he could relax more and shine with confidence in front of his younger colleagues. He would watch as his colleagues got drunk and tried to chat up some company for themselves. The man had never indulged in either of these activities. He was normally driving and certainly wasn't looking for the sort of change or excitement a strange woman would have brought him. His bosses' secretaries described him as a pleasantly calm, polite gentleman, and privately he was very proud of this.

The man was not ambitious to the extent that he might want a showier position or a higher wage. He had nonetheless been promoted several times. Every now and then a position would become vacant within the company for which he was more than qualified, as he had already been taking care of these other responsibilities to cover holiday leave without extra pay, in addition to his own work.

His wife always expressed at length her concerns that something embarrassing might happen to her husband, either at work or somewhere else, if she, the omnicompetent wife who never forgot a thing, were not there to take care of matters. She didn't trust her husband to keep himself or the space he used presentable for other people. This is why he didn't have a space of his own in their house and why his wife bought all his clothes for him.

His wife had never left him at home by himself for as much as a day, unless it had been absolutely necessary due to giving birth or a bout of illness. She never allowed him to do any of the housework. She was afraid – though she didn't dare admit this even to herself – that her husband wasn't quite as helpless around the house as she wanted to believe. If that were the case, all her sacrifices would have been for nothing and she would have wasted her life, spending it as a useless parasite.

The man knew very well that this is what his wife was thinking, but didn't know what could be done about it. She was sceptical, almost hostile, in her rejection of any shows of courtesy and thanks.

They didn't have very much to say to one another and certainly nothing new. In the evenings his wife would recount the events of her shopping trip and the man would talk briefly about what had happened at work. Normally his wife would interrupt him several times to comment on how silly she thought he had been. Sometimes she would interrupt to remind him of something which needed to be done around the house. At times like this the man knew he had somehow offended her: perhaps he had made it sound ever so slightly as though his work and the people at work were more important to him than his wife and his home.

Sometimes they would talk about their children, but even on this subject they didn't have much to say if they wanted to avoid an argument – and this they most certainly did. His wife was of the opinion that their children had all chosen the wrong university, home, job or partner and that they were incapable of looking after their finances or indeed any other matter. Her husband disagreed. He believed he was able to substantiate his arguments far better than his wife did hers, but never had the opportunity to present them fully. In any case the man was proud of their children and wished whole-heartedly that his wife could be too.

He wished that his wife didn't feel the need to justify her usefulness to herself so desperately that it made her break and quash everyone who otherwise might have wanted to love her.

The man arrived home from work.

The time was a quarter to five as he walked through the door. He knew exactly what he could expect to see and hear: plates and part of a meal on the table, the rest on the stove or in the oven and his wife explaining that the food was not quite ready; hopefully he wasn't too hungry yet. She always said this, even though throughout their married life they had always eaten dinner at the same time – five o'clock – and the man had always come home from work a quarter of an hour before that unless they had agreed otherwise.

But now there was no one in the kitchen; no wife, no half-finished meal, not even the smell of food.

The man put his small suitcase and his satchel on a chair in the hall, took off his shoes and walked into the kitchen, looked round the bedroom, came back, checked the living room and began to smile. Whatever this was, his wife had certainly surprised him – something which had never happened before, not since the early years of their relationship. He called for his wife again, shouting out her name, searched upstairs, in the basement and the garden, but eventually decided to heat the stove in the sauna and unpack his suitcase.

Never before had the man enjoyed sitting in the warmth of the sauna as much as he did that afternoon. A liberated silence hung around the house, and in that small, humid room he had the freedom simply to *be* – without having to pretend anything or watch his step. The odd, mundane thought occurred to him from time to time, but his mind easily slipped back to the place where the boundaries between oneself and the outer world disappeared. Even time no longer existed.

The man lost count of the number of times he replenished the logs in the sauna stove. When the large wood basket was finally empty he leisurely got down from the sauna bench, picked up the basket and walked out to the woodshed. It was an old habit, because you weren't supposed to leave the basket empty; he had learnt that, at least.

On his way he stopped at the boiler room. That too was an old habit he had, but one so voluntary and instinctive that the man didn't even noticed he had stopped walking. He listened to the hum of the water tank, and he could feel his eyes heavy as he slowly turned letting his eyes rest upon the various details in the room. The space was warm, clean, soporific; everything was just as it had been.

Except for one thing.

The drain was now situated at the lowest point in the floor. It was still in the same place, but the floor had changed shape. The man got down on all fours to examine the floor's painted concrete surface and the small grille above the drain. There was nothing out of the ordinary about them. Both of them fitted perfectly into the space and served their everyday function.

The man felt a slight chill; he noticed he was somewhat dusty after kneeling on the floor and thought it was probably best to go and have a warm shower. He stood up and took hold of the door handle, glanced around once again and shrugged his shoulders. For a moment it felt as if something were insisting that he consider that room in some way exceptional or noteworthy. After all, it was a boiler room just like any other, nothing special.

With that he returned to the bathroom, stepped under the shower and reached out his hand to turn on the tap.

But the taps were no longer there. In their place was a smooth, modern handle. The man remembered suggesting that they get one of these and a thermostat, because the taps had been in very bad condition and someone had even burnt their hands on them. He had finally relented once he had been assured that such a thing would be a waste of money. Nonetheless the new handle and the thermostat were now in place. The water flowed evenly and at just the right temperature, just like in a good hotel.

Just then the man noticed the array of shampoos and soaps. He had been expecting to see the supermarket's usual sharp-smelling economy brands which irritated the eyes and the skin, especially of those who were allergic to these products, but instead there was a selection of beautiful, good quality, fragrant, allergy-tested products. The man tried them and found them most pleasant.

He turned off the shower and stood for a moment on the spot, water dripping to the floor.

The shower floor was tiled, not covered with peeling linoleum. The washing basket was different to what he had expected, so were the stools, the washing machine, the cupboards and the mirrors. He couldn't remember whether there were supposed to be mirrors here at all. Indeed, he wasn't sure about many of the fixings. Most of them were things he had never consciously paid a second thought.

Wearing a soft dressing gown and a pair of slippers he walked right round the basement and noted more and more small changes. Inside the sauna everything looked slightly different. In the corridor the colour of the walls caught his attention, and so did the rug on the floor. In place of the dark, stuffy food cellar there was now a practical cold storage room. The woodshed looked familiar, even though there were a few strange items there too. Everything was suddenly far more beautiful, more coordinated and of a much higher quality, though not necessarily newer or more expensive than what the man thought he could remember.

The woodwork room was entirely different from before.

The room was in a state of joyous disorder. One corner had been reserved for weaving rugs, the other for carpentry. Competing for the rest of the floor space was an amateur painter's set of tools, folders full of stamps, hiking equipment and items of clothing which looked like they were part of a fancy dress costume – a medieval knight and his damsel in the castle tower.

The man quietly switched off the lights, closed the door and turned towards the staircase.

He opened the door into the kitchen: a pleasant, practical room, cosily cluttered, softly lit; a room which invited one to stop for a moment and not simply dash through into the bedroom to get dressed. He did everything very slowly: strolled, looked around, undressed, put on a set of clothes he had forgotten that he even owned, combed his hair and ran his fingers across the large double bed, feeling how its soft sheets caressed his skin and how the firm mattress pleasantly supported his body. The room was like new and the bathroom was barely recognisable. He was astonished at the sight of the living room: neither stiff, uncomfortable pieces of furniture nor fragile ornaments to be avoided. The bookshelf was not how he remembered it either; now it was full of different books, some old and battered, the ones he vaguely recalled someone ordering him take up to the attic to make room for the chintzy items they had received as gifts.

Upstairs were the children's old rooms. The children's belongings were still more or less in place, just as the man remembered, but still in some way the rooms looked new. Long ago the children had decorated their rooms, and now there was not a trace of adults having the final say, as they might once have done. The man opened the door to a little room which might have been one of the cupboards in the attic, but after a while he realised he had come into the bathroom. The final door upstairs led into a storage room, which was neither small nor cramped, but was filled with all the items the man had expected to find there, and a freezer and a mangle too.

The man opened the freezer and saw a bottle of champagne chilling at the top of the basket. It was something of a surprise to see it there – to see champagne in the house was a surprise in itself – but he picked it up and closed the freezer lid. When he stepped downstairs he noticed that a car had pulled up outside and he thought to himself that the timing was perfect.

His wife stepped inside full of energy and good humour, a bag slung across her shoulder. They met in the hallway and kissed. She explained that she had got stuck in traffic, but that on the radio she had heard a wonderful recording from the same music festival they would be visiting the following summer. The man told her how he felt divine after his sauna and his wife commented on how lovely he smelt.

They went into the kitchen and poured some champagne, put together a light supper on a tray and after short deliberation decided to take it into the living room. There they dimmed the lights and put on a record that the woman had bought earlier that day.

They told each other about their day at work and wondered whether they should go and give their eldest child a hand doing up the garden in her new house; what would be the best way to help their middle child with his sick daughter and when they would get the time to travel to another continent to visit their youngest and meet her husband to be. They had plenty to talk about: the upcoming summer festivals, books they had recently read and what their friends were getting up to. They chatted merrily and poured themselves some more champagne.

Late that evening, when they had both gone up to the bedroom, the man thought how much the world offered him that he had yet to discover, even though he had already lived half of his life. In the mirror he saw his reflection next to that of his wife, and for a short moment he felt that in different circumstances he might have become someone who thought rather differently about things and who perhaps even looked a bit different. It was a curious thought: almost lost and something of a misunderstanding.